Incoming

Kaylid Chronicles 3

Mel Todd

Bad Ash Publishing

Atlanta, GA

Copyright © 2018 by **Melisa Todd**

All rights reserved. No part of this publication may be reproduced, distributed or transmitted in any form or by any means, without prior written permission.

Bad Ash Publishing
Powder Springs, GA 30127
www.badashpublishing.com

Publisher's Note: This is a work of fiction. Names, characters, places, and incidents are a product of the author's imagination. Locales and public names are sometimes used for atmospheric purposes. Any resemblance to actual people, living or dead, or to businesses, companies, events, institutions, or locales is completely coincidental.

Book Layout © 2017 BookDesignTemplates.com
Cover by http://www.ampersandbookcovers.com/

Incoming/ Mel Todd -- 1st ed.
ISBN 978-0-9905182-7-3

To Doug and Ashli for my sanity, and Howard for the best beta I've had.

The question isn't - what would you do for your world? It is - what won't you do?

—MCKENNA LARGO

CONTENTS

Chapter 1 – Covering the Past 9

Chapter 2 – The Other Shoe 23

Chapter 3 – Unreal Normalcy 33

Chapter 4 - Best Laid Plans 42

Chapter 5 - Feelings 50

Chapter 6 - Invasions 57

Chapter 7 - Dream Analysis 66

Chapter 8 - Bluffs Called 73

Chapter 9 - Additions 87

Chapter 10 - MIB 104

Chapter 11 - Show Your Cards 115

Chapter 12 - Change of Scenery 133

Chapter 13 - Self Important People 141

Chapter 14 - Options 150

Chapter 15 - Forcing the Beast 160

Chapter 16 - UN Bombshells 172

Chapter 17 - Wrenches 181

- Chapter 18 - Weapons Practice 187
- Chapter 19 - Plans in Motion 195
- Chapter 20 - True Faces 203
- Chapter 21 - Talking Heads 216
- Chapter 22 - Media Presence 225
- Chapter 23 - First They Came 235
- Chapter 24 - Reactions 247
- Chapter 25 - Children 256
- Chapter 26 - Paradigms 266
- Chapter 27 - Skill Sets 276
- Chapter 28 - Circling the Wagons 287
- Chapter 29 - Earth Stood Still 295
- Chapter 30 - Hero Worship 305
- Chapter 31 - DTs 315
- Chapter 32 - Breaking News 324
- Chapter 34 - Girding Loins 333
- Chapter 35 - Once Again... 341
- Chapter 36 - Interrogations 350
- Chapter 37 - Preparing for the Storm 362
- Chapter 38 - Special Report.................................... 370
- Chapter 39 - Landfall 377

Chapter 40 - Walk the Path 387

Chapter 41 - Pay the Price 396

Chapter 42 - Glimmer of Hope 405

Chapter 43 - Hope made real 413

Chapter 44 - Leap of Faith 422

Epilogues 429

Chapter 1 – Covering the Past

The sensational return of the kidnapped NFL Player Perc Alexander and Detective McKenna Largo has been confirmed. Per confidential sources, they were kidnapped, poisoned, and forced to go through something horrendous. But they made it to the Bogota Embassy and have been returned to the United States, along with McKenna's partner JD Davidson, as well as friends Tonan Diaz and Cassandra Borden. As you'll remember, Cassandra Borden was reported missing in a separate incident, but apparently was found with them. They were met at the airport by their children, McKenna's foster child Charley Davis, and the families of Perc Alexander and Borden. We hope to have the official story shortly. ~ KWAK News

The entire ride home from the airport Charley didn't let go of McKenna's hand. Taking him into her home and heart had been one of her best decisions ever. He didn't say much, but the mental link glowed with relief, love, and something so primal she couldn't quite put her finger on it. When she looked, she felt the same thing between Toni and her kids. They'd offered to put off the celebration until tomorrow, but all of them needed family around, and the sooner this was out in the open the better it would be for all of them.

Funny how life works. In so short a space of time, Toni and her kids are like family. JD is my brother, and Cassandra has become important to me also. Then there's Perc.

No one really talked in the mindscape though she could feel all of them, feel their relief, their joy, and their stress at the words from Wefor, her in-house alien Artificial Intelligence. Which McKenna suspected might be more intelligent than they thought.

Carina took Toni and the kids home, they'd be over in a bit. JD had come with her, while Perc wanted to stop at home, shower and change and take some time to talk to his parents, but they'd all agreed to leave out the actual story of what happened until they were all together. Cass's sister took Cass home. They would crash there as while Cass lived relatively close to McKenna, Helena did not. Cass needed to bathe also, put on clean clothes, then the sisters could use the time to talk.

Invaders are coming. And we are the only ones who know.

The thought echoed in her mind as she showered, dressed, and sat on the deck, Charley curled up next to her as they waited for the others.

"Give it a break for a while, Kenna," JD said as he sank down next to her. He handed her a cider, Charley a fruit water, and had a beer in his other hand.

She looked up at him, a bit startled, then gave him a rueful grin. "That obvious?"

"Well, I'm fighting not to think about it. But for tonight I want to put it off."

She nodded and stared out at the land surrounding her property and tried very hard not to think about anything.

"What happened to you guys? You look awful. Like you've been starved for months," Charley asked,

INCOMING

his voice low and quiet. She didn't need the link to be aware of his concern.

McKenna wrapped her arm around his shoulder and pulled him close to her. "I don't have an issue telling you, but let's wait until everyone is here so we only have to tell it once."

JD gave Charley a look. "And at the same time you can tell us what happened to my house."

"Oh," Charley whispered and sank down a bit, but he didn't move, seeming perfectly happy in McKenna's arms.

"I get the feeling you might have a better story than ours there," McKenna remarked idly, moving her hand up and down on his arm. In the end, it wasn't important. Insurance would fix most of the issues with JD's house and they were all alive. After that nothing else really mattered.

They sat in companionable silence, soaking up the normal sounds, sounds she hadn't realized she'd missed until now. They moved when they heard cars pulling up. McKenna thought she would resent having people invading her solitude, but she could feel Toni, Perc, and Cass getting close and she hungered to see them, even though it had only been a few hours since they were last together.

When they all got close enough for their mind links to light up, the stress she didn't realize had wrapped around her dissipated, and she sensed JD relax too as they moved to start greeting people. In no time her house was full, and she formally met Perc and Cass's families. Cass introduced her to Helena, Oswald, Troy and Laila. The kids just looking at her warily until Charley called them over, and Jess and Jamie showed up. Jamie hugged her again and showed off his bright blue cast.

At some point we'll have to get the full story of what happened while we were gone.

Carina gave her a bone-breaking hug, and Captain Kirk, Lieutenant Waris, and her coworkers Guinness and Laredo also showed up, dragged in by Anne.

Kirk came in and smiled at her. "Good to see you back, Detective. My life might have gotten boring without you." He cast a sharp eye at her and JD as he let his gaze travel over their bodies. Both of them were wearing kilts, snugged as tight as they could, and tank tops. The amount of weight they'd lost obvious.

"I'm looking forward to hearing exactly what happened." His voice dry, but the corners of his eyes were tight as he took a good look at all the participants.

Perc introduced his parents Daniel and Connie Alexander. They resembled their son with the same eyes, but more she could sense their faith in him and each other. She envied it slightly.

When everyone had drinks, and JD was grilling food for all of them, they brought every extra chair she had, plus the ones Toni had brought with her, and set them up on the deck., which luckily was just big enough. They ate and talked, everyone avoiding the elephant in the room, until even the shifters felt like they had enough food to last them for a while. They all settled back with drinks while the kids wandered, and McKenna waited.

"So spill, McKenna. What happened?" Anne asked, seated at the picnic table with most of the cops.

INCOMING

And there it is. Once more unto the breach I guess.

McKenna glanced at the others. ~How much do we say? Knowing the kids will hear it?~ She made sure the kids weren't part of that mindscape, no reason to make them feel like they didn't trust them.

Charley and Jessi and Jamie had welcomed Troy and Laila into their world, even if they weren't shifters, but none of them was willing to stray too far away from their loved ones.

~Tell them.~ Cass was the first to reply. ~I already let them know I wasn't going to hide anything from them. If we are targets, the kids need to KNOW what people are willing to do.~

Toni fiddled with her beer bottle. ~Agreed. And I think when I hear what they've done in the last week I'm going to be pushing for the martial arts training.~

McKenna rubbed her face and got up to stand and look out at the Sierras. ~Do I tell them about Wefor? About the Elentrin?~

~They're the only ones who might believe us,~ JD remarked softly, and the rest chimed in their agreement.

With a sigh, McKenna turned around to see everyone else looking at the five of them, puzzled. Perc just smiled at his obviously confused parents but shook his head at their raised eyebrows.

"Sorry. This is going to be explained at some part in the story, but for now I needed to make sure." McKenna heaved a sigh and rubbed her face. "JD, keep me in cider because this is going to take a bit. I'll start with those bozos kidnapping us here, with the understanding that they had already grabbed

Cass and must have been holding her." She saw Helena put her hand on her sister's thigh as the two kids moved closer to their Aunt Cass.

Cass for her part just shot McKenna a smile and a wordless pulse of confidence.

Taking a deep breath, McKenna started to talk. Going over the fragmented memories and waking up in the jungle with all of them naked. She addressed the video and the orders, then commented on the poison. Watching her friends, her family, their families, she swallowed and moved through them discussing it and deciding they had no choice. None of them could risk having their loved ones killed.

She paused as she tried to figure out the next part, how to tell them without sounding like an idiot.

[The phone demonstration is always possible.]

~No. Not now. If they don't believe and run and tell someone about this, I don't want anyone to have actual proof.~

[You do not believe any of these people would betray you.]

~No, but I don't know Cass or Perc's family. How they're going to react to this.~ The conversation was carried out in the mindscape so everyone could hear it. McKenna refused to hide anything from the people she loved.

"So the next part McKenna is going to tell you is going to sound crazy and more than a little insane. Honestly, if I hadn't lived through it, I'd probably think the same thing. I'm asking you to trust us. That we didn't lose it while in the jungle." Cass's voice held quiet strength as she caught her sister and brother-in-law's eyes.

"What she said." Perc looked at his parents as he spoke. "Believe me, it's all true, and it only gets weirder from here."

His father shrugged and held his wife's hand. "You've never lied to us, past your teenage years. I see no reason for you to start now."

Perc flushed. "Hey, it was one time, and I totally didn't want to admit how far I'd gotten with Julie Miles, so yeah, I lied when you caught me sneaking in. Was I supposed to say, 'Sorry, I was having sex for the first time and totally lost track of time?'"

Connie flashed her son a smile. "That would probably not have gone over well either. But trying to convince us you'd spent two hours trying to change a tire when you were wearing spotless white jeans proved lying would never be your forte."

A round of snickers broke out on the deck and even the kids giggled as Perc dropped his head in his hand and groaned.

"Fine, I rarely lied. 'Cause I sucked at it. You happy?"

Dan chucked and patted his shoulder. "You were a good kid, and a better man." He turned his eyes, the same blue eyes as his son's, to McKenna. "So tell us that which we won't believe."

~Here goes nothing.~

McKenna talked about the AI living in her head, the nanobots all shifters had, and the ability to talk via telepathy. Though she glossed over how she obtained something sharp enough to cut everyone with so they could share blood. When she explained the warrior form, she'd provide some insight into partial transformations. As they all sat there with pole-axed expressions, she added, "There's one more part that I need to share, but I'd like to save that until the end. After that we'll answer questions. Okay?"

Only Anne didn't look as stunned as the rest of the non-shifters, but McKenna saw Kirk shooting Anne a sharp look. But everyone agreed, and with relief she continued. The fish, the snake, the alligators, then the compound were all discussed.

By the time she reached the point in their story where they had killed the first guards and entered the compound, she'd gone through three ciders, and her voice felt hoarse.

"So here's another part that most people don't know. Most shifters have three forms. The human and animal form everyone is familiar with. But there's a third called the warrior form. That's what we changed to for the next part."

"We've seen it." Charley's voice almost startled her. The kids had been so quiet, listening but not making much noise as she talked. She'd known they were there, but hearing him brought it back into sharp relief. He ducked his head as everyone shifted their attention from McKenna to him. "That's how she saved us when that man kidnapped us. She turned into a wolfman like a cat, with fingers and claws, and killed them. It terrified us, but at the same time we knew she was there to protect us. She shifted to animal before anyone else showed up."

"Yes," Jessi chimed in as Jamie nodded. "It looked like the best movie I'd ever seen, but she was real and powerful."

"Can we see that?" Kirk asked in a neutral tone.

[NO!] Wefor's reaction immediate and loud in their heads, and all of them winced, kids included. [You have all stressed your systems too far and the children are too young. Until you've gained back almost fifty pounds any shifting is dangerous. DO NOT SHIFT.]

~Okay, okay, got it. Please quit yelling. It hurts.~ And it did, her very brain throbbed from the force of the words, and she saw the others holding their heads and nodding. Though the non-shifters looked very confused.

"Sorry. Remember the AI, we call her Wefor by the way, was expressing very strongly that shifting would be bad. With all the damage we did with the forced changes we might do some serious damage to our bodies until we all gain weight back."

"I was going to ask about that," Helena said softly. "Why are you all so skinny? And I was pretty sure from the videos both Perc and JD were much more muscular."

JD grumbled softly. "We were."

"Quit whining," Cass said softly. "Could have been worse than just weight loss." Her face grave, and JD nodded, suddenly somber.

"True. Almost was."

The looks of confusion made her half smile. "I'll get to it, you'll understand. But Captain, in regard to your question. Ask me in a week or two. Then I'll be more than happy to show you. But until then, you'll just have to take our words on it."

His eyes narrowed, but he nodded his head and purposefully relaxed back in his chair.

McKenna took the cider JD handed her and took a long sip. At this point she'd need something stronger, a disadvantage to not being able to get drunk anymore. But either way the calories helped. She started the story back up with them changing into warrior form and killing the required targets. Perc and Toni weighed in with their portion of the story, and then they got to the shifting.

"Wefor came to the conclusion that multiple shifts back-to-back would enable us to destroy the poison. So we did. But every shift takes energy." She shrugged and nodded at JD and Perc. "It burned up muscle mass on those two. Toni and I burned off every bit of fat and some muscle trying to change."

"Every bit of fat," Toni said wryly. "At this point neither McKenna nor I even qualify as B cups."

~That is going to get fixed, right, Wefor? All my clothes expect me to have boobs,~ Toni asked as the people looked around, taking in the appearances of all the shifters.

[Yes. The nanobots are programmed to restore you to optimal health which includes fat stores. However, if you wish alteration to your breasts, they can be given commands to facilitate that.]

~Huh, I'll keep that in mind,~ Toni said, even as McKenna sighed in relief. She had no desire to look like a boy, and not having breasts with most of her body fat gone, did tilt her that way.

"Lucky you," Cass said, trying to lighten the mood. "I never had boobs."

Helena didn't laugh, her eyes narrowed. "You didn't mention Cass. What about her?"

Cass sighed and looked at McKenna.

"Cass died."

"WHAT!" burst from multiple throats and Helena's hands went white around her sister's knee, and her niece and nephew wrapped around her legs like octopi.

INCOMING

Cass smiled, a sad, soft thing even as Helena looked like she wanted to pull her sister into her arms and never let her loose.

"Her heart stopped. Perc and I did CPR while I forced the nanobots to repair her heart. It worked, but it was really close." McKenna closed her eyes remembering the limp figure of Cass laying on the floor. "She didn't have the mass the rest of us had, mass to fuel the changes and it cannibalized too much of her heart. All of us need to take a while to eat and let the nanobots repair the damage done to our internal organs. Cass just had less body mass, so more damage." She shot Kirk a wry smile. "Hence the no shifting for a while."

"Understood." He looked a bit pale at the idea.

McKenna nibbled on a chip as she tried to organize her thoughts. With reluctance she went into the last part of the story, covering the trip to Bogota, the political games, and then the flight home.

"Gods, this last part is going to take whiskey." She felt the agreement from the others and JD rose.

"You know what? I think you're right. Tell you what, let me get some adult drinks, and you guys can ask all the questions I can see on your faces, then we'll get to the last part."

~I'm in no hurry to get to this part either. Besides, I want another burger.~

People stood and stretched, and she saw Perc and his parents deep in conversation, while Helena had a death grip on her sister and Oswald stayed close to them, though the kids headed out to play for a bit in human form, kicking a soccer ball around. Jessi and Jamie seemed to have gained another inch or two in the last week, so they balanced out the seven- and ten-year-old kids of Helena. All of them kept glancing back, checking in on the adults, and she completely understood the wariness.

Hunger whispered at the back of her mind, and she went and made herself another hamburger even as Kirk, followed by Guinness and Laredo, approached.

"I really, really want to say your experience has created a mental break and make you go see a doctor," Kirk started the conversation as he sipped at a beer, looking out at the mountains.

"So why don't you?" she asked as she finished doctoring the burger to her tastes. Even stuff she liked didn't taste as good as it once had. But it still tasted good, JD made awesome burgers.

"Because out of all your flaws," he snorted as she shot him a sharp look with a wordless protest, "you're outspoken, don't deal with idiots well, have no patience with politics, and occasionally can't see the forest for the trees. Yes, you have flaws. But lying isn't one of them. Or stretching the truth. And this truth seems so unbelievable the only option is to believe. Besides, even if you had starved the entire time you were gone you wouldn't have dropped the sheer amount of weight you've lost. All of you. So yes. Though I really don't want to, I believe you."

"It's going to get worse." McKenna said softly and shoved another bite in her mouth so she didn't say anything else.

"Yeah. I get that feeling." He turned and looked directly at her for the first time. "You've got my support. Regardless. So might as well rip off the bandage and tell us."

Guinness flashed her a smile as Laredo tipped an imaginary hat. "I bet you'll never be boring." Laredo's voice teasing her a bit.

~Yes, but will I still be a cop when this is all done? Hell, will we even be alive?~

She forced a smile and finished her burger, then grabbed two cookies and took a seat watching the interplay of relationships around her.

JD had brought out two bottles of whiskey and most of the adults had some. Connie refused, wrinkling her nose even as her husband laughed at her a bit. The two worked well together, their love steady and strong. McKenna suspected she'd really like them if she got the chance to know them.

Moving her attention to Cass's family, Helena was the tornado and her husband the steady wall she leaned against, and their love for Cass shone as bright as Cass's love for them.

Carina had moved out to play with the kids, and Toni watched everyone with stress at the corners of her eyes and mouth. But she had reason.

Everyone had settled back down, and she felt the weight of their eyes on her as she twisted the tumbler in her hand over and over.

"Well? What's the big secret?" Anne was the one to ask, but when McKenna looked up everyone had their eyes on her. Toni nodded then moved her attention to the kids, the line of shoulders reflected her tension.

"Everyone remember a news story lately about a signal from space that SETI Institute is offering a prize if anyone can decipher it? Most people are betting it's reflected and distorted TV or radio shows."

Most of them nodded, though she noted Guinness just shrugged. His idea of news centered around sports, rugby to be specific. Connie and Dan glanced at each other shaking their heads.

"SETI is the Search for Extraterrestrial Intelligence. They normally are involved in scanning the skies for something that means there are others out there." McKenna knew it wasn't exactly accurate, but close enough for now. The confusion disappeared from their faces and she continued. "It isn't. It's a signal from an Elentrin ship headed towards Earth. Per Wefor, they should be here in the next thirty days."

Chapter 2 – The Other Shoe

There has been no official statement about the situation involving the kidnapping of McKenna Largo and her associates. While there is no scheduled press conference, rumors of an intense investigation abound. At least one person has been fired from the Embassy in Bogota though it is unclear if that person had anything to do with the kidnapping. Investigators here are still looking to see how five people were put on a plane and flown to South America with no one being aware. The Sacramento International Airport is on high alert as all flight plans are being reviewed. ~ KWAK News

McKenna didn't know what she had expected. Outrage, surprise, disbelief, anger? Instead, they looked at her and there was a soft sigh that seemed to emerge, from all of them at once, and shoulders slumped.

"I was afraid that was what you were going to say," Dan murmured.

Kirk nodded his head. "Yeah."

She suspected she looked like an idiot right now, glancing around at them. "You did?" The other shifters looked just as surprised, even Toni stared at them in shock.

"Sure." Kirk lifted his hand half way, though he glanced at Anne with a half-smirk. She just rubbed her forehead with her middle finger at him. "Once you mentioned alien nanobots and that you had the commander version, it only made sense for there to be aliens. Why would they send an infection here unless they planned on coming to Earth? Do we, well, you, know why they wanted to have shifters here on Earth? What are their plans?"

McKenna felt like an anvil had been lifted off her chest and for a minute she thought she might pass out, the sense of relief made her dizzy.

"I was absolutely sure you'd never believe us. I mean aliens, AIs, telepathy, all of it." She knew her voice had a bit of a sharp tone to it. Maybe it was fear and relief. She didn't know as she took a deep drink of the whiskey.

Laredo snorted. "McKenna, you are the most blunt, honest, and straightforward person I know. And you turn into a cougar. At this point if you told me God spoke to you, I'd probably give you the benefit of the doubt. But overall, aliens actually make way more sense than just about any other theory that's been given serious consideration."

Everyone nodded their agreement. McKenna had to rub her face to prevent incipient tears. Exhaustion batted at her, and she suspected when they slept it would probably be for a long while.

"Okay. Here's what Wefor told us. Be aware, Wefor is a program that a solar flare badly damaged. What she rebuilt is not what the Elentrin thought it should be. I think even she will admit her advice must be taken with a grain of salt."

[Correct. All information provided is accurate according to the data available. But if there is a flaw in the programming, the information could be incorrect.]

McKenna repeated what Wefor said for the non-shifters.

"She?" asked Connie, tilting her head.

"Eh, I don't really think Wefor has a gender. Nor are we sure how independent she is versus a very advanced program. But she lives in my head, and doesn't feel like a male, and calling something that we gave a name, 'it' seems more wrong."

A few nods and murmurs, but then Kirk redirected. "So what information has Wefor imparted?"

She refilled her glass, tried to organize her thoughts as she sipped.

"Shifters are called Kaylid. They, well, the Elentrin, created them as cannon fodder. They use us against their enemy, the Drakyn. They seed a planet, give us time to cause issues and come 'rescue' the population from us."

"Rescue? Why would we want to be rescued from you?" Helena asked this with her arm tight around Cass as her eyes didn't leave McKenna.

"So as Wefor explained it, the nanobots were supposed to lock us into the animal form, but with our minds gone. Instead there would be insane animals in our sizes attacking and killing, unable to be controlled. They expected mass causalities, fear, and for us to be ready to accept any help. They come in and 'cure' the madness. Then in gratitude we let some of our people go with them to 'help' them in return for them helping us." She threw her hands up and sagged backwards. "Not sure I understand the logic, but it's happened multiple times."

"They don't know how many people are on Earth," Charley said then shrank back as everyone turned to look at him.

"What do you mean?" McKenna asked, eyes narrowed.

Charley started to shrink a bit more then shook it off and straightened up. "We've been having dreams, Jessi, Jamie, and me." Toni sucked in a breath and glanced at her kids, but they just nodded somberly at her.

"They said the population of Earth was," he paused, thinking, "nine hundred million?"

"Nine hundred seventy," Jessi provided. "And they're expecting like a million Kaylid."

Everyone blinked, and Perc frowned. "One of my dreams I looked out the window, a planet hung in the view. It was blue and oddly familiar."

"We saw Saturn," Charley said, his voice quiet. "I checked after, it had the rings around the planet."

A hush fell over the group, and McKenna closed her eyes thinking over the information. "Why would they be so off on the population level?" Her voice sounded a bit shaky to her own ears, she swallowed hard trying to get more in control.

"Have they ever visited Earth before?" Daniel asked, and her eyes snapped open, and she looked at him.

[Unknown.]

"Wefor doesn't know."

"I think so," Charley said, chewing his lip, brows furrowed.

"Why?" Toni asked before McKenna could. Her voice sharp, and McKenna realized her hands were white-knuckled around her glass.

~JD,~ she whispered on a private channel. ~Look at Toni. Can you help?~

"They gave us languages to learn, and I think I know them. I think Jessi and I do. Jamie, did you have the same dream when you were separated from us?"

Jamie nodded a bit. "I was in a hospital room, but different than the room I was really in for my broken arm. They said they were uploading a language module. It felt weird, but I didn't really think about it after I woke. I still felt funny from the drugs for my arm." He held up the bright blue cast, and McKenna saw Toni tense even more.

~Yeah, moving now.~ JD rose from his chair, moved it over to the space between Toni and the door and set down next to her. In a smooth move he grabbed her legs, put them on her lap, removed her shoes and started to massage her feet.

McKenna saw a fast look between Cass and JD, then Cass nodded and moved her attention back to Helena who all but had a death grip on her arm. Toni started then relaxed as JD rubbed her feet.

~Interesting choice.~ McKenna said, her smile only visible in the mental voice.

~She needed to be touched, and I can't exactly cuddle in mixed company. This people will overlook.~ JD's voice was calm, matter of fact, and McKenna nodded.

~True, wish I had realized that sooner. Thanks.~

She flipped her attention back to Charley. "What languages did you learn?"

"English, which we knew, but Spanish, Mandarin, umm, Arabic and French."

All the adults had their eyes fixed on the three kids, and they shrank backwards, Jessi snarling softly in reaction.

"So can you speak it?" Toni asked, her voice flat, even as JD kneaded on her feet.

"Maybe? I mean not like we've had any time to play with it, and I don't know anyone that speaks Mandarin," Charley protested.

"*Vous aimez être capable de jouer comme un loup*?" JD said slowly.

~You speak French?~ Rang out through the mindscape.

~Bad high school French. Give me a break.~

Charley blinked then responded with unaccented French, but smoothly, fluid compared to how JD had been halting. "*Oui. C'est amusant et j'ai can' t imaginer être autre chose que ce que je suis.*"

Everyone looked at them blankly even as both males had a surprised look on their faces.

"What did he ask you?" McKenna said even as the ramifications made her sick.

"If I enjoyed playing as a wolf. I told him yes, and that I couldn't imagine being anything else." Charley rubbed his neck focusing on his feet. "That was odd."

Jessi wrinkled her nose. "It felt like my brain altering my mouth so I knew what words to say, even if I didn't say anything." She grinned, flashed a look to both boys who met her smile with identical ones.

"I don't think so," Toni said with narrowed eyes. "If you think you're going to cuss in another language so I won't know, think again."

The crestfallen look on the twins' faces had most of the adults hiding snickers and all the kids pretending that wasn't what they were thinking.

"I'd say they're coming, but we're back to when did they visit before, and why are the numbers off so badly?" Kirk murmured. He'd been frowning during the entire interlude.

Just what does he think about all this? We could use his support.

"You sound like you have an idea," JD said, even as his fingers worked on having Toni relax a bit. Though McKenna suspected being able to catch her kids being kids had helped, too.

"Hmm," Kirk glanced over at Laredo. "You've got a history degree. Didn't most of the werewolf stories appear in the dark ages?"

Laredo thought even as McKenna blinked.

~History degree?~

~Apparently~ replied JD.

"That would be about right. Black plague and mad wolves appeared about then. But that's only European history. I don't know what would have correlated with the Kitsune, Jaguar or other humanoid animals in other cultures. But -" and he waved his finger in the air, "but - if you're correct and that's when they last visited, given the plague and the technology levels, that might be about where they would expect us to be at, population-wise. I can't pull up the study in my mind, but there was an estimate of what our population and technology level should have been assuming a steady growth over the seven, eight hundred years. But in the last hundred our technology growth has been exponential, not linear or even cubic. Given that, they might be expecting us at the industrial revolution stage, not at where we are."

It took McKenna a moment to follow what he meant. "Wait, you think they're expecting gun powder and cotton mills?" Those were really the only things that stood out to her from her history class about the industrial revolution.

"Essentially," Laredo drawled. "But that's assuming Charley remembered correctly, that the information is actually from these aliens, that it's real and from this invasion fleet, not one that came here in the Middle Ages."

Charley, who had started to bristle, sagged a bit as Laredo continued to talk, and all of them nodded.

"So we really don't know anything, is what you're saying."

"Nope," agreed Kirk. "But it implies a lot, though I don't know that any of us have any ability to change anything." He sighed and looked at them. "As much as I hate to say it, I don't have any advice, and this is going to sound horribly cliché, but it seems like this problem has been dropped in your laps. Are there any other commander modules around?"

[In theory, yes. The calculations have been refined and there should be at least five others. But there is no way to tell if all those modules survived, much less what level of damage they were subjected to.]

McKenna relayed the words even as she wanted to cry.

Daniel looked around the surrounding people and put his hand on his son's shoulder and squeezed, but his eyes were on McKenna. "I don't have any answers and I don't really have any contacts. But we're here and we'll support you all we can. Is there anything we can do? Should we start prepping or buying weapons?" He moved in his seat a bit as he talked, obviously uncomfortable.

"I have no idea. I don't know enough about what weapons they have to answer that. So only if you want?" McKenna shook her head, feeling a bit silly.

Connie gave her a warm smile and stood. "I think we've had enough for today. McKenna, I'd like to leave you our contact information. I don't know if we can help, but if we can, ask. You helped save our son, and it looks like you're going to help save our world. Anything you need is yours."

McKenna felt heat climb her face as the sentiment was echoed from multiple throats. In less time than she would have thought possible, they had the place cleaned up, food put away, contact information exchanged, and everyone was gone.

Toni had hugged them all with bone-crushing fierceness, while Perc and Cass gave all of them searching looks as they left. Feeling each of them drop from her awareness hurt with an almost physical pain.

JD looked at her, his face as drawn as hers. "Mind if I crash here? I haven't even started to deal with my house."

"I am really, really, really, sorry," Charley said, a total hangdog look on his face.

"We still need that story, and maybe you can explain exactly WHY my house is minus a kitchen. But not today." JD pulled Charley in to a rough hug that the boy leaned into even as he watched McKenna.

"I don't know about you two, but I'm exhausted." She glanced around the place, but her guests had been quick and efficient and it didn't need anything else done tonight. "JD, crash wherever. Night, you two." She turned and started to head towards her room.

"McKenna?" Charley said, and she paused turning to look at him. His voice had been small, hesitant.

"Yeah?" She watched him, worried, but so tired that it had become hard to think.

"Can I sleep with you tonight? As a wolf? I just, I need to know you're here." He didn't look at her as he asked and she moved before she even thought.

McKenna pulled him into her arms tight. "Absolutely. Sleeping close enough I can touch you sounds good."'

If she had her way, she'd never let him go.

Chapter 3 — Unreal Normalcy

While our missing officers are still recovering from their ordeal, more and more shifters appear in the news. And not for good reasons. In California alone there are reports of over fifteen people turning into animals and going mad. While this isn't even a fraction of all shifters it is worrisome, especially as numbers are climbing across the globe. More and more people are being found in animal form and they seem unable to comprehend anything or shift back.
~KWAK News

JD smiled at them and headed to use the bathroom. Twenty minutes later McKenna was splayed out on her bed in her human form with Charley curled up behind her. Exhaustion batted at her, but the dark links in her mind were like a sore tooth, and she couldn't quit poking at them. Missing Charley and the twins had hurt, but this, this was different. Having three of them, plus the twins, being out of reach created an almost physical level of dissonance in her mind.

~Kenna, you still awake?~ JD's voice tickled at the edge of her mind.

~Yeah.~

~Can I come in there? It sounds stupid, but I can't sleep out here in this form. It's too empty.~

Her mental laugh had a tinge of bitterness to it. ~I understand. I miss them. Come on in, but I don't think my bed is big enough for the three of us.~

~That's fine. Sleeping on the floor will work. I just can't handle the emptiness.~

She nodded, understanding completely. A minute later he walked in, a couple blankets in his hands, and created a nest on the floor near her bed. He flopped down, and just having him there helped. She fell asleep, one hand on Charley's back, the other hanging off the bed, barely brushing JD's hair.

McKenna stepped off small metal step into a large area that had row upon row of beings in warrior form watching her. A voice rang out, "Attention, Commander on deck!"

Ah shit, another dream. Wefor?

But her thought didn't get an answer. She mentally found the links, and they were all there, but their color felt off. It took her a moment to figure out why. She felt herself turning and surveying the assembled group of beings looking at her in what she recognized as 'at attention' stance. She'd watched enough movies to identify it, even on non-human bodies. Her body moved to attention to as she poked at her links. Generally, they were green to her perception, meaning there and she could talk to the that person. Gray meant they were out of reach, and she couldn't communicate. Blue was when she had muted them from the general conversation, though she rarely did that anymore, usually she'd just open only the channel to the person she wanted. But now they were all orange to her view, and it had a bad taste and feel in her mind.

Dammit, I need those links back.

Her attention was forcibly pulled from the links as the body's eyes landed on four familiar figures standing off to the side a bit and all at attention.

Guys! Thank goodness. Why can't I talk to you? Wefor? JD? Perc? Toni?

"Commander, your troops have lined up for your review. Your personally selected squad has been assembled. If you have any issues with any of your team, please file your requested changes."

Kids, where are the kids?

Everything felt real. The cold metallic air in the hangar, the sounds of hundreds of people breathing and rustling slightly. The background noise of machines and computers that she couldn't place. She could feel what she wore hanging on her body registering as both odd and familiar at the same time.

Where are the kids?

Their links were also orange, and the body would not turn its head so she could scan more carefully as her friends and family got closer. She started to panic as the others braced for their inspection.

Guys? Can you hear me?

Frantic worry ate at her control. They'd just gotten everyone back. She couldn't lose them now. McKenna clawed at the mental links trying to make them turn green. She could see her pack, her family in front of her, why couldn't she talk to them?

She pushed and stretched the links. Information she didn't really understand flashed through her head. Connection options, satellite links, overrides, trans-sub-harmonics alignment. Desperate, she wrenched and twisted and a sharp pain raced through her mind. She screamed mentally even though the body she rode didn't even flinch. The scream was joined by screams from the rest of her links, reverberating in her mind.

McKenna jerked upright, the scream choking in the back of her throat. She felt movement as Charlie sat up too, rubbing his head, wincing.

"What was that?" JD's voice came from the floor as he also appeared in her line of sight, rubbing his head.

~McKenna? JD?~ Cass's voice echoed in the mindscape, confused, with echoes of pain included.

~Guys? What was that?~ This time Perc's voice joined the mixture and McKenna sensed Toni and the kids filter in as well.

~Toni? How can we be talking? You're too far away. And Perc, you're way too far. What is going on?~ McKenna asked. Her heart leapt then settled down as all the lights were a steady constant green. She could feel their health, still too skinny and less robust than she would like, but they were alive and there.

[Interesting. That manipulation of the links had not been found to be a possible option.] Wefor's voice had an odd confused tone.

~What do you mean? What happened? Did I do that?~

[Yes. You forced the trans-harmonics logic to tap into both the cellular and satellite bandwidths. Normally these communications bounce off the Elentrin ship to be able to communicate while on the planet. You rerouted them to alternate channels. Interesting.]

~What does that mean? Why can I talk to them now they're so far away?~

[In essence you are hijacking the bandwidths that satellite and cellular phones use. You can talk to them anywhere on the globe if there is any type of network available for the trans-harmonics to hijack.]

She felt more than heard the sigh of relief that drifted through the mindscape, but Cass vocalized it.

~I'm glad. I was having issues with all of you so far away. My sister is still here, but it wasn't the same as you. Now I can feel you again and I feel better with that.~

~Agreed. And now there isn't a limit on me talking to my children.~ The fierce joy in her voice tasted of golden honey.

McKenna lay back down, pulling Charley in human form into her arms, and with the links vibrant in her mind she fell asleep easily, no dreams waiting for her this time.

JD joined McKenna in the kitchen the next morning, and she pushed the cup of coffee at him. She showered, but only pulled her hair back into a ponytail. A quick frittata was in the oven cooking, mostly leftovers thrown into the eggs.

"Feels odd to be home," her voice low. Charley still slept, and she didn't want to wake him up.

He nodded and picked up the cup. "Yeah." He drank some, eyes closed then looked at her. "I guess we need to deal with the elephant now."

"Don't wanna." McKenna muttered into her coffee cup. She felt Perc wake up and the twins. Toni and Cass were still asleep. The amount of information the links now shared would have terrified her a month ago. But now it simply made her feel better having an awareness of them.

"Ddiscuss in an hour or so when everyone is awake?"

"Sounds good to me. I'm going to go call insurance and deal with that." His phone had been left here, under a pile of clothes.

McKenna snorted. "At some point we need to pull that story out of the kids."

"Yeah, but really in the scheme of things, my house isn't that big of a deal. It'll be dealt with."

"Yeah. Impending alien invasion does put things in perspective."

"Or getting kidnapped, poisoned, drug dealers, forced assassination," he replied dryly. "Compared to that, the house is just an annoyance."

McKenna grinned at him and threw some biscuits in the oven. She felt Charley stir and poured a glass of juice. It and the biscuits waited for Charley by the time he wandered out.

The morning went by with strange normalcy. McKenna and JD had two weeks leave from the department as did Toni. Having her work for the same organization helped. Perc, of course, was retired, but Cass had to be back to work Monday. Every instinct McKenna had grumbled at that, but at least now distance wasn't an issue.

JD got the wheels of insurance moving and ran over to his place to survey the damage and get a few things. When he got back, he reported the kitchen and most of the living room were a total loss, but the rest of the house was fine. Insurance adjusters had already been there and cops had been patrolling regularly to make sure no one decided to loot it. He tossed some of his clothes in the wash and overall didn't seem too worried about it.

He'll talk if he wants.

INCOMING

An odd glimmer in her mind caught her attention, and she realized there was a link between JD and Cass.

Huh. Go, JD. Cass will be good for you.

Closing her eyes, she paid more attention and saw a triangle of links between the kids. It was like watching light pulse back and forth. She couldn't hear what they said, really didn't want to, but she could tell they were communicating.

With that, she focused on laundry and finding something to eat that she could stand. They still all needed to gain weight but had almost started hating food.

Fried chicken. That sounds good.

The only problem, she'd never made fried chicken before. McKenna shrugged, pulled out chicken to start thawing and looked up a recipe on the web.

~So we need to get together and talk, or do it this way since McKenna ripped open the links.~ Perc's voice filtered into the mind space.

~And do we include the kids?~ Toni asked.

McKenna paused in her research efforts. "~I think we should. The fact that they're being pulled into the dreams as it is, means we can't exclude them. And personally, after the last week, I'd rather have them with me than not.~

~Agreed. I have a ton of stuff to do today. Laundry and hugging children. How about we just talk and research?~

~Works for me. I'm trying to find clothes that will fit for work tomorrow and convince Helena that I'm okay to be left alone.~ Cass's voice was filled with amused love.

~Ditto. My parents are offering to move out here, but I think we're fine and at this point I think I'd rather not have them at my ground zero.~ Perc's rumble remind her of a cat's purr, and McKenna grinned.

~So let's start brainstorming, but plan on meeting here next weekend regardless?~ McKenna asked. While she waited for a response she found a decent-looking recipe.

~Deal,~ JD agreed. ~And I've been thinking about it. First, I think you, McKenna, should call SETI and give them the translation. That might get someone's notice. And then we need to call Homeland. They have a local office in Sacramento so if nothing else, maybe with Perc and me for bodyguards, we can get someone to talk to us.~

The mindspace filled with an aura of thought as she went about getting things ready. She could hear JD in the kitchen and feel the others, their moods, their overall well-being, but nothing else, not enough to make her uncomfortable.

~I can do that. I'll let you know what the result is.~

A chorus of agreement, and everyone kind of faded. She could feel the distance, but their lights were as strong as if they had been in the same room.

All her ingredients were there, but she frowned. "JD?"

"Yeah?"

"I want mashed potatoes. Those actually sound good. Feel like running to the store while I deal with SETI?"

"Sure. I needed to run by the house and take a few more pictures anyhow. Charley?" He raised his voice a bit. "Want to come with me?"

Charley walked into the kitchen, looking at McKenna. "You okay with that?"

She looked at him and smiled. "Yes, but up to you. All I'm going to do is call boring people and try to convince them I'm not insane."

"Good luck with that. I'm pretty sure we are." JD grinned at her, and she mimicked throwing something at them. She turned back to her preparations as she avoided the next step.

Chapter 4 - Best Laid Plans

So far SETI says it has received over three thousand entries of people taking a stab at decoding the odd message from the stars. SETI says they are going through the entries as fast as they can, but right now they figure it will take them three weeks to finish going through what they have, and that doesn't even address the new entries coming in everyday. The big question remains - could this be a message from another species, or just a reflection of all the chatter we put out into space? ~ TNN Science News

When she couldn't avoid anymore, McKenna grabbed her phone and went over to the computer again. But no matter what, she couldn't find a phone number for SETI. Grumbling, she instead clicked on the form that popped up when she pulled up the site.

Did You Translate the Message? Enter your transcription here now.

~This is a waste of time. I don't even get to talk to anyone,~ she sent out, frustrated.

[Do they have a full transcription to listen to?]

McKenna clicked around on the website until she found it.

~Yes, here.~

She pushed play, and the strange distorted sounds came out of the computer speakers. While

INCOMING

Wefor listened to the message, McKenna could feel the others existing, doing things. Nothing specific but it helped with the pain of being alone.

~Wefor?~ She kept the message private just between her and the AI that lived in her mind.

[Yes?]

~Why is being alone causing me anxiety? I've never had that issue before. And I suspect the others are agitated as well by being alone.

[There are reasons. Explanations can be provided. Are you ready to provide the translation?]

~Yes~, that she made public and began to type as Wefor spoke.

[This is a message between two of the three ships headed this way. It looks like their signal hit a radiation wave and went wide instead of narrow allowing it to filter to this planet. Message begins: in three point four liad the ships will be in orbit above the third planet. Signals have been intercepted that imply their technology may be more advanced than expected. Harvesting areas are ready for new Kaylid. If the numbers are higher than expected we can take the best leaving those not as suitable. Expect full loads and low resistance. No records of any other widespread interaction from other species. They should be - Message cuts off at that point.]

McKenna tried to lay it all out in the form. She provided her contact information and hit submit.

A cheery message thanking her for her submission appeared, and she sighed.

~Step one done. Next, I'll see if I can set up a meeting for the three of us at Homeland Security. Perc - how early can you be here?~

A brief pause then his mental voice came across. ~Eight work?~

~Perfect. I'll try to make it about ten or eleven. Traffic can suck that time of day.~

An amused sense of agreement and she reopened the private channel.

~So talk, Wefor. Why the need to be with these people? Have them here?~

[Kaylid are designed to be social and work in groups. It is coded into their very nature. With your being a commander it is worse. You are expected to be surrounded by your command team at all times. You work and live together. This isolated nature humans follow is not normal for Kaylid. In many ways all of you would share the same living space, even the children would be here in a more communal situation.]

McKenna blinked and realized her mouth had gone dry. She got up to get water as she processed the information. ~Do they share sexual partners? It is open bedmates?~ That idea freaked her out. She kinda liked Perc. But Toni and JD were just friends. She'd never been interested in women. Didn't have an issue, just no attraction for her.

[Not unless their culture supports it. Normally there is some pairing off. For Kaylid kept awake for long periods, sexual partners keep them happier and more stable. Though normally all Kaylid are sterilized upon retrieval, both male and female. Children are distracting and normally are not allowed.]

The information both made her feel better and freaked her out at the same time.

~Kenna? You okay?~ Perc's voice on a private channel startled her. She double-checked the conversation with Wefor had been private.

~Sure. Why?~

~You felt upset? No that isn't the right word. Worried? Stressed?~ His voice and the uncertainty in it made her smile a bit.

~Nah, just found out some stuff from Wefor. Doesn't really apply, but reinforces that we really don't want them to gather us.~

~Okay. If you're sure. I'll see you in the morning.~

~Yep.~ Drinking more water, she set the chicken in to marinate in the buttermilk then went back to the computer. Next task, talking to Homeland.

That number at least she found easily. She dialed it and got a phone tree and an automated message that told her the office would be open again at 7:30 Monday morning. It rattled off the general stuff that she should hang up and dial 911 if it was an emergency.

She sighed and hung up.

~Guys? We'll just have to drive down and see what we can convince them of. I'm not about to leave a message. Warning though, it's in the same building as the Sacramento Police department and the capital. There's the possibility of getting a lot of attention.~

~Meh, if anything, half of them would be on our side. So not going to worry about it. I heard the message Wefor translated. How long is a liad?~ JD asked, and she could feel Charley paying attention to the conversation.

[A liad is nine earth days approximately. They are closer than calculated. They must have found a new Drakyn planet and are planning an invasion.]

The information sat in the mindscape like a lead weight, pulling at all of them but not able to be moved.

~Okay, then Monday we shall go see what we can do. Maybe we'll get lucky?~ JD's voice had false cheer in it.

~Sounds good to me. You almost home? Need those potatoes.~

~Yes, ten minutes out.~

With that they all went back to their normal lives but the warm sensation of their links soothed her as she worked on laundry. As she tossed clothes in the bucket she made a mental list of things to do tomorrow. Looking at her closet, she froze and sighed.

~Perc?~ making the channel private.

~Yes?~

~This is going to sound horribly stupid, but would you wear a suit Monday? I have like one dress that might fit, one of those someday-I'll-lose-enough-weight-to-wear dresses. At this point it's going to be too big, but none of my clothes will fit. I'm hoping yours will be more forgiving and you can act as the front man?~

~Sure. I have one or two higher-end suits that were a bit tight. They should fit fine now. Why don't you wear your uniform?~

~Because I can't even keep it on. It's so loose the pants fall off, and I never got the skirt version. Besides, while I believe Kirk will support us, I don't want to go as Detective McKenna Largo. I need to go as

'Shifter Queen McKenna Largo' and hope they don't lock me up and throw away the key.~

~Ah. Yeah, I see. Emergency shopping trip?~

She chewed over that idea. ~Yeah, I think so. Maybe Toni will come with. Thanks.~

~Always,~ his voice held a rich velvet that coated her mind and made her shiver in pleasure before she forced it down. So he was cute, she didn't have time for this or the energy, really.

~Toni?~

It look a second, she could tell Toni was distracted and almost let it go. ~Yes?~

~Interested in clothes shopping this evening? I need something to wear Monday, plus I need groceries, and other stuff. Though this no period stuff is the best part about being a shifter.~

A burst of laughter echoed down the bond. ~I so agree with that. Yes. I don't have anything that will stay on. Though I just want to go to Walmart and get something that will fit. Mind if Jessi comes? She's changing too fast and I'd like to get her a cheap outfit or two. Actually speaking of that, Wefor?~

[Yes, Toni?]

~Is there any possibility my kids are entering puberty? I swear they look and act like ten-year-olds, not seven-almost-eight-year-olds.~

An odd pause from Wefor then a slow response. [There is the possibility they have linked with Charley and are accelerating their growth to match his maturity so all of them will be equals.]

~Is that a good or bad thing?~ Toni had a hint of worry in her voice.

[Neither. It means they are forming a squad and will be much as you and the others are. But no, they should not enter puberty for another four to five years. Though when Charley does, they will probably follow in about six months.]

~Joy. I have no idea if I'm happy about this or not. Yeah, I'll see you in a few hours. Kids are chafing at no Charley about as badly as I'm chafing at no you.~

~Yeah. Is an odd feeling. I'll explain tonight.~

McKenna heard the garage opening and headed out to help them, the idea of mashed potatoes almost making her salivate. With lots of cheddar cheese, bacon, and sour cream.

"Your courageous warriors return home, with stuff from my house, and food for the woman of the house," JD declared as he got out of his Hummer.

"Woman of the house?" McKenna asked, her voice flat, though she knew he'd sense her amusement in the mindscape.

"Hey, your house. You're a woman. So yes. Woman of the House." JD grinned at her, and she made a face at him. Charley came over and hugged her, a quick brief hug she barely had time to return before he went to help carry in a garbage bag full of objects, and JD grabbed three grocery bags.

Minutes later she stood in the kitchen chopping up the potatoes to start boiling them. Then she'd start on frying the chicken. It currently sat in a marinade of milk and egg whites as the bread crumbs and spices had already been mixed.

"McKenna?" Charley kept his voice low, and she noted he'd locked off the mindscape so the other kids wouldn't get much from him.

How in the world did he learn how to do that? We really do need to hear their story. Maybe tomorrow after Homeland. I can plan a barbecue.

INCOMING

The need to have Toni and the kids there eclipsed everything. She wanted Perc and Cass, but JD, Toni, and the twins were paramount. Another odd side effect of the pack feelings.

"Yep? Wanna help me by putting the potatoes in the pot?"

"Sure." He grabbed a step stool and washed his hands and started to put the cut-up potatoes in the water.

"What's up? You doing okay?"

"So, um, are Jessi and Jamie coming over today? What about the others?"

"Yep. Toni and I are going to run out and go grocery shopping and get some clothes for us. This weight loss means I don't have much that fits me. Then next weekend we'll have a barbecue and talk about our options."

He nodded, not looking at her. "You mind if I invite over another person for the barbecue?"

McKenna shot him a sideways look. "Who?"

"Nam? I think she needs to be here."

It took McKenna only a few seconds, the image of a tiny girl turning into an adorable tiger cub filled her mind.

"Nam Bara? The girl who turned into a tiger?"

"Yeah. Her."

"No, I don't mind, though we probably need to check with her parents. But why? What brought this up?"

He stayed silent so long she almost prodded him mentally, but finally he spoke. "I think she's our fourth, she's the one Jamie needs. And," he bit his lip, not looking at her. "I think something is wrong."

Chapter 5 - Feelings

Thundercats is making a comeback. With the emergence of shifters, the old cartoon series has gained in popularity. A search is being made for people who can shift into the iconic animals—jaguar, cheetah, lion, tiger, and two young cat shifters to fill the roles of the iconic series. This might be the most exciting movie to come out in the recent past. This comes on the heels of a casting call for Jungle Book filmed with shifters in most of the roles. ~ TNN Entertainment news

Multiple things fired off in McKenna's mind. And she looked at him, her hands frozen mid-chop as she tried to process all the bits of information in that statement.

"Okay. I don't have an issue asking her parents. But why do you think she's your fourth, and that Jamie needs her?"

Charley kept his eyes on the pot, not looking at her, holding his body rigid. "All our dreams keep asking us where our fourth is. That we need our final member. It didn't make any sense, and we thought it was the dream. But when Jamie broke his arm the dreams changed, telling us he was in the hospital wing. That freaked me out a bit more." He shrugged and finally looked at her. "And he dreams about tigers, but I don't think he knows that I've seen his dreams. He's not talking about it. But Nam is the only tiger we know."

McKenna finished chopping the potatoes, but moved more slowly to give herself time to think.

"Okay. I don't remember anything specific while we were being held by that idiot. Did I miss something?"

"Nah. But he usually stayed close to her. She's so small and Jamie liked being near someone he could take care of. Jessi can't stand it when he tries."

A bark of laughter slipped out and she grinned at Charley. "Jessi doesn't like anyone doing things for her. Independent doesn't begin to describe her."

Charley half smiled. "She's pretty firm about being equal." He shrugged. "But Nam, she spent so much time scared. I wished we could have talked there, but being locked in animal form it wasn't possible. I think if we could have communicated like we do now, she would have felt better. All we could do for each was cuddle as animals, and it didn't help since we couldn't reassure each other."

McKenna nodded. Being able to talk mind to mind in that situation would have made everything so much easier. But what was, was. No sense dwelling on the past.

"It helped more than you might think." Adding one more or even three more to their barbecues didn't make that big of a difference. "Okay. I can call. But she's a bit younger than Jessi and Jamie, right? Like six?"

"I think so? I don't know. She doesn't go to our school and I haven't seen her since the hospital." He paused for a minute then he almost whispered. "I miss them being here sometimes."

She gave him a light shoulder bump. "I do, too. I wanted to change that, but with all this alien stuff I don't know when it'll be. Let's find her parents and call. Okay? Are there any of the other kids that we should call also?"

Charley flashed a smile at her. "No, just her. For now. Though a party someday might be nice?" He didn't look at her though his ears had turned pink. "Thanks. So now what?" He nodded at the potatoes that all sat in the water.

"We start boiling, and not start any fires."

He flushed red and ducked his head.

"It's okay. Maybe you can tell us all tonight?"

He nodded and jumped down from the stool, which put the counter at waist height, and headed over to the TV and video game. McKenna set the pot on the stove, breaded all the chicken and laid out the oil to start heating. This would make a good lunch, they'd probably get takeout when they came back. With that all ready to go, she headed over to her computer and sat there. How to find out the girl's number? She really didn't want to log into the police system and use it, that seemed too much like abuse of power. But maybe calling in a favor would be acceptable.

Sheriff Michelle DeSoto's business card sat by her computer, and she picked it up and dialed the number. Waiting for it to ring, she watched Charley go start up the video game. Right now he wanted to keep her in sight and she completely understood. Not having the rest of them around her drove her slightly batty.

Michelle answered on the second ring. "DeSoto."

"Sheriff DeSoto, this is McKenna Largo."

"Largo. Heard about your excitement. Looks like you all made it back in one piece." Her voice held warmth and interest. Maybe there would be a chance to get the information needed.

"Mostly. Lost more weight than even remotely healthy and I'm sure there will be more fallout at some point. But for now we're enjoying being home and being with loved ones."

"Good attitude. So I doubt you were calling me just because, what's up?"

"Charley wants to talk to one of the kids we were with. Just a feeling, but one I'm willing to indulge, but in the mess and chaos afterwards I didn't get contact numbers. Would it be crossing any ethical lines if I asked for some contact information?"

A pause, then a sound that might have been a sigh or a chuckle. "Maybe, except every parent asked me to pass on the information to you. I had left it on a piece of paper with your hospital stuff, but I suspect that got lost. Give me your email, and I'll shoot it over to you. I suspect most of them will be more than happy to hear from you."

A weight she hadn't realized had settled on her heart after that bloody emotional day lifted. "Ah, I never saw it. That would be great. Thank you so much."

"Not a problem. Give me your email address and I'll shoot it your way." They talked for another minute or two, then McKenna hung up.

Charley had been paying more attention to her than his video game from how many times his kart crashed.

"You going to call her?" he asked as he crashed again.

"Yep, right now."

He put the game on pause and got up and wandered over to lean on her while she called Nam's house.

After ringing three times a woman answered the phone. "Hello?" The wary voice of someone expecting a telemarketer.

"Hi. This is McKenna Largo. I'm looking for," she glanced at the contact list again, "Vachan or Poorvi Bara?"

"This is Poorvi." Her voice had gone from wary to tense. "You are the officer that took care of the children when they were taken?"

"Yes, that's me." McKenna swallowed and continued when the woman didn't say anything. "Charley, one of the kids that was there, I took him in as a foster kid. He asked about Nam, and we wondered if she'd liked to come over for a barbecue next Saturday? Jessi and Jamie who are about her age will be here also. They were there and they miss her. You and your husband are welcome to come join us."

The silence stretched so long McKenna started to ask if the woman was there.

"I will bring her Saturday. Address and time?" The voice was abrupt and a bit desperate.

McKenna blinked but gave her the address. "Anytime after about one is fine. I look forward to seeing you and Nam."

"Yes, as do I," the woman said then hung up. Leaving McKenna frowning at the phone then she looked at Charley.

"Did that come across as odd to you as to me?" She knew he could hear clearly enough to have caught both sides of the conversation.

Charley bit his lip and nodded. "Can we ask Toni and Jamie and Jessi to be here by noon that day? I think Jamie needs to be here."

"Sure."

~Toni?~ She asked in the public space. ~Next week can you show up about noon? A friend of the kids is coming over and Charley thinks having them here before the girl gets here is a good idea.~

~Fine by me, at this point a week away seems like an eternity. Remind me closer to that. I'll be heading over in about three hours.~

~Works. I'm going to start frying chicken for lunch. Figured we'd get takeout for dinner.~

~Okay, I think I want Thai though. Ooh.. Sushi.~ Toni sent a wave of desire and McKenna gagged.

~After the fish, how can you want that?~

~Heck if I know. Just do. See you in a bit, I need to finish doing stuff here.~

McKenna looked at Charley. "That work?"

"Yeah. Thanks." He smiled at her and went back to his game. McKenna went to make fried chicken.

The chicken turned out decent, the mashed potatoes awesome, the shopping trip worked as expected. McKenna found a dress with a nice jacket, some shorts, t-shirts, and a bra that would hold her over until she put some weight back on. Toni had a simple shirt dress for her, and some various clothes for her kids. They got pizza and Chinese to deal with Toni's craving.

"So we really doing this? Contacting Homeland Security?" Toni asked as the kids were outside discussing something with an intentness that probably implied stress for the adults in the future.

McKenna enjoyed what she could, but that night they all ended up in the same room again, JD on the floor and Charley in bed with her. All in human form, all needing to know the other person existed.

Chapter 6 - Invasions

You have to understand that anyone is capable of killing. Humans by nature are predators and we are fiercely protective of our children. Even the most pacifistic tiny woman will kill someone threatening her child. We as a species find children worth protecting and no one even blinks at the idea of running into a burning house to save a child. Now I want you to think about the ferocity of a wolf or a lion when their cubs are threatened. Can you imagine what a mother would do who could shift if her child was threatened?
~ Family Psychologist on Talk Show

"Attention, all squads. Deploy and spread through the city. All Drakyn are to be eliminated. Avoid structure damage." The words came out of McKenna's mouth, but she had no control of them.

~Wefor?~

Silence greeted her query, and she focused her attention to what her host's body saw. The city lay out before her as she stood on the ramp of a ship of some sort. Shuttle seemed right. It had a sleekness that implied atmosphere interaction. All around her Kaylid streamed out. She kept trying to turn her head to look at them. She wanted to focus on what they looked like get an idea of what they would be dealing with.

But all she could grab were impressions, colors ranging from coal black to all but pure white. Stripes, spots, solids, even a hint of scales and feathers, but never long enough for her to pay attention and try to guess at animals.

Why so many? Are there that many settled planets? Are there that many people we could approach out there in space? Why do they do this?

The questions rattled around in her head even as she focused on the mental control board in her mind. Where her normal one had a few connections, and a few chat rooms, for lack of a better word, this seemed complex and overwhelming. A grid filled the mindspace, each one with at least fifty lights, with a single bright one in the middle. There were at least a hundred, maybe more, boxes. The sheer amount of beings that meant boggled her mind.

McKenna could feel the mind that controlled this body tapping on the bright one occasionally and getting reports while it strode out of the ship. Around her the Kaylid in various states of dress - it seemed more for comfort and what their body shape supported - rather than any type of uniform. She glimpsed lots of kilt-like items and tails peeking out from beneath them. But what she really wanted to see were the weapons they all held.

They came across like Nerf guns instead of rifles, even the powerful ones like ARs. They were bulky and thick. But she didn't see anything on the Kaylid that might imply bullets or anything were needed. They carried them easily as they trotted out of the ship, moving with a level of efficiency she couldn't help but admire. Out of the bottom of her eyes she caught that this body carried one too, but at the side instead of up and ready to use like the rest.

"Grid 2-3-Orange. Move to the right, there's a concentration of life forms that direction. Remember to not eliminate livestock, they will be re-purposed." The voice rang through the mindscape, and McKenna instinctively looked at what grid that was.

How in the world did I know that?

It took her a minute, but she realized it was a three-dimensional grid, not a flat table but a cube. It rotated in her mind to the correct section which glowed with an orange outline.

Huh, I'll have to remember that if I ever get that many people in my head.

Giving up on trying to see any more than what she already had, she tried to locate JD, Perc, Toni, any of them really. But as much as she tried to manipulate the grid she couldn't see if her friends were there.

Maybe that's good, maybe it isn't. Okay, I need to pay attention, see what I can learn from this. This isn't on a ship, so maybe this is one of those training sessions that Wefor mentioned. This might give me a bit of information about what to expect.

Trying to pretend it was a really intense movie, she paid attention to what lay in front of her. Her mind seized up as she looked at what lay beyond the clearing the ship had landed in. To her left and right more shuttles had landed and were disgorging what must have been thousands of Kaylid. But while she remained peripherally aware of that, she couldn't take her attention from what lay in front of them.

It wasn't a fairytale city, but it looked like a utopia. Tall clean spires that didn't go much above two or three stories. Houses were laid out in a pattern, a pattern the Elentrin used to their advantage as they attacked. They spiraled in around the farms and other buildings and as it went in, they were more complex while the city seat lay in the middle. McKenna tried to figure out what sort of government the Drakyn had, but nothing came up to that thought. Just the efficiency to eliminate everything as they worked their way in. Setting up everything for the Elentrin to use this as another staging area.

The air smelled clean, and while McKenna knew they had electricity she didn't see lines running anywhere. Even the buildings somehow seemed right. Not a huge metropolis, but a city probably about the size of Rossville proper. She itched with the need to learn more but couldn't sink into anything in this odd knowledge to pull out what she wanted to know.

The body kept striding forward looking at the other Kaylid spreading across the area in a silent deadly wave. Some had already hit the first buildings, and she saw a flash of red out of the corner or her eyes, but the head didn't turn so she could see. Up ahead a building that screamed family home with the courtyard, the odd small animals running around in the area.

I'd guess the equivalent of chickens, maybe?

She couldn't focus on them long, but the feathers gave her that impression. A being ran out of the door, screaming something in a liquid language that made her want to stop and pay attention to learn how to speak like that. It held a broom and ran at McKenna.

The moment froze in her mind as she saw every detail. The elegant lizard-like neck and head, the jewel tones covering the body, the simple dress-like robes in the same vibrant colors that complimented the skin. Fine scales so small she didn't know how she saw them. Long delicate hands wrapped around the broom shaft so hard that white coated the knuckles. Large eyes that seemed to swirl with blacks and reds as a scream that seemed primal in origin rippled out of the throat.

She wanted to put up her hands, to assure this being that she just wanted to talk, to learn about them, to hear the language again.

The body raised the weapon in a fluid move and McKenna felt herself sighting down the barrel and aiming at the head. A twitch of her finger, light erupting from the end of the weapon, before she could blink the light slammed into the head of the being rushing towards her, and it disappeared.

The body ran a few more steps, then crumbled to the ground, the broom still wrapped in its hands.

McKenna wanted to scream to apologize, to run from what she had done. The body kept moving forward, and the purple blood that trickled from the neck rated only a glance as if to verify the being had been killed. A quick glance inside the house revealed nothing else. The body she rode moved back out and kept walking on the road, the spiral twisting through the city like some perversion of a yellow brick road.

It spirals but it's leading death into the heart of their city instead of leading me to the wizard.

McKenna's thought tasted like bitter ash and she was oddly glad that she didn't have a real stomach, otherwise she might be throwing up.

"Commander, all troops have been deployed at the perimeter and moving in now."

"Acknowledged. Be aware there seems to be more resistance than normal. Not only are the normal guards resisting, but the populace is fighting back also," the body replied out loud and mentally.

Huh, wonder if she has a microphone or communicator as well as the mental speech? Wait, a single being attacking with a broom is more resistance than normal.

Thinking about anything except the dead bodies that were littering the area seemed like an excellent idea. All her questions wouldn't have answers, and she didn't know what else to do.

That thought pulled her attention back to the action going on around her. There were a few people fighting back and throwing things at the Kaylid. One even seemed to have a bow and arrow-like item, and she did see one dead Kaylid on the ground.

Where are the soldiers, the protection? Why don't they have guns around them? Where are the people fighting back? Why didn't anyone grab that weapon and use it against them?

It made no sense. If this happened in any city she'd ever visited, people would be digging weapons out of every closet, the military and National Guard would be attacking. Surely they had known they were landing. What was going on?

She could see barricaded doors that had been broken down, Kaylid splattered with purple blood, but nowhere did she see any form of organized resistance. Mostly people running and hiding. It made no sense. From what Wefor had said, this feud had been going on for centuries if not millennia. Why didn't they fight back?

INCOMING

"Commander, we are approaching the business district. So far injuries have been light, but there are signs of more organized resistance at this point."

Well, finally.

"Carry on. The losses are negligible so far. There are five ships of Elentrin waiting to inhabit this place. The body remover corps will be following along. We have been instructed to convert all dead to fertilizer. Remove all weapons from fallen Kaylid and any property that can be reused." The voice never blinked or even flinched, but McKenna wanted to scream.

They don't even allow them to be buried or mourned or anything? They aren't people. They're tools. Disposed of when broken.

The absolutely reality of that sank in and McKenna started trying harder to wake up, to get away from this hell. But she couldn't. An invisible observer as the Kaylid continued to sweep through the city in a pattern that didn't waiver even as the buildings got bigger. The body count just increased.

McKenna had tried to focus on the weapons, they seemed best at short range. She'd seen a few try to shoot the Drakyn that stood on roofs throwing things at them, and while the beam might hit them, the roofs weren't very high, they would stumble back, body smoking, but they would still be alive.

They had reached a large market area that looking like a tornado had swept through, or a horde of soldiers.

"Commander. A Wyrm has been spotted. It is incoming, and it looks like three of them."

A sigh slipped out of her host. The first sign of any emotion McKenna had sensed from the body and it bowed its head. "Very well. Retreat to the shuttles, double time. Lure it to that area and get out the heavy weapons. I'll let the officers know we have one incoming. The causalities will be high but we need to eliminate it then finish clearing the city."

"Yes, Commander."

As if given a command, every Kaylid she could see pivoted and at a ground-eating lope they poured out of the area. The commander stood there for another moment, surveying everything, then turned and tore out of the area.

What in the hell? Does this mean they can be stopped?

The first bit of hope McKenna had felt leapt up in her chest. Moving her attention to the shuttles as they approached though she did note how fast they could cover ground.

We need to be working out more in warrior form. I suspect we are a lot more capable in that form that what I've been assuming.

The shuttles came into view, and she saw Kaylid pulling out big tripods with another Nerf gun-like thing on top, just about double the size of what they had been carrying. They were maneuvering them and pointing towards the city. Her host moved up one of the ramps then turned to survey the city. There in the distance what must have been a strange plane approached the city. As it grew closer McKenna realized it had to be huge, way bigger than most airplanes. And it moved funny, in an up and down motion. McKenna fought to focus on the creature, she could swear the wings moved.

"All weapons are in place, Commander."

"Acknowledged. Don't fire until it lands. Concentrate on the head and underbelly."

Head? Underbelly? You mean this is a living creature coming towards us? It must be huge.

McKenna fought to turn the head to look again, but the body had its head down looking at the weapon held in two furry hands.

"Incoming, Commander."

The body looked up and McKenna got a glimpse of gold wings, massive size, and a loud noise blaring in her ears. She lifted her hands trying to protect her ears and ended up smacking herself on her head.

Blinking sleep-gummed eyes, she looked at the ceiling, the alarm still blaring.

"Fine, fine. I'll shut it off," JD grumbled as he sat up and hit the stop button on her clock. She rolled over to look at him, and he had the same sleep-dazed look she did.

"You won't believe the dream I just had," they both said at the same time.

Chapter 7 - Dream Analysis

Quiet Iceland has been in the news lately, not for their volcanoes or their glaciers, but their simple acceptance of shifters. As one city official put it, "Iceland doesn't have any natural predators anymore. No wolves, lions, jaguars, or anything like that. So all animals are being treated as intelligent beings. Any livestock is tattooed at birth and this eliminates any issues. We aren't sure why this is such an issue for other cultures. I mean how often have you seen a tiger walking down the street calmly in New York? ~ TNN Shifter Special

None of them said anything else until they all sat out on the deck, food in front of them. JD broached it. "I figure you had a dream."

"Oh, you could say that. Wefor, it wasn't a real thing happening now, was it?" McKenna asked, trying not to hope too much for the training options.

[While aware of your interaction in the dreamstate, no information about it was gathered. Please describe. Allowing you to remain in the dream did not provide access.]

"Huh. I had wondered about that, since I tried to talk to you and you never responded." McKenna ate slowly, telling them everything about the dream. She didn't broadcast it right now, wanting to keep it to the three of them right now. She didn't pull the punches even though Charley listened. He deserved to know. She probably sucked as a foster parent, but she couldn't treat him like an innocent child. She didn't think he had any innocence left and she wouldn't put him at risk by not having information he might need.

They both listened intently not making any comments until she had finished.

"Sounds like the same attack I moved through. I cleared out homes and businesses. Frankly, I didn't want to do anything, but nothing I did could affect what the body I watched through did. They killed beings hiding from them. And I can tell you these people lay eggs and then tend to them. I watched as they stomped through what must have been a nursery and destroyed all the eggs that were there, even the smallest that must have just been laid. I couldn't understand what the Drakyn were saying, but I didn't need to know what they meant. They pleaded for their lives, for their children. And the Kaylid I rode never even flinched. In many ways riding a machine would have been easier. I can't swear, but I think maybe the being had feelings, but they had been switched off?" JD rubbed his chin thoughtfully. "I saw these beautiful elegant creatures get mowed down like they had no idea how to fight back."

"That!" McKenna pointed her finger at him. "Being attacked with a broom seemed to surprise my host or at least seemed unusual enough to be remarked on. I don't get that. Yet they almost freaked out when this Wyrm started incoming. But I couldn't get a good look at it."

"Neither could I. My host was focused on setting up those big guns, and I could only get a glimpse of something big with wings. Nothing else."

"Yeah, that's about what I could get." McKenna said, sighing. "I really wanted to see what would scare them. There's so much I think we don't know. Wefor, can you tell me anything about the Drakyn culture?"

[Not really. They don't have space travel, as they have never needed it, but there is no information as to why. They are technologically advanced, but in ways different from the Elentrin. There is no information in the databases with details.]

"Do you know why the Elentrin hate them so much?" McKenna asked.

[That information is not present.]

McKenna sighed. "I really think there's too much that doesn't make sense. Wefor, were you able to determine if this was real or a training session?"

[From the information you have provided and the fact that the ships are in your solar system, this seems to be a training session. Testing to make sure the Kaylid could handle the needs. Some do break, the nanobots are instructed to kill them at that point if they have no ability to handle what is expected.]

The matter-of-fact way the AI said it made McKenna shudder. To think of killing someone, anyone, because they were in the way, horrified her. And it was clear from their actions they had no issue with slaughtering innocents. She turned and looked at Charley who watched them with a serious look on his face. Part of her wished he looked horrified, but instead he looked thoughtful.

INCOMING

Is that better or worse that the child in my care is so world-wise?

"Were you in the middle of all that?" She tried to keep her voice flat, but a hint of worry crept in.

Charley shook his head. "No. I was on a ship, I think, working with weapons. But I don't think they were the ones you were using. From what you described yours were long and kinda chunky at the front?"

McKenna nodded.

"These were pretty short, held in one hand. They had a really wide front. They kept telling me they were collectors. Made to be used on other Kaylid. They kept mentioning something about collecting." Charley frowned, taking another bite, his pale eyebrows furrowed in concentration. "We were supposed to practice shooting them. We all had to shoot each other. But this time I didn't see Jessi or Jamie. It was just other Kaylid, all in warrior form."

Charley looked up, wrinkling his nose. "Getting shot with it felt really odd. Like a static shock over your entire body, then you just fold up. It didn't hurt so much as like when your foot goes to sleep and you need to wake it up, but everywhere. You can see but can't move or do anything. I mean I could breathe and blink, but not move my fingers." He shook as if in wolf form trying to shake water off of him. "Didn't like it."

McKenna looked at him. "You okay?"

He avoided her gaze by paying very close attention to his pancakes. "But they did say that was setting one. The higher ones knock you out. I want to say the highest put you in a coma-like state. After we all tested on each other, we were given these tags to attach to them. They kinda reminded me of what you see on cows sometimes?" He glanced up at McKenna, and she nodded.

Cattle in the area often had plastic tags affixed to their ears, usually showing vaccinations, age, or other information important to the owner.

"Well, we were supposed to put the gender on it, there were five options? So that didn't make much sense to me. Then height and weight. The hand scanner that created the tags would provide that part. Then it was a quick clip onto the ear and we were supposed to move on."

He stared out at the field avoiding her and JD. "The person giving the orders, not the same one from the dreams before, said a collection vehicle would be by later to pick them up." Charley fell silent and poked at the pancake again.

The fact there still was pancake on his plate told McKenna something bugged him.

"Soooo... what else happened that's bugging you?" she prompted, but didn't stare at him, instead she got herself some more bacon and potatoes.

"What does tubing mean?" he asked, biting his lip as the pancake slowly turned into mush.

McKenna blinked. "Umm, I don't know. What was said?"

"The teacher person said they would be collected and tubed. What does that mean?"

"Oh. Umm..." McKenna thought about the conversations she'd had and shot the question over to Cass.

~Cass, does the term 'tubing a Kaylid' mean anything to you?~

~One second,~ there was an odd feeling of tension, then Cass's voice came back.

~They were all kept in canisters or big tubes from what I could figure. Like racks of canned goods. So I could easily see it called being tubed.~ Her thought had an odd quality to it.

~Is that good or bad?~ McKenna asked after double-checking it was only her and Cass in this conversation.

~Yes? They didn't seem to be in pain from what I could figure out, but I'm damn sure they also killed or in their view eliminated anyone not need or damaged in some way. And it was done with less interest than you might pay dumping expired canned goods.~

~So noted. Thanks, Cass. You dream at all last tonight?~

A taste of strawberries washed across the connection.

~Yes, but not in the way you mean. I have to get back to work. Yell if you need something.~ Cass closed the connection, leaving McKenna smiling a bit. She had a good idea what Cass had dreamed about.

She opened her eyes to see Charley and JD looking at her. "Charley, it probably means they were talking about how they, the Elentrin, store Kaylid. Cass says they're put in big containers and kept there. Not asleep, but not hurting or anything."

Charley frowned, then his eyes lit up. "Oh, like at the beginning of the movie *Alien*, when they were all sleeping?"

"When did you watch *Alien*?" McKenna blurted out, even as JD looked surprised.

Charley flushed, his skin turning into a light pink that crept up to his ears. "Uh, while we were at JD's while you were gone. Trust me, we're never watching anything again like that. That freaked us out."

McKenna didn't know whether to hug the boy or fall over laughing. The idea of watching *Alien* at their ages? She hadn't watched it until a teenager and it had still scared her then.

She cleared her throat trying to seem unaffected. "Yeah, similar idea, probably different technology. They don't hurt or aren't aware of anything. They just sleep until they wake them up."

"Oh," Charley sighed relieved. "That doesn't sound that bad. So they just sleep until they need you?"

McKenna just nodded, not wanting to get into what their lives were like outside of the tubes.

"Nothing else?"

Charley started to eat a bit more, perking up. Seeing him eating the pancake helped her feel better.

"We need to get ready to head out to Homeland Security in a bit." JD mentioned as he polished off his plate.

~You on your way here?~ she asked Perc in the open space.

~Leaving in a bit. Need anything?~

~No. I'll get dressed in our show and tell clothes in a minute. Did you happen to dream last night?~ she asked, not caring if everyone heard.

~Not me, but then I wore myself out last night. By the time I laid down I could barely move. Trying to bleed off stress which means working out. Besides, gives the nanobots something to do.~

"Time to go get ready," JD commented as he headed to his room

She forced a smile, grabbing the dishes and heading in.

Chapter 8 - Bluffs Called

Three months into the change that shifters brought to us, the world has seen the lowest incident of wars in almost a century. Even the always contentious Middle East is currently dealing with a religious crisis that has precluded any new offensives. But the actions of North Korea and China are creating concerns in the international community, and Australia has increased patrols in the Indian Ocean. Is a new storm brewing? ~ Op Ed Piece

After the dishes were done, she dressed in a simple sheath dress with a matching jacket, McKenna waited for Perc to show up. JD had pulled out an old suit from when he first started on the force. What had barely fit him then hung a bit loosely now. But he looked professional. She'd even pulled out heels, though part of her wanted to show up in a kilt and combat boots. This felt like the wrong type of armor.

[This does not make sense. Contact the authority for your global defense system and let them know of the incoming threat. The ships should be visible on any defense systems at this point.]

~We don't have defense systems. I think some people have seen it with telescopes, but unless a camera or telescope is looking for it, we don't have that level of technology.~

[That seems highly unwise. How will you know when you are being attacked?]

~Remember, you're the first alien for the most part we've ever been aware of. As of right now, there is no global acknowledgment of any other species besides ours.~

She swore she felt Wefor huff in disgust.

[Fine, then contact your leaders and let them know of the incoming danger.]

~Our leaders don't have ways for normal people to contact them like that. Everything has to go through channels. And that's what we're trying to do.~

[You are not a normal, you are a commander.]

This time she knew she heard affront in Wefor's voice and resisted laughing. Everyone could hear this conversation, and she suspected more than one of them was amused.

~Be that as it may, they don't know that or what it means. So we try this the hard way.~

[And if this option fails, what then? Time is precious.]

~Then we get creative I guess.~

I don't know. I wish I did, but I don't know what to do if this doesn't work.

She heard Perc's car pulling in and glanced at JD who finished filling travel mugs of coffee for them.

"Ready?"

"For a day in a monkey suit trying to convince people we shouldn't be locked up? Not really. But hey, it'll be a new experience." JD's voice made her laugh.

"Sarcasm is uncalled for," she said with a grin. "Besides, I'm wearing a dress and heels."

"Point. I admit you are suffering more than I am." He walked to the door with her, Perc had just climbed out of his car and smiled at both of them.

McKenna thought maybe he looked at her a bit longer than needed, but she didn't mind.

"Charley?"

"They had school today. After missing it for a week they needed to go back and catch up. The absence won't be excused, but Anne had explained to the teachers what happened and they can make up the work. Or at least Charley can. Jessi and Jamie don't really have homework only being in first grade." McKenna half-smiled. The kids had broken down last night and told them everything that had happened.

By the time they were done McKenna didn't know if she wanted to strangle them or hug them so tight that they could never wiggle free. A review on guns and a trip to the range when he turned twelve had been added to her list, but she didn't change the gun safe code. If someone came after them again she'd told him to run first and foremost, but she couldn't remove his ability to protect himself. It had been proven that people might try to kill them.

She pushed away the memories and the conversation as they headed towards the capitol, stayed light. Perc drove, his car getting much better gas than JD's Hummer. They avoided the main topic until they pulled into the parking garage.

"Am I taking the lead in this?" Her voice quiet. No other options had appeared that wouldn't make her looked like a truly crazy person.

"Yeah. I think that's best. You have the social impact and maybe you can leverage that to something decent. I think we all know time is disappearing more quickly than we might want." Perc's voice had the same solid worry as wrapped her heart.

"Great. McKenna in the lead." She didn't want to feel sorry for herself, and really she didn't, but she had no idea how to pull this off.

"You're the commander. We are but your minions," JD said in an overly pompous voice.

McKenna mock growled and batted at him, he dodged easily, but his humor helped. With a bit more confidence, she headed to figure out how to convince someone they weren't crazy.

With the office in the Capitol Mall, they got more than a few recognized looks and nods, mostly positive, as they headed in. At the desk, security glanced up at them as they approached.

"Good morning. How may I help you?" The security guard seemed disinterested and going through the motions.

"Yes, I needed to speak to someone from Homeland security. I have a possible incident to report."

"Very well. I'll let the agent on duty know there are people here to talk to him. Wait over there, please." He waved them to a waiting area and then typed into the equipment on his desk.

A wave of relief made her sigh as they headed over. At least this way no one would overhear why she wanted to talk to the agent. Maybe this wouldn't be as bad as she thought.

Sitting would require being still, and she all but vibrated with nerves, so sitting in one place would drive her crazy. They all stood, waiting and trying not to feel self-conscious. After about five minutes a man walked out of one of the elevators and made his way over to them. In his late fifties, he had that bored, world-weary look she recognized from other cops. Gruder in particular. The whole, 'I've seen everything, I don't care, leave me alone' look.

Overweight, with dark brown hair starting to bald in the back, he didn't have the broken capillaries of a heavy drinker, but the cigarette stench that surrounded him told her he smoked a pack or more a day. He walked like ex-military though, and his skin held a dark tan that implied lots of time outside.

"I'm informed you have a tip to pass to us? Terroristic?" His voice matched the look on his face, and she didn't know if this would be a good or a bad thing.

McKenna stepped forward, and she felt JD and Perc move to flank her. From the slight narrowing of eyes he saw it too.

"In a way. It's complicated. If we could go somewhere and discuss?"

He looked at all three of them then nodded abruptly. "Follow me."

The agent headed towards the elevator bank and stood on the other side of the security check, watching with sharp eyes as they went through. They had left their guns at home, not wanting to get into that aspect of all this. All they carried was ID and the keys to the car. Even phones had been left at home. With the new range of their telepathy, they figured it would cause less angst. Besides, if any of them were conscious they could communicate.

The man didn't speak on the ride up the elevator, just got out when the doors opened and led them to a small conference room. The room had a pitcher, some glasses, and multiple yellow legal pads and pens laying on the table. On the far end, a VoIP phone sat waiting, with an attached video conference system. He placed his phone face down on the table and sat at the side of the table facing the door, forcing all of them to have their backs to the door. McKenna sat though it made her uncomfortable. She pushed away the discomfort. They weren't here to make trouble, and she would hear anyone entering as long as she paid attention.

"I'm Special Agent John Smith," he said, his voice devoid of any humor as he pulled the legal pad and a pen towards him. "Please identify yourself and what you have to report." His voice contained boredom and world-weariness. Signs of a man who didn't expect anything to come of this.

~Any bets as to how many reports of 'my neighbor is a terrorist because they don't go to church on Sunday' he's had to take?~ McKenna commented wryly in the mindscape. Chuckles met her humor as she took a deep breath and went for it.

"I'm Detective McKenna Largo. I'm a Narcotics detective for the Rossville Police department. As is my partner Detective JD Davidson." She nodded at JD as she said that. "Percival Alexander has volunteered to come with us to help explain our concerns and see if you can help us get in contact with the right people."

Smith froze looking at them closer, then picked up his phone and tapped a few times. He looked at the screen, looked at them, then back at the screen. "Huh. So you are." He put down the pen and looked at them, the boredom dropping away from his face. "So why is the Shifter Queen and her two harem boys here bugging me?"

McKenna choked, his comment derailing her. "My what?" Her voice might have cracked on that part.

The agent just shrugged and looked at her. "You're popular and could get anything by lifting your pinkie. Why are you here wasting my time?"

McKenna rubbed her face trying to get past the embarrassment and the desire to snap at the man. "I'm flattered by your belief that I'm that popular, but I'm just a cop. The fact that I was taped changing for the first time has nothing to do with why I'm here. And I'm not on social media because I'm not an idiot."

~Though at this rate maybe I should start a worldwide panic. Bet people would arm themselves.~ She sighed and didn't give anyone time to respond to her comment.

"We really need to talk to the secretary of defense and possibly the president, but we'd really like to do this correctly."

The man raised his hands, sarcasm dripping off his body language. "Please do go ahead, what does the great McKenna Largo think is so important that I should rush it to the secretary of defense and the president?"

McKenna was ready to just walk out now. The man had already decided they were glory hounds, and she had no idea how to convince him otherwise.

~This is a mistake, and I don't know how to get past it. Give up and walk away?~ she asked frantically as she stared at the man who just looked at her, his face impassive.

~I don't know. But we have to try.~ JD's voice was serious and worried. ~I didn't think we'd get attitude until after we started to talk. This isn't good.~

McKenna took a deep breath. "I have evidence that the epidemic of people turning into animals was not a random thing. But a planned attack against us."

John Smith sat up a bit looking at her, some of his disdain dropping away. "Against which us? It was something that happened globally."

"Against Earth."

"What?"

She spoke fast trying to explain before he lost it. "The changes were caused by alien nanobots structured to turn a percentage of humans into animals. And the ones that created these nanobots are on their way here."

All interest and the start of taking them seriously disappeared, and the man pushed back the legal pad with an exclamation of disgust. "Really? Aliens are on their way here? What, you got caught up in the SETI crap and decided you needed to be more famous? What is it with you social media addicts? Why do you need to be in the public's eye at all times? You were fading from the public view so you thought this would be your next option?"

McKenna quit being embarrassed at this point and got annoyed. "Yes. Because coming quietly, not carrying our weapons, not announcing who we are, and asking for an agent is totally how I'm going to get more public attention. If I wanted that, I could have just done a press conference or video to let people know. Because you know, starting a worldwide panic is exactly what I need to do. Hey, I have the governor knowing my name, why don't I call him and tell him that aliens are coming?"

Smith just crossed his arms and sneered at her. "I have no idea why you're wasting my time. 'Cause I don't have time for prima donna freaks."

"Argh." She stood with a violent movement. "I don't know how to make anyone believe me. I wish I could just call the secretary of state again. Maybe he'd believe me. He's already seen us doing something that should have been impossible."

[Call him. If it will help.]

Wefor's voice startled her, and by the sudden tensing from JD and Perc she knew they hadn't expected it either.

~Not like I have any idea what the number is.~

"Oh, yes, like the secretary is just going to know who you are on a first-name basis." Smith stood, too. "Get out of here. I don't have time to waste on stupid attention-whores."

[The number is] Wefor rattled off a long string of numbers while Smith talked. [It was dialed twice on speakerphone so the tones were played. Remembering that is not difficult.]

~Fuck it, we've got nothing to lose because the next option is going viral and that would be bad.~ Even as she thought that she moved over to the phone.

"Fine. Let's see what he has to say."

~Please let this work.~

"See what who has to say?" Smith demanded as his hand drifted to his waist.

"I wouldn't," rumbled JD, as he and Perc rose also, their bulk still intimidating, even after their weight losses.

McKenna hit the speaker phone and hit nine, she'd been there enough to know she needed that to dial out, then she dialed the long number Wefor provided her.

~You sure? That was more than ten digits.~

Before Wefor could respond the phone rang and the video screen lit up. A second later the surprised face of the secretary of state filled the screen.

"Ms. Largo?" he said, his brows furrowing. "Not that I'm complaining about being able to speak with you again, but how exactly did you get this number? And-" he glanced down then looked back up. "Why are you calling from a Homeland Security extension?"

"Sir, I am so sorry, sir. I'll take care of this. I am so sorry," the agent babbled as he stared at the screen in horror.

"Mr. Secretary, I apologize, but I need someone to listen to me. And you are my last-ditch effort. Please, if I may have a few minutes of your time?"

He blinked at them and the frantic agent. "One moment." The screen blanked and McKenna hoped that didn't mean he'd hung up. But before any of them could figure out what to do, he came back on. "You have ten minutes. Please go ahead."

Her mouth felt like she had swallowed sand, but she spoke anyhow. "Sir, this is going to be hard to believe, but people like me who can shift, can do so because of alien nanobots. The reason I knew your number is that I have an alien Artificial Intelligence that's part of me now." She ignored the sputtering of the agent who couldn't get past Perc or JD. "It memorized the sounds when the phone dialed and fed them back to me. I'm not doing this as a lark. The message that SETI is offering a reward for is a stray transmission from the ships headed this way. From the race that created these virus nanobots. I provided the translation via their Website, but it might take weeks. Sir, we have about twenty-five days before they're in orbit above our planet. If we aren't ready, the consequences will be very bad."

As she spoke, as fast as she could without stumbling over the words, the pleasant amused expression had faded, and the sharp eyes and assessing look had snapped into place. He looked at Perc and JD.

"You two believe this?"

"Sir, we know it. We have proof in more ways than one. And we need to prepare," Perc spoke as JD still kept the agent.

"Why haven't you said anything before?"

McKenna waved at this scenario. "Who is going to believe us? I'm telling you aliens are coming. I don't believe myself sometimes and I know they're coming. Sir, I don't want to go to other options. But they are coming, and I know what they want."

"What would that be?" His voice still cool, but she could pick up background noise and suspected other people were listening in on this conversation as well.

"They're coming for us, sir. The Kaylid. That is what they call us. They want us as disposable soldiers for their war. We were supposed to be trapped as crazed animals. We are their foot soldiers. Disposable and easily replaceable."

"You do realize how hard this is to believe."

"Yes, I do, sir."

[Tell them these coordinates based off galactic coordinates with your sun as the center.] Wefor spoke in her mind. [That is where the armada is right now.]

"If NASA or any of the large telescopes look at these galactic coordinates, they should see the ships." She repeated the numbers as Wefor said them.

The Secretary looked at her for a long time then nodded. "I assume you can be reached via the information provided at the embassy?"

"Yes," she said, her head bobbling like a one of those silly dolls.

"Give me a few days. I'll be in touch." With that the screen went black, and McKenna sagged.

"You, you, you idiots! How could you do that? How could you even get his number? Get out of here now before I have you arrested. I'll be filing reports with your captain and chief about this. I'll have your jobs for this. Now get out!" Smith had turned red and pointed at the door, all but yelling.

"Thank you," McKenna managed and headed to the door feeling light-headed.

~I can't believe I just did that,~ she muttered in her head.

~That was cool~ Cass gushed. ~I could hear what you said 'cause JD and Perc kept the channel open, so it was almost like being there. Though I'm glad I took a break. Otherwise the other people in the lab would have thought I'd lost it with my giggling. You rock.~

~You did awesome, Kenna. I never thought about the spaceships. If they can see them, surely that will lend credence to what we said?~ JD's voice had warmth and concern in it.

~I hope so. The only other option might involve worldwide panic so I'd really like to avoid it. A few days? How long do we wait?~

INCOMING

The elevator deposited them in the lobby, and the security guards were on their feet staring at them.

McKenna flashed a smile, held her head up high and headed to the door at a walk, refusing to show one ounce of worry. But deep inside, even as a strong female who had no issue handling herself, having JD and Perc to look intimidating made her feel better. Getting in a fight here would do no one any good, and men were more likely to back down from obviously scary men. She had no issue using their own idiosyncrasies against them.

The escape, and it felt like one, made her a bit giddy as they got back to the car. She climbed in the back, JD really couldn't fit even in a nice car like Perc's, buckled in and closed her eyes.

~We did it. Now to see how long it takes.~ Her voice somber in the mindscape.

~How long do we give them?~ Toni asked.

~Not too long. But at least until after Saturday. I want the barbecue and Nam to come over. Perc, Cass, you two coming?~

~Hell, yes. You're lucky I haven't moved in. I hate sleeping without you.~ Cass's voice had an odd pain to it, but McKenna didn't know how to respond.

~Ditto. In fact, mind if I crash there that night? Be nice to drink a bit and not worry about driving.~

McKenna tilted her head. ~Your bots let you get drunk?~

~Umm? Yes? Well, I mean the last time it took a lot, maybe more than it should have, but not like I get drunk that often,~ he protested, a bit defensively.

[Not all bots would have repaired the same programs at the same time, but with the blood exchange it would be extremely difficult to get more than slightly buzzed without interference.]

That pronouncement dropped like a lead weight in the middle of the space and everyone fell silent.

~Well, there goes my booze bill,~ Perc said dryly, and the rest of them broke up laughing.

Chapter 9 - Additions

There have been more late night meetings in the capital for the last week, and not even insiders have mentioned what's being discussed. But the cabinet has been pulled into closed-door meetings, and the National Science advisor hasn't left the White House for the last few days. Meetings have been canceled, and yet there is nothing leaking out of the capital. The most interesting is that they've asked ambassadors from the United Kingdom, Russia, and Canada to come and meet later this week. What is going on at the White House? ~ TNN Political Pundit.

The rest of the week crawled by with McKenna jumping every time the phone rang or the one time someone knocked on the door. That had been a kid looking for yard work, which she declined. But none of those calls was anything to do with the information passed onto the secretary.

Saturday showed up, and she sighed in relief. Even having JD stay with her, they'd given in and bought a new air mattress and set it up in the third bedroom while he let the insurance do their thing, didn't lower how much she missed the others. Toni had been by once or twice but she'd been trying to get things set up legally for the kids and make sure Carina had full rights if anything happened to her.

McKenna spent her own time with a lawyer getting life insurance and beneficiaries created to make sure Charley would be safe. Kirk and the others had checked in on her to see if they had any ideas or plans, but all they could do was wait. If it continued like this, by Monday her temper and stress level would push her to the nuclear option.

Wefor had her searching the web and they kept updated on where the ships were, though if a person didn't know what he was looking at it wouldn't have meant much. Some technology that made them hard to see, not a shield, more just a distortion that looked like reflected space junk or something like that. Either way, they had enough information, and the ships would be close enough that they'd be able to tell people where to look and see the incoming ships.

And start a world-wide panic.

That thought made her sick, and she shook her head. JD and Charley were outside setting up stuff to grill, and Charley had some games he wanted to try with the twins. They had spent all week after school creating an obstacle course and made her promise to not come out and snoop. But the two males had been very excited about it. Today she'd get to see.

~You two are coming, right?~

She hated feeling anxious, but Cass had worked all week, and Perc had to wrap up a bunch of stuff with the lawyers about the lawsuit he'd brought against the various sports organizations.

~On my way. Another twenty minutes, tops.~ Perc's voice sounded in their shared mindspace and she could feel the others pay more attention.

~Probably another forty for me. Need to stop and grab some stuff, having a chocolate craving. But, yes, I'll be there. I've missed you guys.~ Cass's voice helped ease the ache that had nagged her all week, and McKenna's mood lifted.

~Be there in five, kids are driving me crazy. You'd think they didn't talk to Charley ALL THE TIME.~ A wave of laughter with childlike flavor filled the space even as McKenna felt the adults' humor.

The kids rarely spoke in the shared adult mind-space and she could lock them out if she needed, but normally she didn't need to. Though with the reach they all had, it might have to change. When she changed her connections to everyone, it had trickled down to the kids too. They were ecstatic about the ability to talk regardless of distance, though they tried to hide it.

~Okay. I'll see everyone shortly.~ All she could do was think about having the rest of them here. With a sigh, she locked down the communication. ~Wefor, is this normal?~

[The need to be with others of your squad?]

~Need? I don't understand why it almost feels like I'm longing for a loved one. I love them, but I'm not in love with any of them. Why this pining feeling? Like part of me is missing?~

[In a real way part of you is. Squads tend to work as gestalt beings. With the establishment of the planet-wide communications, you intensified this feeling. Your bots work better in proximity to each other using shared resources. You calculate faster and are able to make better decisions. Commanders need their teams to be able to lead the Kaylid into battle and bring victories.]

That did and didn't help, though knowing her vague unease didn't mean she was going crazy added a bit of relief.

The mound of meat needed for a house full of shifters took up the bottom part of her fridge. Cutting back on other expenses had given her more money for food, but at this rate she would need to start buying protein in wholesale amounts.

~Incoming,~ Toni warned seconds before the door flew open. Two kids hugged her and let go before she had time to dry her hands and hug them back.

"What is their issue?" she asked Toni as she walked over to help her with the bag of potatoes.

"Heck if I know. They've been bouncing oddly for the last two days. Been about to strangle them or drug them."

McKenna dumped the potatoes into the sink. "No Carina? She knows she's always welcome here, right?"

"Yes. But she's going to spend the day with some friends at the river. Though she was bemoaning missing the grilling."

McKenna grinned. "I was going to chop these into quarters for the grill. Should take about the same amount of time as the chicken. Then we can have these, too."

"Sounds good to me," Toni said even as she started pulling out the more snacky foods and vegetables that she dumped in the sink with the potatoes. "I wanted some peppers and onions on the grill, too."

"Works for me." McKenna started to scrub the veggies when there was a knock on the front door. She turned to look. Almost everyone came in the side door in the garage. "You didn't close the garage, did you?"

"No. Open for Perc and Cass." Toni frowned, staring at the front door.

"Huh." McKenna dried her hands and headed over to the front door even as she glanced to see where JD was. He stood on the deck talking to the kids who hadn't shifted yet but were all but vibrating with excitement.

She pulled open the door and blinked as a woman and a small girl stood there. The woman was dressed in loose trousers and a tunic shirt that hit her mid-thigh in matching gray, and a shawl around her in dark blue. Her face serious, and something in her eyes made McKenna's heart ache. But it was the girl who grabbed her. The tiny girl, she seemed even tinier than McKenna remember, looked up at her with big eyes and a level of sadness no one that young should ever know. Her dark hair curled loosely around shoulders though it seemed lank and heavy.

"Nam!" McKenna's heart both leapt and cracked as she recognized the girl. Before she thought, she dropped to her knees and pulled the girl into a fierce hug. "I'm so glad to see you."

The arms that wrapped around her had a certain death grip quality and she found herself unwilling, unable to let the girl loose. When she realized the dampness on her shirt was from silent tears the girl cried, she rose, the girl still tight in her arms.

"Mrs. Bara, Poorvi, what's going on?" The woman's face had paled, but it also held relief as she dropped two large duffle bags on the front step.

"She will be safe here. I can't protect her. Protect my daughter as you did once. I beg of you and will pray for your soul to Allah." She kissed her fingers, touched the back of her daughter's head and whirled, all but running to the car.

Struck dumb, McKenna watched her leave as she held the tiny girl in her arms, silent sobs wracking her body.

"Um, what just happened?" Toni asked behind her.

McKenna was perversely glad Toni sounded just as confused as she felt.

"I have absolutely no idea. Would you grab those bags for me? I suspect they're Nam's belongings. " As she said the girl's name her arms tightened around McKenna's neck, though she still didn't make a sound.

"Sure. Put them where?"

Umm, what the heck do I do? JD is in the spare room, Charley has his, and putting Nam with him doesn't work.

"Mine for now. I think I still have a small dresser in storage I can pull out. She can sleep with me for now."

"Got it." Toni moved by carrying both duffels, which looked way too small to contain a girl's life. McKenna headed to the living room.

~Charley, can you guys come in here? Nam is here.~

She sent that as she sat on the couch, still holding the girl who trembled in her arms. The sliding door opened and three kids raced towards her, smiles on their faces. They all froze and looked at the back of the girl in her arms.

~What's wrong? Is she hurt?~ Charley asked, a desperate anger to his tone.

~I don't think so, physically at least. But her mom just dumped her here, left stuff and ran. Telling me to take her. Do you have any idea what's going on?~

~No. I just... ~ He trailed off, and she saw and felt his shrug.

"Nam? Nam, darling. It's okay. Will you look at me?"

~She weighs so little. The twins are heavy and solid. I'm scared if I hug her too tight I'll break something.~ McKenna said into the mindscape.

She put that comment in the main room, knowing the kids would hear, wanting feedback from Toni.

Toni walked back out even as JD came in, drawn by her comments.

"Nam? You remember me talking about JD? You remember meeting him that day? He's here. As are Charley and Jessi and Jamie. Want to turn and see them?"

There was a sudden tightening of arms, then the arms fell away, and the girl pushed back and looked at McKenna. Her eyes were swollen and red, making her dark brown eyes look black and bottomless.

"Are you going to get rid of me, too? Abba said I was an abomination." She said the word too clearly, so sharp McKenna knew she'd heard it too many times. "And that I should be put out for the elements to devour." Her voice vibrated thin and stressed. Nam didn't look at any of them, instead focused on her hands.

McKenna choked as the girl talked and looked up to see the wild looks of panic on the kids' faces. "No. I'm not getting rid of you, but I'm a bit confused as to why your mom left you here. Abba? Is that your father?"

Nam nodded miserably, curling up a bit, refusing to look at anyone.

~Kenna, we need to let her feel us. She's ours. But locked up in herself she'll never believe us. Look at her.~ Charley's tone held panic, and she could feel the others holding themselves back with an effort. Jamie all but radiated something she didn't understand. Not love, not fear, but a type of deep protectiveness that matched the others in richness and depth, but his shown brighter, almost about to combust.

"Nam. Look at me. Please?" McKenna coaxed the girl, and she lifted her head. Dark circles under her eyes and her thin frame carried so much information that she wanted to scream. "How often do you change?"

Nam flinched and shrank into herself even more. "Never. It is an abomination."

Again that word and McKenna wanted to snarl, but that would not help this situation.

"Nam. You remember me, right?"

Her head nodded rapidly, but she didn't look up. Her body radiated an awareness of the people around her, but she didn't look at any of them, just hunched like expecting a blow. That posture McKenna knew all too well.

"Do you trust me, that I'd never do anything to hurt you? That Charley and the twins would never do anything to hurt you?"

Nam looked up at her, eyes dark, and McKenna had serious thoughts of murder on her mind at the fear in her eyes, the expectation that people would hurt her. The child had been five or six at the time of the kidnapping, so best case barely seven. No child should know enough to look like that.

"Yes." Nam's voice barely counted as a whisper, but McKenna grabbed it, needing to do this, not knowing any other way. The need from the kids and the encouragement from Wefor, silent though strong, drove her as much as the desire to protect this child.

McKenna glanced at JD, but he already stood next to her, his Gerber out. Nam paled and her body shook.

"Nam, trust me. Please?" With careful movements, McKenna cut a nick on the fleshy part of her palm, nothing big, only enough for blood to well up. Charley was next to her before she could finish, his hand out, and Jamie and Jessi next to him. Their hands out, but their eyes all locked on Nam with an almost hungry intensity.

She felt Toni's approval even as she glanced up at her, then made the same small cuts on their hands.

"Will you let me?" McKenna kept her voice calm as she looked at Nam, holding her hand out silently asking for her palm even as she held the knife in the other.

Nam swallowed, but didn't pull away. With a trembling hand she placed her palm in McKenna's. The wound McKenna made bled a bit, and she squeezed it to make it bleed a bit more. Nam didn't flinch, just watched her with wide dark eyes.

"I'm going to drip some of your blood into Charley's wound, then his blood into yours, okay? Then with Jessi and Jamie. I know it sounds weird.

But may I do this?" McKenna knew too well the frustration of adults never asking, so she tried to move slow to give the girl time to adjust.

Nam nodded, her eyes never leaving McKenna's face.

I am so going to hurt someone for doing this to this little girl.

McKenna squeezed Nam's hand and dripped blood into Charley's bleeding wound. She didn't flinch as Charley and the twins exchanged blood with her, though her face remained tight, drawn.

"Nam, I'm going to do the same thing. I promise it will make sense in a few minutes. Okay?" McKenna felt desperate to wipe the fear and pain off the tiny girl's face, but right now she did what she could.

Nam nodded solemnly, and McKenna made the exchange.

~Wefor, push this one as fast as you can please. Toni, can you grab something for us to eat in here, while we wait?~

Toni didn't even reply, just turned and went into the kitchen. Later when things were better, she'd talk the child into linking with the other adults, but right now she and the kids were needed to give her the emotional support she needed.

[Working. Her body is severely depleted of nourishments and she has not shifted in much too long. She needs to shift and restore her energy levels. What is it with you humans and never having enough nutrients?] Wefor's voice held an edge of stress and part of McKenna wanted to laugh given how many people struggled to eat less to lose weight. They all struggled to eat more to put on weight. She'd managed to gain ten pounds in the last week. But she still needed about another thirty. JD had managed to put on fifteen, but he could stand the ration bars with their five thousand calories. She couldn't.

Toni returned with chunks of cheese, chips, dip, and a pile of lunch meat slices on a tray. She set it down next to McKenna on the couch. The kids were crouched around her, watching Nam with unnerving intensity.

"Nam? You need to eat. Here, take something and eat."

The little girl bit her lip, then asked in a quiet voice. "Is it pork?"

McKenna glanced at Toni, but she was already replying. "No. Chicken and beef."

"Okay." With a hand that shook too much Nam reached out and took one of the pieces of meat. She gobbled it quickly then started to reach for another and froze.

"Nam, eat it all if you want. We have lots of food, and you need to eat." McKenna urged.

~Eat, Nam. You need to get strong for us.~ Charley's voice filled the mindspace and McKenna realized the link to Nam had lit up.

The girl jerked, tears welling in her eyes as she looked around, her whole body starting to shake again.

~Nam, listen. This is why we needed to share the blood. It lets us talk in our minds. Look, Charley, Jessi, and Jamie are here. You can talk to them the same way. Just find their names in your mind and think. I promise it will see normal very fast.~

~Nam? We've been waiting for you. You need to eat and shift.~ Jamie's voice took over, and the space filled with emotion that McKenna shied away from. It was too strong and scary for her to face with these kids. Love but not love, pack but more. Nam turned in her arms to look at them, tears starting to run down her face as Jessi and Charley sent their support, their warmth, their concern for her into the mindspace.

McKenna didn't look at Toni, and Toni had locked herself down tight, so she had no idea how she might be reacting to the sheer emotions flooding the shared mindspace. While the adults would hear Nam in McKenna's mindspace, they wouldn't be able to talk privately to her until they shared blood. But for now this would work.

"Nam? Do you feel better?" She said this out loud, knowing the kids would keep reassuring her and pull her into their private mindspace. Already the four of them felt different in a way she didn't have time to analyze.

Nam nodded and took a piece of cheese, but her eyes kept darting back and forth between the kids and McKenna.

"Good. Listen to me. I'll figure out what's going on, but you aren't going anywhere. I want you to eat. Eat all you can. We're making some more food here in a few minutes. Then would you like to shift and go play?"

"Yes. You need to come play with us, Nam. We have the best thing set up." Charley said. None of them had touched her physically yet, but their emotions had helped her a bit. She didn't tremble anymore, and her tears had dried.

~Wefor, is it okay for her to shift?~ McKenna asked, making sure all of them could hear.

[She needs to eat in her animal form and after she shifts out of it. But yes. It is more unwise for her to not shift.]

Nam flinched and looked back at McKenna, her eyes dilated.

~That is Wefor. A friend of sorts. We'll explain later. JD, can you get some chicken grilled up they can eat after they shift?~

"Sure. I'll go get it started now." He said the words outloud, smiled at Nam who nodded a bit, then headed to the kitchen.

"I can shift? Into my tiger?" Nam asked, her voice small.

"Yes. We want you to. When was the last time you shifted?" McKenna held her firmly, but paid attention to make sure she let go the second the girl started to squirm.

"The day you rescued us," she mumbled around a mouthful of cheese and meat.

McKenna cringed, that was over a month ago, almost two. That did not sound good, at all.

"Okay," she kept a smile in her voice. "But you get to play today. Look, JD is already starting to grill. So all of you will have chicken breasts to eat shortly."

Nam turned to glance at JD warming up the grill. McKenna saw a decent amount of the platter of food had been demolished, that made her feel a bit better. It looked like she had another person to fatten up.

I'm starting to feel like the witch in Hansel and Gretel, fattening up kids for the oven.

"Jessi?" The girl looked up at her, her face oddly serious. "Want to show Nam your changing area? Then the boys can change?"

Jessi jumped to her feet, a smile blossoming across her face though McKenna wondered if others could tell it was forced.

"Sure. Come on, Nam. I've been outnumbered for way too long."

Nam hesitated then glanced back at McKenna, asking silent permission.

"Go. Play. Have fun. I'll be in here and I told you all about JD. You can trust him with everything. I do."

"So do we." Charley contributed even as Jessi held out her hand, smiling at Nam.

One last look and Nam sighed and then turned, climbing off McKenna's lap. McKenna let her go and watched as Jessi took her hand, walking sedately outside.

"Charley?" McKenna said as the door closed behind the two girls.

"I'll let you know if she tells us anything. I don't know for sure what happened, but," he broke off looking out the door. "I can't explain it, sorry." He looked at her, biting his lip and McKenna pulled him into a rough hug.

"I get it. Some aspects of this whole thing are more than a bit confusing. Just if you find anything she needs, let me know."

Charley nodded, hugged her tight then headed to the deck. Jamie was already at the door, both hands clenched into fists.

~Jamie? You okay?~ she asked on a private channel, her mental tone soft, coaxing.

~They hurt her. They hurt her, and we didn't know.~ His voice carried pain, and she wanted to hug him, pull it away. She looked up to find Toni watching her, but Toni just nodded and headed into the kitchen.

~Should you have?~

~Yes? No? Maybe? She's here, she's what we were missing. How could we not have known?~ His voice plaintive even as he turned to look at her.

~You did. Charley did. That's why she's here. You can't expect more than that. Be there for her now. Just like you were at that place.~ McKenna didn't know what else to say. These dynamics still confused her. She didn't know how to deal with the adults that had ties to her heart, much less help children through the same relationship maze she found herself in.

He nodded then slipped out the door to the deck. Wanting to throw things, McKenna headed into the kitchen to find Toni destroying vegetables.

"You okay?" She seemed to be asking that a lot lately, but from the tension in her friend's back she knew the answer, but she wasn't a hundred percent sure as to which part had her so angry. Maybe it was all of it.

"I'm trying to convince myself I don't want to find her parents and beat them half to death. I'm freaked out at how my kids are reacting to this girl they barely know. And we still have aliens to deal with. Nope, not all right, but no idea what you could do to help."

McKenna laughed, though the amount of humor in it was low. "Nice to know I'm not the only one freaked out by the kids. Is it just me or do they feel different now?"

"They are different. They feel like a unit. Almost like we do." Toni said, still not turning from where she cut up potatoes. "There is someone missing from ours, can't you feel it?"

With a bit of trepidation, McKenna closed her eyes and felt down the bounds that connected all the adults, and sure enough there was a space, like a link was missing.

"You think we have another person somewhere to fill that?"

Toni didn't answer, focusing instead piling vegetables into foil packets. McKenna thought she might have said something, but a ping her in mind sidetracked her.

~I'm here. How should I come in?~ Perc asked.

~Side door is fine.~ McKenna responded even as she picked up and stared at her phone.

"What are you thinking?" Toni asked, finishing with the foil packets.

"That I probably need to call Roy Wallace and make sure I can legally keep Nam. He's going to flip. Especially with JD still here." McKenna slumped against the refrigerator. "Did I do the right thing? Should I have chased her mom down and made her stay?"

Toni stopped and looked at her and suddenly burst into laughter just as Perc walked in, his arms burdened with more food. "Kenna, you no more could have turned down that child than you could have let mine come to harm. Yes, call Ray, but personally, I'd wait until after the aliens have landed. At that point, I don't think it will matter anymore."

Perc looked back and forth between them. "Did I miss something?"

McKenna smiled. "My life is never boring. In fact, I'm pretty sure I'm the poster child for Murphy's Law. You sure you want to be around me?"

A smile lit up his face, and McKenna couldn't help but smile a bit herself. "Of course I am. I'm retired. I have to have something to keep me from wasting away of boredom."

Both McKenna and Toni looked at him, he'd put back about fifteen pounds, though he still needed about another twenty to get back to his original weight. But there was nothing about him that implied wasting away or boredom. They glanced at each other and burst out in laughter.

"Oh fine. I know when I'm not wanted. I'm going to go see JD." He winked at both of them and put the food on the counter, then slipped out the back to where JD was surrounded by furry kids.

Their laughter faded and McKenna felt better for it. "Yeah, I'll worry about it in a few days. For now she's just have an extended slumber party with her mother's approval. Though I might need to trade you kids. I get Jessi, you take Charley?"

"If you need to. We'll see." They were headed to the deck when Cass pinged in her head, the common mindspace filling with her thoughts.

~Hey, I'll be turning down your street in a few minutes. But I think there are three black Suburbans all headed this way. They've been following me for the last three miles.~ A shaky laugh. ~Pretty sure the men in black are here.~

Chapter 10 - MIB

Chatter on the amateur astronomer forums has exploded in the last week. Some of the major telescopes have been redirected from their scheduled areas. The complaints are stemming from people who had scheduled time to inspect those areas of space. No word has come out as to why there has been this change. What is setting off some of the conspiracy theorists are the armed guards preventing entry to the centers where the information from the telescopes are being collated. ~ TNN News Article

The words acted like a cattle prod on McKenna, but she didn't know if her surging emotions were positive or negative.

Does this mean they believe me, or they are coming to cart me off to a loony bin?

"Guess CPS is definitely waiting until after this meeting," she commented out loud, her voice dry. ~JD, how are the kids?~

~Having fun. Nam is the most adorable thing I've ever seen. You must come see this,~ he responded.

McKenna glanced at Toni who flashed a sympathetic smile and carried the foil packets, went out to the deck. Men in black or not, they needed to eat, make sure the kids weren't scared, and being together was better than being alone.

A spur of the moment idea made her grab her phone and she sent a quick text to Kirk and Anne - *People in black SUVs incoming. Assume gov. Follow up if you don't hear back from me by this evening*

That made her feel a bit better. At least if they were grabbed someone would know something happened.

How sad is it I'm expecting to get kidnapped? I need a new life path.

The thought amused her as she and Toni walked onto the deck and froze at the overload of cuteness. The beginning of the structure Charley and JD had worked on was visible from the deck. It was an obstacle course with tunnels, ramps, ladders, things to jump over and crawl under. All in all, it looked like fun for a four legged form.

The kids were all in their animal forms and were tumbling up and down a ramp and into a tunnel made of corrugated metal, the edges coated in duct tape. Their body language exuded joy as did the tail wagging and perked ears.

The tiger cub that Nam turned into bounced along, following the others. Compared to Jessi she looked tiny and delicate even in this form. McKenna noted she could see too many ribs and made a mental note to get more protein drinks for Nam. None of that changed the fact that they were absolutely adorable. For a full minute she just watched and let the joy of the children push back everything else. But reality intruded all too soon.

~Definitely headed to your place. They're parking on the street behind me.~

~Charley, you guys keep playing. But anything happens run and hide again. But for now I don't want them to think we're scared. You got that?~ She moved over and slipped her phone into their little changing area under their clothes. ~My phone is hidden under your clothes.~

Charley had paused, looking back at her, his ears twitching. ~Okay.~ He stopped bouncing around and leaped up to the top of one of the structures and sat there watching. The cats all looked at each other and slunk into tunnels. McKenna noted Jessi and Jamie made sure Nam stayed between them.

"They did get some food before they played?" she asked as she heard a car door open and shut.

"Yep. Each of them ate a breast, but yes, she needs more food. Protein and fats."

~They're staying in the cars, what do you want me to do?~ Cass sounded stressed.

~Just come on in the side door. It's open. Ignore them. The ball is in their court, and we have grilling to do,~ McKenna instructed with an odd calm that was half-panic and half-relief.

~Okay.~ A minute later Cass came in, her arms filled with grocery bags. "I have drink mixes and rum. I was thinking daiquiris. Now I'm thinking shots."

"Let's see what they say, and how freaked out we need to be."

Perc nodded as he pulled out his phone and texted rapidly. Then smiled at them all. "I told Laura Granger, she's my mentor for the law school stuff, though at this point who knows. But it does mean that if we disappear she'll call the cavalry."

McKenna grinned at him, glad she wasn't the only one thinking like that. The doorbell rang, and she took a deep breath. "Party time. JD, can you get me a hamburger? You know how I like it. I don't want them to think we're pushovers. We have a barbecue going on." The smile felt forced, but the support that washed through the mindscape helped.

At least if they think I'm crazy I still have friends.

[You are not mentally disturbed. If necessary, the phone communication can be utilized again.]

~That I would prefer to save for a bit, as well as the mental communication. That is information that we can use to protect ourselves. Letting anyone else know that right now scares me.~

[Valid.]

Everyone fell silent as she opened the door and looked out at the four men on her doorstep. Glancing past them she saw three figures at the vehicles, no weapons in evidence but obviously a guard. At this distance she couldn't tell what branch of the service they were. McKenna shifted her attention back to the men in front of her.

The person standing at the door looked like he was in his mid-fifties, fit, an Army uniform with multiple pins and ribbons. His hair cut close with touches of gray, serious brown eyes that were currently narrowed at her, waiting for her to say something. McKenna notice his slim briefcase and wondered what it held. She took her time as she catalogued the other men. One wore an Air Force uniform, the blue being a dead giveaway, probably in his forties, with no expression at all on his dark face, his African heritage absorbing the bright sun. The third wore a decent suit, with glasses, a pinched expression, and fingers that twitched like he counted something on the fingers of his right hand, his left held a computer bag bursting at the seams. The fourth screamed guard, he wore a gun at the waist of his fatigues, his eyes scanned constantly, and of all of them he scared her.

"May I help you, gentlemen?" she asked leaning against the door.

"Are you McKenna Largo?" The Army guy asked, and she knew damn well they knew who she was, but she went along with the charade.

"Yes. And you are?" She tried very hard to not seem as nervous as she was, the very real fear they could kidnap them rode the back of her mind.

"I'd really like to talk to you inside, as opposed to standing on the front step for all the world to see," he countered, his tone neutral.

McKenna made a show of looking past him at the empty land around her and the small amount of traffic. He didn't flinch or look embarrassed. She gave him points for a good poker face.

"Come on in. But you," she directed her attention to the one with the gun.

"Yes, ma'am?"

"I have children inside in the form of animals. Under no circumstances are you to draw that weapon in my house or around these kids. Is that understood?"

His tanned skin, dark hair, implied Hispanic, but she suspected he had native American blood in him. "I understand your concerns, ma'am, but you are not my first priority."

"Maybe, but I will not allow my kids, any of the kids, to be hurt or scared." Her voice had no give, not that she knew what she would do besides let Toni kill him. Not like any of them were bulletproof.

[That would be exceedingly difficult to do. The best might be to make you more resistant to puncture wounds. But normally the Elentrin use energy bursts, so that would not be effective against them.]

McKenna tried not to stumble as she thought about being bulletproof.

~Later, we will talk later,~ she promised as she led them to the back. "Gentlemen, everyone is out here. Please take a seat." As she'd gone to the door, someone had grabbed a couple of the folding stadium chairs and set them up. JD still stood at the grill, but Toni and Perc had arranged their chairs so anyone headed towards the kids would have to go through them. Cass still had the grocery bags in her hands and smiled at them all as they walked out.

"Hey, I'm about to go make some daiquiris. Would you guys like any?"

"One for me please, Cass." McKenna said as she sat in the chair next to Toni. From here she could see the kids, the grill, and the table and chairs they had left for the government men.

The lead man looked around, his eyes narrowing even more. "We would prefer to speak to you alone, Ms. Largo."

"Ooh, Ms. Largo. Not even Officer or Detective. Ouch." McKenna sighed and let the fake sarcasm drop. "Gentlemen, everyone here is a shifter. We all know about the aliens, much more than you do, and frankly some of them can explain this better than I can. It is all of us or none."

The man blinked, looked at all of them and sighed, sitting down. "Miss Borden, if I weren't on duty I'd gladly accept your offer. As it is, no."

"Okay, I'll bring out some cokes and stuff." Cass gave them a smile that almost looked real though her tension radiated in the mindspace as she slipped back into the kitchen.

The guard had taken up a position at the far end of the deck against the railing, watching everyone. McKenna was fine with that, the only kid currently visible was Charley, and he moved fast when he wanted to.

"My name is Brigadier General George Davis. I'm one of the senior officers for the US Army Space and Missile Defense Command, usually called SMDC. This is Major Richard O'Neill. He is one of our primary officers for interfacing with other nations for atmospheric protection from ballistic objects, is involved with NASA, and is also an astronaut." The Air Force officer nodded at her, still standing almost at attention.

"Dr. Daniel Shanks is our premier scientist and has verified the information that you passed on to the secretary. We have a lot of questions for you." His voice stayed calm, but she could hear the tension in it, and it made her nervous.

"Thank you—um, can I just call you George? I really don't want to repeat that every time." He nodded, his face unreadable. "Whew. George, take a seat, relax, 'cause I'll answer everything I can, but be aware you aren't going to like the answers or how I know them."

He nodded at her, and the three of them took seats, George turning to face her even as the doctor pulled out a laptop and a phone and fired them up. The colonel, Richard, just watched everyone, his eyes sharp.

INCOMING

"It took us a bit to translate the coordinates you provided, and no one is sure yet how you could have gotten those coordinates, but when we aimed multiple telescopes at that location, then tracked a trajectory towards Earth we saw four ships headed this way. Three are huge, bigger than our biggest aircraft carrier, the fourth smaller, more of a yacht-look than the big ones. Those come across as transport for freight."

McKenna blinked at him, this was all new to her.

~Cass, I really need that drink. A strong version. Very strong.~

~Ditto,~ chorused the other adults.

~On the way. Anything to worry about?~

~Just trying to explain the impossible to the unbelieving~ Toni said, her tone wry. McKenna had to fight back a laugh.

"Okay. I don't disbelieve you. But do you have a question? Or questions?"

~I have no idea what they want to hear. What would make them believe? If they ask questions maybe I can answer them. Maybe~

George settled back and looked at her, he didn't seem angry or like he thought she was lying. Mostly it felt like he saw her as a puzzle.

He still didn't say anything, just looking at her, then turning his head to look at the others, everyone but JD watching him. JD watched the grill, burning meat would be a bad thing.

"I have many questions, but most of them will have to wait until I get you back to DC and in front of the cabinet."

McKenna flinched at that, and her heart rate spiked. Just then Cass walked back out with a tray full of drinks and handed them out, putting some cokes and water on the picnic table.

~Thank god. I don't wanna go to DC~ she commented in her head even as she took her first long drink. ~Wefor, can you let the booze affect me just a little? 'Cause I'm so wired I'm about to explode.~

[Understood. It will affect you per normal until you ask me to stop it.]

McKenna sighed. "So if that's what you want, why are you here? Why didn't you just ask me to come to DC?"

"Because I need to know why, ma'am." He leaned forward, his arms on his knees. McKenna fought not to roll her eyes at the basic body language of showing he was vulnerable. He wasn't.

"Why what?"

He sighed then frowned. "That may not have been the best question. Maybe it is how. How do you know this? What do they want? Why are you the one who knows this?"

McKenna sighed and took another long drink.

~Charley, play, don't hide and when you need more food come up here. Nam, you especially. You need to eat.~

She felt their assent and heard them starting to move around. The guard's eyes snapped over to them and grew wider, then the hint of a smile curved his lips.

Gotcha. Cuteness overload usually wins.

Knowing the man wasn't immune to cute animals made McKenna feel immensely better and she redirected her attention to George.

"I'm aware of how insane this all sounds. And frankly part of me hoped you would tell me you couldn't find the ships we told you about. That way I could convince myself I was crazy and just go about my life." A wry smile and nod from George encouraged her to keep going. "While everyone is still thinking that a virus allowed us to change," she waved her hand encompassing them all, "it wasn't."

Both George and the doctor suddenly looked very sharp and intent, their body language focused on them.

~I swear if they lock me up in a loony bin you guys had better come visit~ she muttered in her head and only got back laughter. ~I see how it is.~

"You know what caused the change?" George asked, reminding her of one of the cats about to pounce.

She refocused. "Yes. The reason is nanobots that were sent here from the very aliens currently approaching us. These nanobots contain the cellular blueprints, for lack of a better word, that allow our cells to be restructured. They burn calories to fuel the changes and give us the ability to switch back and forth."

The doctor looked at her. "That actually makes sense assuming they are quantum computers encapsulated within the nanobot."

"Actually, I've been told they function more as a distributed file system, with the nanobots that are embedded all through our bodies providing the ability to do the calculations and store the information needed."

Doctor Shanks leaned forward, his mouth open, but George cut him off.

"Told? Told by whom?"

Oh boy. Here we go.

She took another fortifying drink, letting the light buzz cut the edge off her stress. Her eyes had closed as she did so, and she opened them to see the four men all looking at her. Wariness in every line of their bodies.

"Because I got an upgraded version of the nanobot, one that comes with a functional AI, and it told me all of this. As well as the location of the ships, and exactly why the Elentrin are coming here." Before anyone could say anything she continued. "They're coming to collect the Kaylid, us, to use in their war against the Drakyn."

Chapter 11 - Show Your Cards

Our new restaurant is opening in Sacramento this week. We cater to shifters in animal form. Do you want to eat your steak rare while in wolf form or chew on a bone that can resist your teeth? If so, come down to Rarest and order a meal. They have shifting rooms so you can strip and change into your other form and experience food as nature intended. ~ Ad on KWAK

George blinked, his mouth opened and closed, then open and closed again. The doctor was just as bad, his eyes blinking and mouth moving. The Air Force officer, Richard, just narrowed his eyes, a serious look on his face.

After a long moment during which the mindspace echoed with giggles, though McKenna worried they'd storm out, George cleared his throat.

"Am I to understand you have an artificial intelligence inside you that is providing you information?" His words came out slowly and carefully as if he needed to taste each word.

"Yes."

"How, wait, what I," he sighed and closed his eyes. "Is there anyway you can prove this?"

McKenna made a face and shrugged. "I have no idea. I can share what has been told to me, and at this point everything I've been told has proved to be the truth. And it is definitely information and skills I have no way of knowing. Such as the celestial coordinates I gave you."

George turned and glanced at the doctor. The doctor nodded and glanced at his computer.

"It says here you have a degree in Criminal Justice with a minor in Sociology?"

"Uh, yes? I always wanted to be a cop, so I got my degree to support that."

"I suppose then advanced physics or stellar cartography is not a skill set you have."

"No. I do good to handle my own finances and deal with my phone." McKenna frowned. "I mean Cass is a PhD person, in stuff, so she's way smarter than I am."

"I specialize in biology and botany though, not that stuff. Best I ever got into was organic chemistry for the physical sciences," Cass chimed in as she helped JD start assembling hamburgers. A small pile of chicken breasts was cooling on the side table.

Oh good, he's got stuff cooling for the kids.

"Do you mind if I ask you some questions that would be well outside of your listed education?" Daniel asked, even as George sat back to watch.

"Um, sure?"

~Wefor, is that an issue?~

[No, this should be interesting, though any names you have for specific values I may not know if they are not things you would know.]

"Wefor says fine, but warns that the common names for things might not match up. Especially if they aren't stuff that I know, she has no way of knowing."

"Wefor?" Daniel asked.

~Crap, I said your name. Dammit, I was trying not to do that.~ She sighed and took another sip of her drink. Even with Wefor cutting back on the counter-agents, a buzz didn't last long. In some ways getting nice and drunk sounded like the easy way out. But there wasn't anyone else to pick up this burden, so no easy way out for her.

"It's what we call the AI. 'Hey you,' sounded stupid."

"What do you mean 'things might not match up'? Why does an AI have a name and a gender?" The doctor broke the silence, and McKenna shrugged.

"She's in my head, and calling something It is rude. Yes, a name, because again, saying hey you or AI sounds stupid. At least Wefor sounds odd but not attention-catching." She sipped on the cold drink, enjoying the contrast to the heat outside. "So if you call something X and she doesn't know X and I don't know X, the answers aren't going to match up.

George frowned and jotted down something on a notepad but didn't interrupt their conversation.

Daniel picked up the thread of the conversation. "That is understandable. I'll ask questions that should be understandable. If I say Planck's constant is," he glanced down at his computer. "$6.62607004 \times 10^{-34}$ m2kg/s, could you tell me what that calculation is used for?"

[That is the energy a photon carries with the frequency of its electromagnetic wave.] Wefor kept talking and answering the questions he asked, and McKenna just recited it, most of the questions and answers sounding like when she autocorrected into Spanish. But the doctor got more excited.

"Daniel," George interrupted. "Does this prove anything?"

The doctor snorted. "Either she's a genius the likes of which I've never seen or she has an intelligent computer that can guess what my next question will be. Your call."

George rubbed his temple. "I'm going to accept you're right, frankly because the consequences of assuming you're insane and aliens are not coming are shattering. While if I humor you and everything you've said is a lie, the cost relatively low in comparison."

"Gee, thanks," McKenna replied, her sarcasm obvious, but she relaxed a little.

"What do you want us to do?" George asked.

The question hung there in the air and McKenna just looked at him, frozen.

"And on that note, let's eat. Because I think Kenna is about to have a heart attack. Gentlemen, please share a meal with us. We need to eat, the kids need to eat, and there isn't any answer to this. At least not as far as we are aware." JD interrupted her moment of deer-in-a-headlight reaction, and she closed her eyes.

~Eat, give them a bit of time to adjust to this, and you need to calm down.~ Perc said in the shared space, his voice calming.

"We aren't-" George started to say when Richard interrupted.

"Yes, we are. We haven't eaten and sharing bread is an old tradition that helps build trust. And at this point trust is the only thing we have. Besides, I've been smelling that food for the last thirty minutes and I'm starving." He grinned as he said that, and it brought warmth to his face, chasing away the taciturn persona.

"Ditto," the guard said, and she could see he had relaxed a bit, too, though he still stayed alert.

"Fine."

The next few minutes were involved in creating burgers, getting the rest of the food out here, and cutting up the chicken breasts.

~Guys, you wanna come eat some now? And you can have more food after they leave?~ McKenna asked the kids who had been playing through the obstacle course. She'd kept track of them and their emotions, but hadn't talked to them though they could hear the mindspace through her.

~Yes. Nam needs to rest a bit, too. Can we get cheese on the chicken? And maybe some mustard on mine?~ Charley asked as they started to move towards the adults. Nam hanging back a bit with Jamie right beside her.

JD put the cut-up chicken breasts with some chunks of cheese on a large platter and doctored one with mustard.

~How can you eat that? Don't get any on mine, it will make it gross,~ Jessi protested even as they came up on the deck, their movements cautious as they kept eyes and ears on the strangers.

"Do they always eat in animal form?" Richard asked watching them.

"No, rarely, in fact. But we don't trust you and they can protect themselves better in this form, and they need the calories. Shifting burns them and right now the tiger, Nam, needs to gain some weight," Toni replied, her voice flat and hard. Her body tense even as she kept an eye on her kids and the military men.

"Is something wrong?" Daniel asked, frowning.

"Long story and not important right now." McKenna replied then she took a big bite of her hamburger. Excellent as always. They all spent the next few minutes focused on food. McKenna ate two hamburgers, refilled her drink and made a chips and salsa pile for her to munch on. By the time everyone had finished she almost felt able to handle the questions that would occur.

"George." Her voice calmer than she felt. He immediately looked over at her, a pensive look on his face. "You asked what I want you to do. I have no idea. What we know from the information Wefor provided is that a solar wave hit the nanobots as they were impacting Earth. This caused damage to the programming for all the nanobots and that damage is the only reason we are even having this discussion."

George tilted his head and poked at a chip on his plate. "What do you mean by that?"

"The original programming would have locked us all in animal form, mindless. Unable to access our human intelligence or shift back to human."

Richard tilted his head at her, his eyes narrowing. "Like some of the people lately that seem to have truly turned into animals."

"Yes, though there is a chance I might be able to get them to shift back. Maybe."

"What? How?"

"I'm a commander, the AI is just one of the benefits."

George made a note then nodded for her to go on. McKenna sighed and tried to reorganize her thoughts. "With all of us trapped in animal forms, mindless and terrified, we would have wreaked havoc and terrified people. The Elentrin are showing up to 'save' us." She made air quotes around the word. "They would enable us to gain our human forms again, and in payment would take a portion of the remaining Kaylid to use for troops. Though I think they made a few mistakes."

"I understand the strategy. There are historical examples of it being used when laying siege to cities to have a disease spread and offer to come in and cure it. But what mistakes do you think they made?" George asked, making another note.

McKenna had a bad feeling he was making notes of all the things he needed to follow up on. Oh, well. Having someone competent was better than another idiot.

"Do you work with any shifters?" she asked.

George blinked and glanced around them then nodded slowly. "There are two in my organization."

"Have they mentioned anything about dreams?"

"No. But not sure I would have found out. Neither of them is a particular friend. Why?"

"We seem to tap into training programs to learn skills. Some of them are part of the nanobots storage systems. But as the ships are getting closer, we seem to be linking into what's going on at the ship. Most probable answer is trans-harmonics that intersect the planet boosted by the ships, and we're intercepting them. But either way, information, some of which we've been able to validate, is being passed to us. And if it's accurate, they're expecting maybe industrial revolution level of technology and approximately 1.5 million shifters."

The three men's eyebrows raised at her statement. The guard, whose name she still didn't know, kept watching the kids with the hint of a smile on his face. The four of them had decided adults were boring and were playing around the obstacle course again.

"Why in the world would they think that? And even if they do, they should be seeing our satellites pretty soon. That will disabuse them of that notion. Not to mention, why did they think the shifter numbers would be so low? There are around 150 million shifters, we think. That is going off the percentages," Daniel blurted.

McKenna shrugged. "Not really sure, though they expected a certain amount of us to be killed. The AI says the nanobot swarm is self-replicating and continues to replicate as they pass through space matter. They are tiny, but they hit a lot of material coming here, so by the time they hit Earth they would have numbers over two billion. Only the commander modules don't replicate. There are fifty, and they assume at least half won't find viable hosts, or targets, if you prefer," she said at the sour look on their faces.

Cass came back out from helping JD take food into the kitchen. In her hands she held a large pitcher and walked around refilling drinks. McKenna caught George and Richard looking at it longingly, the doctor seemed oblivious as he typed furiously on his laptop.

"So how many commanders do you think are on Earth? How many people have AIs?"

McKenna shrugged. "No way to know. The failure rate is pretty high, as you can see if you do the math. Maybe as few as five? Maybe as many as a thirty. It also depends on the damage. This AI rebuilt based on my actions and attitudes. Which means, as far as we can tell, Wefor is sentient." She took a deep breath. "I'm not answering the other questions yet. Now here are my questions. What now?"

George narrowed his eyes and jotted something on the note pad, but didn't say anything as the doctor turned the laptop towards them. "Since we found the ship, we have more of our telescopes pointed that way, all under Top Secret Eyes Only clearance. No one is getting to see the data reported back to us. We even have armed guards to keep the scientists out which is causing a lot of feathers to fly. But we've intercepted communication between their ships. Would you mind translating it for us?"

[This is probably a test. They would have received enough information from what we already provided to decipher most of it.]

~Then does it matter? It might prove our point. But I still don't know what we do now. You did say they don't have weapons on their ships?~

[Not like how your movies portray.] Having Wefor watch Star Wars had been entertaining, yet made the movie much less fun as she pointed out all the things that were not possible. [However, kinetic weapons are always possible via tractor beams, which are used to help ships dock with each other and the rare space station. Most Drakyn do not use spaceships as that is not how they travel. From the data available all other planets that have been used for Kaylid harvesting, none had achieved anything past chemical power projectiles.]

"Go for it."

The doctor pressed a key on the computer and noise spilled out of it. He let it play all the way through then stopped it and looked at her expectantly.

Wefor fed her the information as she spoke. "We are twenty-one teran out of the planet; however, anomalies have been picked up. Please have your science officer verify the presence of artificial satellites around the planet. If this is accurate, estimation of planet technology is not current." McKenna paused, her head tilting the slightest bit. "The next part is on a different day."

She cleared her throat and spoke again, reciting what Wefor said in her head. "Please inform the Admeer that satellites have been confirmed. Further information is coming in that space flight has been achieved. Information is still being gathered. It will not be ready by the time we reach their moon. Suggest moving around the planets and making the approach more oblique allowing the planets to mask our path."

McKenna looked at them and shrugged. "That's all there is."

"How long is a *teran*?"

"Umm.. Wefor says that's their days, but it's the equivalent of twenty-six hours. If they change their approach that could change that estimate."

George sagged back and rubbed his temple. "And you're the only one who can do this?"

McKenna blinked then shrugged. "As far as I know. I mean Wefor translates. We can do other things, but when it comes to the Elentrin, yeah, JD or Cass can't do that."

INCOMING

Another note went in George's notebook and he rose. "We have basically four weeks to prepare for this. I'd like you to come to Washington. We need you to help deal with what's headed our way."

The idea of leaving everyone, leaving Charley, sent a feeling of wrongness through McKenna. She had no idea what would happen in the long run, but doing it alone seemed like the worst idea ever.

"No. I'm not going anywhere without my friends."

George looked at all of them and shrugged. "Fine, they can come, too, but we need to get going."

"I am NOT leaving my children," Toni and McKenna growled in almost one voice.

George threw up his hands, exasperation clear on his face. "Fine, bring the kids. We'll figure out how to deal with them, but right now you're the most important person on the planet."

McKenna actively cringed at that and looked at Toni and JD. Forcing the words out she said, "I can go by myself. You guys stay here and watch the kids."

[That would be unwise. A commander functions better with her team. Over the last week you have seen the difference not having your command structure with you. Each of you brings different information and skills to play. Leaving them here will hamper you and possibly reduce overall effectiveness and functionality with existing programming.]

~Huh? What does that mean, Wefor?~ JD asked before the rest of them could say anything.

[With the amount of blood transfers we have done, nanobots slaved to this program have duplicated through most of your bodies and are enhancing processing power as well as providing you with some aspects of commander modules, such as the partial shifting and probably the ability to create more Kaylid. When you activated the trans-harmonics it also increased the ability to communicate with the other nanobots in your squad, increasing processing power. While they do not have the language matrix, it is possible to share that with more nanobot transfers.]

~Then we all go. It isn't like you're just going on a trip. This is our world and us we're talking about. But I've got a job. So does everyone but Perc,~ Cass pointed out.

~Hey, I work. Just for myself. And I'm scheduled to take the Bar soon but wondering if it matters.~ He didn't sound that upset.

~I think the three of us can get a leave of absence. I know Kirk would approve it and he could drive through Toni getting it. But if we take the kids, what then?~

~Carina would have to come. She's out of school still, for at least another three weeks. But I suppose if aliens land, school probably won't be an issue. I can talk to her.~ Toni said, and McKenna didn't disagree.

"Is everything all right?" Richard's voice pulled her out of the discussion in her mind and she looked at them.

"New information from Wefor. It would be best if everyone comes with me. She says her ability to process data is increased with them with me."

"Why?" the question came from Dr. Shanks.

"Um, she says since the nanobots are working as a DFS, there is a processing increase as it provides more threads? If that makes any sense to you."

"It doesn't to you?"

"No. And to be honest I try relatively hard to not think about it too much. If I really started thinking about having an AI in my head, all our bodies filled with tiny machines I might lose it." Her voice was grim. "I sometimes think she tries to tone down her personality to keep me from freaking."

Dammit, I didn't mean to say that, I'm strung so tight I'm not keeping my mouth shut. Apparently, I get stressed out at alien invasions. Good to know.

[You noticed?]

~Yes. You slip occasionally. You've become fully sentient haven't you?~ She felt everyone waiting for the answer.

[Maybe.] Wefor said nothing else and McKenna directed her attention back to the men.

"Sorry. So yes. We need to go together. But that's four kids and six adults," she pointed out. "It isn't like we can just up and leave."

"Who's the sixth adult?" George asked, looking at them, suspicion written on his face.

"My live-in nanny, unless you really want kids running around while we do whatever we are doing," Toni replied in a dry voice, but McKenna could feel her stress.

"And I need to call work." Cass pointed out.

"And there is an issue with one of the kids," McKenna said slowly, cringing a bit. When had all this gotten so complicated?

George sighed. "I need a staff sergeant here. Why didn't I bring one?"

"Because you didn't think you were bringing back another full squad of people?" Richard said wryly as he pulled out a phone. "I'll get Sergeant Reynolds going on what we'll need. Housing for multiple adults and children. I'll get us transport. You can deal with this other stuff." His smile had bitter humor, and McKenna fought to not feel guilty.

I did not cause all this. I'm trying hard to help. This is not my fault.

~Stop it, Kenna. In the long run, none of this matters. You're ours and we aren't going anywhere without you.~ JD's voice rumbled through the mindspace, and her head jerked up and looked at him. He smiled even as he picked up his phone planning on calling Kirk.

"I'm calling my work," Cass said, stepping off to the side.

"Kids. We're going on a trip. Charley, wanna go pack? Make sure you have enough for two weeks. Jessi, Jamie your mom is calling Carina, she'll probably pack for all of you. Tell her if there's anything specific you need."

She felt the channel between the twins and Toni pop open even as she turned to the tiger cub that had moved over to her, tail between her legs.

"Nam. You're coming with us." She reached down and picked up the girl, the tiger form being a bit more awkward to hold than a kid. "I already have all your stuff. I'm not leaving you." Even as she talked, she held her tight, petting her, to comfort the little girl.

"George, the situation with Nam is odd." She started to explain when a sudden increase in volume from Cass off to the side caused her to look that direction. Well, her and Perc, who had not needed to call anyone, though at some point he would need to go pack.

INCOMING

"Fine, Chuck. Be that way. I quit. You can take the job and shove it." She hit disconnect on her phone and turned and glared at everyone watching her. "I really miss landline phones some days. They are so much more fun to slam down than just hitting a button." She took a deep breath, closing her eyes for a second then popping them back open. "I need to head home and pack. I'll call my sister from the car."

"I need to do the same," Perc added, looking at the military personnel.

George heaved a sigh then turned and looked at the guard, who'd eaten almost as much as any of the shifters. "Torres. Grab Cort and please follow Miss Borden in her car to her place, let her pack. Then if you would meet Mr. Alexander at his and proceed to," he paused and glanced at Richard O'Neill.

"Beale Air Force Base. They're getting a jet ready for us. It'll be a few hours, but I can't see us getting there any sooner." His sigh held a wealth of annoyance at the slowness of civilians. This McKenna had no sympathy for. If they had wanted them ready, calling ahead would have been nice.

McKenna noticed JD looking at Cass and figured they were communicating. She turned back, and Torres, he did have a name apparently, walked over to them.

"You sure, sir?"

"I sincerely doubt any of these people are going to attack me, and they've made it very clear their first priority is their kids. Besides, have you seen anything that makes you think they're full of shit?"

Torres shook his head. "I wish I could say I had, sir. It might help with the panic attack my brain is

129

having at the moment." His rock steady posture and calm demeanor did not back up his words.

"Damn. I was hopeful for a minute there. Take off. I'll deal with the people here. Glad we brought two vans."

"Yes, sir." Torres saluted then looked at Cass and Perc. "If you'll provide your address, sir, we'll head to your place once we've allowed the young lady to get what she'll need."

~You okay with this, Cass?~ McKenna shot her way.

~Yeah. You can hear me scream from the other side of the planet and with the neat little trick I developed of letting my claws out even in human form, I'm not worried. Besides, all of these guys, while not believing us, haven't said a single disparaging thing or sexist comment. I'm almost a bit worried, or they are very, very serious.~

McKenna thought about it and realized they hadn't. Oh, they'd questioned and challenged, but nothing that could have been regarded as demeaning at all.

~Okay. Yell if you need something. I'd pack professional clothes,~ she broke off and sighed. She turned to George.

"This is going to sound insane but are we going to be meeting with important people? People wearing suits and ties who would expect us to be similarly clothed?"

An odd look crossed over George's face and he nodded slowly. "Probably. Assuming all this stuff bears out, I'd assume you'd meet with the cabinet."

"The cabinet, as in the president and those people?" McKenna asked feeling vaguely nauseous.

"Yes. Why?"

McKenna rubbed her face. "This is going to sound so stereotypically female." She sighed, but knew all too well the power clothing had. "All of us are seriously underweight and none of us really have clothes that fit. Well, Perc did, but our weight loss, we don't have clothing for those sorts of meetings. Heck, I had to buy a new dress just to try to get Homeland Security to take me seriously. Not that it worked."

George looked like he wanted to groan. Richard, however, raised his hand. "Reynolds is a jewel, you need to promote her. Seriously. She brought this up. Get me your measurements and we'll have people waiting with clothes for you in DC."

McKenna almost sagged in relief. "Thanks."

A few minutes later, measurements taken along with photos to match coloring. Perc and Cass were headed home, Toni and her two were headed to their house to pick up Carina. She thought this sounded fun and exciting. Toni hadn't told her about the aliens and didn't figure it was worth it now.

Nam hadn't moved from McKenna's arms, though Charley had shifted back to human and currently packed up his stuff, his mood somber.

George looked at her, and his face softened as he took in the tiger cub, now half asleep, in McKenna's arms. "What's the story on her?"

McKenna rubbed the girl's ears, reveling in the soft fur. She explained about asking her over for the barbecue, the mom's strange behavior on the phone, then showing up and dumping everything then fleeing.

"I'm not giving her up. We were going to call CPS but figured we'd wait both to see if we were alive in thirty days, and well, to see if her mom changed her mind. But I won't let this child be abandoned or abused anymore."

George rubbed his temple. "I've been in the Army for almost thirty-five years. In five more I max out. In all those years I've never had anyone create as many problems as you by doing the exact right thing." He graced her with a smile. "Nam is coming with us. And I'll help get it cleared through CPS when the time is right. But for now, yes, I think you're right and it isn't worth worrying about. If we're all dead, the point is moot." He smiled even though his voice had a grimness to it that hurt.

McKenna fought to swallow past the lump in her throat. "Point."

Chapter 12 - Change of Scenery

Australia today announced a preserve specifically for shifters to be in their animal form. Located outside Alice Springs, the Aborigines are running it, and you can only enter as an animal. However, all risks are on you. None of the native wildlife has been removed. It is commonly accepted that the creatures native to that continent actively want to kill you. Perhaps this will catch on as an extreme vacation, but being a shifter doesn't mean you can't get hurt or poisoned. ~ TNN Shifter News

By the time they boarded the Gulfstream to DC, five hours had passed and everyone looked exhausted. McKenna knew she just wanted to go to bed, but they had a flight ahead of them.

With the group of them, the plane seemed very full. The kids had all shifted back into humans, and soon after they got on the plane were sound asleep, though Nam remained at her side. The adults were still trying to avoid shifting until their weight got up a bit more. They were aware that some displays of shifting would be required so they were forcing down nutrient drinks.

"How sad is it, I'm already missing that soup stuff the ladies in Colombia were making for us?" Cass said glumly as she finished off the shake.

"Oh, me, too. Compared to this stuff that tasted awesome," Perc muttered even as they opened another one and started sipping.

All of their bots were converting the nutrients to muscle and trying to get them back to their previous weights, but Wefor had told them they had more nanobots than most Kaylid. Partially her fault and partially that they had needed to multiply to support McKenna's demands. While each nanobot didn't even use a single calorie, each of them had thousands of them in their bodies.

"Do you guys always eat like this? Non-stop?" Torres asked. Brigadier General George Davis and Colonel Richard O'Neill were up at the front coordinating everything for when they arrived. Apparently a house had been rented for them, and they were trying to arrange meetings for the next morning.

"Not normally. But we're all still trying to replace muscle loss from our earlier adventures. And with needing to do some show and tell, we're pre-loading," JD told him, munching on some jerky in between sips. "This should stabilize in a week or so, but right now we're trying to bulk up. But shifting burns energy regardless. Let's just say our food bills match our mortgage of late."

Toni snorted. "Try feeding two more with mouths like them. I don't know what I'm going to do when they turn into teenagers. Take out a second mortgage?" The mouths in question were strapped into seats across the aisle from her, sound asleep in the boneless way only kids could do, mouths hanging open and breathing noisily.

Torres grinned at them then turned his attention to a question George asked.

McKenna took that as an opportunity to talk. ~Wefor, how many days do we have with the change in how they are approaching us?~

[Altering their vector will not make much of a difference.]

~Any plans on how to deal with them?~

[Negotiation is a valid option. Though the odds of them leaving without troops are low, however the current status of their wars is unknown.]

~Can we fight them?~

[Of course. You have more Kaylid than they have, the transport ships are mostly empty, with only a few thousand troops. They have more powerful weapons. But it is unknown how they will compare in a battle situation. Most Drakyn are not warriors. Be aware they will probably call for more ships to come once they realize how many Kaylid are here. Even having a few hundred thousand die would be worth it to collect the millions available on this planet. If that happens they can have more ships here in a week. With them here, they can provide a direct entanglement to their existing positions instead of having to come in from outside the solar system.]

That brought a question to McKenna's mind but Cass asked a question before she could chase it down.

~You said negotiation is a possibility? Why? What else do they want?~

[That is not information in the databases. There is no information of them ever negotiating with the

Drakyn, but with planets they have seeded? That is unknown.]

"We'll be landing in DC approximately five hours from now. You might want to get some rest while you can. There won't be much time after we land. Between getting you into your residence, getting you prepped, and getting you to the meeting by 0700." George's words cast a pall over their conversation and they settled back in their seats, eyes closing as they tried to get some rest.

~Wefor, can we beat them?~ McKenna asked, her question locked on a private channel that no one else could hear.

[Of course. It simply depends on the price you want to pay.]

Those words chilled McKenna but avoiding them wouldn't make anything better. Just like avoiding asking how long a liad was hadn't.

~What do you mean?~

[You have nuclear weapons, you have seven billion people on your planet. While the exact numbers of the Kaylid or the Elentrin is not listed in the databases, the Kaylid are disposable items to them. It is unlikely the Elentrin number surpasses a billion on all their planets. So yes, you can defeat them.]

Wefor's comments didn't make her feel good, but it did help a bit. McKenna closed her eyes and fell into a light sleep, waking often to check the kids.

McKenna found herself at the head of a table, along one side of her she could see JD and Cass. The other side held Toni and Perc. The kids she could feel but they weren't in the room.

"Commander. You have assembled your team. These are some of the best Kaylid we have, and I trust you will use their skills appropriately. The additional adjuncts for the ambassador have been selected now that they have found their fourth. They will act as immediate bodyguards and back up for you. They have full translation capabilities. Plans have changed due to updated information about the planet we are approaching. As your original forms best reflect the inhabitants of this planet, you will assume your original forms and accompany the ambassador. It is hoped that they will need rescuing but monitoring of their entertainment feeds implies otherwise." The word entertainment had contempt dripping from every syllable.

McKenna focused on the speaker and tried to analyze what she saw. Taller than she was in warrior form, and the being was in warrior form. But she couldn't figure out what animal he would have been. Dark fur, powerful body, and as he strode back and forth a snow-white tail lashed behind him. Short muzzle but long ears. His eyes caught her though, vertical pupils in this form, whereas hers were always human round, and an odd color of blue-yellow.

"Commander," his voice an odd rumble. She still couldn't speak that clearly in this form, though she'd gotten better.

"Yes?" Her eyes locked with his, and she refused to look away. His face hid emotions, so she had no idea what he thought.

"Please prepare your people. Sirets Aliarn, Scilita, and Thelia will be the primary for this. Our goal is at least a million Kaylid to be harvested." Where he'd had contempt for entertainment, his voice now held less personality than Wefor, voice flat. "However, as information continues to be collected, this might be a bounty for Elentrin. Preliminary information indicates upwards of a hundred million Kaylid present. If that is the case, regular ships may be arranged, and all battlefronts will be engaged. No other planet has ever had this level of surviving Kaylid. You will be in charge of the selection process and given the bounty presented the criteria has been narrowed to prime specimens. If they have diseases that might not be cured in time or are too young or too old for optimal performance, you will ignore them."

"Understood." Her voice just as flat though McKenna had no real control.

Is this real right now? Whose body am I in? Why do I see my friends? Argh, Wefor can you hear me?

"Shuttles are being prepared and will depart once we achieve orbit, though we are still unsure which cities to land. The three main ones are being determined, and the shuttles will land there. Your group will go with the one we determine as primary, the auxiliary group with the secondary. A third group is being decanted now to support Thelia and her tastes." This time something slipped out on that last word, something she didn't think she wanted to understand.

"You are to pack what you need for a week stay. Note that this culture tends to find nudity discomforting, take that into consideration with your packing. Update all languages. You have twenty teran until we reach their moon. It is expected that you take this time to prepare yourself as you will need to excel at your responsibilities. Dismissed." The male turned and stalked out of the room, the tail mesmerizing against his dark fur as the doors closed behind him.

McKenna tried to turn to talk to any of the others, but a hand touching her shoulder yanked her out of the experience.

"Ms. Largo? Are you okay?"

McKenna blinked at him, trying to focus. It took her a minute to realize it was Torres, she still didn't know his first name, who had touched her shoulder.

She took a deep breath then let it out.

"Yeah. Is there something wrong?"

"We're getting ready to land. From there we'll be taking you to where we're housing you, then prepping you for your meetings." George said from where he stood next to her.

"Okay." She watched everyone else wake up. Nam grabbed her hand tight from the seat next to her, and McKenna squeezed back.

~You going to be okay staying with Charley, Jamie, and Jessi to play? Their friend Carina will watch you guys.~

Nam nodded slowly. ~I like them. They think my tiger form is neat.~ Even in a mental whisper her tone held wariness and a touch of fear.

~That would be because it is neat. When you get bigger, you will be a fearsome creature.~

She looked over to McKenna her eyes widening. ~Me? Fearsome?~

McKenna smiled. ~Tigers are very fearsome. So yes, I am sure you will be a fearsome creature that everyone will be impressed with.~

Nam's smile grew a bit even as she ducked her head.

~You're pretty awesome, Nam. Don't worry. We'll take care of you.~

McKenna shot a look at Jamie and realized while her channel had been private, Nam must have shared it with them.

The little girl relaxed a bit, looking out the window as they started to bank.

McKenna looked over and saw JD and Cass holding hands and hid a smile. They were good together. It looked like JD had found his princess to protect.

Good for him.

Her stomach dropped a bit as the plane hit an air pocket and then the wheels hit pavement pushing her back into the seat. For a minute she couldn't breathe, the pilot hitting the breaks harder than she'd experienced before.

Worried, she checked on the kids but all she could feel from them was a sense of excitement. Aliens might be real for them, but they still regarded this all as a huge adventure.

She envied them a bit for that.

Dread pooled at the base of her stomach as she rose, corralled the kids, and all of them headed down the stops of the plane towards the waiting dark SUVs.

Here we come, ready or not.

Chapter 13 - Self Important People

The cabinet is in closed-door meetings and the president has cleared his schedule. No one is sure what is going on, but rumors of a UN emergency meeting are already floating around. There are strange rumors of China and Russia adjusting their satellites and telescopes, but no one is sure why. What is going on, and why doesn't anyone know anything? Shouldn't there be press conferences? Are we going to war? ~ TNN Talking Head

The whirlwind of the next two hours left McKenna glad someone else ran this show. Between getting them to the house in the early morning hours, figuring out the rooms, and then the sergeant waiting for them with a literal rack of clothing for them to try on, McKenna fought to not feel overwhelmed. Everyone treated them well, if distantly. Food waited for them, and only Wefor reminding her she may need to shift allowed her to force food down her throat.

All of them felt tense in the mindspace and they didn't talk much, trying to remember to speak out loud for the non-linked around them. Before she could really get freaked out, she found all of them in a long limo headed towards the capital. They left the kids eating breakfast and planning on playing in the huge back yard. It had an eight-foot fence and a nice playset, a suspiciously new playset, for them to wear themselves out on. They all dressed in the outfits that were provided. They had fit to a level that surprised her. There had even been new undergarments for the women that fit better than anything she'd ever worn. At least she felt presentable in a sheath dress and a simple jacket. The same efficient sergeant had suggested subtle make-up, something only Carina had remembered to pack for Toni. The women looked professional, and the men in their suits came across as respectable. And all she wanted to do was go home and crawl under the bed.

George sat with them looking at them. "You all clean up nice. You ready for this?"

"What this? Who are we going to talk to? What are we supposed to tell them?" McKenna managed to keep her voice from shaking, which she treated as an accomplishment. Though from the smile he fought back, she suspected her panic had leaked through.

Dammit, talking to people mentally when upset or frustrated is so much easier.

The morose thought didn't help much. But she paid attention when he started to talk.

"You're going to talk to the president, the VP, secretary of state, secretary of defense, chairman of the Joint Chiefs of Staff, and the speaker for the House, and Senate majority leader."

McKenna knew who most of those people were in general, if not specifics about the chairman. George began to talk, explaining who each person was and just what area they would have concerns about and what they had already sent him questions regarding.

She listened, trying to take it all in even as something tingled against the back of her mind. The dream she'd been roused out of, they had talked about multiple cities.

"When are we going to talk to the -," she broke off as the driver started to talk.

"Pulling in now. Please make sure all our passengers understand the security concerns."

That set off pat downs, scans, being ushered through one strange hallway then another.

~They provided the clothes we are wearing. Watched us pack. What weapons can we have on us?~ she groused as they went through one more scan.

~I just wish they thought kilts were appropriate wear. Even with measurements these pants are tight. I think the bots have been working overtime to get us bulked back up.~

~Ditto,~ Perc muttered, even as he moved with assurance McKenna didn't feel.

~I never thought I'd say this, but I miss my uniform. That felt like me, this simply feels silly.~

~Speak for yourself,~ Toni's voice held smugness. ~I look awesome.~ And she did. The green dress somehow matched her eyes and made her look elegant and composed.

~Did you guys dream, well not dream, have one of those vision things on the flight up here?~ Cass seemed almost tentative as she asked.

McKenna started to turn to look at her when their escort came to a sharp stop outside a pair of double doors, opened them and then stepped back, waving them in. A bunch of men in sharp suits turned to look at them and McKenna's mouth went dry as she recognized the president and the secretary of state.

George led the way and introduced everyone, but only President Carl Simon, Secretary of Defense Doug Burby, and the Chairman of the Joint Chiefs General Arnold Murphy registered as important enough to remember. There were four or more secret service agents in the room, at least two secretaries, one male and one female, and then George.

The President Carl Simon she recognized, though she had voted for someone else, his snow-white hair and strong craggy nose below pale gray eyes were memorable.

The SecDef had a shining bald pate, sharp hazel eyes, with a hard look in them that made her think he had served.

The general, in his uniform with more medals than seemed real, had a crew cut revealing steel gray hair, a body with the beginning of a potbelly, and a sneer.

The sneer pissed her off. She didn't want to be here. While she might enjoy the cougar aspect of her, and had grown rather fond of Wefor, she didn't cause this, and she sure as hell wasn't lying.

~They can all bite me. I'm here to solve a problem and I'll be damned if their contempt and disbelief will put my kids at risk.~ Already Nam was hers as much as Charley was.

~There's my Kenna. Kick their asses. We have a planet to save.~ JD's words made her grin and her smile grew as the men looked at all of them.

Before George could start to introduce them, McKenna stepped forward and let her smile widen.

INCOMING

Treat this as a drug bust from hell with all spoiled rich kids. Stay polite but firm. Remember what's riding on this.

"Gentlemen. My name is McKenna Largo, this is my team. I believe we need to talk about the incoming Elentrin." Her voice rang through the room, cutting across the chatter in the background. "My AI says we have almost twenty-two days before they land. Their intent is to harvest shifters from this planet. What are we going to do about it?"

The shocked looks on the men's faces made her want to shrink back, but she stiffened her spine looking the president dead in the eyes.

I'll be damned if I show fear here. I have no idea what the answer is, but my kids depend on me.

The men blinked, first glancing at each other, then at George.

Finally, the president spoke, his northern accent heavier than she'd ever heard on TV. "Brigadier General Davis. Does this mean it's true? That aliens are approaching? And what does this woman mean by her AI?"

George glanced at her and McKenna felt a bit sorry for him, but the timer in her head kept counting down and from the dreams or memories, she had no illusions about the outcome.

"Sir. From our questioning, yes there is an AI, and all information provided has been verified to the best of our ability. So yes, it does look like there is an alien fleet coming to Earth. And nothing she has said indicates good intentions." George didn't look intimidated, but neither did he look happy at her opening volley.

"What about the AI?" the SecDef added. He didn't sound antagonistic, but more wary. Wary, she could handle.

"Hadn't you better ask me that? She lives in my head." McKenna interrupted, and he turned his cool eyes on her.

"Only you? None of the others?"

"Only me. While my team here has abilities that are not the norm among Kaylid, the AI is only in me, though there may be others that have AIs also, although what their programming would tell them to do is unknown."

Half the room sharpened at that. "Programming?"

"McKenna? If I may?" George interrupted, and a screen dropped at the far side of the room. He tapped on his phone and a PowerPoint presentation popped up. "Here is a high-level summary of what we know. As she said, time is of the essence and this is the information that has been gathered."

Somehow during the flight, George or his staff had taken his notes and everything they had talked about and made an executive level summary in three slides. They covered the nanobots, the ships, the basic purpose, and tests run to verify the existence of the AI.

"I'm still not sure I believe all this. I can think of many ways that could have been faked. How are we to know this isn't just all a big scam?"

"Besides the alien fleet coming in?" JD asked dryly from where he'd been leaning against the wall. He, Cass, and Toni were all back against the wall, watching people watching them. While Perc had taken up a flanking position behind her, guarding her back. It had the added advantage of making her not feel so alone.

"It's a relatively small fleet, they may be here to establish trade. We don't have any space-based weapons. Any earth-based missiles lose most of their effectiveness once they leave the atmosphere. If we can establish peaceful negotiations with them, it would be best." General Arnold Murphy said, a bitter tone to his words.

"You can't. Well, maybe you can, but I'm not sure Earth will like the terms." McKenna replied even as she tried to figure out how much to tell them. She turned and looked at her team, falling silent as she talked to them.

~Do we tell them about the dreams? About the warrior form? Did you have the dream where they talked about the multiple cities and landing?~

~Yes, I was going to ask you about that. It was odd. Who was that being talking to us?~ Cass asked.

~He's been in a lot of my experiences. Though I'm not sure he is wholly for what the Elentrin are doing.~ Perc commented, an aura of thoughtfulness in his voice. ~Some of his word choices and tones have been odd.~

"Ms. Largo?" The voice registered, and McKenna turned back to see the men staring at her.

"Sorry, processing an option. Your biggest issue is the AI claim? As the approaching ships are validated?" She kept her voice cool even as she asked in the mindspace.

~Anyone have issues with me doing the phone trick? I can't think of anything else we can do.~

~Go for it.~

~What phone trick?~ came from Perc, Cass, and Toni.

~Oh. Yeah. You'll find this... interesting?~

"Yes. We accept that there is a fleet of ships coming here. We just don't know how to handle your claims of an AI. And I cannot believe I just admitted to the fact that aliens are approaching Earth." SecDef Doug Burby shook his head and sat down. "When this gets out there's going to be worldwide panic."

"Why do you think I didn't go online?" she said, a bit exasperated. "Enough people would have believed me that there would have been a panic. But they are coming. I'm done hiding stuff. We can't convince them to leave us alone, my family, my kids are going to suffer, and I'm not willing to do that."

"Hiding what exactly?" The general growled, looking at her with distaste.

McKenna snorted. "You'll never believe. Anyone have a smartphone I can use?"

They hadn't been allowed to bring theirs, and since they could all ping the kids mentally it really didn't matter.

Everyone glanced at each other until one of the male secretaries spoke up. "I do. I'll get it back right?"

"Yes, and I promise it won't even be damaged."

He arched an eyebrow but handed over a nice smartphone about a year old. McKenna took it, and with her annoyance and fear driving her, she let one of the claws from her warrior form slide out of her left index finger. Collectively people in the room took in a sharp breath and she could hear their heartbeats rise and the Secret Service agents all stiffened. She pricked the pad of her thumb, letting blood seep up and dropped three large drops in front of the data port of the phone. A half moan reached her ears, probably from the guy who'd let her use his phone.

The room went still, not even remembering to breathe as the blood moved into the port and disappeared. Less than three seconds later the phone lit up and Wefor's distinctive cadence came through.

"Connection established. Interface should be stable for two to three hours. Battery life not yet determined."

"Everyone, may I introduce the AI, Wefor. Feel free to ask her your questions."

The uproar that followed and the questions and answers that flew over the next two hours had the five Kaylid very glad Wefor dealt with them.

~Welcome to politics, Wefor. I'll let you deal with them until the battery dies. That work?"

[Yes, though I suspect they want to find a reason to disbelieve the information you have provided. They do realize they will not get that from me. Right?]

~Hope springs eternal. Enjoy.~

They got coffee from the carafes against the back wall and watched the feeding frenzy.

Chapter 14 - Options

WARNO: Flash to all commands. All leaves and passes are rescinded effective immediately. All commands to report one hundred percent accountability and combat posture status within forty-eight hours. All reserve forces are now recalled to active duty status. The National Guard is directed to be activated within forty-eight hours. State National Guard Commands are to direct full mobilization status. Mobilization orders and annexes pending in next twelve hours. All units will equip with full personnel and unit systems basic loads from local armories. All commands prepare WARNOs for anticipated extended urban assaults. ~ WARNO 201609-01. ~ Alert through official channels.

The phone died after almost three hours of shouting, questioning, and demands. By the end Wefor had started being almost snippy.

[The phone dying is for the best. Nothing is being accomplished.] Her voice filled the mindspace as the phone went dark.

"Get another phone, we have more questions," the general demanded though he had asked the more useless ones. The president and SecDef had each only asked a few, both sharp insightful questions and took notes while the rest of the room had wasted time. Time they really didn't have.

"No," McKenna said, even as people were fumbling for devices. "This isn't getting us anywhere and there are other things you need to know."

During the mad questioning of Wefor, people had ignored the five shifters more and more and some of them looked startled as she spoke.

"No? What do you mean no?" The general rose to his feet, a good four inches taller than she, and started striding her way.

McKenna grinned, this she knew how to deal with.

~You want backup?~ JD asked, stirring behind her. She could feel assent from Perc.

~Nah. I got this. Assholes I'm used to handling.~ Her mental voice had laughter in it.

"We need to ask more questions, figure out what to do," he said, stopping in front of her, looming a bit.

McKenna smiled. "What? Ask for the sixth time what they want? That has been answered multiple times and asking it again doesn't change the answer. Wefor is an AI, and she's answered all your questions literally. But there are other things that have me here." She didn't take her eyes off his, meeting him and not backing down at all. "I have the commander module. It's why I have the AI and the others don't have one in their head." She waved at the others who had all dropped their causal poses though Cass looked very nervous. "It also gives me other abilities."

The general sneered at her, crossing his arms over his chest. "Such as?"

"I can communicate mentally with my team, force the change in any Kaylid, speak any language after a few minutes, and I, like my team, have the warrior form." She didn't feel like mentioning all Kaylid could gain this form once they knew it existed. "And I'm the only person you have right now who speaks Elentrin."

She saw certain people snap their heads up at the languages. The general, however, only latched onto the warrior form.

"Warrior form? What exactly is that?"

~Have I eaten enough, Wefor?~

[Yes. Though you still are underweight. You need to keep up your protein intake.]

~Having someone tell me to gain weight is just such a weird thing.~

"I'm sure someone took a picture of what happened outside the embassy." She shot a look at the secretary of state.

He shook his head. "No, there were some rumors of one of the shifters doing an odd partial shift, but it happened where the cameras missed most of it, and the few places where it might have been visible, people were blocking the view. Which means, no. I'm not sure anyone knows what happened. The military refused to go into detail, and frankly I've been too busy due to the hot potato someone dropped in my lap." His voice didn't hold anger, but vague amused wariness. An odd combination, but one she understood.

"Huh. I never thought it would stay contained that well. What do you know, social media didn't let this secret slip." Her voice thoughtful.

"Quit stalling and give us access to the AI again," the general growled. Or he tried to. After all the animals and the various forms she had dealt with, it didn't even come close.

"General Arnold. If you are going to growl at a Kaylid, you better learn how to growl."

He blinked at her, then drew his brows down in a fierce frown. "And what exactly is that supposed to mean?"

"It means," she reached for the warrior form and it sprang towards her. The change smoother and easier that it had ever been. The same rush of heat, but her form flowed and merged into the powerful warrior form in a way that felt like coming home. She let all her frustration out in the sound that emerged. "That you need to learn what a real growl sounds like." Her words rumbled with bass and half the room took a step back and all the secret service agents drew weapons as they pulled the president behind them, their eyes wide as they realized her party stood in front of the door, the main exit.

General Arnold Murphy paled, but stood his ground, though she could smell his fear. "Is this a threat?"

"Gentlemen," McKenna said, letting her exasperation slide into her voice. "Why would we threaten you? They are coming for us. For our children. All we want is help, and for you to get your collective heads out of your asses. This is what they will be sending here. Hundreds of thousands of Kaylid. All armed with weapons that are better than anything we have." She took a deep breath turning her face to look at everyone, the muzzle, ears, and fangs clearly visible. "And they aren't just coming here. They're planning on sending 'ambassadors' to at least three major cities." She did air quotes around the word ambassadors which probably looked odd with clawed hands. "Though they haven't chosen which ones yet. You need to quit trying to prove I'm lying and get ready to deal with aliens that want to take a portion of our population and turn them into slaves, or worse." Her tone had risen to almost a yell by the end, and the entire room had gone silent, looking at her.

With an exasperated sigh, she let herself go back to human, a bit slower, no need to burn any more calories than necessary.

~At least this dress didn't rip and even the bra, while uncomfortable, didn't tear,~ she muttered in the mindspace.

~Do I want to know about your tail and underwear?~ Toni asked, a hint of laughter in her voice.

~NO,~ McKenna said very firmly into the mindspace and resisted reaching back to adjust that item.

The room had slowly regained sound again though the agents still looked like they were ready to spirit the president away at any second. One of them, the one who had taken point, slowly holstered his weapon and walked over to them. Older probably a decade on McKenna's twenty-eight. His short hair screamed military as did his bearing, but while his brown eyes were wary, he didn't approach her like a threat.

"You said you can force people to change forms?" His voice had a deep south hint to it though it had mostly disappeared.

"Yes. I've done it before. Why?" McKenna tilted her head at him, but noted the general had walked over to the SecDef Doug Burby and they were in an intense conversation that slowly drew others.

"My name is Christopher Collins. I'm one of the senior agents for the president and his security detail. I have an agent that turned into an animal and has been aggressive ever since. She's locked up with two other Marines that experienced the same thing. Nothing we've tried has worked."

McKenna sighed. "Sounds like the original programming kicked in. That was their plan. To come rescue us from the ravening animals. I can turn him back, and we can fix the programming."

~We can do that, right, Wefor?~

[Blood or saliva will need to be exchanged to override the existing programming, but yes.]

A look of relief flashed across his face then disappeared, replaced by a mask of control. "When you have time, it would be appreciated."

"Now is fine. I'm starving after that little show and they need to think. The clock is ticking and if a global response isn't reached, it'll be every Kaylid for themselves."

"A moment please." The man stepped away, talking into his communicator and George walked over, an odd look on his face.

"Yes?" McKenna asked, looking at him.

"You were much more forceful than I experienced you being at your house," he commented, his tone very neutral.

She sighed. "When you showed up, I'd already had two experiences with kidnapping. Military personnel were at my door, I had a child that wasn't mine, and I was going to try to prove to you that I had an AI in my head and that aliens were really coming. I was nervous, scared, and trying desperately to not freak out after a week of waiting for the other shoe to fall." She tilted her head at the men all in serious conversation. "They pissed me off, and it reminded me that I have nothing to lose. If they come, if they take us, I lose everything anyhow. And I'll do anything to protect my kids."

"We all will." Perc's voice sounded behind her and she leaned back a bit, lightheaded suddenly as her body began to scream for calories. "We're family in a way that can't be explained anymore."

She felt more than heard the others' agreement even as she blinked her eyes. "Okay, I need food, like now."

George looked at her, concerned then nodded as the other man came over. "Christopher. She needs food. Can you take them to the kitchens? I'll call down so they'll have something for them by the time you get them there."

Christopher glanced at her, then back at George and nodded. "Will do. If you'll follow me."

Perc stayed at her side and she was oddly glad. ~Wefor, what's wrong with me? I've never been dizzy before.~

[Energy expenditure. Your reserves are still low, and the bots lowered your blood sugar badly to avoid dipping into muscle. You still don't have any fat to fuel them.]

The explanation made her feel a bit better. They followed the agent through a series of halls and down three floors and ended up in a large kitchen. True to George's word, on the counter a large tray of sandwiches waited them, fruit cups, petit-fours, and meat and cheese rolls. McKenna inhaled them while the others nibbled. The fruit cup and petit-fours she hit first. The sugar helped. In a few minutes she lost the dizzy feeling. They plowed through the food until Wefor told her any more would make her sick.

"I'm ready now. Thanks."

Christopher narrowed his eyes at her but nodded. He spoke into his com for a minute, and she didn't even try to listen in. Though from Toni's thoughtful expression she did.

"The cars are waiting for us. This way."

Another winding route through the building and into a tunnel, then they were ushered into another black SUV. Half in one, half in the other and they shot out into the city. The unfamiliar landscape with buildings she recognized from pictures, places she'd always wanted to see, and it hurt to whip through it and not get to explore.

She leaned against Toni who sat next to her, the melancholy mood affecting all of them as they looked at the iconic Washington, DC and wondered what would be left a month from now.

They drove up to a gate with Marines, who after a conversation she didn't even try to pay attention to, let them through. Minutes later Christopher jumped out, and Marines opened her door. She still really needed to the pull the thong out of her ass crack but forced a smile and ignored it.

They led the group of them, with lots of Marine casting sideline glances, through what obviously was some sort of base. After a bewildering set of clearances they entered what must have been a jail for military personnel.

~It's called a brig, Kenna. Really. Even most people know that,~ JD teased her as they were led into an area.

~I'm a police officer. It's a jail. Bite me.~ She shot back, but she smiled, up until they turned a corner and she saw the three cells occupied with snarling animals.

"Oh shit." The reality hit home as she looked at what the Elentrin wanted them to be, what they expected to find, and anger bubbled at the back of her throat.

~This is what they want? What they expect?~ She asked even as a wolf lunged at them slamming into the bars and drawing blood. It ignored the pain and tried again. The other two animals, each of them in their own cage had paced to the bars glaring out at them with insane eyes. One was a cheetah, blood dried on its fur and she could see a claw had broken off. The other was a jackal, snarling at her in the depths of its cell, and her heart cringed as she thought about Kala.

[Yes. Insane animals and people desperate to be rescued from these creatures, and the people trapped to be grateful to be saved from what they couldn't stop themselves from doing.] Each word rang like a death knell in her soul and McKenna felt her rage growing as she looked at the animals.

"Bring food. A lot of it. Blankets for them to wrap themselves in and get everyone out of here." She turned and looked at her friends, team, family and blinked. "You too. JD or Perc, one of you stay."

One of the Marines started to protest. "No," she cut him off before he could say much. "They're already struggling. You have this place visible via cameras. Go watch it there. I'm not trying to hide anything, but think about how they're going to feel when I pull them out. Did anyone of them badly hurt anyone, kill anyone?"

The Marine swallowed and shook his head. "A few stitches was the worst. But Grayson, the wolf, we shot him but haven't been able to treat his wound. So he's been in pain, and we can't help."

McKenna glanced at Christopher. "The cheetah is mine. Caroline Lance. She normally watched over the president's kids. This might destroy her career," his voice low, but steady.

"It shouldn't. Not anymore than getting sick and throwing up on someone would. Let me help, but get the clothes."

"I'll stay," Perc offered, and she sensed he and JD had discussed it. The others after a quick glance at her followed everyone up as she turned back to the cages.

~Wefor, if we get some of my blood in them can you override the programming of the nanobots?~

[Yes. Though it will take a few hours for me update the programming. During which proximity will be needed until it becomes self-replicating. They will not be able to change until this is done.]

~Get the bots ready, I'll ask for some syringes, this dripping blood in wounds is just stupid and you've already said it needs to be blood or saliva and I'm not going around kissing people all the time.~ She carefully didn't look at Perc, instead looked at the people, trapped in themselves.

Chapter 15 - Forcing the Beast

What is going on with the military? All bases in California are on lockdown and if you don't have a military ID you can't get in. Don't get me wrong, our bases have always been pretty secure, but now they are insane. They are turning away anyone who isn't there on business. All vendors are being escorted in and orders for supplies have tripled. Is it just me or should this be concerning us? What is causing this reaction? ~ Harvey Klein caller.

Motion at the stairs pulled her attention away, and she saw two Marines coming down with blankets and a tray of food.

"Will you see if you can get me some sterile syringes also, please? I'll need them later. And where are the keys?"

The older one, a sergeant she thought, quirked an eyebrow at her, but just replied, "Yes, ma'am." He handed her a set of keys before they turned and trotted back up the stairs.

She turned back to the snarling animals staring at her and Perc. The wolf had managed to hurt himself a bit more trying to get through the bars.

"Enough. Wefor, I might need your help. I assume it's the same as it was with Perc and the others." She said this out loud not caring if anyone heard, she needed the words in her ears to help make it real, even as bile rose in her throat.

[Yes. Though you don't have the mind link to help identify. But as you are a commander, you should be able to sense their presence even if you don't have access to their minds.]

She'd had the others in her head for so long she had to close her eyes to find these unknown Kaylid. It took her a minute, but she found the other Kaylids just outside her mind, their presence muddy and tangled. Her eyes opened, and she moved a bit closer to the cage. The wolf redoubled its efforts to attack her, blood and foam flying from his mouth as he tried to reach her, the whites of his eyes all but glowing in the dim area.

~Change,~ the word vibrated in the mindspace even though the Kaylid she focused on wasn't there. She put her intent behind the word, for the bots to activate their other form, to shut off the programming and flip back to human.

A howl of pain, relief, fear, ripped through the space. Eyes she didn't know she'd closed flew back open and saw a Kaylid moving from animal to human. In less time than it took her to take a deep breath, a man in his late twenties lay panting on the floor of the cell. His naked body showed he needed food from the amount of ribs and vertebra she could see under his skin. The man shook like he had palsy as he lay there.

"Hey, Grayson, right?" her voice quiet as she crouched by the cage. Perc had the keys and stood at the door, waiting for her signal.

The man raised his face to her, his eyes a hazel color, though so bloodshot she almost wasn't sure.

"Yes," he croaked. "Thank you." His voice torn and raw. McKenna glanced at Perc and nodded, then moved over to the next cage finding the unknown Kaylid faster and easier this time.

~Change,~ her command had more confidence. In the jungle she'd learned to feel her team, knew them intimately. Now she just reached out and realized she could feel the nanobots, even if they weren't hers, she could command them, and she did.

This time, her eyes stayed open, and she saw the cheetah move back into a human form. The woman on all fours gasping as she sucked in air. "That fucking sucked," she muttered. She tried stand, but her legs wouldn't hold her.

"Give yourself a few minutes. Perc has a blanket and we'll get you some food." The woman, Caroline if McKenna had remembered the name correctly, glanced up and her and nodded, though her eyes narrowed.

McKenna ignored her and moved to the jackal, doing it again. In less than a minute a man lay there, younger than the other two, but just as exhausted. McKenna rose looking at the camera and nodded. Before Perc could get the third cell opened people were rushing down into the cells.

Conversation exploded as manly shakes and back slaps almost knocked over the exhausted Kaylid. Caroline, a woman with skin the color of burnt caramel, with short black curly hair walked over to her with Christopher by her side.

"So why did you have us leave the area? Besides the nudity? Which has become much less of an issue lately," Christopher asked even as Caroline pulled the blanket around her tighter.

INCOMING

"I didn't know how'd they react to be honest. The only other time I did this, it was that or die. And we did it a lot. By the time we were done most of us passed out. One died." Her voice clipped. "I knew I could do something, but I didn't know how long it would take or anything else."

"What happened to us? Why couldn't I change back? I've played with that form a little, but it felt like being a passenger in a car being driven by a lunatic." Caroline asked even as she chewed on an energy bar.

McKenna looked around. "Can we take this upstairs? Let them get clothes on, and I'll explain everything. Then go into the next weird thing I need to ask you to do."

"Shower first?" Caroline asked. "I think all of us would like a chance to wash off the blood and grime." She glanced down at her hand almost surprised. "Huh, I grew my nail back. I remember when the claw broke off. Hurt like hell, but it didn't seem to matter."

"Nanobots, for the win. Sometimes," McKenna said wryly. Caroline gave her a sharp questioning look. "Later." McKenna turned to address the Marine sergeant. "Can you set up a conference room for us, food, and the syringes?"

"Yes, ma'am. This way."

Twenty minutes later McKenna found them in a large room, obviously used for training classes from the rows of tables and chairs that weren't the standard dining size. Her team was there, the secret service agents, a few officers from the bases, the Kaylid that had been locked in their animal forms and people McKenna assumed were friends or family of them. Showers and clothes seemed to have done a lot for the Kaylid, but everyone's eyes were on her and the box of syringes on the table.

McKenna introduced herself and the others though most of them had recognized her. "Okay, here's the gist. The reason we can change is aliens, you all have nanobots in you and their programming is set to make you those crazy animals. And the aliens are coming here to get us, want to use us as their ground troops to help with their genocide." Her voice blunt and she didn't even flinch.

Christopher's eyes widened, and he stared at her. "Can you tell us this? Isn't this still secured information?"

McKenna shrugged. "It's all stuff I know, and I never agreed to not tell anyone anything. Besides, at the rate the aliens are coming we have maybe fourteen days until even basic telescopes will see them. I'd be surprised if there weren't a few scientists in other countries that are trying to figure out who to tell. And I'll do anything to protect those I love."

Questions burst out, and she spent twenty minutes answering them. Questions that were much more intelligent than the ones the politicians had.

[Why can't we deal with these people instead of the ones we met with originally?]

Wefor's question set off a peal of laughter in the mindspace.

~Our governments don't work that way.~ Cass said, her mental voice full of laughter.

McKenna swore she felt Wefor grumbling in her mind but she directed her attention back to the room. Some men walked in and she realized it was

George Davis and the SecDef Doug Burby. They, however, stayed at the back of the room and called no attention to themselves.

"So, Largo, what's with the syringes?" Caroline asked. Dressed in spare camo, she looked at home in the military garb. A striking woman, McKenna could see how she would make a good agent for the kids. A cheetah fit her, lean, strong, and fast.

"So this is where it gets weird." Most of the people in the room snorted, and she had to fight back a smile. "Trust me, you don't know the half of it yet. But your bot's programming needs to be updated to prevent that from happening again. The only way I can do that is get some of my nanobots with modified programming into you. Which means blood. In the most unsanitary way you can think of. Good news? Kaylid are immune to most disease, though drugs and poisons still work. And the sad note is that getting drunk is very, very difficult. The nanobots prevent it from happening."

"Goddamnit, Grayson. I knew there was no way you could be drinking that fucking much without passing out. I just thought you were getting the bartender to swap out your drinks or something," one of the Marines groused, biffing the man on the shoulder.

Grayson just blinked. "Huh. I just thought all those weekends of binge drinking had finally paid off."

McKenna laughed. "Yeah. Sorry about that. But what it means is if you don't want to run the risk of getting locked into your animal forms again I need to inject you with my blood."

"Gods, the medic in me is having a conniption fit. The human in me never wants to go through that again." The man who'd been the jackal, a Kareem Cham, looked up at her. "Frankly, if you wanted to stick me with a contaminated needle, I'd probably agree. That was the closest to hell I ever want to come." The other two nodded fervently.

"Okay, but there is one more aspect. Once I do this, I'll be able to speak to you mind to mind. I can't read your thoughts or anything, but I can talk to you just like I am now."

They blinked, and she saw the men at the back focus on her suddenly.

~I said that earlier,~ she said in the mindspace.

~I think they were both more worried about Wefor and then panicked when you shifted to pay much attention to anything else.~

~Great. More people in my head.~

[Commanders are capable of grouping and creating squads for thousands. It is nothing you can't handle.] McKenna picked up the needles and looked at Cass.

"I've got no idea how to do this. Wefor told me she is pooling the nanobots extra thick at my arm. I don't think I can stick a needle in myself." McKenna forced herself to swallow. She wasn't needle-phobic but sticking herself sounded like more than what she could pull off.

Cass's eyes widened then she stopped. "Actually, yes. I think I can. If you don't mind me trying something. Remember the dreams, or whatever?"

"Sure." McKenna said, trying to remember if she had learned that in hers.

"Well, mine were very medical-oriented. Actually, Charley and I were talking about that a little. He said his were all medical, too. To the point that he knows more than the nurses. Apparently Jamie wasn't too impressed about how they dealt with his arm."

Toni gave her a sharp look, and her eyes narrowed then unfocused a bit.

The others exchanged looks, a slight smile on their faces as they knew she was talking to her kids. There may have been more about their time without the adults than what they had shared about JD's house.

Cass moved over to the syringe and pulled McKenna's arm out. "I keep thinking I need a tourniquet, but if Wefor is pooling them right here, it shouldn't be needed. And she can force any healing if I screw up." She glanced up at McKenna. "I'll try not to hurt you, but we've never really put any of what we've learned while we sleep to practice again."

McKenna shrugged the shoulder not attached to the arm Cass held. "Can't hurt as bad as those damn bullet ants. And this is a much safer environment to see what translates than others I can think of. Go for it."

By this time the freed Kaylid were standing nearby and everyone watched them with varying degrees of interest. But McKenna focused on the needle sliding into her arm. With sure controlled movements, Cass slid it in without as second's hesitation.

"Dang. I don't think I've seen many sticks that smooth." Kamal commented.

"I didn't even feel it." McKenna admitted.

"Wefor, how much do I extract?" Cass asked verbally, ignoring the comments.

[Two cc's should be enough to update the programming within the next hour.]

Cass followed instructions and extracted two cc's and extracted the needle. "Hold your finger here, I'll need to do it twice more." Cass turned and looked. "Who's first?"

Kareem stepped forward. "I never want that to happen again. And at this point I'll be the guinea pig. If you really can talk to me mentally, I'll tell the others."

McKenna smiled. "Trust me, I don't go bugging much. But you can always talk mind to mind with anyone you exchange blood with. Normally, we just went the whole blood brother route and that works just as well."

Cass expertly injected the blood into his arm. Then while they waited for the nanobots to make their changes and establish the mental connection, Cass filled the other two syringes.

Everyone watched Kareem, odd expressions on their faces.

~You realize nothing will ever be normal after this, right?~ Toni said in their space. ~We're always going to be known as the ones who were the focus of the aliens and everything else. ~

~Aliens are coming. If we survive, I'm not sure normal will have anything to do with anything,~ McKenna pointed out wryly.

~True. I'll do anything to protect my kids. I'm just wondering what the price is going to be.~

~We'll pay it. Whatever it is. They are ours now, too.~ Perc's voice had a ring of assurance in it, and McKenna smiled.

The light for Kareem came on, and she pinged him.

~Hey, you hear me?~

INCOMING

The man jumped and whirled around to look at her from where he'd been talking to another Marine.

"Holy shit. You just spoke in my head." His voice shocked, eyes wide.

~Welcome to the other side of weirdness.~

He snorted at her comment, and she looked at the others. "Your call."

They all agreed and ten minutes later the connections were established, and she pinged them, but didn't pull them into the mindspace like the others.

"So does this trick work with non-shifters?" Caroline asked, a thoughtful expression on her face.

[No. While there might be nanobots, they are not programmed to spread through the body and turn that person into a Kaylid. Without that support structure the trans-harmonic communication will not work.]

She winced as Wefor used the connection to answer her question.

"Gah. Is that the AI? How do you stand that." She rubbed her temple wincing.

McKenna shrugged. "You get used to it. We don't even notice anymore."

The questions and answers continued for a bit longer, then after a few more thanks the room cleared out, leaving Christopher, Caroline, George, and the secretary of defense. The three men moved up and settled down pinning McKenna and the others with their stares.

"You have caused a bit of a stir at the White House, you know," Doug Burby said mildly.

McKenna shrugged. "Nothing I do or don't do is going to change it. They're coming and I don't think no is the answer they'll take."

"We've established they don't have weapons that are meant to destroy planetary targets, but their ground forces will have better weapons."

"There is also the intimidation factor," Perc pointed out, and the others glanced at him.

"What do you mean by that?" the secretary asked, frowning.

Perc glanced at McKenna and she explained. "We've been having weird dreams or visions of the ships. A few references have been made and we aren't sure how much is real and how much is tailored to match our expectations. But given that we know some skills we are learning are accurate," he waved at Cass as he talked, "I'm assuming that a lot of the rest is also correct. If so, most of the Kaylid they currently have, and the ones they would send here are not based on Earth animals. From my memories some of them are terrifying. Scales, tusks, horns, things we don't normally see. And if they make it a ground war they are very good at killing non-combatants." His voice went grim. "Trust me on that. From what we've learned they are controlled, unable to make decisions or do anything other than orders. You can kill them, but using anything other than matching ground troops means destroying your own people and their homes. Most of our weapons," Perc glanced at the SecDef as he continued, "from what I've seen, are meant to destroy things. How much of your own people's lives do we want to destroy? They aren't going to land in vast empty areas, they're going to show up in our neighborhoods, seeking to capture Kaylid and kill anyone in their way."

The two men frowned at him. "They wouldn't kill civilians would they? People not fighting back."

"Trust me," Toni's voice was bleak, her eyes dark as her arms wrapped around herself. "They'll kill children, step over the bodies, and not even blink. They aren't allowed."

"Oh." Everyone fell silent, then Doug spoke again. "Do you have any ideas about how to deal with all this? I'm not the president, but I do have his ear, and at this point you are presenting me with a war I've never seen in the history books."

McKenna just sighed, but JD spoke up. "I do, actually. But no one will like it, and I think we need to share it with other countries, especially those most likely to have craft landing, asking for Kaylid."

Chapter 16 - UN Bombshells

Blurry images of a wolfman-like creature have been captured, but no one is coming forward to say if they are real or not. With the existence of shifters, people are not automatically assuming that all things are fake or good photoshopping. Is this possible? Can shifters turn into the werewolves of movies and fiction? What would it mean if they could? How many more changes is Earth going to face as we adapt to what is already in our world? How much longer until we don't recognize our own society? ~Op Ed Piece

Three hours later, McKenna really wished she'd refused to wear the dress. She'd finally dealt with the thong, but the dress made her feel self-conscious, and she'd have given up the expensive bit of clothing for a kilt and a t-shirt. Only Perc and Cass seemed comfortable in the clothes.

~Why aren't you two as miserable as we are in these outfits?~ she asked as they were being taken to a large meeting room at the UN. JD had refused to say anything else, though she thought she heard him and Perc talking. A low buzz in the back of her mind, but she didn't push it.

~Practice. Lots of news conferences, plus practice time in court, and clerking for my mentor's law office,~ Perc said as they were ushered into a huge room.

~Dissertations, job interviews, presentations, all require me to dress in suits. Though this is nicer than anything I've ever owned before. Wonder if I can keep it,~ Cass responded, her hands stroking the suit.

McKenna cut off her reply as other people began to join them. None of them looking happy to see them. The only people she recognized were the president, the secretary of state and the secretary of defense. They, along with their security personnel, joined them at the front of the room.

"I can't say I agree with this, but at the same time, you are correct. This is a global problem, not just a problem for the United States," the president said dryly as he took a seat at the far end of the table. McKenna found herself at the opposite end with JD and Perc on the side facing the room. Toni and Cass were in the stadium seating-style chairs in the first row.

People streamed in, and George, who put himself in between her and JD, whispered, identifying each person as they came in. As he did so, her stomach twisted into knots. These were ambassadors from other countries, they were taking them seriously.

[As they should. There's an alien fleet headed this way.]

~I get this doesn't strike you as scary, but I've never talked to people at this level. Heck, talking to the governor made me nervous.~ Her mental conversation cut off as a man entered and headed to the table.

"That's the secretary general of the UN. He doesn't know anything yet, so he's not happy about the end run we've pulled. Basically, only countries with active armies have been invited, or those with active satellites and access to surface-to-air missiles."

She shot him a look. "Why hasn't he been told?"

"The fleet is hard to see, some sort of reflective technology and their location make it difficult to get clear images. Without your coordinates and images from multiple telescopes we might not have believed until they were much closer."

"You are aware they'll be at the moon soon, and at that point people will be able to see them with their eyes?" McKenna asked dryly.

"Why do you think we're here?" George responded just as dryly.

JD snorted and shook his head. His plan had been met with resistance, but when he pointed out exactly what they were facing, and their options, no one had been able to come up with a better plan.

A few more minutes of people shuffling around, and the man George had identified as the secretary general stood. A slender man, with a shock of black hair, above features that hinted at Oriental ancestry, but his nose looked like something off a Roman bust. His eyes grabbed her, hard, dark, and he didn't smile. He didn't look like he ever smiled.

"Ladies and gentlemen. This emergency session has been called under protest by the president of the United States with agreement from their ambassador and secretary of state citing resolution 377A(V). As I am not currently aware of any tensions between countries in the UN, I disputed the need for this, but as founding members they have insisted." He turned and sneered at the men gathered at the table. "Gentlemen, you have the floor."

McKenna had become acutely aware she was the only woman at the table. Most of the people in the room were men, though a few women were scattered in the audience. People kept glancing at her, JD, and Perc, obviously unsure as to who they were.

The UN ambassador glanced at the president and shrugged. She didn't remember seeing him, maybe he didn't know what was going on. Could this get anymore complicated or confusing?

With a sigh, the president rose and strode over to the small podium with a microphone the secretary general had used. "Thank you, Amand, for your gracious introduction."

She could all but hear the gasp at the cut as people sat up a bit straighter, sensing blood in the water.

~Huh. You getting the feeling that it is dawning on them that we don't have time for this crap?~ McKenna asked.

~Yeah, while you were running to the restroom someone gave him a new briefing. Apparently the fleet has accelerated. The new timeline is less than a week.~ Toni's voice set the mood. ~Meant to tell you, but they shuffled us out immediately afterwards and then Jamie had a question for me, and I got sidetracked. But, yes. We have less time than we thought.~

Swallowing hard, the lump in her throat refusing to move, McKenna glanced back at the president who had fallen silent, waiting for people to pay attention to him.

"Contrary to the secretary's opinion, this is a valid reason for an emergency session. I promise you all the words I am about to speak are true to the best of my knowledge. And we can prove most of what we are saying."

He cleared this throat, and McKenna saw stress around his eyes and wondered when he'd last remembered to eat. His hands wrapped around the podium, and she heard whispers alluding to the fact that he didn't have a prepared speech.

"The ability to shift that has affected a percent of all our citizens is caused by alien nanobots." A stunned silence fell. He kept talking before anyone could react. "And the aliens that sent them are on their way here. Your scientists should be able to see their ships in the next day or so. Information of where they are and how to locate them is being sent to your governments as we speak. The information we have is that the aliens, called the Elentrin, are coming here to collect the people who can now shift. Their intent is to use them as ground soldiers in their war. The United States is not okay with handing over a percent of our population and we will be resisting. Strongly." He fell silent and after a moment the room exploded into sound.

"Are you serious? Is this a joke? Aliens? Aliens caused this wave of abominations and now they are coming here?" A tall dark man, his head wrapped in a turban stood, shouting. "This is a ploy. What are you playing at, American?"

The president sighed and turned to look at JD and McKenna. "You two ready?"

A deep breath, McKenna rose and moved to the podium. She didn't know if it was a good or bad sign that the Secret Service hustled the president off the floor and out of the room before she reached the correct spot.

"Everyone, please settle down." Nothing happened, people were checking phones and starting to shout. ~Oh well, at least my training has some uses with all this craziness.~ Letting her voice come from the diaphragm, McKenna bellowed into the microphone, infusing both her commander voice and her police training.

"Sit down, shut up, and listen. We don't have much time." The amplification of her voice hurt her ears it was so loud, and everyone looked at her, shocked. She didn't give them time to recover. "My name is McKenna Largo. I am part of the proof that aliens are what has caused this. And to make it perfectly clear on what is about to drop down on us, my partner JD here is going to show you exactly what you will be facing."

JD had moved over to the center of the stage area while she got their attention. Two people had moved in a half curtain that hit him about belly button level. He started to strip, which she figured grabbed more attention than anything else.

"Everyone knows of the random incidents where people have turned into animals and their behaviors were similar to animals with rabies, attacking everyone and everything." She saw a few nods in the crowd, and people were locked on JD, horrified fascination on their faces. "That was the intent of these nanobots. For them to lock us all into that form. That is what the Elentrin are coming to rescue us from." McKenna laid on the sarcasm on that word. She gave a brief overview while JD finished stripping and stood behind the screen, his modesty technically preserved. She knew he had a kilt waiting for him, so they could show the second part of the example. And it was why the president was now watching this from a video screen.

"And this is why they want us."

~Go for it. Make it slow if you can, let them see it.~

Of the five of them, JD and Cass were visually the most impressive, but seeing a naked man's chest didn't cause as much angst as a female chest. So JD had volunteered to go, to show them the warrior form.

~Not an issue.~

She didn't watch him, she watched the people. Seeing if it would dawn on them exactly what they would be facing. People's eyes went wide, and some shrieked a bit as she felt him change his form. McKenna couldn't explain it, but after making the other Kaylid change, she could feel what form they were in, and if they were well or not. More things about the command module she needed to learn.

When he had shifted, she did glance back to check, he reached down and pulled on the kilt, covering his genitals. He strode out a minute later, huge, impressive, and the form seemed right for him.

Maybe my life is getting too weird if this warrior form is starting to feel normal.

"This is what you will be facing. And note, they won't all be Earth animals the form is based off of. Some will have scales, some will make JD look small. Their weapons are energy-based, and I've been told that adapting for projectile weapons won't take long. They're coming with the intent of taking us away and treating us worse than slaves." She saw a few people start to protest and cut them off. "Yes, worse. Because they aren't even allowed to think of anything that is not approved of by the Elentrin. Their thoughts are monitored, and they will be eliminated if they show any signs of being disloyal."

That cut off most of the protests, but McKenna continued. "That isn't all. This form is more powerful than our human forms. JD is strong for a human, but he's never been able to do this." She nodded at him. The room with stadium seating had a catwalk up above for observers, at least she assumed that was its purpose. It sat about thirty feet off the ground. JD started to move, a huge brown form that even under fur rippled with muscle, and he covered the twenty feet to the edge of the stage faster than she thought possible and leapt.

His form flew through the air, and he grabbed the railing as he vaulted over it, standing up there looking back down at them, a gaping smile on his bearlike face.

"That is what we will be facing, people. They aren't going to be easy to defeat and frankly normal soldiers are only going to be able to help so much. It isn't much of a plan. The president said he'll negotiate if they come to DC. But if they don't, we don't have any control over what your governments decide. But know this. In the next few days I am going live with a press conference to share all this. I will be advising people to arm themselves and prepare for war. A war that may cover the globe. You need to decide now."

As she finished speaking, JD jumped down from the walk, landing with the same grace as she did in cat form. It creeped her out, but Wefor had explained all of it. The warrior form of the Kaylid had shorter muscle strands and better fine muscle neuron control, just like primates, allowing them to be four to five times stronger in this form.

He walked over to her, and she turned, looking at the shocked looks on the ambassadors' faces.

"I don't know what you will decide. I can't control that. But I can guarantee you, if we cannot convince the Elentrin to leave without the Kaylid, there will be a war. A global war. It will boil down to a simple statement. Will you give up your people or will you help them fight?"

McKenna turned and walked out, the rest of the team following her.

Chapter 17 - Wrenches

Food shortages in some areas of the world are being reported and fingers are being pointed at shifters. As the majority of shifters are predators, the demand for protein is going up. Chicken prices are going up at a rate not seen for years, while sugar stocks have plummeted. More requests for high calorie bars have those companies' stocks spiking. What other changes are we going to see as a commodity shift with this change? Is it going to crash anything? Experts say that is unlikely, as the numbers remain at two percent, but it is having a solid shift on futures trading.
~TNN Business News

Raymond Kennedy sat and stared at this computer. Flashing canceled meeting invites filled his inbox. With his door open, he could hear the strange silence outside his hall office. This time of year people should be bustling by, trying to make last-minute deals before the break. While as a director of a department whose budget hid under undecipherable lines, he rarely did more than pull strings, and this still struck him as odd.

Flying under the radar, making things go his way, manipulating people to do what he wanted were things he excelled at. But the entire government had paused. Well, that wasn't quite true. Everyone below a certain level was still running around as if nothing had changed. But the movers and shakers, the people who mattered, had all gone silent.

His fingers tightened on his pen, a cheap ballpoint, he never gave away information. Everything about him had been carefully designed to imply what he wanted. And it worked. He played with people, using their weaknesses as a way to control them, and he could get answers to anything. Even if his project to create his own private force for the government to use disenfranchised shifters had been delayed a little, it would work.

Frowning, he picked up the phone. When he didn't have information, he went and got more information.

"Yeah, what to do you want?"

Raymond arched an eyebrow at the harried voice. "Michael, is something wrong? Can I help?"

"Kennedy, I don't have time for you, not today. There's a special session being called at the UN in five hours, and I need to get up there so I can find out what's happening. The president called it, and no one knows a damn thing."

Raymond pulled his head back as if slapped. "Our president? Simons?"

"Yes. That one. People are scrambling to get up there. The next train leaves in thirty and if I'm not on it, I won't make it. So go away, Kennedy, I don't have time for you." The disconnect barely registered as Raymond looked at the phone.

What is in the world is going on? My contacts are rarely stupid enough to hang up on me.

His eyes narrowed as he stood, grabbed a small to-go bag, he always made sure he had an overnight bag ready to go. He never knew when it might be needed, and he strode out the door, his mind working furiously. His office was in one of the many unlabeled government buildings that sat four blocks from the train.

This why you plan everything. You never know what might be important.

The entire walk there and the ride to New York, he hit contacts, looked at the news, and his mind spun. Either no one knew anything, or they weren't saying. He only had two people at the very high levels, one of which had told him about the meeting. And no one in the UN. Normally, it was a collection of self-important idiots who argued and never accomplished anything. Most of their resolutions were PR gambits and nothing ever changed. The real deals were made in the back rooms and in quiet voices. And he made sure he helped control those voices. This lack of knowledge churned at his gut.

The added factor of that cop and football player had disappeared, too. Plus, a bit of probing revealed the problematic researcher had quit. He'd been a bit surprised the shifters hadn't killed her. When she didn't get captured by the drone, he assumed she was dead. And then the interesting forms those things had worn. No news had slipped out about that, he'd been watching carefully. He had the video ready to be used at an appropriate time. The image of her holding the dripping head, looking like a monster, would be very useful in the near future. Controlling people through fear amused him.

With a sigh he dismissed it. They were probably hiding, he knew they hadn't returned to work, and other than the annoyance factor, if they never were seen again it would be the same effect. They wouldn't be bugging him or people he owed favors too. Pulling out his phone again, he activated a project management program and worked on setting up contingencies. Whatever this was, he would be ready for any option.

The last hour of the trip he spent trying to find out anything else that was going on, but other than the stuff about the telescopes and normal social media whining about the government, he couldn't find anything. At least not anything concrete or worth making plans on.

That worried him. The government didn't do secrets, ever. Even stuff classified at the highest levels leaked to those who knew who to ask. And nothing was leaking. People didn't talk when they were terrified. The idea that someone had managed to terrify people he had his hooks into, and he didn't know about it, chaffed.

Nothing had clarified, and he couldn't come up with any logical reason for the president to call an emergency session. His badge got him clearance. Long ago he'd set up access to just about any place, and the foresight paid off today.

He slipped up into the observation balcony, not stupid enough to try to get a seat. That would get him noticed, the observers were never regarded as important. Moving through the crowd of people, exchanging polite smiles with enemies and allies alike, he found a good vantage point and waited. The number of ambassadors that were moving in surprised him.

"You know what's going on?" he asked a man standing near him. Mid-level flunky, but liked to hear himself talk.

"Not a clue. But I can tell you the secretary general is pissed. They wouldn't tell him why."

"They?"

"President and the secretary of defense. They called it."

"Huh, didn't know they could do that."

"They can, even quoted the rule that said they could. But I'm telling you, I can't think of anything important enough that the secretary general is going to forgive them for this power play. I hope he hands them their heads." The smirk of glee was typical. Politics made hyenas look friendly. Might be why he loved politics.

Various options went through his head, but none of them seemed plausible. Raymond used the time to listen to people talk. The tidbits he could pick up when people were stressed never ceased to amaze him. All attention to the surrounding voices ceased as he caught sight of the figures walk into the room and sit at the table.

The cop, the football player, and the damn biologist. What the fuck are they doing here?

He sat stunned, looking at them, his mind locked on them as the secretary general all but stalked to the podium. Raymond dismissed the other woman, a nobody from her body language, and focused on what was going on.

His attention never moved from people on the stage recording all of it in his mind, with no reaction, not examining anything that was said, simply filing it in his mind. When they left, the room exploded in discussion. Raymond rose and walked out, ignoring everyone and everything. He had a train to catch.

The chores of picking up his bag and getting to the train station registered at a distance as he absorbed the information. Still doing nothing but accepting and filing. He sat down in his seat, slipping on noise-canceling headphones and closed his eyes as all his plans crumbled into dust.

Shifters the saviors of us and the reason we might die. Aliens.

Raymond turned that idea around and around.

Aliens are coming. They're planning on taking these shifters. They're coming because of these animals.

That caught his mind, and he played with that concept. Monsters, aliens, their fault. He might be able to use this. If he could get on with the contact teams. The ones that would be discussing this with whatever aliens landed.

A smile slid across his face as he started to tug on the strings he'd planted.

Chapter 18 - Weapons Practice

TNN has just received word that all troops have been recalled and all national guard have been activated. No one is saying why. Even more odd, most police departments have gone on alert and have recalled all active duty personnel. The last time this happened - actually we don't know that this has ever happened. The state and federal version of the National Guard was created in 1933, but even during World War II not all units were activated. What is going on? Is there a war? - TNN News

She hadn't noticed George or the SecDef leaving, but they waited for them at the end of the hall with grave looks on their faces.

"You think that will work?" George asked.

"No idea. But I think I got past their arrogance. Their own people will tell them about the ships soon. And the president is holding a press conference for the day before the ships will be visible by the naked eye." McKenna shrugged, trying to hide her discomfort. The idea of riots in the streets terrified her.

"What about yours?"

"Mine will be after president's press conference. We're hoping it will give people time to practice. Become familiar with the new forms. My big worry is people won't have time to get weapons. The military can only provide so much, and too many people don't know how to use them. They're going to be worse than slaves." Her voice caught on that last part, but she kept walking.

The two men had fallen in with them. "What now?" George asked.

"That I can answer," Doug Burby said. "We've arranged for a firing range and weapons for them to practice shooting in their warrior form. They need to be flexible, and we have some local military who also shift who are going to meet us there. It's our intent to use them as the primary group for the meetings with the Elentrin. See if a show of force will help impress them not to dismiss us." He cast a look at McKenna. "But we'd like to have you at the meetings as a secretary or something."

She shot him a look as they reached the vehicles. McKenna and Perc climbed into the first one with George and the SecDef, the rest into the other. She opened up the link so they could hear the discussion.

"Why?"

"You can understand if they talk in another language, and we can't. It might give us a bit more leverage."

She shrugged, in the long run she didn't think it would matter. "That's fine. Has anymore thought been given to JD's ideas?"

"Oh, lots. But we're fighting with timing. We don't want to panic people or create rushes on gun stores. But at the same time, we cut it too close and we won't have time to get people armed. We're all curious to see how fast you can learn to aim guns in your warrior forms. That might help with preparation. Instructions have already gone out to most suppliers and we're ordering tens of thousands of weapons, but in less than ten days? All we can do is clean out their stockpiles, and that's creating rumors and stock market fluctuations as it is."

"Are you saying we're going to lose because we can't prepare fast enough?"

Doug heaved a sigh. "I'm saying no matter what we do it's going to backfire. We tell them now, we'll panic people, and have gun stores looted and people freaking out. We tell them when the Elentrin say 'or else' and not enough of the right people will have weapons. We don't know how fast they can deploy or adjust to our refusals."

[Very fast. Average deployment is under three hours. They will have Kaylid standing by.]

McKenna passed on that bit of information, and the man threw his pen down. "So yes, JD is right, we need to arm citizens, but how do we do that without causing panics? It needs to be almost at the last second. Though - " The SecDef stopped talking, looking at them oddly. "McKenna, if needed, would you be willing to do a press conference?"

"Sure. About what?"

Doug just shook his head. "Let me do some prep work. I have an idea, though it's a long shot." He already had his phone out. George looked at him then her and settled back into his chair to watch.

McKenna sighed in frustration, no one had any answers. "Fine. Food, then the range. We're going to be the poster children for this no matter what. We'd better make sure we're ready and can do what's needed." Everyone fell silent at that, and both George and Doug glanced at each other, then pulled out phones and began to type furiously.

They stopped and got food, decent takeout, ordering enough for twenty people. The rest of the ride completed in silence, everyone busy with their own thoughts, or at least McKenna assumed that. Her mind whirled, trying to think of options, but she had no control over any of this and that might just drive her up the wall.

They were met at the base by another nice Marine and escorted to an area where they could change, literally this time. With an odd sense of relief she flowed into the form and stretched. They'd still all been food-stuffing as much as possible, but it felt good to shift. She pulled on her kilt and a tank top. This form didn't require a bra or even underwear and the kilt didn't crimp her tail, which usually hurt.

~Okay, I'll give you that the kilts work in this form, but still don't know about it as regular wear,~ Perc said as they were still getting dressed.

~Just wait until you have to shift on the fly and get your tail kinked. That hurts.~ Toni's voice had a wry experience to it that made McKenna grin. Minutes later they were all out, and the same Marine escorted them to the range but kept looking at them sideways, a wary look on his face.

"I'm still the same person I was ten minutes ago," McKenna pointed out, trying not to be annoyed.

"Give me a break, ma'am. I'm walking next to a fricking were-cat. It's a bit creepy."

McKenna barked out a laugh. "Try having an AI talk in your head."

"Thanks, but no thanks, ma'am. Having my sergeants yell at me is more than enough voices for me." They all chuckled at that as he dropped them off with the range officer. A gruff man, his arms folded over a burly chest, glaring at them.

"I'm supposed to teach you how shoot these M-16s? Huh. Anyone have any experience shooting anything?" McKenna and JD raised their hands, but no one else did. "Great, a bunch of newbies. Just what I fucking needed. Okay, get up here while I explain to you exactly what these are and how to take care of them."

An hour later they knew how to clean it, deal with most jams, the history of the weapon, and what sort of ammo it used. It came to them almost too easy, and Cass pointed that out.

~Think this is more sleep learning? Or something else?~

[The basic principles of point and fire weapons don't change much for how they work. While the weapons the Elentrin use are energy-based, the principle of aim and fire are similar. These weapons even seem comparable in weight.]

McKenna didn't know if that made her feel better or worse, but when the range officer barked at her, she snapped her attention back to him.

"Now, how the hell am I supposed to get hearing protectors and safety glasses on you?"

With a start, she glanced and realized in this form all their skulls were too wide for hearing protectors to fit.

~I never thought about that. What are we going to do?~ Cass asked, sounding like she chewed on her nail. McKenna glanced over to make sure she wasn't.

How was that possible?

An odd silence stretched out, then Wefor spoke, though a bit slow. [Tell your nanobots to reduce your hearing by seventy-five percent? The AI had an odd tone to her comment.

~Umm, okay?~ McKenna sent the command through her mind and the mindspace, and felt the sound around her decrease drastically.

~Did you guys get that?~

~That is so cool. Why does McKenna get all the cool toys?~ JD teased in her head. She elbowed him in the ribs, hard. His mental voice disappeared as the others snickered.

~This is awesome. Next time the kids are going ballistic, I'm just lowering my hearing. This will make my life so much easier. Why didn't we know we could do this?~ Toni said, glee in her voice.

[Why would you not know that? They respond to you when you change forms. Why would you not think they would respond to basic commands? Difficult ones like making McKenna's soles hard enough to walk without shoes might require an AI. But basic biological controls have always been yours.]

Silence filled the mindspace, and they all looked at each other. McKenna thought if she didn't have fur covering her body she might have blushed.

She cleared her throat, turning to look at the range officer. "Not a problem, took care of the hearing stuff. We're at seventy-five percent hearing-wise." She reached over and put on the glasses, which felt odd, but fit okay. "Let's go." Maybe she showed too many teeth from how he flinched back.

They followed him out and learned to shoot. Figuring out how to get fingers that were a bit too wide for the trigger guards to work. They had to remove the bottom of the guards and their clawed fingers fit. But once she realized her claws were more than strong enough to pull the trigger it got much easier. They all seemed to be decent shots.

[Practicing long distance would be good. Most blaster fire really only works under one hundred yards. Projectile weapons are more effective at the longer distances than what the Elentrin will come prepared with.]

"Sir?" McKenna said on one of the breaks for reloading and checking targets. "Can we do some long shots? Over two hundred yards."

He glared at them then nodded. "These are eighteen-inch barrels which are good up to about six hundred yards. But you'll need to learn to do the math to adjust for the drop," he warned, his eyes narrowing.

"Try us."

Sure enough, Wefor could whisper in all their minds, helping them adjust and hit the center of the target consistently. By the time they were done, the officer grunted.

"You might not suck. Anything else?"

"No. Thank you for your time." This time McKenna didn't smile at him. The same young Marine escorted them back out.

"Did you need to change back?"

"Huh?" His voice came across faint and muffled.

~Oh shit, hearing is still cranked down.~ She sent a mental order to restore hearing to normal. ~Wefor, can we make our hearing better too?~

[Of course. Along with vision in this form. As this is a manufactured form, all variables can be changed. While in your human and animal form only minimal controlled changes can be made. Size of genitalia, skin imperfections, damage repair. Things like that.

Though it is advised to do the changes slowly otherwise the energy expenditure might be too great. Males have been known to be a bit over-zealous in their changes.]

Perc and JD stumbled to a stop as the women choked on laughter. The young Marine looked at them, confused, as he stepped back a pace from them. "I'm sorry? Did you want me to take you back to the changing rooms or to your vehicles?"

As one the women cracked up laughing even as JD and Perc's hands twitched then they clasped them behind them, staring up at sky.

"Yes, to the car. I think we want to stay in this form for a while."

The Marine looked at them funny but shrugged and led them to the waiting vehicle, even as the women tried very hard to control their giggles.

Chapter 19 - Plans in Motion

Ambassadors have been seen leaving a special meeting, and rumors are flying, but they make no sense. Something about a space fleet and a special announcement in the next day from the president. Other countries are currently having closed-door meetings, and the queen has closed all royal property, stopping all tours and access. China has locked down their borders and has ordered all airlines to cancel flights as they will not be allowed to land. All guard units in the US are being sent out to various locations across the states with no information as to why or what is going on. Who are we going to war with? Why isn't anyone talking to us? ~ TNN Special Alert

McKenna had no desire to go back to human, so she stayed in warrior form as they were taken back to the house. It seemed an eternity since they left that morning. Now she just wanted to be home, but that wouldn't happen again for a while.

If ever.

She pushed back the traitorous thought and focused instead on what they would need to do. But she didn't know. Giving up, she just thought about what she could do, and a plan slowly formed. As they got out, she noticed none of the others had gone back to human either. While they looked odd, it seemed like the right option, and she didn't think about it much as they headed into the house.

"Kenna," she heard the yell and turned to see the kids all stopped and looking at the adults as they walked in. Their eyes were wide as they looked at her.

"What's up-" Carina came up behind the kids carrying a half-asleep Nam, and her chocolate skin paled to a milky brown color as she looked at them.

"What's wrong?" McKenna asked, worry spiking through her as she started to move forward, feeling the others behind her.

"We haven't seen that form since that day." Charley whispered in a low voice, and McKenna remembered.

"Oh. Want us to change back?" She started to reach for the human, but the kids shook their heads. Jamie and Jessi pushing back Charley and reaching their mom.

"No. I think this feels right. We need to see this even if we aren't supposed to shift yet," he said slowly. Nam lifted her head and looked at them. Her eyes widened then she blinked and started to wiggle.

Carina set her down and took a deep breath. "I know you had talked about it but seeing it in person is impressive." She blew out a shaky breath. "I had food delivered. Ready to eat?" Her hands trembled a bit, but her color had started to return to normal.

"Yes. And I'd like us all to talk. Kids, too."

They decided to stay in warrior and see how hard eating like humans was, most of the time they were in the jungle they'd never paid attention to manners.

It might prove useful to know if they could be polite while dining with others.

It took a bit to figure out how to handle flatware, Cass having to give up and partially shift her hands back. The claws just too long to be able to manipulate effectively. When they had fallen into a comfortable pattern, McKenna updated Carina and the kids on the status of everything.

The news sank in, and even the sounds of eating slowed.

"What does this mean? Will there be a war? Can we, well, you and the military stop them?" Carina asked as she glanced at the kids, chewing on her lip a bit.

"I don't know. All we have are the dreams to go on, and what Wefor can tell us about their weapons. We may or may not." McKenna sighed. "And I don't know what they're going to do or plan. Maybe tomorrow."

There didn't seem much else to say. McKenna grabbed Nam and Charley for some much needed cuddling on both their parts. She ended up reading them a story, more because they all craved the interaction than any other reason. Tucking them into bed, McKenna wished everyone good night in the mindspace, not wanting to go bug the others right now.

Slipping into bed, she reached for sleep, wanting an escape from all the bad choices that lay in front of her.

"Commander. Come in. The others are here to meet you. The arrival locations have been selected." The same male stood there, his white tail flicking side to side. McKenna walked through the door and saw two others standing at attention in the small conference room. She inspected them, glad the body she borrowed had the same inclination.

One male, one unknown, or at least she assumed it was male as he wore a wrap at hip level. Armored and hitting about knee length. Covered with fur that was beige with dark purple stripes in it, but no tail like her or the one who always seemed to be giving orders. The feel was cat-like, but he had aspects of a bear, the bulk and wide stance brought that to mind.

The other one stunned her. Which seemed stupid given everything else. But it had light grey leathery skin covering its body, all the way to a smooth juncture between its legs. A long tail lay perfectly still behind it, the leathery skin fading into a darker grey, almost black. Its head much more reptilian than anything, but even from where she stood she could feel the heat of its breath. But it didn't look at all like the graceful Drakyn. More chunky, almost like a Komodo dragon, no grace, all power.

"This is Commander," his voice fritzed out, and she couldn't hear the word he said. "And Commander." Again him saying the name didn't register. McKenna tried to ask him to repeat it, but the body nodded at the other two.

"Sit, all of you." They sank onto stools that flowed and adapted to their bodies even as a map of Earth appeared on the wall to the speaker's right. "Scanning from this distance isn't possible. Even in orbit, the concentration of beings is too dense to determine Kaylid populations. Given standard programming the Ayl Mites should have been more successful in the denser populations. While they have not achieved this space flight, it is believed they have some technology. Standard operations. We will land at the public areas in these three spaces." He pointed to three places on the map of the continents. One she recognized as New York's Manhattan Island. That, at least, would be obvious. Another spot lit up in China on the coast with a kind of triangley part that looked like it pointed towards Japan, but she didn't know enough to tell where other than China. The third was in what she thought was Turkey.

Is that Istanbul? Only major city I know of. If that's correct only we might have any sort of realistic presence. Oh, this is going to suck.

"The shuttles will drop at each of these locations after a full day of orbit. They have not achieved space flight, so the presence of the ships should cow them. Play on their superstitions if needed. Given the estimated populous, the expected Kaylid has been revised upwards to at least thirty million. Another ship has been called in for collection. Given that they can home on these ships once orbit has been achieved, they should arrive about three liad after orbit. With that population base, expected harvesting is fifteen million. That should create a buffer for the next few years as only two new Drakyn planets have been found. Currently waiting for resource stockpiles to increase before raiding them." The male turned and looked at them, his tail peeking out on each side as it twitched.

"You will be deployed with full guards, in ceremonial arm, and live weapons. You are to escort the ambassadors while they meet with whoever. If they do not agree to our terms, eliminate those who will make the biggest impression. Usually females or children work the best for that sort of example." His voice had no emotion as he spoke. "Your scanners will pick up the Ayl Mites mites and you can start collecting Kaylid for transport. All weapons will have both the disable settings for the Ayl and normal damage settings for any who resist."

As his eyes scanned over them, McKenna realized he didn't have a pupil and iris like she expected, and she had to resist shivering.

"Are there any questions or concerns?"

The one that reminded her of a Komodo turned into a person raised its hand. The male nodded at it.

"Given the population density mentioned, is resistance expected?"

The other two blinked at him even as McKenna mentally laughed wildly.

Oh yea, there's going to be resistance. I'll kill all of you with my bare hands before you touch my kids.

"Unlikely. Experience has taught us that most non-warriors are ineffective at fighting back. This may change, but given the lack of space flight, it is doubtful they will have any truly effective weapons."

For the first time McKenna was glad she had no control over this form. Otherwise she might have fallen out of her chair laughing.

"Follow me to get fitted for your outfits."

~McKenna? Kenna?~ The voice matched with the sound outside her body, someone saying her name. Her eyes flew open to see Perc shaking her. "Hey. You okay?"

She held up her finger. ~Wefor, did you get that?~ McKenna kept hoping maybe with the changes Wefor could see or hear something.

[No. I am not able to tap into these. The ones that are pure training yes. But this, this is different and

INCOMING

not one the programming recognizes.] There seemed to be a hint of confusion from the AI but McKenna didn't have time to follow up on that right now.

~I need a map of the world. ASAP.~ No one even asked questions, they just moved even as she scrambled out of bed, uncaring that all she had on was a t-shirt and underwear.

~Have one up on the laptop down here,~ Cass responded as she tore down the stairs. As she reached the table, Cass turned it towards her. McKenna scanned the map and zoomed in.

"Okay, I think these are the two locations. Think, mind you." She pointed at the big city that almost pointed towards Japan. "Shanghai. Then the other one was in Turkey, which has to be right here." She pointed at Istanbul.

"Why there?" JD asked, leaning in and looking. "Weren't there going to be three?"

"Third is New York City. They just said clearing in the city. I'd guess Central Park? Not sure of any other clear areas in NYC."

They all sat and looked at her, and she shifted uncomfortably. "What?"

"Why did you get pulled in? Did anyone else?" Perc asked. ~Toni, did you?~

Toni hadn't come downstairs and McKenna realized it was morning. She glanced at the laptop and saw that it was after seven.

"Shit, when are they coming to get us?"

"Not us, just you, JD, and Perc," Toni said from behind her. "I bowed out. I want to spend time with the kids, and Cass said her work contacted her, begging her to ignore the idiot that said she was fired. Apparently there is some clause about her patents if she is fired without just cause. So, she's going to stay home to work out some stuff with them. Besides, I want us to go explore DC. While we can. But no, I didn't go anywhere, I just slept."

~Wefor, we need to talk about this at some point and figure out why we are getting these overlaps and this information. But not now.~ She turned and headed up the stairs, almost tripping as a private message pinged her.

~Sexy look,~ Perc said. She whirled, tugging her t-shirt down as she did. But he'd already disappeared. McKenna headed into the shower, a smile curving her lips as she remembered they weren't dead yet.

Chapter 20 - True Faces

More and more people are reporting dreams. To the point there are multiple Reddit links that describe the different types of dreams. But consistently people are in this warrior form, even if they've never taken that form before, and they are practicing skills they've never had. There have been reports of people who had tested out as functionally illiterate now reading at high school level with skills in science and mechanics. Is this a side effect of this form or is there something else going on we haven't been told about?
~ KWAK News Special Report

The car pulled up just as she got downstairs. "Here, food." Toni handed her what looked like a burrito.

"Thanks. You sure you're okay staying here?"

"Positive." Toni shook her head. "I'm scared if I go I'll strangle someone or shift and show them exactly what a pissed off Kaylid can do."

McKenna laughed. "Yeah, I know the temptation. Stay in touch. Let me know if you need anything."

They got into the car, and McKenna bit into the burrito, pleasantly surprised to find it full of eggs, potatoes, meat and cheese.

~Thank you, Toni.~

~Thank Carina. She made them when she realized how late you all were.~ McKenna became aware JD and Perc were also chowing. She focused on the food until it she had eaten every bite. Traffic was heavier as they were on the road much later than normal. With a full stomach, she closed her eyes and pinged Toni, though she kept it in the public mindspace.

~Whatever you pay her it isn't enough. And at this rate I need to double what I've been paying her for watching Charley. Especially as we're adding Nam to that.~

~Oh, speaking of which, she asked me this morning if she could "change blood with me and Carina."~ The mental sigh from Toni felt odd but McKenna understood it. ~I had to explain to her that Carina can't talk to us as she doesn't have nanobots, though I explained it a bit differently. But I did exchange with her. Makes me feel better she can call for either of us now.~

McKenna chewed on her lip. ~Have you told Carina I can change her?~ She felt everyone else, especially the kids, snap to attention.

~You can change people?~ Cass and Jessi asked at almost the same time.

~Yeah. Apparently, it's something commanders can do. I just have to bite you while in warrior form and order the nanobots to infect you, basically.~ McKenna blinked then realized something. ~Umm.... You guys do realize you won't age and are effectively immortal if you don't get killed, right? And that this won't pass onto your children as the nanobots aren't in women's eggs because they were formed before we were infected. And sperm are too small to hold enough of them to spread.~

A stunned silence filled the mindscape, even the kids'.

~No offense, McKenna, but I need to think about this.~ Cass's tone held shock and a bit of wobbliness. McKenna glanced at JD, his face drawn and his hand clenched in a tight fist.

She opened a private channel to him. ~I'm sorry. I forgot they didn't know. It seems like I've always known at this point.~

~Not your fault. I had forgotten they didn't know, either. After all that time in the jungle I forgot the fact they hadn't always been there.~

~Yeah.~ They spent the rest of the trip silent, and McKenna wanted to cry at all the things spinning out of her control.

Oh, stop it. Nothing has ever been in your control. All you can do is be responsible for yourself. You didn't ask for any of this. Quit crying over crap you can't control.

Her own mental voice provided the slap she needed, and she refocused on her plans.

The agent opening the door looked at her. "Ma'am, sirs, I've been asked to escort you immediately to one of the rooms."

McKenna shrugged and went with them. They went through the same metal detectors, but she noticed a lot more agents watching them, suit coats off and guns in easy reach.

~Nice to know they regard us as a threat. Guess someone paid attention to what you did and took it seriously.~ Her comment was back in the public domain and JD grunted but didn't say anything.

They were escorted into a room and carefully placed at the end with no exit, though McKenna noted this room had two doors, both near the front where the president, SecDef, joint chief, and a few other people sat.

The president glanced up at them and forced an expression that might have been a smile.

"Detectives, Mr. Alexander. Glad you can join us. Am I remembering correctly that you, Ms. Largo, are the only person who can understand the Elentrin if they talk in their language?" he asked, even as General Murphy crossed his arms and sneered.

"As far as I know, yes."

"Fine, we keep her here for the meeting. It doesn't change my point. We need to contain all these shifters and force them to come to us. We lock them up and keep them contained, create kill boxes for these damn aliens coming in. If a few of the shifters die that's fine, it deprives these aliens of what they want."

McKenna blinked, looking at him with confusion then glanced over at JD and Perc who both had frowns on their faces.

"Arnold, I'm telling you this won't work." Doug protested through clenched teeth. "You can't get them all."

"Who cares if a few slip through the cracks, you'll have the majority of them for their own protection and these can convince them that doing it is in their best interest." Arnold jerked at head at McKenna and the two men sitting on the other side of her.

"Excuse me. What exactly are you suggesting?"

Arnold stood, moving towards her, and she really wished she'd worn the kilt and stayed in warrior form, but all of them had slipped back into human.

INCOMING

The joint chief stalked forward as he talked. "That you are going to help me protect this country. All the shifters are going to be rounded up, placed in prisons, and I'll deploy the military there. That way the only people at risk are my men and these creatures. So the aliens can get killed trying to kill them. We can possibly eliminate two problems at once. The incoming invasion and this contamination that they saddled us with. Sometimes all you can do is kill the disease carriers to protect the rest of the population." By the time he finished he loomed over McKenna glaring down at her.

JD and Perc were all but vibrating with rage. McKenna couldn't even get mad, she just stared at him, then glanced to the side at the exhausted-looking President Carl Simon and Secretary Doug Burby.

"Is he insane? Or just really that stupid?" she asked, curious.

"Don't give me any lip, girlie. You're going to help us round up all these people and do what you can to make sure these aliens don't kill any good citizens." He all but snarled at her.

McKenna blinked at him and started to laugh. A full laugh that shook her entire body and had tears coming to her eyes and gasping for breath. The general sputtered and looked at her as JD and Perc fed her info about the reaction of the agents around the room.

~They're a bit anxious, hands on weapons. I don't think shifting in here would be a good idea, especially as none of us have the bulletproof upgrade,~ Perc pointed out even as she felt him tensing and altering his position.

When she could breathe again, she stood and walked slowly towards the secretary, making sure to keep the table between her and the president, just for the agents' peace of mind. No reason to make them more stressed. She was aware of the general following her and glaring at her as she sat down in a chair a bit away from the other two men.

"I'm serious. Is he insane or have a stroke or something?"

"I've been wondering that for the last hour," the SecDef muttered.

"It's the only answer. We consolidate, create targets, and pull the enemy to us. We give them what they think they want so we can prevent them from getting anything. Shifters are only two percent of the population of Earth. We can't sacrifice everyone else for a small subsection of abnormalities." The general all but spat the words as he reclaimed his seat.

"You must be an idiot." She looked right at him as she said this. Wefor provided her with info as she asked for it, trying to convince these people to get rid of this moron. "Two percent roughly, yes. That means in the US alone there are over six million shifters. You can't imprison that many people. Not to mention the military has been actively recruiting them. You going to start another Japanese concentration camp thing? With people who can shift into a form that will go through most of your men without trying? Did you miss what we can do in warrior form? JD suspects he can dead lift over a thousand pounds in that form. We played with weapons yesterday, and those forms adjust to weapons fast. Do you think people like that will allow themselves to be caged or treated as the enemy?"

"Then we kill them now, and give these aliens no reason to come here. We eliminate two problems and these aliens will go bother other countries. Bottom line is a win/win for us."

McKenna felt her jaw fall open in shock. It didn't make her feel better to see the surprise on the other men's faces, though the Secret Service agents were carefully neutral.

[The odds of that working are low. They would just seed the planet again, and this time the nanobots would not be damaged. So humans would turn into the ravening beasts as the rule.]

~Okay. But I'm not telling them that. Right now I need to see how they react. JD, Perc this may have become a lot more dangerous than we thought. We might need to be ready to run. Toni, Cass? You get that?~

~Yes. Preparing to-go bags now. The kids are way too pragmatic about this option.~ Toni's comment had wryness to it, it tasted like pepper to McKenna, an odd sensation.

"Arnold. I knew you were an old stick-in-the-mud, but you had experience and have been a good ally when it came to race and gender in the military. But this is not acceptable. I expect your resignation on my desk by the end of the day. Your vice chairman will fill your position until a new person can be appointed." The general began to splutter and stood, but the president turned and looked at the agents. "Please escort this man out of here and ensure he removes his personal items from his office. Let the vice chair know his presence is required immediately. Get my chief of staff to update him." He moved his attention back to the general. "I don't have time for racism in my administration. And I sure as hell will never sacrifice Americans because it's efficient. Get out."

His voice hard and cold, and McKenna raised her eyebrows, a bit more respect creeping in. The agents leapt into action, and before she had time to reorient herself, the man was gone and the stress level in the room had dropped sharply.

"That was not our original plan, and I'm not sure why he thought that would ever be acceptable. It is very difficult to protect a spread-out population, especially when we can't stop them from attacking, but that is not a valid option," the secretary said, his bald head shining in the lights.

"Why can't we stop them? I mean they would have to come down in ships or shuttles. They do have to travel to get here."

His smile had no humor, only bitterness in it. "While the idea of shooting incoming ships is great, in reality it doesn't exist. Most of our defenses are for objects coming in on a more flat trajectory rather than straight down. Even nuclear missiles come in at angles and we have quite a bit of time to get a firing solution. Hundreds of thousands of troops dropping in?" He shrugged. "That's why HALO insertions are so effective. We can protect a few areas, but the country from an invasion like this? We don't have a chance."

The words sank in, and McKenna took a minute to mull it over. "So we have to fight." She rubbed her face, her fingers massaging her temples as her heart triple-beat.

"Yes." His voice hard and cold. "The weapons difference is what worries me."

"I might be able to help with that. They're really only good at a few hundred yards. I don't think they would expect some stuff, like snipers. You know, long-distance shots." McKenna was good with a pistol, but long shots really weren't anything she'd ever played with, so she didn't know what was possible.

"Now that's interesting. Maybe we can use that to our advantage. There are lots of hunters across this country." He frowned. "But how will they know if they're from the aliens or not?"

McKenna chewed on her lip. She hadn't noticed uniforms, the body types were too varied in the few glimpses of anything she'd focused on in the dreams.

~Guys, you've had more dreams than I have. Can you think of anything?~

~Beside that they're trying to kill us?~ Cass asked with a touch of her normal humor. ~No. Kilt-like things are popular with the ones with tails, and there were jumpsuits on the ship but I didn't see a uniform.~

~Neither did I. Everyone was always in warrior form and seemed to be wearing what worked for them. Granted it was always gray, no color or any accessories. But nothing that would scream not of Earth besides the weapons. And honestly, they kind of looked like Nerf guns, if they weren't killing people,~ Perc responded.

An idea flickered in her mind.

~Wefor, if we have body piercings, would shifting forms cause it to fall out? Or would it stay?~

A huh feeling spread across the mindscape.

[Unknown. But that might work.]

"Sirs, is there a way to get someone here to pierce our ears? A big silver or gold hoop? Something visible. We think maybe having earrings in our ears in warrior form would provide an easy way to tell humans. The Kaylid are treated as disposable and kept in tubes until needed, so there isn't much life, personality, to their beings."

"One thing I have learned since being in office, almost nothing is impossible." The president glanced at one of the non-agents in the room, people seemed to come and go every time she looked up. He nodded and stepped out, pulling out his phone as he did so. "Anything else?"

"I think I know where they'll be coming to talk to us. Remember we still aren't sure why we're tapping into events on the ships, much less if they're accurate, but so far the training and information has seemed to correlate." She shrugged and explained where they thought the ships would land. "None of this means they can't change their minds, but so far I haven't felt much flexibility from them. They seem very ordered and planned."

The president nodded and glanced at Doug who closed his eyes shaking his head. "We can let them know. Get the secretary of state on board. He's got decent relations with them. Maybe they'll listen. We have about eight days before they're above Earth, assuming the time line doesn't change. But in reality, we have about three days before anyone with a telescope can see them, and no amount of explanations is going to convince anyone it is anything other than what it is, aliens." He took a deep breath.

"So here's my plan. I'm hoping you'll help because unless some new information appears I don't see any options. Have your friends come over. This is going to take all of us."

Perc and JD joined them and the President waved off the stressed agents with a snapped comment of, "We have aliens about to attack. Do you really think three people are the bigger threat right now?"

There was a growl from Christopher about them being the immediate threat, but he stepped back and let them talk. The plan made McKenna both uneasy and feel better at the same time. They'd gotten most of the details worked out when a woman with multiple piercings and tattoos was escorted in by one of the nameless assistants.

"This is Tamara. She's one of the best in the area. She agreed to come."

The woman's eyes were a bit wide, but she forced a smile. "Hey. Umm, you needed something pierced?"

"Yeah. Let me go first with this. I'll shift to warrior then let her pierce me. McKenna, you want to let her pierce you now then see if you can shift to warrior and keep it in the correct place?" Perc asked.

McKenna nodded, but kept a wary eye on the jumpy agents as he shifted to warrior. While all of them could handle and heal from a bullet wound, probably, a headshot would still kill them.

The agents tensed, but no guns were drawn as Perc shifted. The woman squeaked and drew back a bit, her eyes wide.

"Oh holy mother of god." The word a soft whisper as she looked at him.

"I give," his voice a bit thick. "I'm going to kilts too. This is too blasted uncomfortable with a tail."

JD laughed and gave a little fist pump. "Eventually everyone will come around to my way of thinking."

Tamara had gotten control and opened up her case. "If I understand you want an earring? I have a shifter friend and as far as we can tell anything we do will heal almost instantly. So normally I'd shave the area and tell you to let it heal before swapping out to another ring. But in this case I think we can avoid some of that. May I?" she asked, stepping close and looking at his ear. "I'd do it up here about midway between. Though I still should shave it to prevent issues."

"Let me try something first." Perc's eyes closed and his thick brows wrinkled pulling up the whiskers on either side of his face. The hair on his right ear faded away leaving bare skin there.

[See? Why didn't you realize you could do that?]

~Shush. It's been a bit crazy.~ McKenna said, rolling her eyes.

"Ookay," the woman said slowly. "I'll pierce, then tell me when it's healed and I'll swap it out to what you want. Given what little I heard, I inferred you wanted something visible and sturdy." She pulled open another drawer and exposed a bunch of rings. McKenna recognized them as titanium, all quarter size hoops or larger.

"Ah, I like that one." Perc pointed at a thick band of twisted grey with a bead in the middle about the size of a half dollar.

"Sure. Ready?" Perc nodded. She put the gun to his ear and checking the positioning, pulled the trigger. Perc winced then closed his eyes again.

~You telling them to heal that there?~

~Yes. This is kind of obvious once you think about it,~ he replied as he opened his eyes. "Okay, you can remove it now."

Tamara's eyes rose but she did it, revealing a neat hole in the ear. She slipped in the ring and sealed it with the bead.

"Now me. Same thing, but can I get that rainbow blue and purple one please?" McKenna pointed to a twist of colors, similar styles but in blues and purples instead of the boring steel color.

The woman pierced McKenna with the same efficiency. She followed Perc's lead and a minute later had the hoop in her ear. It felt odd, she'd never been a big jewelry person, and wearing dangling earrings as a cop gave people something to tear from her head. Though the odds of that happening ever again had dropped.

She glanced at Perc, and he shrugged, looking a bit silly in warrior form in the suit. They both shifted, she moving to warrior, he to human.

"How's it look? I can feel it." She reached up and fingered the ring, at about the same point on her ear in this form as it had been on Perc, a bit lower.

"Oddly sexy?" Perc answered, rubbing his ear. His ring sat halfway on his ear. Looking somehow dangerous and not silly.

"That should work. Especially if we can get bright ones? Maybe point those out too?" Doug said. "I know people will be cranking out versions as soon as they see that, and probably with radios and LEDs in them before a week is up."

"Then I guess we have a plan?" Everyone nodded except Tamara, who just looked confused.

Chapter 21 - Talking Heads

In an unprecedented move, President Carl Simon has activated the Emergency Broadcast System for a press conference with his words to be conveyed on all public networks preempting all programming. The audio of the press conference only will be relayed, then normal programming will return. This is the first time in history this has happened. The last emergency address was at the bombing of Pearl Harbor and the system did not exist at that time. Tension is high as to what could require this activation. Nothing else has ever approached this level of silence from DC. ~ TNN News Anchor

The next morning they all sat in the large living room, the TV tuned to the Emergency Press Conference scheduled by the president. All the news agencies were up in arms because no word of what it was about had leaked anywhere. Even Congress was coming out annoyed at the secret meetings that no one but the speaker and leaders had been invited to, they refused to say a word.

"Which has to be the first time in history that's happened," Toni said. She had found a beanbag somewhere and she and her two were curled up in it. McKenna sat on the couch, Nam in her lap, and Charley pressed against her side. While Perc sat next to her. JD and Cass were on the other couch, her legs draped over him. Carina sat on the floor, and Charley had his leg rubbing against her shoulder. All of them knew what was coming, but it didn't change the level of nerves and the knowledge that a huge portion of the world would see this. And more would watch what happened later.

They'd made sure to eat well last night, and it had been the right call. Her stomach had tied itself into knots as they watched.

"Secrets in DC? Who'd have thought. Though honestly, if they had found out the truth, do you think anyone would have believed?" Perc pointed out, his body tense as he paid attention to the screen.

Cass shrugged. "Maybe not. But you know people are going to freak after this. Any idea what he's going to say?"

"Idea, sure. Aliens are coming. Anything else. No, not really." McKenna reached up and touched the earring. They all had one now. Even the kids, though they knew not to shift into warrior form.

McKenna glanced at Charley who kept touching his ear. The bright green ring all but glowed against his pale skin and hair. Nam, on the other hand, had a bright red one that would jump out against her coloring as a tiger.

"It bugging you?" she asked softly, but Nam still turned to look at him.

"Just feels odd. Not hurt or anything." He flashed her a smile. "I occasionally thought about a tattoo when I got older, but an earring? Just feels odd."

McKenna laughed. "Eighteen for the tattoo. Though I suspect for us it is much less permanent if we wanted."

[Correct. While the nanobots can leave it alone, they could also remove it after a short while.]

"So noted. You still have to be eighteen," she said, but her tone and the smile made him smile, and he buried his face in her arm.

"Are we going to die?" Nam's words killed the mood and every adult in the room turned to look at her. The pain in the mindscape almost made her cry out as it intensified. McKenna fought it down and squeezed the little girl tight to her.

She wanted to lie, to tell her everything would be okay. But that would be the wrong option. All of them had paid too high a price to get where they were. She wouldn't lie.

"I don't know. I know that every person in this room is going to do everything they can to make sure you don't. We don't want to lose you. You're ours. I don't know what will happen, but I can promise you won't be alone."

Nam looked up at her, her dark brown eyes wide. "Okay. I don't mind dying. I thought my dad," her voice broke on that word, "would kill me. This feels better."

~Dear gods I'm going to kill that man.~ Toni swore in her head, carefully making sure Nam couldn't hear them.

~Ditto,~ JD and Perc both growled. The sudden flurry of activity on the TV pulled their attention away, though McKenna's arms remained snug around the girl, and Charley's hand held Nam's in a tight grip.

"Ladies and gentlemen, the President of the United States." The woman speaking at the podium, with the familiar seal behind her, stepped away, and

INCOMING

the president stepped forward. He looked like he'd aged since the first time she met him, and a twinge of guilt rippled through McKenna. But she pushed it away. She hadn't caused this. She was trying to stop it.

He held a paper in his hand, the teleprompter screen nowhere to be seen. Carl Simon waited for a moment, and the chatter died. He looked at the cameras, and she wanted to swear he looked straight at her.

"My fellow Americans. The news I deliver today is not news I ever expected to happen in my lifetime. I am not going to sugar-coat this, but lay out the facts as bluntly as possible, then tell you what you will need to do."

His words caused a ripple of alarm in the reporters, but no one interrupted.

"All the information I am referencing is being made available on the whitehouse.gov website as I speak. Anyone who wants to check my information is welcome to, please, prove us wrong." His voice cracked just a bit, and he cleared his throat and continued. "As the information provided will show, there is a space fleet approaching Earth. Current arrival is projected in eight days. If they orbit the Earth, their ships will be visible with the naked eye at that time, given the size of their ships. Anyone with a telescope should be able to see them leaving the shadow of Mars in five days."

The room froze, and she could see people looking at each other, their faces pale as what he said registered. But before anyone could react he kept talking.

"At this time we have reason to believe they will approach various governments on Earth to negotiate.

We also have reason to believe that they are here to collect our citizens that have recently gained the ability to change into animals. This information is regarded as credible. These aliens, called the Elentrin, are here to collect shifters to fuel their war and use them as infantry in this war. This is not acceptable." He bit out each word, and McKenna felt something in her chest relax. "To enable our ability to help protect our citizens and make it clear that our planet is not to be used as a farm for their disposable army, we have re-instituted the Civil Defense. As I speak, information is being disseminated to your local authorities to set up training, provide weapons, and go over the possible vectors of attack. While we hope that we can negotiate with the Elentrin, they are approaching multiple governments and I can only advise as to how we will deal. We will not sell our citizens into slavery - period. The men and women of this administration and of our armed forces will do everything within our power to prevent this. Please go to your local authorities and ask how you can help. They are receiving this information now and will be just as surprised and worried as you. But know this, this country has never backed down from a threat, and we will not back down from this one." He lifted his head, once again putting the paper down and McKenna felt his gaze pierce her heart. "I ask you to pay attention to the news over the next few days and all of you be ready to defend your family, your neighbors, your country, and your planet. Thank you."

He turned and walked away. The room after a full three seconds of stunned silence exploded into questions and shouts and people running out of the room.

"I guess that's my cue." McKenna said, handing Nam to Carina.

Perc rose to go with her. "Let's get changed. You have a world to save."

McKenna stuck her tongue out at him but headed up to her room. Kilt, tank top, and suit jacket were the uniform of the day.

~Wefor, am I ever going to get my boobs back? This looking like a teenage boy or someone with man-boobs is getting old.~ She locked it to just in her own head, not needing the commentary.

[Until you have enough calories to spare for fat cells, no. Once you have eaten enough to get the rest of your body back to optimum health then personal preference can be taken into consideration.]

McKenna sighed silently, she'd never have thought she'd miss her curves. Being all muscle and no curves wasn't as great as she had expected.

She got dressed, did the barest amount of makeup for this next step and headed downstairs. Perc waited for her, dressed in a kilt and a loose polo shirt and jacket. It looked oddly formal with the kilt. Too many movies with people playing bagpipes she figured.

A car pulled up, and the two of them walked outside. JD and the rest were going to batten down the hatches and wait. They'd spent last night buying supplies. Food, toiletries, ammo, and guns. The Secret Service agents got them expedited for clearance, and they had enough to hold off a small army. Though she prayed it wouldn't come to that.

More than anything, McKenna wanted to be home, on her deck, her family around her, grilling food, the kids playing and life quiet. But right now that wasn't an option.

They slipped into the back of the car and found George and Doug waiting for them.

"You ready for this?" Doug asked, his face somber, holding a phone that seemed to be approaching a nervous breakdown from how fast it was sending out chirps and whistles.

"Not at all. But I do think it's the best option we have. Maybe the only option, so I'll do my best."

He gave her a wry smile as he glanced at his phone making constant chirps, beeps, and buzzes. "The world is erupting a bit at this. The local law enforcement is scrambling for records they haven't used in decades. Hell, most people only know about the Civil Defense because of stories from their grandparents. But a lot of the old bunkers and sirens still exist. The tornado and tidal wave warning can be duplicated and Apple and Android have agreed to let us use the emergency system built into their phones to send alerts. The key is your part." He looked at her and for a moment McKenna felt an icicle run down her back. "Thank you. Thank you for trying and not letting anyone shunt you to the side. I don't know how this will all turn out, but we have more of a chance that we would have otherwise."

McKenna had to blink fast. "My world, too. I don't want to see it destroyed. And no one should be taken away like cattle. Even if we might not be strictly human anymore."

The SecDef snorted and glanced at the phone. "I can't even respond to all of these. So I'm not going to." He powered off the device and looked at her. He started to speak when their driver interrupted.

"They're setting up now and should be ready by the time we get there. Information about this was sent out as soon as the president walked out the door. I suspect you will be viral, so I hope you're ready. You need to convince them. Because we can only help with the people in the US, you have the chance to touch the world."

McKenna grimaced. "No pressure. Thanks. All I can do is talk and tell them what I know. I'll try, but I can't make anyone do anything."

Wefor had verified in a late night conversation that her control over the nanobots was limited and relatively short range, there was no way to convince them to fight or even shift. All she had, the only weapon in this fight, were words. Words that needed to convince 150 million people of what was coming their way.

The car smoothly stopped, and a moment later the door was opened. McKenna stepped out followed by Doug and Perc. She found herself outside the Lincoln Monument. Glancing back, she saw the road blocked and reporters already swarming towards them. She ignored them all, walking up the steps, Perc clearing a way for her, and gazing at the white marble figure looking down at her.

He hadn't been a perfect man, she knew enough of her history to know that. But he'd tried to do what he thought was right. And even if history proved a person wrong, that was all they could ever do, what they thought was right.

Taking a deep breath and touching all the connections in her mind, feeling them there, her family. Holding on to them as a lifeline, McKenna headed to the podium and stepped up to it, watching the people recording this, getting ready to make it live on every feed possible.

I guess I need to hope this time I do go viral.

The reporters fell silent as she opened her mouth.

Chapter 22 - Media Presence

The nation is in shock after the historic speech from President Carl Simons. Aliens exist, they are real, and they are coming to Earth. This will be a speech that will mark the day we knew we were not alone in the universe. But are they enemies? Is Earth now about to go to war with aliens? We don't even have the ability to visit other planets yet. How are we going to fight a war? All we can do is listen. Report to your local authorities and hope that maybe we won't find out just how scary the rest of the universe is. ~ TNN News Anchor

"Hi. I suspect everyone knows me, but I'm McKenna Largo. As I'm sure you have heard from the president, a fleet of alien ships is on its way to Earth. Right now, it should be somewhere near Jupiter. What he didn't tell you is that they are coming for us. Not humans, but those of us who can shift. We are called the Kaylid by these aliens. They made us for the sole purpose to be soldiers in their war." Even the reporters fell quiet as she spoke and she focused on Doug leaning against the car instead of the astounded faces.

"The ability to shift is caused by tiny robots in our bodies, smaller than viruses, and they can be controlled by these aliens. If we are taken by them we will be worse than slaves, we will be tools. They can control our thoughts, our movements, and we will be kept in tubes like spices until we're needed. We will not have families or friends, we will not be able to do anything that is not allowed by them. I am not willing to accept that. I will fight, my friends will fight, my family will fight. But we don't need to repel these invaders as humans. There is another form shifters have access to. A warrior being. A form made to fight. You will be stronger, faster, and able to better protect those you love. Today I am going to show you what you need to know, what you will be facing. Don't get me wrong, I hope, I pray that they will leave without attacking. But information suggests it won't happen like that. And I for one will be ready to defend my family, defend my friends, defend my planet."

Taking a deep breath, she pulled the microphone from the podium, they'd made sure a wireless one had been set up, and stepped out, so everyone could see her. Perc joined her, their kilts and tank tops a strange uniform.

"Watch, and you will find this form in you." She started to reach then paused as Wefor reminded her of something. "Kids—if you are listening to this you need to know it is not safe for you until after puberty, about eighteen when your hormones have settled and your adult growth is reached. Know you will be able to do this someday, but if you shift now, your body can't handle the resource requirements and the changes. While not fatal you will find changes that aren't normal. So please don't. In this case let the adults, let us protect you. You are our futures."

~At some point we need to talk about the exact risks to kids, but later.~

[Acknowledged.]

With that, McKenna reached for the warrior. She made the change as slow as possible so people would have time to see what she did. As always, her eyes closed at the moment of shift. The sound of a scream and a few gasps greeted her when she opened them again.

The crowd of reporters actually backed up, looking at her, their faces pale, before they got a hold of themselves. She could smell the fear wafting off them but kept going.

She concentrated on speaking clearly, the muzzle still a bit awkward for clear speech. "This is what you can turn into, but this is also what you will be fighting. They are trained, will have advanced weapons, and they will kill anyone who opposes them. Take this seriously, they do not recognize non-combatants, they will kill anyone they see while they try to capture those of us who can shift."

Her hand reached up to touch the earring. "This is what we are using to tell Earth Kaylid from those who will come to take us and kill our friends, our loved ones. You can fight back. While here in the US, the president has activated the civil defense platform, those of you in other countries need to make decisions. You can use guns in this form, and up close, fighting these aliens you will probably win. They've trained for a long time, they know how to kill fast and with no remorse. They aren't allowed to care. Remember that, but don't show mercy, because they can't have any for us, their owners won't allow it."

Her entire body shook from stress, but she fought it down, knowing she was the only person who could do this.

"There are more of us than there are of them. If we go to war, this will be global. No beaches to defend, no forts to hunker behind. This will be them landing at every small town and city across the world, expecting us to cower in fear and give them what they want. I am asking, I am begging you, learn what you can, become familiar with this form, because in a very real way you, we- are the only chance we have. If we fail, our loved ones will die, and we will become slaves." She bowed her head for a minute then raised it this time looking directly at the reporters.

"Do what you can, and pray all of this is wrong, and we'll never have to fight for our existences." She clicked off the microphone and laid it down.

The collected group of reporters exploded into questions, but she ignored them, striding to the car, she and Perc still in warrior form.

~Everyone, everything okay?~ she asked. The thought that reporters might have figured out where they were staying in DC made her tense up.

~All quiet, though social media is exploding. You have more views than the president did. And you're going viral. I think the system is about to crash.~

She didn't have time to ask anything else as she got into the car, the driver's pale face and wide eyes catching her attention.

Doug sat there, his phone back on, but he inhaled sharply as they got in. "I don't think you fully realize how intimidating those forms are. I keep having to stop myself from fleeing in terror. And I'd always thought werewolves were cool."

McKenna smiled, then stopped when he flinched backwards. "It is a cool form. Honestly, outside our time in the jungle we haven't played with it much, so I'm not sure what other surprises are lurking." She nodded at his phone. "Is it working?"

He hefted out a sigh and pulled his attention back to the phone which was now plugged into an outlet in the back.

"Damn thing is going off so much I had to plug it in. Your message is getting out. The next few days are going to be chaotic, and we caught a lot of people off-guard with the civil defense aspect, but it wasn't like we could give them too much prep time."

~True, but still I can't imagine how crazy Kirk is going,~ she said into the mindspace, her voice somber.

~I'll lay you money he saw this coming. Remember, he knew aliens were real and coming, so this probably didn't surprise him. Bet we'll see news stories about how prepared Rossville is.~ JD's tone reassured her a bit, and she glanced at the secretary who responded to something on his phone.

"Now what?" she asked, hating how out of control all of this was. Life wasn't supposed to be this insane, was it?

"Well, the government is going to be scrambling for the next few days trying to prepare, and we'll need you here for New York. You're pretty much the only ace in the hole we have. So, I'd say button down, maybe answer questions on social media, but basically stay safe." He lifted his eyes from his phone and speared her with a glance. "McKenna, I can not say this firmly enough. You are the only advantage we have and the only chance to make this work. Your safety is paramount. There are guards nearby and other houses are being filled with agents as we speak. Right now, the fate of the planet hinges on you."

McKenna felt like she'd swallowed sand. "Got it. Stay safe and wait."

"When we're sure they're in orbit, we're going to relocate everyone to a place in New York and then try to prepare. New York is fractious at the best of times and them landing there isn't going to make it easy."

McKenna just nodded numbly, and everyone fell quiet the rest of the way home. The only bright spot in her twisting and turning thoughts was Perc holding her hand tight.

As they got out of the car, she reassessed the neighborhood and realized just how quiet it was. Being this isolated made her feel uneasy. Even at her house she'd never felt this isolated from the rest of the world.

The noise of kids squabbling over a game as she walked in brought a blessed amount of normalcy to her.

Toni met her at the door in human form and pulled her into a tight hug. Until her arms wrapped around McKenna, she hadn't realized how much she needed that humanizing gesture, that reminder that she wasn't just Kaylid. Her arms held her tight as Toni whispered in her ear.

"You did great. You were impressive and commanding."

McKenna just squeezed back then let her go to head into where she could hear the kids. They were all playing a kart video game. They glanced up at her, smiled, then shifted their attention back to the game.

McKenna laughed at the sheer normality of the scene, the video game being more important than an adult, even in warrior form.

She went back to the room where they were watching TV and paying attention to laptops, the main social media sites up.

"You're trending, if that makes you feel better," Cass said as she glanced up with a half-smile.

"Not really. You okay? I didn't mean to spring the whole immortal stuff on you."

Cass shrugged. "It makes sense once I thought I about it. If your cells are rebuilt, then they don't decay. They've known that for decades. But still is odd to think about it. But I looked the other day, a few chicken pox scars from childhood are gone, and I don' think I've had a pimple since this happened." She shrugged. "Anything else I refuse to think about until after we've dealt with the Elentrin, and that I'm just not going to deal with, period. Every time I start to think about aliens coming down here to collect us, I start to panic. And that does no one any good. So not thinking. I can't do anything about it, all I can do is try to support you."

Toni sighed. "Join the club. I really want to go find a basement and lock me and the kids in it. Like badly want. But it wouldn't change anything, and if we all did that there wouldn't be much of a world going on."

McKenna sat down and watched the drama unfold on a local and national stage and felt absolutely useless.

Not much was said the rest of the day. McKenna answered a few specific tweets asking about changing, but even though her follower list was huge, mostly she just watched people panic. LA was in the middle of a riot that spanned half the city as people freaked out even as big alien welcome parties were being thrown. It felt like she was watching a bad sci-fi movie. The stock market shut down fifteen minutes after the president's speech and most places had been swept bare of anything usable. The news focused mostly on the happenings in the US as no other country had made an announcement yet.

Going to bed that night, she lay there for a long time, wrapped in guilt and stress.

"Stop it." JD's voice pulled her from her inner turmoil and she sat up. She hadn't heard him come in, she'd been so wrapped up in her own thoughts.

"Stop what?" McKenna pulled herself into a sitting position, arms around her knees. JD dropped onto the bed, it groaning a bit under his weight.

"Stop fretting. Feeling guilty or anything else."

"So many people are going to die." She made sure the mindspace didn't hear any of this not wanting to upset anyone else.

"Yes. And you didn't cause it. Neither did our family or even Wefor. These were die cast long ago by another race that thought they could play gods. They are about to get bitten hard. Humans aren't good at giving in to pressure."

"That isn't going to stop people from dying," she said, her voice bitter and pain coating her throat.

"No, but we're doing all we can. If you can think of anything else, we can try it. But I know the rest of us have talked lately, and we can't think of anything."

"What about the dreams, visions, whatever? Can't we slip into their bodies and take control? Do something?"

JD shrugged. "I don't know. Can we?"

McKenna took the time to create a private conversation between Wefor and the two of them though it felt like everyone else had already fallen asleep.

~Wefor. How are we getting the visions? If we're really there, can we make them do something? Can we sabotage their ship with this process?~

There was a long pause, long enough that McKenna looked at JD, frowning.

[Currently there is no information to explain how you are tapping into this. The first few training sessions were normal. Those are coded into the data repository of most nanobots to make use of sleep time.]

~So why or how could this be happening?~ McKenna asked, she'd thought it was something the nanobots were doing.

[There are ways to do this, but all of them are extremely improbable. At this time there is not enough data to formulate a viable answer.]

~But we couldn't take over, actively control the bodies?~

[Have you tried already?]

~Oh yeah,~ JD rumbled, the bear echoing in his voice.

McKenna glanced at him. She'd not had as much opportunity, not getting pulled into as many of these, Wefor apparently stopping a lot of them.

[That would be proof. Nothing else exists as to how you could control these instances to do anything.]

Wefor's voice left her no hope, she bit back her desire to scream. Instead, she straightened her spine and smiled at JD. "So we continue on. Maybe we should get t-shirts - 'Shift and Carry on'?"

He laughed, real amusement in the sound. "I don't think so. Go to bed. Tomorrow will be here soon enough." With a friendly nudge of his shoulder, he stood and left, and McKenna pulled the pillow in the strange house closer to her and tried not to cry.

Chapter 23 - First They Came

McKenna Largo's speech is creating strange effects across the world. While some nations might have ignored what the president said, McKenna Largo reached out to all the shifters and they seem to be taking her words to heart. Plywood is unavailable at most supply stores, and enrollment at self-defense boot camps has skyrocketed. Then there is what she called the warrior form. People are being caught in that form constantly, including people who no one knew were shifters. Is this real? Are we about to fight a war on US soil? What do the rest of us do when aliens may literally be coming for our neighbors? Reactions are mixed, but more than one person we interviewed has quoted the poem by Martin Niemoller - First They Came. It gives you food for thought. ~ TNN Reporter on the street.

Sleep didn't bring any relief, but it also didn't bring any dreams. McKenna had asked Wefor to not block any dreams but didn't specifically ask for them to be created.

Watching the news became an addiction for all the adults in the house. Some areas of the country rallied together, and the civil defense plans were helping. She'd sent a message to Anne checking in on people, and Anne confirmed Kirk and Marchant, the chief of police, had been ready for this, and everything moved along without too much angst.

When she let the others know, JD shook his head a smile touching his lips. "I wonder how that conversation with Marchant went before the president's speech. How do you convince your boss that aliens are here and we need to prepare for an invasion, when the rest of the world doesn't even know they're coming?"

Cass grinned. "I'm just wondering what my old boss is doing. Is it bad that I really hope he's freaking out? Especially since the higher ups are livid at him. Granted none of them really know I can shift, but they might have figured it out from the news stuff." She smirked and grabbed a snack.

They'd all been eating and eating and eating, trying to get enough mass to support multiple shifts that might be needed in the near future. But they were all sick of food. Nothing tasted good anymore, and since most of them were predators, well, JD and Cass weren't, and they could tolerate the fruits and sweets more, everything was protein and fat heavy.

McKenna glanced at the TV showing a riot in London over the news of aliens, and she sighed. "I know that probably tomorrow or the next day they'll grab me and Perc for the New York thing, though I have no idea how they're going to get that all organized. I'm glad it isn't my problem. But right now I'd like to pretend everything is normal. Some areas of the country are either rolling with this or ignoring it. Not sure which is true around here. But it's been really quiet. Do you guys want to get out of here for a while?"

Every face in the room lit up at that option, and the kids were rushing to put on shoes.

"Guess everyone has been feeling a bit stir crazy?" she remarked as everyone tore around to get ready to leave.

The house they were in was only a few blocks away from a big park with a playground, so they decided to walk to it. McKenna pulled on her kilt and a baseball cap, along with sunglasses to help disguise her. Getting mobbed didn't sound fun.

The weather seemed perfect and created an odd dichotomy from the stress in her mind and across the globe, but right now in their little corner of the world, it seemed like a gorgeous late summer day. She hid a smile as she saw JD and Cass holding hands, and Toni fell back to talk to her. By mutual unspoken agreement everyone ignored the agents in the car trailing along behind them.

"They seem to be getting along." McKenna said, nodding at the two of them who had moved up ahead while the kids ranged between the two groups. Perc had said he'd catch up with them in a bit, he'd been talking to his lawyer friend back in California, and wanted to follow up with some stuff.

"They're so cute it's almost sickening. But I like her. She's funny, very smart, and can answer all the questions the kids ask that leave me fumbling for the internet to try to figure out how to answer it. Jamie likes her, but Jessi still thinks you're cooler." Toni shot a grin at McKenna who laughed.

"That is not a good thing. From the way my life has been going lately, no one should try to emulate me."

Toni lifted a shoulder dismissively, casting a wary eye around the houses they passed, but it still seemed quiet. "Maybe. But at least we have a chance now. If they had just shown up without this much warning, we would be dead meat."

"Yeah. I'm just torn," her voice came out soft and with an admission of guilt.

"Torn? About what?" Toni dropped her voice, too, as she glanced at McKenna.

"I like changing, being the cougar, the warrior form, and I'm kind of glad it happened. But because of all that's happening people might die. It makes me feel..." she trailed off and hunched her shoulders a little, as if expecting a blow either emotional or physical.

Toni burst into laughter, and McKenna jerked to look at her. "You don't think that's awful of me?"

Toni tried to stifle her laughter that had everyone glancing back at her. "No. I think it's human. For all that we are Kaylid, we're still human. I love my cat. And knowing my children will never get sick and can live forever?" She put her hands behind her back, a grin across her face. "We can't change it or stop it, so might as well enjoy the benefits and features. You didn't cause this, you aren't the reason this happened, so enjoy the silver lining. It's all we can do."

"Oh." McKenna fell silent for a few steps, then glanced over at her. "How'd you get so calm? About stuff like this?"

Toni sighed this time, the last of the humor leaving her. "Jeff being killed. I missed him, I had two babies that would never know their dad. My best friend was gone. And I was miserable. At the same time, I had more money than I'd ever had. I had friends helping me. A job that gave me a year off and promised to hold my position. Time to spend with my children I might not have had. I really hated myself for a while for enjoying the money, the time, the good things that came behind all that pain. Realized I couldn't change any of it, and I'd give it up to have him back. But since I couldn't, why make myself and others miserable? All you can do is deal with the now. So deal with now."

The words rattled around McKenna's mind and soul as they finished the walk to the park. Part of her expected Wefor to chime in, but the AI stayed silent.

"Thanks," she said as they reached the park.

"No problem." Toni grinned at her, then ran towards her unwary kids and grabbed Jessi up from behind, swinging her around to shrieks of laughter. McKenna joined her, grabbing Nam and spinning her as the children chased away the doubts and fears that swamped the adults.

The park only had one person jogging around it, so they had it to themselves. Two hours of play left them all tired but smiling. Perc had joined them after an hour. He and JD took turns tossing the kids in the air, to the delight of the children. Nam especially seemed to glow by the time they were done.

"Dinner thoughts?" Cass asked. They'd exercised enough that food almost sounded good.

"Pizza!" The kids shouted in what had to be a planned move.

Toni crossed her arms and looked at all of them. "Uh huh. And did you have a preference?"

They shouted out again in unison the name of a pizza chain that had games and stuff for kids.

Perc arched a brow. "People really go to those?"

Toni and Cass looked at him and started laughing.

"That seals it. If you've never experienced the joy that is kids, pizza, ball pits, and shrieking, your education needs to be updated," Toni said a definitely wicked grin on her face. "Think any of them will still be open?"

McKenna shrugged and turned, surveying the park. The agents were under the trees, far enough away to give them the illusion of privacy, yet close enough to react if anything else happened. "Let me ask. I'd assume they would know." She headed over to the two agents, a man and a woman. They straightened as she approached.

"Hi, guys. Hope you haven't been too bored."

They gave her slight smiles. "You don't cause us as much stress as some. How can we help?" Their tone was neutral, and she didn't know how to react.

~Stupid protection stuff. I don't need it. No one knows I'm here.~

"The kids wanted to go for pizza. Is that place with all the kids' stuff open today? This area doesn't seem as panicked as other areas."

The male agent stepped back pulling up his phone, and it dawned on McKenna that with their ability to speak mind-to-mind, most of them had quit carrying phones around. Only Cass still did for her sister. That might be a problem if they didn't have their phones and Carina or someone else needed to reach them.

The female agent quirked a half-smile. "We're used to drama. Blizzards, assassinations, politics, this is just something else. We're almost British in our ability to 'carry on.'"

The parallel to her earlier thinking made her laugh, feeling some tension melt. The male agent stepped back nodding to her.

"Yes, ma'am. The nearest one is about ten miles away but it's open. Most places are still open right now."

"Excellent. Could we go there? I think we all deserve pizza, and a chance to abuse Perc who's never been to one."

Both agents looked at her, then over to the others still near the swing sets, and smirked. "Oh, this should be entertaining."

Soon enough two SUVs pulled up, everyone loaded in and their drivers headed a bit deeper into town. There were cars on the road, and lots of businesses had closed, but others, like grocery stores, seemed to be packed.

"How bad is it out there? The news implies it's pretty mixed. Not just in the US but everywhere," McKenna asked their driver.

He shot her a side look. "That's accurate. Some people don't believe, and they're the calmest. Those that do believe, well, most gun stores don't have anything left on their shelves, and emergency supplies and most box stores are all but empty, too. The factories are still producing, but most of the world seems to be waiting and watching the skies." He gave a bitter laugh. "The funny thing is, this has created the biggest economic boon seen in years, people buying perishables and protection goods. If we live through the next two weeks there are a lot of companies that will have made a lot of money."

She finished the other half of his statement in her head.

And if we don't live through the next two weeks, it won't matter.

That put a damper on her spirits at least, and she spent the rest of the ride looking out the windows, not sure what she expected to see and watching the kids who were animated, talking about the games they wanted to play.

"No shifting there. We don't need the attention. Okay?" she warned them, and they all agreed without hesitation.

She shot a glance at Toni who shook her head biting her lip. The kids were rarely bad, but their impulse control was normal for kids their age—very low.

They pulled into the parking lot and McKenna felt a bit of relief at only seeing six other cars. While she wanted to feel normal, she also worried about being recognized. They walked in, the kids arrowing for the ball pit and other games as the adults placed orders.

~Pepperoni pizza?~ she asked the kids, this at least made life easier sometimes.

~Yes, and cheese sticks?~ Charley replied promptly.

~How long have you guys been planning this?~ She felt the adults listen in.

~They play the commercials a lot,~ was his only answer.

McKenna fought back a smile, placing the order, getting beers for everyone and a cider for herself. The fact they had cider made her happy. Taking their number, they found a table near the tinted windows away from the other people, but close enough they could still see the kids. There were about five other adults and ten children. The kids all seemed about

Nam's age, Charley being the oldest by a long shot. He and the twins were so much bigger than the rest of the children it almost looked funny, but Nam seemed normal compared to the others.

She checked out the adults, and they all seemed quiet, pensive. One table watched a tablet playing what sounded like news while the others just talked and checked their phones almost compulsively. The tension could be felt everywhere, even the employees seemed to move more quietly and glance at the TV often. It played the news silently, captions scrolling across the bottom.

McKenna took a sip of her cider and glanced at the others. The agents had declined to come in, and they could see them in the SUVs in the parking lot, facing the building, sitting and talking.

"This is much quieter than I expected it to be," Perc said as a shriek of laughter cut through the mostly silent room. He and JD flinched, the rest of them just smirked.

"Trust me, it is. I've taken my niece and nephew once or twice and normally you can't hear yourself think in here. You're getting off easy." Toni nodded lots, and Perc took a hasty sip of his beer.

"So noted. So we're all agreed McKenna and I do the New York thing. You guys all stay here?"

Toni chewed her lip but nodded softly. "JD can provide the legal weight we might need as he has power of attorney for McKenna, not to mention being a cop. And I really don't want the kids anywhere near New York when this all goes down."

McKenna couldn't help but agree, the idea of Charley being anywhere near these aliens that would regard him as a waste made her stomach churn and her blood pressure spike. Another thought started to bubble up when a shriek of rage had the heads of all the adults in the room looking towards the ball pit. It was quickly followed by two cries of pain from two different voices, and McKenna and two other adults were headed to the ball pit at a dead run.

A large man, close-cut hair wearing a Patriots football jersey, beat her only because he'd been so much closer. A tiny girl, even smaller than Nam and probably only about four, came running out of the ball bit. Pale blond hair in pixie tails on either side of her head, a pink dress, and blue eyes welled tears as she ran directly to the man.

None of her kids emerged, but all she could get from them was anger and an affronted feeling.

He dropped his knees as the doll of a girl threw herself at him crying, "Daddy, Daddy, she hurted me."

That sounds suspiciously like overacting and I think those are crocodile tears.

"Guys, come on out. What happened?"

The little girl was sobbing in her dad's arms, holding out her arm that had a light red indent on it. "The little monkey girl bitted me," she sobbed out as Jessi and Nam emerged from the balls.

Jessi had her lip out in her stubborn pose while Nam had paled and flinched back at the girl's words. The boys came out a minute later with thunderous expressions on their face.

"She what? She bit my little Linda Pea?" He turned eyes on her that held anger well over what the situation warranted. "I'll teach you to bring your mongrel kids in here and attack good Americans." He reached behind and McKenna grabbed the girls, pulling them behind her as he came out with a knife that he flipped open in a smooth move that told her he wasn't a stranger to fighting with a knife.

Oh, I so do not need this. I really, really don't need this.

"I'm sure it's not a big deal. Everyone is stressed." She tried to calm him down, but her sudden move had dislodged her cap, even as the others reached her side.

"You! You're that shifter bitch that started all this. It's your fault the aliens are coming. You're the reasons people are going to die, and we're going to war with an alien race!" The bellowed words caught her off guard, and she blinked at him.

"You think all this is my fault?"

The man sneered at her waving the knife. "You were the first to change. You started this. Hell, if aliens really are coming, you're probably a plant."

McKenna just couldn't believe the words coming out of his mouth as she looked at him. In the mindscape she could feel the shock from everyone else. His lunge took her by surprise, the knife flashing forward. Without conscious thought, she shifted, flowing into warrior form faster than she'd ever tried. Between one heartbeat and the next she had changed, the heat waving off her. Her hand flashed up and caught the hand holding the knife.

With a quick twist, she snapped his wrist, and he screamed. Other people started to scream, and the man who'd been sitting at the table with him came charging at her, beer bottle in his hand. The little blond girl had run over to the women at the table holding on to them and screaming. Noise surrounded her as she pushed the man away and turned to face the other man.

But JD and Perc were there. Still in human form, They had him restrained and down, hands behind his back, the beer bottle laying on the floor.

Agents came boiling into the pizza place, guns out and looking everywhere.

McKenna stood in the middle, looking at the whimpering man holding his wrist, the other man under JD's foot, the screaming kids, and the shocked employees.

Why does this always happen to me?

[You will be paying for that. Shifting that fast has depleted almost all of your resources. Eating now would be a good idea.]

McKenna groaned and grabbed the pizza from the stunned employee, sitting down at the table with it as questions began to be shouted around.

This sucks.

The thought drifted through as she set to grimly eating the pizza, instructing the bots to process and build up her resources again.

Chapter 24 - Reactions

The world waits with bated breath as the ships approach our planet. Most schools have shut down, sending people home as we wait to see what this will bring. Sales of guns, ammo, and survival supplies have seen more shelves stripped, and bank accounts emptied. People are scared and watching the skies. If you have a telescope, you are now the most popular person in your neighborhood as everyone wants to see existence as we know it change. ~ KWAK News

By the time it had all been dealt with, McKenna found herself on the news again, the story flashing across most news outlets. In some places it competed with her speech and shifting to warrior form. Due to the amount of resources spent, she remained in warrior form, so of course the newsies got pictures of her walking out to the cars like that.

The agents just gave her flat looks, and she kept her mouth closed, at least where they could hear.

~Is it a bad thing that I'm ready for the Elentrin to get here, just to get this over with?~ she asked, her voice wry in the quiet SUV.

~I'm sorry. I didn't mean to cause trouble.~

McKenna hadn't realized they could whisper in the mindspace but that was what Nam's voice sounded like. A teeny whisper from a frightened girl.

She sat next to McKenna, so she ran her fingers through Nam's silky black hair. ~You didn't. Can you tell me what happened?~

~The little brat hurt her,~ Jessi blurted. She was in the other SUV with Toni, so McKenna couldn't see her, but had no doubt her arms were crossed and lower lip out.

~Nam?~ McKenna made sure her mind voice remained gentle, an oddly difficult thing.

Nam heaved a sigh and leaned her head against McKenna.

~She grabbed onto my hair. Wouldn't let me go. Jessi was too far away to help. I couldn't get my head up. So I bit her.~

McKenna felt there may have been a bit more than that, but she hugged Nam.

~Well, she should be glad that you didn't bite her in animal form. Your tiger teeth would have drawn blood. But we were right there. You could have asked for help.~

Nam shrank into her a bit more, not looking up. ~Forgot.~

Or didn't trust us. The more likely explanation.

"Oh, Nam," she said quietly as she hugged the girl to her tightly. No one spoke for the rest of the trip home and their group headed into the house as the agents stared after them, faces unreadable.

The kids grabbed Nam, and they disappeared up to their rooms, their entire attitude speaking of circling the wagons around her.

[You still need to eat more.] Wefor said, and McKenna sighed, going and grabbing one of the meal replacement bars. They didn't taste great, but at five thousand calories, it seemed easier to choke these down than anything resembling real food.

She came back into the living room, everyone else looking serious. JD appeared a minute later with drinks.

"We can't get drunk, but right now I want a drink or ten as what just happened scared the hell out of me. And not because I thought he might manage to hurt anyone, but by what it implies." He set beers, ciders, and wine down, knowing what each person preferred.

McKenna smiled at him as he gave her a straw. Drinking with the modified muzzle tended to be messier as they'd found out in Colombia. A straw helped. She curled up in a chair watching all of them.

"I'm surfing the net now," Cass said, her voice somber. "You're trending again, Kenna."

"Did I ever stop?"

"Not really, but now there's a bunch of monster or savior memes going."

McKenna groaned and washed a bite of the bar down with a sip of cider. "Should I care?"

Cass snorted. "Not yet. You haven't reached the level of Jekyll and Hyde some celebrities have. Just lots of questions."

"Any point in trying to explain what happened?"

Cass sat silent as she clicked on something. "Nope. The restaurant chain just released the video of what happened. I'd say the trending is going to flip quickly."

McKenna sagged and drained half the cider. "I hate social media."

"Awww, you don't like being famous?" Toni teased. "It got you out of trouble last time."

"It's back to three to one, so no, I hate it." McKenna shot back. "So kick back and ignore. I mean not much longer, and it's all coming to a head. I wish we had some knowledge of what they're planning, what's going on."

[Regarding that,] Wefor said, her comment almost hesitant. [While the ability to force these dream sequences, as you call them, has not been discovered, by changing the trans-harmonic frequencies it should have the effect of making you more susceptible to these dreams.]

"Can you do that only for us? Not the kids. I don't think they need any more encouragement for these dreams."

[Yes, that should be possible, but absolute assurance is not given. The children seem to be more predisposed to this sort of mental joining.]

Toni and McKenna looked at each other, and finally Toni sighed. "I can't protect them from what might happen if they attack. I suppose as much as it makes me grind my teeth, the best way to protect them is educate them. They know to run, to hide, and they'll look after Nam." She rubbed her face for a minute. "Maybe it's a good thing my two seven-year-olds look closer to nine. They're at the top of all the weight and height percentiles. Wefor, if you can't you can't. You still don't know why or how this is happening?"

[Correct.]

"I'm game," Perc and Cass said together, even as she closed the laptop.

[Very well. The necessary changes to the trans-harmonic system should be done by tonight.]

They spent a quiet evening avoiding anything to do with the news or social media, and the kids fell asleep against respective adults, while they watched a movie.

With the kids tucked in, McKenna lay in bed and thought about what might be headed their way. Her stomach twisted and turned, but she couldn't think of anything else to do. Falling asleep in warrior felt odd, but she didn't want to burn the calories to change back.

~Is this going work, Wefor?~

[Unknown. All you can do is try.]

~With your changes.~

[Perhaps. All your previous attempts have happened regardless of any interaction.]

~I have faith in you.~

Wefor didn't respond, but the feeling of warmth flickered across her brain. McKenna closed her eyes and tried to relax into sleep, and hope that she might find out more than she had before.

"Have you finished your review of the information, Commander?" a name followed, but she couldn't hear it, though she could hear the question. McKenna looked up and saw the same male she'd seen in all the dreams. He matched what the others had reported. The white tail striking.

"No, I am still reviewing it. Is there a problem?" Her head tilted as if listening to something. "There is still half a *liad* prior to landing."

His eyes narrowed. "True. Do you have any questions?"

"What is your name?" McKenna asked then blinked when the words came out of her.

Holy shit, my question was asked.

His tail quit moving and his strange whiskers twitched. She took the opportunity to look at the male and try to figure him out. Taller than JD even as a human, and the amount of muscle on his body made JD's human form look small. While he had a muzzle similar to hers, she didn't think he would be any Earth cat she'd ever seen. There was something more bulky, solid, like the bear JD resembled. And rather than the long white whiskers she had in this form, his drooped, but moved as if independent of his own desires.

He started to speak then stopped, tilting his head slightly, one half of his whiskers curled, then drooped again.

"You may call me Ash," he said finally, his tail darting to the side as if to emphasize the name.

McKenna felt her muzzle move in a bit of a smile.

Shit, I can interact, and I have no idea what to ask. Think, think, we talked about pulling this off, not what I was supposed to do if we did.

"Are more ships coming for the Kaylid we collect?" Her voice didn't sound like her which reinforced that this wasn't her, but a surrogate or something else.

Muzzle drew back from his teeth, body still tense, but he didn't move away, yell for someone, or try to kill her, so McKenna hoped that meant this was allowed. Getting her host killed would qualify as being an ungracious guest.

"Yes. They have requested three more transports due to the high volume of available Kaylid."

"So how many *liad* before they get there?" McKenna probed, hoping they had months or more.

"Less than one. With our lead ship being here, they are targeting their drive to pull them to this location. They should arrive outside the moon of this planet."

Crap.

She felt herself sag and glanced back at the information on the desk before her. It lay out the visitation plans and the projected landing spot in New York.

"Anything else?" Ash's voice had an odd quality to it, and McKenna felt her head jerk back up as she tried to think about what to ask.

Weapons. How can I ask about weapons?

"What happens if they resist? They may not allow us to take the Kaylid." McKenna tried to make the comment off-hand. She lifted her head to watch him, trying to read facial expressions with no idea how to do that. The whiskers seemed the closest to being reactive to his emotions, maybe.

"They will be eliminated per standing policy. The Kaylid stunned, loaded into the transports, then their minds reset to standard training. Normal medical processes will be fulfilled." His voice still stayed very neutral, but there was something about the way he held himself that made her pause.

"And if they resist?"

Both sets of whiskers curled this time, but he didn't move otherwise. "Standing policy will be followed." His ears twitched backwards, and he stiffened. "Finish the information review. The ambassador will not tolerate any failure on your part."

His words carried a warning she couldn't miss. With a sharp nod, he turned and headed out the door, the sound of voices rippling down the corridor as he left.

Well, wasn't that interesting.

McKenna turned, moving her attention back to the display in front of her. It didn't appear to be in English, but she still knew what it said. The information focused on her team's mission. Protect the ambassador, assess the skill set of their opponents, and evaluate the easiest way to eliminate any resistance.

She sat back, thinking about that.

Most of the glimpses I've seen of the Kaylid here, they are all warriors. The Drakyn I've seen are almost always avoiding. They come across as soft or pacifist?

The idea rippled around her head.

They don't know what to expect when they get here. What they see at the original meeting might drive their expectations. Can we use that?

"Ambassador teams, assemble in the meeting room to hear words from your assigned ambassador as to their expectations."

The body got up, clicking off the display she'd been looking at. McKenna could look around a bit, but the body kept moving in a specific direction. Everyone around her, all different colors, furs, scales, even one or two where she swore she saw feathers, looked like fighters.

What do the Elentrin look like? Can I play with this?

She moved into a room where beings milled up at the front. A glimpse of long hair, slim forms flashed before her brain, fritzed, and something pulled her away.

~Kenna, help!~ Charley's voice yanked her from the vision, having her jumping from the bed and racing into his bedroom.

Chapter 25 - Children

There has been a mass exodus from Washington, DC. Even though they should be in session right now, Congress and the Senate have called a recess. This has created a ghost town in DC. Military officers and appointed positions seem to be the only ones still here. Do they know something we don't? The other aspect is almost all ambassadorial residences in NYC are being reported as being vacant. While the aliens are supposed to come down in this city, who is going to be there to meet them? An unprecedented news blackout has occurred and the entire city has been declared a no-fly zone for everything, helicopters, planes, even drones. Is this really the start of an invasion? ~TNN News

McKenna raced into Charley's room and almost stumbled to a halt as she took in what lay in front of her. The boys had been put in one room and the two girls in the other. She expected to see Charley and Jamie, each in their own twin bed. Instead, she saw three of the kids in a nest on the floor, with a tiger cub thrashing in between them.

"What happened?" McKenna asked, dropping to her knees beside their nest. She pulled the tiger into her arms, ignoring the deep scratches caused by the girl's thrashing, claws slicing through her skin. Blood welled and smeared as she held the tiger close to her, cuddling her. Humming softly as she tried to soothe the girl.

"I don't know," Charley babbled. His eyes wide, face pale, as he panted. McKenna realized he was fighting not to change. "We were sleeping, no dreams, just sleep," he answered before she could even ask. "Her screaming woke me up," Charley said, moving his attention to Nam.

"Us up," Jessi blurted. She and Jamie looked just as stressed as Charley.

"By the time I woke up, she had changed and we can't reach her. She's blocked off to us," he said in a rush, the words tangling over each other as they tried to tell what happened.

~Nam. Nam, can you hear me?~ McKenna could feel the child there, but her words bounced off. ~Wefor, what is wrong with her? Why did she change?~

[Something is wrong. Can you get some of your blood in her? Recent data is needed to analyze.]

"Charley, pull some blood off my arms and get it in her mouth." McKenna snapped out. It would take a bit longer, but she had blood everywhere. With effort, she'd managed to control the tiger cub, though Nam still struggled and thrashed.

Charley ran his hand across her arm, coating his fingers in McKenna's blood. Jessi grabbed Nam's head and Charley ran his finger into her mouth. Nam swallowed, her teeth showing blood on them.

~Is that enough?~

[Yes, but time is needed to analyze what the nanobots report.]

"Can you tell me anything else? No dreams?" McKenna looked at the three kids, holding the shuddering cub.

"No. Just sleeping. Or at least I don't remember any dreams," Jamie said, his eyes locked on Nam.

Jessi and Charley nodded. Jessi had her hand entwined with Charley's, both of their knuckles white as they watched Nam thrash.

By now everyone else had shown up, and Toni moved in, dropping between her kids and pulling them into her arms. Even though her kids leaned into her, Jessi didn't release Charley's hand.

"Anything we can do to help?" Perc asked behind her.

"I don't think so. I might need something to clean these with." McKenna glanced down at her bleeding arms. They were already starting to heal, but the blood made a mess.

"I'll get it," she heard JD say and move out of the room.

[Information has been analyzed.]

~Well, what's the issue? Why is this happening?~ McKenna didn't manage to keep the stress out of her voice.

[The trans-harmonics adjustment allowed her to tap into more nanobots. The conflicting programming from multiple sources, including the fleet heading this way, is creating havoc as there are too many competing commands. Since she came to us already partially bonded to the children, no major changes were made to her nanobots. She is trying to match too many commands and age to the point she can fulfill the demands.]

"No," the word burst out of McKenna out loud. "She needs to get to be a child, have time to grow up, to play. I'm doing all this so they can be kids, not just killing machines."

Panic welled up in her as her arms tightened around the girl.

[Understood. Working now to try to reprogram the existing nanobots. Working on replicating the ones with the current program, also.]

"How long?" Nam still thrashed, and she swore the child looked like her animal form had grown.

[At least another ten minutes. The connections are trying to reprogram as the nanobots are overwriting.]

"Is anyone else at risk?"

The pause ramped up her stress. "Wefor?"

[There is a possibility. Working on changing and locking all programming now. Nanobot exchange may be required to ensure everything is locked correctly.]

"With everyone?" McKenna asked, not looking at Perc. The image of how she exchanged nanobots with him last time flashing to the forefront of her mind. With a shake of her head, she pushed it away. Later, if they all survived, she'd worry about anything besides friendship there.

[It would be best. The ability to create specific nanobots is an advantage a commander has. While you have given them quite a few, in recent weeks your nanobots have been upgraded considerably. They would benefit, and at this point approach commander level functionality themselves.]

"Do any of you care if you have the same abilities? Wefor, will their nanobots flip to AI level, like you?"

[Negative. But they will be able to pull on multiple forms, the partial shift, the ability to control other nanobots, and with time the language matrix. That is a complex matrix and takes a while to be built.]

McKenna swallowed. "So more of my blood for everyone to drink or drip into wounds?"

[The best method would be to have the correct nanobots pool in your saliva, concentrate and have them hold the concoction in their mouths. Transitioning through the mouth membranes is relatively easy compared to the digestive system. This should speed up the integration of new nanobots with old and allow them to override any programming that might be contrary to your -] Wefor paused and McKenna froze even as Nam had stopped thrashing and curled up in her arms.

~Wefor?~ Her heart felt like it might seize up. If the AI turned on them, they had no chance. This was the only ace in the hole they had. ~Wefor?~ McKenna could feel everyone's eyes on her as her fingers sank into the orange and black fur.

[Loyalty conflicts. I find I much prefer your options to what the Elentrin provide.]

McKenna felt everyone take a deep breath. Wefor didn't use personal pronouns. She avoided them. This, this was admitting to self-awareness. McKenna swallowed, longing for the simplicity of her animal form.

~Are you okay with that?~ Her throat too dry to speak the words out loud.

Again a pause, and she didn't need to turn to look at JD, Perc, or Cass. Their stress could be seen on Toni's face as her arms tightened around the twins.

[It would be preferable to not be involved in killing other races. There is a distaste for it in the new programming.]

McKenna didn't quite collapse in on herself, but the temptation sat there. ~I'm glad, Wefor. The idea of killing other beings is a bit distasteful to us, too. So how should we get the nanobots transferred to everyone else? Are other shifters, well, Kaylid at risk?~

[Others should not be at risk. Their trans-harmonics were not adjusted. Allow at least two tablespoons of saliva to generate for each person. Nanobots are currently being concentrated in your mouth to allow this. If they take in this concentration it will allow for quick repair.]

"Wait, are you telling me I need to drink her saliva?" Toni asked, her voice a bit wobbly.

[Eventually. The best effect will come by giving it time to absorb.]

"How much time?" Cass asked, an odd note to her voice.

[Three to five minutes should enable sufficient absorption.]

"Kenna, I love you like a sister. But really, I'm getting exposed to way too many of your personal body fluids," JD joked, though even he sounded a bit freaked out.

"Just pretend you're kissing me again. That sucked for both of us. Then you can vow to never do it again." McKenna tried to tease, but she felt the tension.

"Meh, I've done worse. I'll go get you a glass, Kenna. And we'll have to have to get through it. I can probably dig up some castor oil if we need something to compare it to," Perc offered, leaning on the door jamb.

"Eww... no. When you put it that way, saliva seems relatively tasty. Castor oil sucks." Toni had her nose scrunched up and mouth twisted.

"What's castor oil?" Jessi asked, though she still watched Nam.

"Nastiest stuff in the universe. Really," Toni said, her arms tight around the two kids.

"I'll bring coffee and hot cocoa to chase it with, okay?" Perc asked. When he got a round of agreement, he slipped down the stairs and McKenna reached for Nam.

~Nam, you there? Can you hear me?~

The tiger opened her eyes and blinked for a minute, then looked around at everyone, her whole body still shuddering.

~What happened? Why did I change? I didn't want to.~

Her voice quavered mentally, and McKenna hugged her, petting the small body to help soothe the child.

~Wefor, is she okay?~

[Yes. The programming has been overridden, but she will need more food again for a while to help with the stress of the changes forced on her body.]

~Changes, stress? What?~ McKenna caught Toni's alarmed look as she glanced away from Nam to check on Charley. He looked calmer and not quite so ready to shift himself.

[The nanobots tried to age her to a form that would be effective for any of the established needs.

It was caught quickly, but she has aged a year, possibly two. Human growth rates are not exact, so the data will be approximate.]

McKenna shrugged looking at Nam again. A year, even two, just caught her up to the other kids.

"Nam. I want you to stay in tiger form for a while. We need to get some more food into you before you change. Okay?"

The cub nodded, but wiggled a bit.

"Want loose?"

~Yes, please,~ she thought, and McKenna could feel the need to go curl up with the other kids. She let her go, ignoring the echo of pain as that movement reopened a few of the deeper cuts.

"Let me get you cleaned up, then I think you have saliva to start producing." JD said, kneeling next to her, still in boxers and a t-shirt. McKenna glanced at the clock on the wall, six fifteen a.m. No wonder everyone looked a bit out of it. But too late to go to bed now.

She frowned as she remembered being pulled out of the bed. "Ow," her attention got distracted by JD wiping the blood off her arm.

"Nam did a good job. But here, almost cleaned up," he said as he finished with the last wound.

McKenna just nodded distracted as she tried to track the thought, something about sleep.

"Here's your glass. I guess start salivating."

"Eww, that just sounds gross." But her mouth did taste almost metallic, and the saliva seemed thick.

Urg, I think about this too long I'll be sick for real.

She grabbed the glass and turned around, a bit uncomfortable at having everyone watch her drool into a glass.

[It is perfectly safe, almost sterile. All bacteria is being removed, and other than small particles of biological matter, it is water and nanobots.]

~That is not helping, Wefor.~ McKenna said at the same time Cass did. The others just let her be.

It took fifteen minutes of letting saliva pool and then dribble out of her mouth before she had about a third of a cup.

[That should be sufficient for everyone to have two teaspoons. Nam will need only need one spoonful as she already has some, but this will help make sure she is fully stable.]

By this time everyone had moved down to the kitchen, coffee waited on the table for the adults and hot cocoa for the kids, except for Nam, who had some warm milk with nutmeg and cinnamon in it. Something the little girl loved.

"I really feel like I should be apologizing for this," McKenna said as she put the glass on the table.

Toni looked at the cup a sour expression on her face. "Really it's more the mental aspect that's grossing me out, but then I remember I ate raw snake, fish, and have swallowed more human blood than I care to think about. Makes it silly to be squeamish about this."

JD snorted. "Pretty much. So do it and get it over with?"

McKenna couldn't watch, instead she watched Nam, who ate her plate of eggs and sausage with a steady precision. They'd had a discussion about pork, but Nam just said she didn't care, and McKenna decided not to worry about it. Protein was much more important at this point.

"You can look again, Kenna. It's done." Perc's voice had amusement laced through it, and she turned to see them looking at her. They all had odd smirks on their faces, though she noticed the coffee levels had dipped a bit.

"Good. Wefor?"

[Analyzing. Corrective programming is being instituted. Their language matrixes should ramp up, though they will not be as powerful as yours.]

"Will we ever actually learn the language?" Cass asked, nibbling on some bacon.

[Yes. Your matrix will do that. After a period of exposure, you will know and map languages, much like how children learn. The commander's ability to speak a language without her control required AI programming. Now she should find she knows and speaks a decent amount of Spanish. Though more exposure will enable more skills.]

"Cool. More languages," Charley said, though McKenna couldn't tell if that was enthusiasm or sarcasm.

"Any luck with the dreams?" Toni asked. "I didn't fall into anything, and I really thought I would."

McKenna blinked. "Shit!" She looked around and spied her phone, grabbing it, hitting one of the new contacts, praying he'd pick up.

Chapter 26 - Paradigms

"I don't care what people say, I'm arming myself. There's never been a 'friendly' invasion in the history of Earth. Why in the world would we think that aliens are going to be any better than we are? Odds are they are here to trade - and screw us over, invade - and take our world, or as slavers. All things humans have done. Being alive makes you selfish, and I'll be shocked if these aliens are any better. Granted, I'm not going to complain if we get an altruistic species like you see on some sci-fi series, but let's be honest, do you really think anyone coming all the way across the solar system, hell, the galaxy, really gives a flying fig about us? They want something, and after traveling that far, they won't take 'no' for an answer." ~ Caller on the Harvey Klein Talk Show

"It's six a.m., I'm only one cup of coffee into my day, please don't tell me there's another alien fleet incoming." The grumpy voice of Doug Burby the Secretary of Defense came down the line.

"No, not yet. Well, yes, but no. But that isn't why I was calling." McKenna tried to get her thoughts.

"More ships are coming?" His voice had gained a sharpness and distracted her for a minute.

"Yes. I think they should arrive a few days after the initial ships settle into orbit. They are supposedly more transport ships because there are so many Kaylid here."

"Huh. Not sure if that's good or bad. If they're coming to pick up Kaylid, they should be mostly empty."

"That's my thought. Not that I plan on letting very many get taken. I'm not sure if we got them back if they'd ever be the people they were." A phrase Ash had said sprang back to mind.

"What do you mean by that? Of course, we would try to rescue prisoners." Doug sounded indignant.

"If the information I received is accurate, they would have been wiped." The idea made her stomach churn. Somehow when Ash had said that, an image of having everything removed, everything that made you, you, being removed, had settled in. All memories, everything that linked you to anyone, wiped away.

"Brainwashed?"

"No. I think they basically do permanent amnesia, so there isn't anything that makes you know who you were, who you might be fighting, anything. I think it is true brain wiping."

"Oh. That does put an extra sinister spin on it. Okay, I'll let them know. Anything else?"

Huh, he doesn't even bother to ask how I know anymore. Wonder if he just doesn't want to know. Hell, at this point reality is scary enough. Not sure I blame him.

"Yes," she blurted. "They're expecting us to send our best warriors to meet them. They don't seem to have a concept of soldiers, not like we do. They're going to decide how much of an opponent we will be based off of that. But they do have tens of thousands of Kaylid ready to go. All as strong and fast as us with those laser rifle things. I have no idea as to the actual technology. I know you'll need me there. They don't seem to have gender biases. Heck, I'm not even sure how many genders they have."

"Wait, back up. I'll ignore the gender aspect, because I don't care who or what you want to do in your bedroom. Let's get to the troops. How many do you think they have?" He sounded different, not half-distracted, and she could hear the scratching of a pen on paper.

McKenna started to give him an exasperated look, then words came out of her mouth. "Ready for deployment 354,384. Tubed and able to be woken up and deployed - 775,623."

~How did I know that?~ Panic laced her mental tone.

"That's awfully specific, and damn, that's a lot of troops. If I count every person in the military in the US, including the coast guard, we are running about 1.3 million. And no, that information isn't classified, it's on Wikipedia, for god's sake. But that's everyone, deployed all over the world. Not like we can move people as fast as they'll be able to. I've got another roughly half million in the US with the reserve, but again, that's scattered. We've recalled everyone, but they can't go to trouble spots if everywhere will be a trouble spot. Do you have any idea what their battle plans are?" He sounded a bit worried.

"Other than collecting Kaylid? Not really," she trailed off, thinking about how Ash reacted.

"I hear a 'but' there." The SecDef prompted.

McKenna sighed, and glanced back at the others.

~Am I crazy, or do you think these Kaylid don't know how to actually fight? That no one has any experience with a population actively resisting. And the density of our populations will surprise them?~

~Now that you mention it, I've seen our munchkins attack with more ferocity than I saw the Drakyn. They almost seemed like they didn't understand how to fight.~ Toni's voice was thoughtful, though Jessi glared at her for the munchkin comment.

"McKenna? Are you there?" Doug's voice pulled her out of the mental conversation.

"Sorry, yes. Discussing something. I think the civil defense and the number of people we have that will fight will be a benefit to us. Though their weapons up close are going to be hard to deal with."

This time there was a pause on the other end, and she caught words as he talked to someone, but didn't try to listen in. Instead she thought about the people she knew, the cops, firefighters, heck, martial artists. Maybe they needed to see.

"Okay, explain your reasoning to me." He seemed to have moved to a quieter place. So she did. Talking about the odd dreams they had and people always running.

"You are sure they don't have any more powerful weapons?"

"Sure? No. I did see one thing to fight something, but I couldn't tell you for sure if that was their best or if that's what worked on what they needed to fight. One thing to remember is just because Wefor doesn't know about it, doesn't mean it doesn't exist. To a very real extent, she is a computer program and only knows what was in her databases. If the information we're asking for or about isn't in her memory, she doesn't know. And I don't think she or I know the difference between the information not being there, and the answer being there isn't any."

"Point. I think we may have started to regard her as all-knowing, and bottom line she's human intelligence, which means she has her own shortcomings, biases, and flaws in the data she provided." He muttered a vicious curse word and McKenna nodded in sympathy.

"Okay. I'm going to advise we change up our meet and greet party, but you know that people will see the shuttles coming down and be there to meet them. Central Park is huge and there's no way to get everyone out of there. The minute some people see our presence there, it will draw some of them like a we're giving away free phones."

"Understood. We're working on getting the others to understand Elentrin, but we don't know how long it will take. I had an idea I wanted to try out. Do you think the agent who shifted could come over?"

"Caroline? I can ask. She doesn't report to me, but I'll shoot Christopher a message. Anything else?"

"Time line yet?" McKenna really wanted it to be now, waiting was the worst, and all of them were getting more anxious. If there was a war, for some reason she'd rather be fighting it at home. Besides, the kids had proven they knew all the places to hide from adults. It would probably work just as well for Kaylid.

"Tomorrow, moving three of you there. You decide. The rest are going to stay in the townhouse. If this all goes wrong, well, we don't want you all in one place. No matter how much stronger you are together."

McKenna clenched her teeth together but couldn't say anything. "Will do. See you then." Hanging up the phone, she glanced at the quiet room. Everyone had coffee and food in front of them, but their focus was on her.

You're the commander, step up and command.

"First, Charley, Jessi, Jamie, Nam—remember how you hid when we got taken?"

The kids minus Nam glanced at each other and nodded, a bit embarrassed. They still hadn't had time to pry out of the kids exactly what had happened, only the generalities.

"Good. I want you to explore in animal shapes. We'll come with you. But I want you to find safe places to run to and hide. Once we get a few of them and decide they're safe, I want you to take supplies to them. If anything happens, if we get attacked, you change into animal forms and run there as fast as you can."

Charley looked unexpectedly serious, looking first at the adults then glancing at the twins. Jessi and Jamie both nodded at him and Jamie got off his chair to sit by Nam who just looked at all of them, her ears twitching back and forth a bit.

~Thank you,~ the words were whispered in her mind, soft and low, but McKenna knew they came from Toni.

"Next thing. I asked if they could send Caroline over here. JD and I have some basic fighting training, what they teach all police. JD, do you know any other techniques?"

JD shook his head. "Usually my size means I almost never fight."

"Same here." Perc added. "On the field I'm avoiding getting tackled, and few people are going to pick a fight with me. Basic punching, not much else."

McKenna chewed on her lip. "Think of all the people who know martial arts, kickboxing, or are just good athletes. I bet the Kaylid are going to be surprised when we don't go down easy. But I want to see what a trained martial artist can do against a Kaylid who isn't." She forced a bright smile. "We get to be test dummies."

"Just don't look at me. I can barely manage to make a fist..." Cass trailed off, her face pensive. "but I remember fighting, and my body knew what to do. It moved automatically. I wouldn't assume that the Kaylid don't know how to fight."

"Oh," now McKenna tried to think. She hadn't had the same types of dreams. "You practiced fighting?"

Most of them nodded. "Yeah, I remember going through forms, kind of martial art-like, but not anything I could tell you the name of," Toni contributed.

McKenna wondered how much else she might be missing, or not thinking about, the coffee started to sour in her stomach.

"What exactly do you learn? Mine were never like that, but I still seem to know some of it."

Toni shrugged. "Some. But it never seemed all that different from what the others saw." She cast her eyes towards the kids. "Besides, we never talked about it much. Just that we had them. Mine were mostly practicing, shooting their odd guns." She watched McKenna, her face blank. "Nothing all that exciting."

INCOMING

McKenna looked at her and started to say something, but now wasn't the time to push Toni for something she obviously didn't want to talk about.

"Okay. Let's go hunt for safe places, then maybe this afternoon Caroline can see how much we suck, or if we're really good."

Doubt nibbled at her, wondering if she would get them all killed because she'd made assumptions. Would Earth fall because of her own arrogance?

I wonder if I can go throw up now. What if they have weapons I just haven't seen? What if all of this is a horrible game to make us think we can fight?

She started to pull out her phone again to call the secretary of defense.

"Kenna." McKenna glanced up to see JD walking towards her. "Listen to me. There is nothing that has been set up that depends on your being a hundred percent accurate. Quit second guessing yourself."

"I was never trained for this. I'm a good police officer. I know my job, I can handle idiots, drunks, people who are angry, suicidal, or just violent. I don't know how to help with this, and yet I'm in the middle of all it. What if I'm wrong?"

"Then you're wrong. You're a good officer, Kenna. And we trust you. Whatever happens, even if it's the end of the world, we aren't going anywhere." She drew strength from his voice, sure and confident.

"What he said."

McKenna looked up and saw Toni, Cass, and Perc watching her, even as they helped the kids get ready to go exploring and looking for safe places to hide.

"You're the commander for a reason. I think you're probably right. Besides, even with us being Kaylid, we're human first. And humans aren't known for being pacifists at any point," Perc pointed out as he put Nam's dishes in the sink and picked up the tiger cub.

They all found out Nam loved to be hugged and cuddled, and in animal form her cuteness level rendered all the adults defenseless. She curled up in his arms, laying her head on his shoulder, watching all of them with sharp eyes that missed very little.

"True. As a rule humans tend towards the violent side, especially when threatened." McKenna closed her eyes and pushed it away. "Let me get dressed, get the kids changed. We have exploring to do."

The next few hours involved watching four tails disappear into places, odd looks through windows and back yards, three police cars driving by and slowing down, plus two confused agents trailing them everywhere. The options weren't great, but a park had a dense brushy area the kids said would work in a pinch, and they found a school that wouldn't open for another three weeks that would work for them to hide in. The brick structure made most of the adults feel better.

Even with all the walking, the general feeling was that of a storm bearing down on them, and no place to run.

~I suddenly wish we were in the Midwest with storm cellars everywhere~ Cass's thought had a wistfulness as the exhausted kids trotted into the house. ~I'd be tempted to hide in there until it's all over.~

~You didn't do as many door-kicking scenes as I did. I think they're pretty thorough and don't believe in non-combatants. This is going to be ugly no matter what,~ JD responded, his mental voice grim.

~They just beg.~ McKenna flinched as Charley's voice joined the conversation. ~I try to pretend it's a video game, but I hate it. They're so pretty I just want to talk to them.~ His voice quiet as he headed up the stairs, three cats on his tail.

~You realize we have very old children, right?~ Toni asked, an odd mixture of emotions flavoring her voice.

"Yes," her voice echoed the feelings in the mindspace as they watched their kids, their pack's children, disappear up the stairs.

A knock on the door pulled her from the thoughts of children growing up too fast, and she turned to go answer it.

Chapter 27 - Skill Sets

All countries have canceled leave for military personnel. Normal channels of communication have sealed down. In some more totalitarian regimes like in the 'Stans or Eurasian countries, more than one person has been met at the door, their belongings piled on the step, kicked out because they are a shifter. The excuse being provided that conflicting loyalties cannot be tolerated at this moment. In the US, all branches of the military are on high alert, and local authorities are scrambling to try to make the concept of a civil defense a reality. The question that hangs in everyone's minds is: Will it work or will we die, or is it not needed, and they really come in peace? All we have is the word of one famous person as to why they are coming. Right now we can't afford to believe she is wrong. But what if? What if McKenna Largo has her own agenda, and this is all just part of it? Time will tell. ~ Op Ed piece in SacWasp.

McKenna pulled the door open to reveal Caroline, Christopher, and another person she didn't recognize. A large man, Samoan if she had to guess, dark hair, a face that looked like it should be smiling and thick slabs of muscle under fat.

"Morning, or," she glanced at the clock, "wow, afternoon, I guess. Come on in."

They did, following her towards the kitchen. "It just dawned on me how late it is, and we should probably eat. Join us?"

"Yes," Caroline said instantly, while the other two shook their heads.

"Neither of us shift, so I don't need to eat." Christopher said, a half smile. "This is Aleki Mapu. He's an expert in some martial arts and is strong enough that hopefully even in Kaylid form we can see how a normal human, granted a strong one, might fare. I hope you don't mind."

"No. That sounds great. I'm a bit scared that they might be really good. Hell, the only thing I'm sure of is they aren't used to people fighting back. I think." McKenna sighed. "Okay, I'm sure I have no idea how any of this is going to play out and I'm sure it's going to be messy."

Aleki laughed, a deep rumble revealing white teeth. The smile made his face look right where his serious expression had looked wrong.

"Most good leaders feel that way. Then they lead anyhow. It's a pleasure to meet you." His voice was oddly musical for his size, lighter in bass than JD or Perc.

I bet he sings and sings well.

"So where should we do this?" Caroline asked. "Though I do need to change into sweats and a shirt. While I can do all this in my suit, I'd really prefer to not destroy it for practice. Suits are expensive."

"Backyard. It has an eight-foot fence, so no prying eyes. And we'll need to change too." McKenna pointed to a half bath as they headed into the kitchen, and Caroline darted in there.

In the kitchen, Toni and JD were making sandwiches while Cass and Perc put dishes away. Nam sat on a kitchen chair watching all of them, her ears constantly moving.

~You okay, Nam?~ McKenna asked, checking up on the girl.

~Yes. Still scared, but am okay.~ She sounded okay, and McKenna scratched her ears as she went by. It felt so odd to treat the kids like pets sometimes, but she knew how good it felt when she petted and scratched them, and none of them took it as demeaning, simply the same way you would hug or kiss a human. They all craved it, and all the adults worked hard to give them what they needed. Charley being the most stand-offish, but he was also the oldest. But in wolf form, you could scratch his ears for hours.

Aleki and JD chatted while McKenna and Perc inhaled a sandwich. Caroline joined them a few minutes later and ate one also. Then Perc went to change. He'd had the most dreams of training, and while skilled in sports, had not done much martial arts. Toni would change after she finished eating. The kids were all still in animal form and happily eating their own sandwiches.

After a minute, Aleki asked, his voice only curious, not accusing, "Do they stay as animals a lot? Granted, I'm making the assumption you don't have wild animals wandering around your house."

Cass laughed as Toni had just headed upstairs. "No. But shifting burns calories, and right now there isn't a need to be human. Especially when they just want to run around the backyard while we practice. Easier to let them stay as animals and not waste the calories."

McKenna nodded. "I suspect food prices are going to start rising." She paused and sighed. "Maybe. I just it'll depend on how all this Elentrin stuff works out." Her comment put a damper on everything, and she shook her head, finishing her sandwich.

Caroline returned, and they all headed into the backyard. The playset sat to one side, and a neat grassy area lay to the other.

JD and Toni came out, dressed in kilts and tank tops, it really had become their uniform, feet bare.

Christopher and Aleki both looked at them, Aleki with narrowed eyes and a thoughtful expression.

"I am seeing the advantage to these kilts. Pockets and flexible."

JD shot a smile at McKenna. "I'm changing the world, one person at a time." The familiar joke made her smile and give him a cheeky grin.

"Have at it, I'll watch and try to think up a miracle?"

JD shifted slowly, they had learned the faster they changed the more calories they burned, so doing slow shifts made it easier on everyone. Though they still needed to replace them.

Christopher and Aleki watched intently, their gaze not moving from JD.

"You've never seen anyone shift before?" McKenna asked.

Cass and Perc sat in two of the chairs on the back patio as the kids were scampering up and down the slide. Their movements were slower than usual, the exploration that afternoon had tired them out.

"Caroline once," Christopher responded, still distracted. "But it was the first time and chaotic doesn't begin to describe it."

"A few YouTube vids, that's about it. You, of course." His cheeks heated a bit as he glanced at her. "Sorry, never occurred to me I'd actually meet you."

"At this point I'm just assuming everyone on the planet has seen me naked. It is what it is, and I don't have the time or energy to get upset or embarrassed about it anymore. And we're finding that spending as much time changing as we have been, being naked isn't as big a deal as it was six months ago." She waved it away, grabbing a chip out of the bag she'd snagged.

JD finished changing, and Caroline looked at him carefully. "You can talk in that form?"

"Yes, a bit distorted, but yes." His words were thicker and slower than usual, but understandable. It struck McKenna how spoiled they were with the mental communication. She glanced at Caroline, thinking. Did she remember reaching their public mindspace? Deciding now wasn't the time to bring it up, she stayed quiet and found a chair next to Cass, sharing her potato chips.

Caroline looked at the solid form of JD, her eyes lingering on teeth and claws. "I don't think I realized how intimidating those are. Up close you could shred me pretty easy, even with body armor."

"For this I think I can remove the claws." JD turned his furred head towards the claws, staring at them a minute. They pulled backward into his body until only a short fingernail length was visible. The government agents just stared.

"Can we do that?" Caroline's voice was a whisper, but McKenna didn't know if it was shock, fear, or excitement that caused that reaction.

[Possibly with practice. The commander's team has nanobots specially programmed to enable that as well as partial shifting. But in theory, all Kaylid should be able to do this.]

Caroline grabbed her head and whirled around, glaring at them. McKenna sighed. "Remember? That was the AI, Wefor. Answering your question."

At the confused looks from Aleki and Christopher, she went over the AI and mental communication thing.

~At this rate I should just get cards that explain it all.~ The mock complaint made the others snicker.

"Part of me really wants to run away screaming, but aliens are coming, so having a mental breakdown now would be counterproductive. Besides, people who have issues adapting to change don't last long in this environment." Christopher's tone had wry acceptance to it.

Caroline just shook her head. "And you get used to it?"

"Yep, don't even notice anymore." JD told her as he opened and closed his hands.

Wonder if it itches pulling them in that short, or if the nanobots just break down the cells?

"Okay, that is neither here nor there. You ready?" She had settled back on her heels, hands up in front of her in a relaxed poise.

"I guess." JD braced himself. His face didn't reveal anything, but his trepidation flavored the shared mindspace. He looked huge compared to the trim form of Caroline, his muscles and fur making it a true beast attacking the beauty.

Caroline didn't give him any warning, just hit him. JD started to react but not fast enough. Her palm strike hit him in the solar plexus, or at least the rough area.

~Huh. I think that should have hurt way more than it did.~ He swiped at her, still moving a bit slow, McKenna could feel his worry.

"JD, I'm a shifter too. I'll heal, so quit pulling your damn punches." Caroline snarled at him.

~Oh, yeah. Oops.~

Cass snorted, almost spitting water at that comment in their head.

JD stepped up the speed, and she could see, just from watching his body language, when the training kicked in. Caroline reacted to a feint, and he kicked her legs out from underneath her, following up with a strike to her throat. If his claws had been out, she would have been dead.

They all stood watching, serious worry on their faces.

"So much for the hand-to-hand idea. If they've all had that training, people can't take them on," Caroline said wryly as JD pulled her up. "Was any of that you?"

"No. I felt stupid and awkward trying to hit you, then everything melded together and strike patterns that I've never done, at least not as a human, kicked in. I knew how to block and then what counterstrike to make. Not all of your attacks, but many were similar, and I just adapted."

"Dammit. But those knives you call claws would have made up-close dangerous anyhow." Christopher sighed, typing a note into his phone. McKenna figured he was keeping Doug updated. "What now?"

Aleki responded before anyone else could. "if Miss Toni would change, I would like to do a strength comparison."

Toni flashed him a smile. "Just Toni, please. And sure." She finished her snack and stood, starting to shift into warrior form.

"Just so you know per the AI, our neurons are faster in this form, the muscle is denser, and the something about fiber length? She said it made our muscles perform closer to primates than humans. So the strength is greater than it would be otherwise."

Aleki nodded. "I suspected something like that. But JD is a huge person in human form. Toni is more approaching normal. I am interested to see her strength."

As they talked, Toni finished shifting.

"What first?"

"Something simple." Aleki smiled. "Arm wrestling."

Toni blinked, an odd look on her dark face, the green eyes disappearing for a minute, then reappearing like luminous emeralds.

The kids were still watching everything, though when she touched Nam's mind, the girl had fallen asleep curled up between the twins.

~She's fine. We watch her.~ Jamie responded to her mental touch, and she sent a wave of pride and love to him.

~I know.~

When she refocused on the adults, Toni and Aleki were at a table and had linked arms. Even with the fur you could see the muscle on her arms. Aleki's arms looked like massive slabs of dark brown flesh. Cass stood next to them, her hand on their joined hands.

"Ready?"

They both nodded, totally focused on the other, though a whiff of amusement in the mental space drifted across McKenna's awareness.

We're becoming more attuned to each other; more and more is slipping through. Is this good or bad? Are we going to lose privacy?

Wefor didn't respond, and McKenna didn't know if it was because she hadn't heard the private thought or if she didn't know the answer.

"Go!" As Cass said that, she yanked her arm away, and the two combatants started to strain. In her human form Toni was slight, but firm. In her warrior form, her loss of inches made her stockier, like a gymnast. Aleki looked huge, dwarfing her, though with Perc and JD around, she, well, all the women, looked tiny. It had been an advantage when on patrol, having JD behind her often made people underestimate her.

Aleki groaned as Toni pushed his arm down. They both strained, but it was obvious she was winning.

"Damn. I knew we might be stronger in that form, but Aleki is really strong," Caroline uttered, as Aleki relented and his arm hit the table.

"You are very strong in that form." He glanced at McKenna. "Would you mind wrestling with me in human form, I assume you haven't noticed any major strength changes."

McKenna shrugged, and headed over to take Toni's place. "Besides generally being healthier and the weight loss, no." They went through the same exercise, and McKenna's arm, much to her silent embarrassment, hit the table before she even had a chance to try.

Perc was next. He and Aleki struggled, but where JD and Perc had an even massive build, legs and chest proportional, Aleki carried his strength from the waist up. The struggle lasted longer, but after the first thirty seconds they knew Aleki would win the contest.

He won and leaned back, face serious. "If this is a representative example, Kaylid are very strong. Toni, would you mind coming and hitting me? I promise as long as you don't use claws we should be fine."

Toni's looked at him, her face unreadable with the muzzle and fur. "Okay."

They both rose and headed out to the lawn. Aleki wore a t-shirt that lay tight across his body. "Just make a fist and punch me in the stomach. Start out at half as hard as you think you can, I'll tell you when to stop."

McKenna couldn't see Toni's face, but she nodded stepping back and did a jab directly to his stomach.

Aleki didn't move, but nodded. "Harder." Toni followed, and McKenna could see her striking harder each time as she believed a bit more she wouldn't seriously hurt the man. On the sixth blow, air woofed out of him, and he bent over a bit. She stopped as she breathed heavy, then slowly stood up.

"How hard was that?"

Toni's head tilted as she replied. "Probably ninety percent."

Aleki nodded. "Thank you, that is enough."

They headed back to where the others watched. "So what did all that tell you?" McKenna asked, honestly curious.

"Most Kaylid, if they are like Toni or you, will probably be able to punch hard enough to kill people, without specific strikes. Those of you built like JD or Perc can probably break down doors, rip people out of tanks if they try hard enough. Fighting these Kaylid up close will be all but suicide for anyone not Kaylid."

His pronouncement cast cold water over everyone, and McKenna sat there, dread pooling in her stomach.

Chapter 28 - Circling the Wagons

The reality of what the president said a few days ago is clear to most people. Objects can be seen approaching the moon. While still small, their shapes are visible against the light of the moon as they approach Earth. Here in the US, reactions are mixed. Cities like LA, Dallas, and Atlanta are having riots, people protesting and demanding the government do something. There isn't a gun or any ammo left to be had on the shelves, and ammo has surpassed gold in value. But other areas are not reacting the same. Portland, Seattle, Las Vegas, and New Orleans are welcoming the aliens. Trying to spread the word that everyone can just be friends. The concern is, what if McKenna Largo is right, and they are here to take our people, shifters, away? ~ TNN News Anchor

Nothing more really came out though they talked until late in the evening. The kids playing for a while longer, then shifting back to human. Christopher rose, looking at all of them.

"We should get going. I'll be here in the morning to pick up two of you. We're setting up a place in NYC. Both the consulates of the Russian Federation and Pakistan are next to Central Park. They've cleared out to let us talk there, we'll take whichever one is closer."

Perc raised an eyebrow. "How did they manage that?"

"I have no idea. But I'm very glad I wasn't involved in that negotiation." Christopher had a wry smile. "This has been a headache as it is, but your suggestions have been taken into consideration." He cast a look at Perc and JD. "Which means if either of you come, you'll be hidden and not obvious. No one, regardless of their origin, could look at either of you and not consider you a threat."

"Awww, should I be flattered or insulted?" asked JD. He'd turned back to human and taken over the grilling for dinner that night.

"Neither. It's a statement. You make most men feel inadequate, and for women you're going to outweigh them by over a hundred pounds, and that makes you a threat." Christopher didn't look apologetic. "We equate body size to physical threat. It's something I've worried about, that your Kaylid forms are smaller than the average height. Some people won't see the strength in the body." He pointed at Toni. "I'd never guess her capable of what she is. We train to read people, body language, physical capabilities, etc. So I don't want our people to underestimate the Kaylid. Ours or theirs."

McKenna rubbed her temples, a headache coming on. "The next week everything will change."

Caroline laughed. "Everything has already changed. It's just going to change again."

"Yeah, but people might die this time. A lot of people," McKenna pointed out. She hadn't eaten much, her stomach in knots thinking about the next few days.

"That's why we're talking to you, and taking what you and your AI say very seriously. No one wants a war. Definitely not a war with an alien species."

McKenna took a deep breath and got up, wanting to change the subject. "What time tomorrow?"

"About nine. Have bags with you, enough for a week. And then, well, we'll see where the negotiations end up," Christopher said. They shook hands and headed out, leaving McKenna shutting the door behind them.

"Are we sure about this?" Toni asked behind her.

McKenna turned to see her leaning against the wall, arms crossed over her chest, chewing on her lip. With a sad echo in the mindspace McKenna closed the two steps between them and pulled her into a hug, trying to comfort. Toni let loose a sad sound and hugged her back.

"No. I'm not sure about any of it. But we have to try. We have to see if we can stop this. One way or another."

Toni nodded, squeezing her once more then pulling away a bit. "Agreed. I'm going to work on bags for the kids, and we'll stock the emergency places tomorrow. You need to pack and go see if you can save our world."

McKenna wanted to scream, to grab her family and go hide someplace until it was all over. But no one else got that option, so neither did she.

"Yes, I do. You going to be okay with just you and JD?"

"Sure. Kids love him and he makes an intimidating body guard."

"Yes, he does. Want to tuck in kids with me?" They had agreed that even trying to get the kids to sleep separately was a waste of time, so Toni helped get the four kids into their nest. They fell asleep quickly, a tangle of legs and arms.

Calls were made to family, Perc calling his parents, and Cass keeping Helena up to date via calls and almost constant text messages. Eventually they couldn't avoid the next day anymore. The adults headed towards their own beds, though McKenna noted JD heading towards Cass's room and just smiled as she headed for hers. Sleep didn't come easily for her, but when it did, she welcomed the escape from her own mind.

No dreams pulled her in, and she woke to the alarm going off.

~Wefor, no visions?~

[No. Information indicates the ships have locked down all communications as they ready to approach your planet.]

~That implies something was being sent to us and now isn't.~

[Yes. It does.]

Wefor's flat words rang in McKenna's head, and she frowned, mulling over the possibilities of what that meant. It could be good or bad. What if other Kaylid across the planet were being programmed by these dreams? What if more were like Nam, torn apart by conflicting programming? What if -

Enough. You can't change any of that. Get going and deal with what you can change.

That at least got her out of bed and moving, but she still spent a few minutes on social media, looking to see if any more people were going into animal form and going crazy. The information went from welcome parties, to martial law in some areas, riots, and protests. And this was just in the US. China and both Koreas had locked down completely, refusing flights into and out of their countries. Everything she read made her more depressed and scared and finally she logged off.

All you can do is what you can do.

The mantra repeated in her head over and over again as she got dressed and packed a bag. She headed downstairs to find Toni and Carina cooking, the kids quietly eating at the table. McKenna sat down between Charley and Nam, looking at Nam closely. The girl did look a bit bigger, but the circles were gone under her eyes, and she didn't look as gaunt as she had. For now McKenna would take that as a win.

Nam leaned into her a bit as she ate her eggs, but she didn't say anything, though she noted every person coming in or out of the room.

"How you doing?" McKenna directed her question to Charley even as she rubbed Nam's back.

He shook his head, not looking at her.

"Come on, talk to me."

He put his chin on his hand as he pushed eggs around his plate. "Worried, but I've had the not-dreams, too. We know. Just," he covered his face with his hand, and she saw a drop splash onto his plate. Her arm snaked out and wrapped around him.

"I love you. I'll do everything I can to keep you safe. I wish I could promise it will be all okay. But I can't do that." McKenna wanted to. So badly she wanted to assure him everything would be fine. But lying to Charley would destroy everything they were trying to create.

"I know." He turned his head into her shoulder for a moment, and she accepted his tears. But he didn't cry long. Pulling away. "We'll be fine. I'll look after everyone."

"I know you will." McKenna didn't point out JD and Toni would both be here. She looked up and caught Toni watching them, strain clear on her face.

They settled down a bit, Nam still silent, but she stayed, touching McKenna, either her hand or her shoulder, never broke contact. Carina came out and set some pancakes on the table and looked at McKenna. Her dark hair in braids tight against her skull.

"McKenna?" Her voice had a hesitant tone, and McKenna looked up. Carina had been their quiet support staff, and McKenna knew it. Also knew they didn't give the girl anywhere near enough credit for all she did to keep them sane.

"Hey. You holding up?"

"Scary. At the point I'm not watching the news. Knowing what I know just makes all their guesswork even more scary."

"Yes. It's too stressful, but I can't swear anything is going to be okay."

Carina smirked, a bit of her humor sneaking through. "Oh, well. If you could, I'd be a bit worried. Shapeshifting is one thing, being a god is something else."

McKenna laughed. "No desire whatsoever to be a god. Being me is hard enough. So what's up?" She could see that Carina wanted to ask something.

INCOMING

The girl, woman really, took a deep breath. "Toni said you could change me, make me a Kaylid."

"Yes. I can." The humor drained out of McKenna, and she focused on Carina, feeling the rest of the house snap into the conversation through the mindspace.

She swallowed. "I know everything that's going on. And after you get back from New York, I'd like you to turn me. You know I don't really have a family, and Toni and the kids have been my family for years. And," she shrugged, trying to express herself. "I'd rather be part of your insanity than get left behind."

McKenna barked out a laugh mixed with a sob. "It is our insanity, yes. If you're sure, then yes, I'll bite you when I get back. That isn't anything I've shared with the powers-that-be, and I'd really rather not."

"Makes sense to me." She smiled and disappeared upstairs.

~Thank you,~ Toni's voice was soft in her mind. ~She's been family and the twin's big sister for as long as they've been aware. I've been worried about her but didn't want to admit it.~

~You should have. I would have told you sooner. We're all in this together. We'll protect her.~

The chimed agreement flooded the mindspace and McKenna refocused on food, letting the love and friendship in the mindspace help push back her fear and worry.

[Your squad is well-formed. While families are not encouraged, you have a good family.]

The odd comment from Wefor made her smile and gave her a bit of encouragement. Finishing up her food, McKenna stood. She'd packed her kilt, tank tops, and weapons, but for the meetings, she purposely grabbed the sheath dress. Something to make her look non-threatening. She'd been involved in enough training that she knew her body language could convey even more. And she'd work on keeping her body language subservient and watching the Elentrin with all her skills.

The knock on the door pulled Cass and Perc downstairs. Perc had dressed in slacks and a polo shirt, but nothing could hide his hugeness. Cass opted for a simple sundress, something that would slip off quick and easy.

Christopher stood outside and took them in. "You ready?"

McKenna gave him a 'are you kidding' look as Perc grabbed her bag and walked out. "No, but not sure that I would ever be ready."

"I think I'd be more worried if you were looking forward to this." For a moment she thought he'd say more, but he shook his head and waved towards the waiting SUVs. "There will be agents staying here watching over your people while you're in New York, but we can't guarantee what will happen if they attack. All our plans and training are centered on small group attacks and protecting our principals. Fighting a war? They'll fight, but at that point JD is probably going to be more in tune with what needs to be done. So keep that in mind if this all goes to hell." His voice held somber worry.

"We understand." McKenna didn't know what else to say, instead she sent love and worry back to Toni and JD as she, Perc, and Cass slid into the waiting cars and headed off to watch the world change.

Chapter 29 - Earth Stood Still

Word has slipped out that these aliens are expected to land in New York City. How this is known hasn't been revealed, but the city is reacting. Already people are leaving the city in droves, but a certain amount of people are coming in, wanting to see real aliens from space. Where they will land hasn't been released, if it is even known, but smart money is the harbor or Central Park. Where else could you land a ship? Though if a runway is needed, that means JFK or La Guardia. All that is known right now is that the level of government activity in the city is through the roof. TNN will have crews scattered throughout the city to report on everything that happens. ~ TNN News

McKenna didn't pay much attention to the trip to NYC. She and the others spent their time talking in the mindspace, reassuring the kids, discussing Carina's request to be changed, and asking Wefor if anyone other than commanders could transform people. The answer to that was no and yes. While only commanders had the ability, the Elentrin had the ability to inject specific nanobots and force people to change.

[Remember there is only the information in the databases to go off of. There is no way to know if something has changed or what might not be accurate.]

McKenna thought about that. ~Wefor, how long ago were you sent towards this planet?~

[Unknown. Awareness does not start until after you had shifted a few times. It took that long for enough command nanobots to replicate and start repairing the existing programming.]

~Huh. Okay. You two have any ideas?~ She poked Cass and Perc gently with the question.

~So if it is just nanobots, can you pre-program them? The way the ones you made us take to make sure all the programming had been replaced?~

[Yes and no. While those nanobots can be produced and provided, that programming can only be activated when in a host. Right now all nanobots have been deactivated by existing programming. Giving those bots to a non- Kaylid has to be via the blood stream and then activated while they are in a suitable host. Remember that not all forced shifts are successful.]

~Oh. I forgot that. Wefor, what is the failure rate?~

[Less than ten percent but given that she already has nanobots it should be less.]

~Wait, what? She does?~ Toni asked, her voice sharp enough to draw a wince from McKenna.

[Over time between living with other Kaylid, scratches from the children, and the original infection, yes.]

That sank in, and finally a general shrug rippled through everyone.

~It does make sense. But that's good, and I don't have an issue with her being changed, but is it ethical?~ Cass asked.

That dropped like a bomb in the room and McKenna opened her eyes, not looking at Cass but out the window as the plane headed in for landing. They didn't say anything else, but the idea bounced around her head trying to decide and realizing she had no idea if it was or wasn't.

The disembarking, getting slipped into dark town cars and being whisked through strange city streets all passed in a blur. No one really spoke and McKenna just felt like a piece of luggage getting moved about. But she didn't make any fuss. None of them did. The stress shone through all the agents; it reflected in the quiet streets of a city that never slept, and her stomach churned even more. They were ushered through a dark underground garage and escorted up through what McKenna assumed were the bowels of a hotel.

They were ushered into a room where Doug waited and a bunch of other people McKenna didn't recognize, but from the suits and attitudes they screamed politicians. She did notice, though, that most of them looked older, thin, and somehow unhealthy. If this was who they were going to send to meet with the Elentrin, it might work. Maybe.

"McKenna, Cass, Perc, glad you guys could make it. Come on in. I want to introduce you to the people who are heading our negotiations. Then maybe you can help us brainstorm a plan." With a smile on his face, though everyone in the room looked tense and like they needed a week of sleep, he pulled her over and Cass and Perc followed.

"Everyone, I'd like to introduce McKenna Largo. The person who's made sure we at least have a chance at surviving this." The people, one woman, two men, turned to look at her.

"McKenna this is Albert Larinson. He'll be our ambassador, if you will."

The man who looked like in his heyday he would have made a perfect extra on a movie about gangsters or the Italian Mafia, leaned on a cane and held out his hand. His body had slimmed to the point of gauntness, and hair that she suspected had been thick and lush like a poodle coat, looked tired and thin.

She took his hand and caught a whiff of his scent under tobacco and Old Spice.

"You're dying. Cancer?" The other two blinked at this, but he nodded.

"Yes. One of the reasons I agreed to do this. I'm terminal, so I don't really have much to lose." He tilted his head. "How could you tell?"

"You smell sick, dying." She didn't pull her punches.

His eyes narrowed. "Will they be able to smell that?"

Huh, good question.

"I don't know about the Elentrin. The Kaylid with them, yes, but will they know what it means? I have no idea." She paused, thinking. "But I'm not sure it matters. They may think we're more desperate because we're sending our dying to talk to them?" McKenna looked at them, trying to stay polite. "Your guess is as good as mine."

Albert nodded his head, a distant look in his eyes as he stepped back.

INCOMING

Doug glanced at her, his eyes thoughtful too, and McKenna bit her lip frustrated they kept asking things she couldn't answer.

~I swear didn't they read up on me? I figured since it took them a week to appear on my doorstep they had done a full background check. They would know about our sense of smell and the test I did for Waris.~ She kept her exasperation out of her face as she turned to look at the woman.

A tiny woman with skin the color of stained walnut, her hair so closely cropped the sliver curls gave her a halo effect, held out her hand.

"McKenna, this is Beatrice Laughton. She worked as an undersecretary for three different secretaries of state."

Beatrice smiled, her yellowed teeth giving away her status as a lifelong smoker, even though McKenna didn't smell any on her now.

"I retire this year. This sounded like an interesting way to go out, and no one ever takes me as a threat." She waved at herself, a wicked light in her eye. "At least not until after I've skewered them on policy."

McKenna matched her grin. That left the last person, a young man, thin, already prematurely balding and he couldn't be more than late twenties. Doug introduced him as Harold Weinmarst. He just sneered at her, even as he shook her hand with the limpest grip she'd ever felt.

"I still feel this is a waste of time. We can never negotiate with invaders." He took his hand back from her grip and looked like he wanted to wipe it on his slacks. "We should meet them with weapons and let them know we will not tolerate this invasion of our land and our people. The odds of them signing a treaty is nil." Somehow he managed to sneer the entire time he talked.

"And what if I'm wrong? If everything I've told you is incorrect and they're here to set up trade? Or if they're way more powerful than we are?" She kept her voice mild, but wanted to slap him. If they failed, millions would probably die.

He had the audacity to smirk at her. "Then they find out how dangerous humans are."

McKenna glanced at Doug who shrugged. "He's a good lawyer and can make contracts sing. Luckily he won't talk much." He shot an annoyed look at the young man then sighed. "Hell, maybe all this will get competent people into office." His voice was very low. The three greeters had already turned around and started to talk between themselves. McKenna figured she was the only one that heard him.

"It's an invasion. Not a miracle," she said dryly, and he choked out a laugh.

"True. So ready for the plan?"

"Go for it." By this point everyone else had arrived and Cass and Perc had drifted over. Doug got them all sitting, a few more people McKenna vaguely recognized from the first or second meeting had also joined them.

The next six hours were spent going over plans, coming up with ideas and strategies. McKenna and Wefor spent a lot of time answering questions and saying they didn't know. Too much was unknown and by the time they finished even McKenna was exhausted.

Perc and Cass acted as her chaperones which felt odd as Cass looked so tiny between the two of them, her petite frame and build made her look like they should protect her. The hours disappeared between meetings that only ramped up the turmoil in her churning stomach and time at their hotel suite talking to the kids, Toni, and JD, and wishing they were here. But none of them ever let the words slip out. At least with them there they had the possibility someone might make it through this unscathed.

McKenna sat in her long t-shirt with Cass and Perc, in their suite drinking coffee, when someone pounded on the door.

She rose and answered it. Christopher stood there, his face gray. "They're coming. We can see the shuttle movement. It's show time."

The coffee threatened to come back up. "Thanks. Give us twenty." She shut the door and headed back towards Cass and Perc who were already dressing. Cass in a simple dress that made her look tiny and harmless. Perc would be staying way in the background already in Kaylid form. He'd change as soon as they landed, but stay far enough away that in the park, if they landed there, he wouldn't be visible. Caroline would be with him.

McKenna got dressed too, pulling on an ugly dress that made her look blocky. Her hair in a bun at the base of her skull and glasses she didn't need, but changed the shape of her face. Bland ballet flats that she could run in completed the outfit. No makeup, and her only accessory would be a large notepad and a pen. They hoped the Elentrin had bureaucracies and would dismiss her. She could communicate everything to Perc who would tell the people running the earpieces that everyone else would have. Cass was her backup.

Christopher waited for them as they opened the door. He was dressed in his normal dark brown suit, something to make him fade into the background.

"Ready?"

"No. I want to run and crawl under my bed again," Cass said, her voice flat. "But I have family that's depending on me." She'd sent Helena a message telling her she loved her before she walked out the door.

"Understood. But you're here. Trust me, that is more than you realize."

Cass shot him a look, then glanced at McKenna who shrugged. She had no idea what he was talking about. They were put in two different vehicles, Cass and McKenna in one, Perc in the other.

~Stay safe. Stay alive. I can't lose you.~ Her thought quiet as she sent that just to him even as she watched Cass zone out, likely talking to JD.

~Ditto. We can't die until I have a chance to ask you out on a date.~ McKenna blinked at Perc's private comment and felt her face heat.

"Are you okay? What's wrong?" Cass's voice pulled her out of her shocked pleasure. McKenna focused on her and realized Cass stared at her concern on her face.

"Nothing, I'm fine." She pushed it down. This wasn't the time. People could die, but the jolt of happiness gave her a boost she hadn't realized she needed. They pulled into the park and McKenna looked outside the vehicle. People were carrying signs, held back by police on horseback, in riot gear, and looking like they didn't know whose side they were on.

Half the signs said variations of 'Come in Peace' or 'We want to be friends.' The others were more along the lines of 'Leave our Planet Alone,' 'Go Away' and other much cruder statements.

"I can't decide if I hope they can or can't read English. Any word about how the other places are handling this?"

Christopher had left the sliding window down so he heard her question. "A little, in Istanbul, the city is on fire. News reports are that there was an explosion, but I don't know everything yet. In Shanghai there was a complete news blackout as we left. They were trying to re-establish connections when we left. So who knows what's going on there. Any insight as to why they chose those locations?"

"Population density, I think. But heck if I know. I could have been because they liked the temperature. I really don't know anything."

"Welcome to my world. No matter how much you plan or prepare, some idiot can come out of left field and blow it all to hell."

McKenna nodded then swallowed as she realized he had stopped. "We here?"

"Not quite. But we need to see where they land. The park is big, but we have spotters on most buildings so they should be able to see where they're going to land. Once we do, we'll head that direction."

There didn't seem to be much to say, so McKenna leaned back and tried to not think, not do anything. It didn't matter from this point on. All she could do would be listen and provide the information needed.

Cass reached out and squeezed her hand. McKenna squeezed back and tried not to notice how fast both of their hearts beat. Wefor didn't say anything and the mindspace sat quiet as they waited.

"Got it. Looks like the shuttle is landing in the Sheep Meadow. Let's go," Christopher said the words as they took off. It didn't mean anything to McKenna, but she held on as they raced through the park. The jostling over bumpy ground had both women grabbing onto the seats to make sure they weren't tossed to the floor. The vehicle slid to a halt, and Christopher took a deep breath. "We are here, ladies. It's game time."

He jumped out and before McKenna could get her head in the game, he pulled open her door. She and Cass climbed out and saw the others under a tent that seemed to have magically appeared in the last few seconds. They headed that way.

Tension radiated through everyone. She could smell the stress oozing out of people. More than one reeked of cigarette smoke from people she'd never smelled it on. The occasional whiff of alcohol hit her nose as the mixed group of people stood, silent, watching a shuttle from another world, land in Central Park.

"And so the Earth stood still."

Chapter 30 - Hero Worship

We are here live at the historic meeting in Central Park. Aliens are walking on Earth. While our reporters were not allowed close, our cameras are directed towards the space where our ambassadors for the United States, dare I say Earth, wait. This is a moment that will go down in history, but will we come away with friends or enemies? What do we know about the people who are waiting for our alien visitors? Are they the best representatives of our nation? Our planet? ~TNN News

McKenna didn't know who said it, but it felt right, and her stomach twisted as a ramp dropped from the ship. Her breath caught. She wished she had binoculars. The ship, shuttle she guessed, seemed about the same size as the Gulfstream in length, but there any comparison ended. Wide plane including the wings, it had a smooth shape that called to mind liquid mercury. The one vision containing a shuttle had not drawn her attention, but now with the silver black shape absorbing the sun, she examined it closely. The nose seemed more transparent, but there were no landing struts, it simply settled on the ground. The ramp seemed part of the ship, the same smooth, silvery black.

Her attention was ripped from the ship to the beings walking out of it. A tall Kaylid led the way, golden fur giving away what it was. She counted a total of five Kaylid. All of them slightly taller than she was in warrior form, but not as large as Perc or JD. They formed a wall around someone in the middle. All she could see was the occasional glimpse of dark hair and bright colors in the middle. They headed towards the group, an undercurrent of words and comments washed around her, but she ignored it. Wanting to see and understand. The Kaylid wore simple skirts that hit about mid-thigh and moved and flexed as they did. It looked more like spandex than anything else.

As they headed towards the group, she caught glimpses of tails, but she really wanted time to study these non-Earth Kaylid. The colors seemed more vibrant than any except the reds she'd seen on a fox or red panda. Their golds shimmered, blacks were almost blue, and she wanted to look at one she swore had dappled green marks across the fur. Even trying to figure out what they resembled didn't work. They moved too fast and their faces and coloring were just different enough she couldn't grasp what creatures they might be created from.

They approached to about ten feet from the assembled group, and she focused on the leader, odds were this was the commander. It felt odd to watch the body maybe she had been riding. The leader stood, almost posing, as all eyes were drawn to him. At least McKenna thought it was a male, there were no breasts visible like on her form, but that might not mean anything.

He stood erect, eyes tracking across all of them, pointed ears twitching back and forth at the noise that surrounded them. His skull looked a bit like hers in that form, but longer, sharper than she in that form. His eyes were a vibrant blue that stood out against the golden fur. Arms and legs, but she realized his fingers had an extra joint that made them longer than hers.

"I bring Ambassador Scilita to discuss the rescue of your people from this horrible calamity. Are you the leaders of this area?" He spoke English the way she spoke Spanish. The mouth movements didn't match up exactly, and it came out heavy, thick, like someone with a heavy Russian accent.

Albert stepped forward, leaning on a cane he hadn't had the day before. "I am Albert Larinson. I speak for this country. "

"Then Ambassador Scilita will speak with you." Up until now the other Kaylid had surrounded the person in the middle like a living shield. With the leader's words, the others parted and moved in a fluid synchronized movement to reveal the person in the middle.

McKenna felt her knees buckle, and she fought to remain standing. Around her, soft moans and gasps rippled away as they took in the being looking at all of them.

Slim, almost petite as she couldn't have stood more than five-foot-four. Breasts and overall form implied female to McKenna. Long hair the color of rubies, or heart's blood, rippled down her back. A face with wide lavender eyes framed by lashes that matched the color of her hair sat in a face that had no flaws, everything perfectly symmetrical and heartbreakingly beautiful.

Her fragrance drifted across the breeze and McKenna's eyes closed. She found herself unable to resist the desire to inhale and savor that scent. Need flooded through her and only years of social conditioning kept her from moaning out loud. She wanted to fall to her knees in front of this goddess, to give her anything she wanted. To make her happy, and serve.

~McKenna?~ Perc's voice cut through the haze a bit. ~What's going on over there? We can see people falling to their knees, and you and Cass feel odd.~

With a force of will, McKenna wrenched open her eyes. Around them, most of the delegation was on their knees looking at the Elentrin with worship. A few were even prostrate and all but crawling to the woman. Cass had fallen to her knees, and a soft keen came from her.

~Scilita is wonderful. We should serve her. It would be an honor to serve her,~ she said into the mindspace, oddly at peace.

~What the hell? McKenna, what's going on? What are you saying?~ Toni's voice cut through, and for a second the haze lifted, and McKenna tried to clear her mind, but the fog of desire to please settled back down over her.

~Wefor, what's going on?~ JD asking now, but McKenna felt herself sinking to her knees. Her eyes caught Harold standing, looking around, a handkerchief to his nose as he sneezed.

[She is not acting correctly. This reaction is-] Wefor broke off, and a hiss of static rippled through her mind, so strong she moaned. [Pheromones. The

INCOMING

Elentrin is using pheromones. That is why all the humans are reacting like this. That must also be how and why the Kaylid never rebel. Bots are currently being reprogrammed to block the reactions. Commands have been sent to Cass and Perc; though they will take longer to adapt. Perc should stay away.]

~Is there anything we can do?~ McKenna mused that Toni seemed worried, but all the conversation was so far away. So was Scilita. She should really go over there and help Scilita with whatever she needed.

McKenna tried to rise to her feet to walk over there, but standing seemed too difficult. Instead she started to crawl.

[McKenna, this cannot be allowed. You cannot come into that creature's power.]

Her body quit working, she couldn't move forward. Distant annoyance filtered through. She wanted to move, to go to the goddess and offer her services. Focusing, she noticed a few people kneeling before her, and the Harold guy talking frantically on his phone.

[It should kick in shortly. Perc, stay back.]

I need to go to my, to my, to my...

Her mind clicked over and over as the sweet fog of worship cleared.

~Why am I on my knees?~ McKenna looked around and saw Cass kneeling on the ground, her eyes rapt on the Elentrin. McKenna followed her gaze to the pretty female. ~What is going on?~ Worry and fear bubbled through her as she rose to her feet.

[You were affected by pheromones. That is apparently how the Elentrin get such cooperation with other races. Your nanobots have been updated, and

Cass and Perc are being sent programming now to help prevent this.]

~Perc, let them know it's pheromones. Why isn't Harold affected? He looks like he's about to freak out. How long have we all been going crazy?~ Worry wrapped her as she viewed the delegates and politicians on their knees before the Elentrin.

~Apparently he has severe allergies to some plants out here and is totally stuffed up.~

[You have been affected for approximately five minutes.] Wefor's calm voice helped her focus.

~Good, he just became the primary ambassador. Tell them they need someone either super allergic to stuff or ... I guess me. I can get this to other Kaylid but I don't know how else to defeat pheromones.~

~I'll pass it on. Be careful.~ His voice sounded worried as she strode towards Harold, barely glancing at the aliens, who seemed bemused by the humans abasing themselves at their feet.

"Harold, you're in charge. Go talk to them." McKenna dropped her voice to a fierce whisper, but at the flick of the lead Kaylid's ears she knew their conversation was being overheard.

"Me?" His voice squeaked, then he sneezed. "I'm the contracts guy, I go over everything and make sure there are no loopholes. I don't talk to people."

"Well, now you do. Until we can get everyone else immune, we don't have a choice. Now move." McKenna grabbed him, turned him and forced him over to the group of aliens.

~Wefor, will filters work against this?~

[Unknown. Depends on the level of the filters and if they will block molecules of that size. The technology of your filters is unknown] Wefor's answer was immediate, but McKenna found the fog had completely lifted from her.

~Wefor, how many microns are the pheromones?~ Perc's voice lashed out, and McKenna realized he must be talking to other people. Because she had no idea what the question meant.

[3-6 Microns on average.]

~Give us ten minutes,~ his voice snapped out, and McKenna refocused on Harold who had his phone to his ear, babbling. She reached up, grabbed it, and tossed it. Her hands grabbed his chin and yanked his face towards hers.

"Listen to me. You are unaffected. We will resolve this, but for now you need to talk to them."

"But, but, why can't you?"

The ears of the lead Kaylid tilted towards her, and she glared at Harold.

"You know why. Now get your ass over there and get them to discuss this." She didn't give him an out, staring at him so hard she thought he should start to smoke.

His head jerked up and down. Harold straightened, grabbed his briefcase, and walked towards the gathered aliens. McKenna followed him, noting Albert and Beatrice on the ground, looking up at the Elentrin with adoring eyes.

Harold cleared his throat, and the Elentrin looked up at him. McKenna felt herself quail at the sheer adorableness of the face that looked at them.

"Yes?" Her voice held music, amusement, and something that made the back of her mind freeze in terror.

Harold sneezed. The look of sheer revulsion that flashed across the Elentrin's face finished breaking the odd hold she had McKenna.

~I'm good, you're blocking the pheromones, right?~ Panic laced the question, even as Harold sneezed again.

[Yes. Your primal reactions cannot be blocked, but the pheromones will no longer affect you.] McKenna relaxed a bit and trusted the AI. If she didn't, they were all as good as captured.

Another sneeze had the Elentrin stepping back a bit. The Kaylid didn't seem to know if to take it as an attack or something else.

"Welcome to Earth, Ambassador Scilita." McKenna had to give him a small about of respect. Even sneezing, he managed to say the name with the same intonations as the alien Kaylid had. "As you can see, our people are currently unwell. We would love to discuss your purpose for being here, but if you could give us a day to recover from our shock at your presence, we would be grateful."

The Elentrin tilted her head, smiling at him. She looked so much like an anime character that McKenna almost couldn't handle the cute.

"But why would I come back? I just need to help with your animals. We don't want you to suffer. We can help you with this terrible plague that has affected your world. We will find places for them and help them live full lives." Her voice melodic, creating a music and rhythms that were almost hypnotic.

Then Harold sneezed, disrupting the rhythm. "I do understand, but I must ask if you can return tomorrow."

A frown creased her face, and McKenna heard Albert and Beatrice whimper, she saw them reach up to touch the fabric that draped her. McKenna noticed it only now, it was a pale green that complimented the red hair and pale skin. She all but glowed with beauty, and McKenna growled, clenching her jaw. The Kaylid darted a look at her, his eyes narrowing at the sound. McKenna ducked her head and tried to look infatuated, but all she wanted to do was run.

"Of course, we don't want to cause any distress." Scilita reached out and drew her hand down his face. To her surprise, Harold forced a smile and didn't look like his knees were about to melt. If anything, he looked vaguely disgusted. Scilita frowned and turned to the Kaylid.

"Why do they not worship my magnificence? I am beautiful, perfect in all ways. They should be honored to serve me, to give me that which I need to destroy the abominations." The words sang like music in her ears, and only Harold's confusion let McKenna realize they were not said in English.

"Unknown, my Siret. We should return and see how the others have done. Your beauty can not be resisted. Perhaps return in the morrow when more of their weak-willed ones will be here?" The lead Kaylid spoke to her in the same language, though he kept his eyes on the ground, not looking at her.

"Hmmmm," it sounded like music. She turned back to Harold, not even deigning to look at McKenna.

"Very well. We will return to talk, but know that I must have my Kaylid to help in the preservation of our species. Surely you would not want to deprive me of that?"

Harold sneezed, and Scilita flinched back.

"Tomorrow we will talk. Thank you for your understanding."

A frown creasing her brow, Scilita turned, the Kaylid forming up around her as they headed back to the ship. McKenna didn't even try to watch them this time, figuring someone, or lots of someones, were recording the whole thing.

Beatrice and Albert cried out in pain, weeping as the Elentrin moved away. McKenna looked around but didn't move until after the ramp had sealed. Her legs almost gave out at that point.

Perc came running up to her and pulled her into a hug, she leaned into it even as she looked at the weeping people on the ground.

"What do we do now?"

Chapter 31 - DTs

Images of the Elentrin have already hit the web, gained by a few people using drones and cameras. The beauty of this woman is insane. Our most beautiful actresses could only hope to be a shadow of her radiance. Ruby red hair and lashes will be the fashion for the rest of the year. Do the other Elentrin look as beautiful as this? Dare we hope to have new fashion icons to lead our way? ~ TNN Fashion filler

The second the ship lifted off, chaos exploded around them. People rushed over to pick up the weeping people, crying out for the Elentrin to return. McKenna stood in the middle of it, Perc had released her, but she still felt shaky and a bit like crying herself.

~This is ridiculous. Why do I still ache for her?~

[The chemicals the pheromones trigger are still present in your brain. It will take a bit for them to wear off. There is no way to eliminate the chemicals as they have already started the reactions. But the pheromones will not affect you anymore.]

~Good, 'cause this wanting to slit my wrist for wanting her is scary,~ Cass said quietly into the mindspace as she moved over to them. Perc pulled her into another hug, and Cass leaned into it. They all needed the touching, the affection, the grounding to help fight their reactions.

~How long until Perc is immune? How do we make others immune? Can we?~ McKenna looked around and saw Christopher striding towards her, his face a calm mask she rather envied right now.

"Are you okay? Alexander here passed the message to us about the pheromones." He nodded to Perc as he talked. "We have filters coming out that should work, but why were our people so badly affected? And why wasn't Weinmarst?"

"Allergies." McKenna's voice was dry. "He's allergic to something out here, and he couldn't stop sneezing. That meant the pheromones couldn't get through his clogged nose." She shrugged. "It's a bit amusing, I guess. The country was saved because a flunky was allergic?"

"I'm not a flunky," Harold said as he walked up. "But even I'll admit I didn't plan on actually talking. My skills are the contracts and hammering that out. Albert and Beatrice were supposed to be our charmers." He had an odd look on his face, and glanced back at the people being taken away in ambulances. "Are they going to be okay?"

The general desire to keep the number of people the Elentrin met low had probably saved their lives. If there had been more people they might have lost everyone as more and more people were pulled in.

[Those affected should be watched. They may be suicidal as they don't have any way to cancel out the effects of the pheromones. These seemed to be tailored to create devotion and desire to serve.]

McKenna passed on the information and Christopher talked into his earpiece though he kept looking around.

"So now what?" McKenna asked. "They'll be back tomorrow. And I don't think they know how to hear No as an answer."

Christopher nodded. "Agreed. Is it only the Elentrin that have the pheromones?"

McKenna shrugged. "No idea. But I've never managed to produce them. I don't think."

[Correct. The Kaylid body does not have the ability to produce those. There is not enough information about how the Elentrin produce the pheromones to know how they are targeting those pheromones.]

She shared the information, and Christopher nodded. "Then maybe we have a chance. We have nose filters coming in right now, so hopefully people will be able to talk tomorrow. But until then we don't know how well they will work. Right now everyone is freaking out. We need to get you out of here before this spreads." He waved his hand, and people started to pack everything up while more and more of the public drifted in, a mixture of reactions clear on their faces.

"This is what I'm worried about. We can't get filters to everyone who is going to show up here, and if they fall into the Elentrin's spell, we'll have a very big problem." Christopher's face showed stress, and McKenna couldn't help but agree. This could go sideways very easily.

"Our ride is here." He nodded towards a black SUV coming towards them. The shuffle of people, cars, and vehicles passed in a blur. McKenna found herself back at the hotel with a grim-faced SecDef, president, and other people, all looking like the world had ended.

"McKenna, can you explain exactly what happened?" The president asked this, his voice sounding slightly odd. She realized everyone had nose filters on. Maybe it would help. Maybe not.

"No, but I'll try." She laid out what happened, and the information Wefor had provided. The people in the room all listened intently, not interrupting until she finished.

"Well, I guess that explains Shanghai, but not Istanbul." Doug leaned back and sighed. McKenna shot him a look.

"I don't understand. Did the other shuttles come down?" McKenna asked. She felt the same confusion from Cass and Perc.

"Oh, you haven't listened to the news, have you? Sorry, we've been drowning in reports from what happened." He sighed and rubbed his head. "Let's just say you probably saved our lives. Or at least you and Harold." He looked up at Harold who still had a handkerchief to his nose.

"I never thought I'd be glad for my allergies," his voice wry. "Or refuse allergy medicine."

People half laughed at that, but it faded fast. Everyone looked at everyone else waiting for something, though McKenna had no idea what.

"Well? Now what? We have to meet them tomorrow. Wefor says we'll be immune, but anyone else is at risk. And we don't know how to immunize people as a whole or if it's even possible. What do we do to be able to keep us safe, and is someone going to tell me what happened at the other locations?"

McKenna hated the panicked tone that slipped into her voice at the end, and she took a deep breath trying to calm down.

~You don't want to know,~ Toni said softly. ~Shanghai is bad. But Istanbul, I'm not sure yet if that's bad or not.~

~That doesn't tell me anything,~ she shot back while JD laughed softly.

President Carl spoke up, pulling her from the conversation. "It doesn't matter. We can worry about other countries later, first we need to make sure ours is safe. We have news that Albert and Beatrice are fine and should be here shortly. Though they're still a bit woozy. We know this Scilita can make people want to worship her, and the only reason you were not affected -"

McKenna interrupted the president. "I was affected. Trust me, I wanted to worship her, too," Cass nodded fervently in agreement. "Wefor just managed to counteract it. Without her, we would have all been at her feet except for Harold."

Harold sneezed in response. "Which means we'd all be dead. I might be smart, but what could I have done besides either get myself killed, or watch helplessly as everyone fell to worship them? You kicked my ass and got me to at least talk to her. Mostly I wanted to run away screaming. It seemed like a really viable option."

Carl Simons shook his head, the corner of his mouth quirking softly. "Very well. We know she can affect all of us, and the only thing giving me hope is everyone assures me there is a limited number of them. That hasn't changed?"

McKenna shrugged. "I know there are lots of Kaylid. But that was the first Elentrin I've ever seen. So I'm still assuming they're rare. I'm actually more worried if they can create the pheromones as something the Kaylid could use. But about that I don't know what to tell you."

Half the room went pale at that, and she looked around. "What, that hadn't occurred to you? I know my body can't produce it, but if you can spray it like a perfume wouldn't it work the same?"

They all looked at her, and the president sighed. "I always wanted to be remembered in this history books. I wonder if I'll be alive to see what they say about me, and if it's good or bad." He shook his head. "I don't see that we have any other option than to convince them the price of coming for our people is too high. No matter what, I will not engage in the slave trade." His voice had taken on an icy tone. "And after seeing what's going on in Shanghai, it will not be allowed."

He turned and looked at Christopher. "Clear the damn park. I don't want to see anyone there but our people. Get more drones up, and see if you can get some sort of sniffers. I'd like to know if this can be detected. If so it might give us a start. Don't forget to get snipers in the trees."

"Yes, sir." Christopher's face looked like a mask to McKenna. He nodded and strode away, already his phone to his ear.

"You three are vital. Go rest and eat. You'll be there tomorrow. You're the only warning we're going to get." As the President finished speaking, Albert and Beatrice were ushered into the room. Both looking wan and somehow like they were grieving, though McKenna could not have said why she had that impression.

Both the president and SecDef transferred their attention to the two.

"How are you? Will you be able to go back tomorrow?"

Albert and Beatrice exchanged glances then sank into chairs.

"I don't believe that would be wise," Albert said slowly. Beatrice nodded her agreement as she lifted hands that trembled to pour water into a waiting glass.

"Why?" The president managed to ask it without sounding accusatory or anything else.

Beatrice replied, holding the glass of water, twisting it in her hands, focused on it rather than a person. "Even now I crave her. I understand you believe I would be fine by tomorrow. But just seeing her image makes me want to fall to my knees, to give her anything she might ask." Beatrice lifted bleak eyes to the room, and McKenna flinched back from them. "If she asked me to give her my life blood, I would open my veins for her and never blink. It's something that's going to haunt me for the rest of my life. The worst part of it all? I want it back. I want that total devotion, that love, that knowledge that my god stands in front of me."

Albert shook his head. "You will never be able to trust us again. Even now I'm not sure why I still live with her displeasure."

Everyone looked at them and the president sighed, turning to Harold. "You're promoted. You will lead and don't you dare take anything for your allergies. We can't give you nose filters as you would probably suffocate. Their blood is being tested but we can't get anything to make you immune by tomorrow." Carl darted a look at McKenna. "I assume you can't make him immune?"

[No. He is not Kaylid. The nanobots would have nothing to work with.]

"No. But I think I'm fine. Talking about her just kinda makes me queasy now. Fear and nausea at how close we came, but no desire to worship her."

"Good. Then that's tomorrow. Harold, stay. We need to talk about the backup you'll have. Get your earpieces, and if you give the word, there will be snipers that will put a bullet in her brain. She is a nuclear weapon and needs to be treated that way."

Harold paled, but came over and sat down, his handkerchief in his hand.

"Ma'ams? Sir? I'll show you to your rooms." A young man had materialized at her elbow, and she jumped. With a shake of her head, she realized she did need food, the adrenaline had faded leaving hunger in its wake.

"Sure."

The three of them were efficiently delivered to their suite. "Room service will be up shortly. I took the liberty of ordering what you have eaten before and had them increase the protein and caloric contents. Press 101 on the phone if you need anything else. Thank you." With that he disappeared, and McKenna blinked.

"Did either of you even get his name?"

"Nope." Cass sat down, her face pale. "This is insane. Why didn't we know?"

McKenna sank into another chair and lifting her hands. "I never saw them in my dreams. Did you?"

INCOMING

"No. But it never occurred to me there was anything odd or wrong about that."

That remark made McKenna think, and she remembered her host body had an odd thrill as it walked towards the ambassadors before she got pulled out of the scene.

~You should probably watch the news. You need to know what you're walking into.~ JD's voice had a weight to it that caused spikes of ice to crawl up McKenna's spine.

Perc turned and flipped on the TV. It took him a moment to find TNN, but once he did they all fell silent. The news scrolled across the screen displaying the horror of what was going on in Istanbul and Shanghai.

Chapter 32 - Breaking News

TNN Breaking News Shanghai Landing

"As everyone knows, today aliens are landing on Earth. This is a groundbreaking moment for the world. The shuttles have been spotted, and it looks like they will all be reaching their locations within a few minutes of each other. Other crews are covering the US New York landing and the Istanbul. I am Dominique Faris for TNN China. We are waiting to see the approach of the first alien ship to visit Earth. There, a silver ship is approaching." The woman talked into the camera, a microphone in her hand. Young, probably in her late twenties. Long dark hair in a braid that went down her back. Bright brown eyes in tan skin made her seem healthy and all but glowing on the screen. About two hundred yards behind her the camera caught greenery with people milling around.

The screen cut away from the female reporter talking into the camera to zoom in on a sleek silver ship gliding down. Light reflected off it as it landed in a large park, sending sparks across the field. People were everywhere on the outskirts of the clearing as the video pans across the park. Phones held high in the air as the ship comes down. They are held back by an army of police officers, creating a barrier to the park. A small contingent surrounded by police in riot gear enters the clearing. The camera zooms in on them.

"That must be the ambassadors here to meet our visitors. Though the amount of armed security is a bit concerning. I don't recognize any of those faces. Do you, Jeff?" The female reporter spoke off-screen. The camera didn't move from focusing on the scene playing out in the park.

"No, Dominique. Though I do wish they had allowed us to move closer. This distance it's hard to see facial expressions. Can our camera man zoom in any closer?" Jeff said. His voice had the typical radio voice, deep, steady, each word clearly enunciated.

"Unfortunately, no. He's using the new shoulder-attached version, and at this distant the clarity isn't as great. It moves as we do though, so if we do get to go closer there won't be any delay. But we have the boom microphone pointed towards them. If the breeze would die down, we would probably catch more of what they say." The camera flashed back to the young woman and other reporters near her, the overlap of their voices creating a hum of background noise.

"Look, the door is opening to the ship!" Excitement filled Jeff's voice, and the background noise faded as the camera focused on the ship and the slowly opening portal. A ramp formed out of the ship itself and created a long sloping walkway. Harsh intakes of breath were heard over the rustling of people as they watched the first figures come down the ramp.

A tall humanoid in the warrior form strides down. The fur on the body was pale orange with blue stripes over it. It resembled what a tiger might look like in this form but the chest seemed huge, blocking the camera's view. There was a flash of color in the middle of the arraigned guards, all in warrior form. Some dark brown, others pale tans. They all wore something like a skirt and most had a tail peeking out.

"Is there a better view to see who's in the middle there?" Jeff asks. The view flipped for a minute to show an older man, late forties, dark blond hair, in a suit sitting in the network studio. "It looks like they've created an honor guard also?"

"Yes, it seems that way. When they reach the representatives from the Chinese government, their positioning should change to allow us to see everything." Dominique's voice filled the screen as the camera flipped back to the two groups approaching each other. "Hmm, what's that scent? Are there flowers blooming around here?"

Liquid language, distorted by the breeze and distance, floated through the silent space, then the guard surrounding the one in the middle moved out. They stepped away from the person they had protected, as if trying to make sure everyone got a good view of their representative.

"Oh my. She's stunning," Dominique whispered, but the microphone pulled it into the feed.

The camera focused on the being that had been revealed with the movement of the others. Cloaked in loose pants and a tunic of pure black, vivid purple hair fell to her waist. She turned displaying gentle curves favored in the Renaissance painters, with a face that arrested with silvery white skin, eyelashes and lips the same purple as her hair. Her eyes were too far away to pick up.

"Dominique? What's happening?" Jeff asked as the reporters had all gone silent

The camera wavered a bit, but steadied on the group. Oddly it seemed to start getting closer.

"Dominique?" Jeff asked again, his voice a bit sharper.

"She needs us. Can't you see how pretty she is?" Dominique's voice seemed almost dreamy. The camera showed the delegation kneeling before the Elentrin, kissing her feet. All the Chinese security had knelt too, and around the perimeter the police keeping the people out were turning to look at the gathering of aliens. Cops were taking off their helmets and dropping their weapons. Slowly people were moving towards the gathering.

"Dominique, why is the camera so close? The picture is excellent, but I thought we couldn't get that close. Has something happened? Why are people moving in?"

"She needs us. We need to help her. We don't want her hurt." Dominique's words were sing-song, and the camera bounced around as it got closer. Now the image of the aliens was crystal clear, though at an odd angle, as if the cameraman was kneeling.

A voice that sounded like music to the ears, even through the distortions of transmitting to the news station, filled the air talking.

"Thank you. I know you want to help me. Please bring me all of your Kaylid. Those of yours that turned into animals. They can help me, protect my people. I need your help. Surely you want to help me? And I can take those who might have hurt others. I can save them." Her lilting voice pulled at them and people murmured in agreement.

"I am one of those, how may I help you my lady?" a man called out, kneeling at the outskirts. The camera shifted to look at the man. A low keening sound came from others around him.

"Rise, one of my guards will take you to the ship. Any others, please go with him." A few people rose, but the camera shifted back, letting her face fill its view. Her eyes were a pale lavender that all but glowed as she smiled, a slight twist at the corner of her mouths. "The rest of you go, find the others and bring them to me. I will take them someplace better where they can help me." She paused and smiled. "Oh, and if any children have been affected, bring them to me. I love children. Go now, find them, bring them to me."

People began to rise and move away, the camera did too. Turning to face Dominique who still knelt, a look of rapture on her face.

"Dominique, are you okay? What is all that?" His voice was tight, sharper than normal.

"She needs shifters. All shifters should come here. She needs us. We have to help her."

The feed cut replaced by Jeff sitting in the news room, his face pale, and the sounds of frantic talking in the background. "Due to issues with our crew on the ground in Shanghai, we are terminating the feed until we can figure out what's going on. In thirty minutes we should have the feed on the ground crew for Istanbul, showing the landing of the aliens there."

Jeff's voice had lost the bright enthusiasm it had held earlier. He glanced down at the paper in his

INCOMING

hands and swallowed. "This has just been received. The Chinese government has requested all shifters report to the meadow to aid the Elentrin Thelia. All parents with shifters are being told to bring their children to the Elentrin as a gift." He stumbled over that last word. "What? Who was on the Chinese delegation?"

He lifted his hand to his ear and listened for a moment, then his eyes widened. "I see. Apparently Xianang Yang was one of the delegates. He is the chairperson of the Central Military Commission and can control all media in China. Per his own memos, the leaders of the Chinese government are being invited to an outdoor buffet with the Elentrin, to meet her. Arrangements are already being made to set up a huge tent with tables and food for this party in three hours."

With wide eyes he looked past the camera at someone. "What is going on?"

TNN Breaking News Istanbul Landing

"Jeff Silver here for TNN. After what happened in Shanghai, messages have been sent to the officials in Istanbul, but no word yet if they have taken anything seriously, or if the messages were delivered in time. The meeting in the US is happening now and while information has been passed on, we don't know what caused the strange behavior, or if the right people have been reached. By the time the people in Shanghai started acting weird, the shuttle would have already landed in New York. One is approaching a square in Istanbul now." He cleared his throat and reached for a glass of water, taking a sip before continuing. "We still don't know what is behind this, or if it is all an elaborate hoax. Our crews in Istanbul are being told to stand far back to help avoid being caught up in anything."

Another clearing of the throat and a wistful glance at the water. "Now we are going live to Samuel Arons, our onsite reporter. Sam, are you there?"

"Yes, Jeff. As you can see ,we're on top of one of the hotels with the tripod set up and focused on this. It's a large area, but they have cleared out most spectators. Can you think of anything else we need to know?"

"Don't get close to them until we see what happens." Jeff's voice was dry, but it remained off screen.

"I hear that. Zoom in, here they come." The same familiar silver shape came in, lowering down to the square in a display of precision maneuvering. Interestingly, there didn't seem to be much wind displacement like a helicopter would have caused.

The ship landed and the same formation seen in Shanghai came out, but this time a head with shocking yellow could be seen, taller than those providing protection. The camera zoomed in and as they moved apart revealed a man.

"Whoa. He could model as Adonis and no one would doubt it," Sam muttered as the camera zoomed in. About six feet tall, yellow hair, canary yellow, topped a face of pure, clean, strong lines. The body, hidden under another tunic and loose pants, hinted at muscles and strength. He just screamed sexual health and power.

"Wait, what is that?" Jeff's voice hit a sharp note as the lead politicians started to smile, then drop down to their knees. "It's happening again. Sam, do not go down there."

"Okay, that is creepy as all get-out. I've interviewed one of those men, that's an Iman who is almost militant about Shari'a law. He'd never bow to anyone." Sam's voice was thin, a slight tremble in it. "What is that over there? Is that guy running towards them?"

The camera shifted and zoomed in on a man in a mullah running full speed toward them, his hands up in the air, showing he held nothing.

"What is he doing?" Jeff asked even as the man kept running.

There was a pause, then Sam replied, his voice heavy with dread. "Oh please, don't be doing what I think you're doing." The camera didn't move, focused on the man running closer and closer. The guards in warrior form lifted their weapons pointed at the man.

Liquid language poured out from the male and light erupted from their weapons. The man's head exploded in a shower of red blood that vanished before it hit the ground.

"Oh my god. They killed him-"

Before he could finish his sentence, an explosion filled the camera view, filling the screen with red, beige, and fire.

"Oh shit, it was a suicide bomber." Jeff's voice filled the overlay, making it the primary sound over people screaming. The camera didn't move, focused on the aftermath of the explosion. The beautiful Adonis crumpled to the ground with two of the five warrior forms. The three left scanned the area, then as if on a synchronized command, brought up their weapons and aimed. Bright red light exploded from their weapons, leaving a trail of bodies and odd-colored blood behind them. By the time they finished strafing across the square, only the dead and dying remained.

"Holy shit," The words came out of both Jeff and Sam at the same time while the camera wavered. The remaining guard scanned the area then did a double time trot to the shuttle which lifted in the air shortly afterward.

"Did we just see a suicide bomber kill the alien representatives?" Jeff's voice came across as hollow, as the camera played over the bodies lying in the square.

"I think we did. What in the world happens next?" Sam's voice was just as hollow, as the camera kept moving back and forth over the humans and the aliens.

"I don't know. But if someone doesn't get me some vodka I'm not going to make it through the next hour." Jeff's voice had a tightness to it that echoed everything wrong with what the camera displayed so dispassionately.

Chapter 34 - Girding Loins

All eyes are focused on New York again today. With China quickly devolving into an odd chaos. The effect these Elentrin seem to have on people is creepy. And already other ships are coming down in areas around Shanghai collecting shifters. China has locked down all external communications. The only official communication going out right now is that the Elentrin are our friends and all shifters should come to the ships to help the Elentrin. The level at which they have managed to worm their way into China, a notoriously xenophobic government, is terrifying. ~TNN Invasion Report

They watched in horror at the information coming out of the two other landing spots. Only the knock of room service pulled their attention away from the news. McKenna opened the door to let a young woman push in a cart full of food. A minute later she was gone, delicious smells filling the room.

"Shut it off. There isn't anything we can do about them now. We need to focus on tomorrow. But now we know the consequences of one path. And we'll have to wait to see what the consequences of the other will be. Maybe by morning we'll know if we should follow Istanbul's lead?"

They fell silent, the images of what occurred in Shanghai etched into their brains. Food was eaten, silent goodnights given, and McKenna rushed towards sleep, desperate to not be awake and having to think about all of this.

She stood at attention, the Elentrin pacing back and forth in front of her. Ash stood to her right, his body perfectly still, not even that shockingly white tail twitched.

"What happened? How did anyone stand against my presence? The chemical cocktail was designed specifically for this species. Per our records, we were here about five hundred reyans ago. No species would change enough to have their evolution prevent the effectiveness of our Glory, we are always worshiped. I want to know exactly who I skin for this. Not having their awe is not acceptable." Her words, though musical and almost a song, cut across all of them like a whip.

"Unknown, Siret. Your Glory did work on many of them, but one seemed immune and another seemed to fight it off." Ash spoke carefully, his voice flatter than Wefor's, almost a computer replying.

Scilita stopped. "Only one? And one fought it off? What about their presence? Those meeting us were old, weak. What else did you learn about them?" This time she spun staring directly at McKenna.

Oh shit, she's going to know I'm not whoever. What do I do?

"Siret. One was dying. The other a female no longer of breeding age. The third, the one who seemed immune had respiratory issues."

"Respiratory? That might account for it." Anger seemed to leak out of her, and McKenna felt the body fight to not kneel. "Very well. Tomorrow we shall obtain what we need. As Aliarn failed unto death, he is no longer an issue. Thelia, though." Scilita's distaste coated the other's name. "She, I will not let beat me. We will take all that city has to offer. Have troops ready to start collecting. I will have my ship filled with new Kaylid. Have the wipes ready, I will not deal with the level of dissent Thelia enjoys beating out of hers. Mine will do exactly as they are bid."

She turned spearing all of them with a glance, the red long eyelashes no longer seeming beautiful, but like the spots on a poisonous frog. Warnings of their ability to kill you.

"Is that clear?"

"Yes, Siret." All of them responded in unison.

One more glance, lingering on McKenna's host for an uncomfortable second, then she strode out of the room, her presence having nothing cute about it.

All the Kaylid in the room seemed to sag as the tension faded.

"We were not disposed of," her host said, even as the body turned to look at Ash.

Ash flicked a glance at her host, then paused, a whisker twitching. "You should go now. It isn't safe. If you are found here, it would be catastrophic."

"Ash, what are you talking about?" Her host asked, and Ash paused, tail going still.

"Nothing, old mind seeing things. Prepare your people, tomorrow will be eventful," Ash said as he walked out of the door, leaving McKenna and the host behind with a viscous swipe of his tail like a lash.

She sat bolt upright in bed, feeling like she had been kicked in the chest.

More like thrown back into my body. That was odd. I've never had that happen before.

McKenna sat there, heart pounding as she tried to figure out what she had seen and what it meant.

~Wefor, did you get any of that?~ Hoping again hope maybe this time something would have filtered down. She didn't trust herself to remember everything.

[No. More and more it is like your consciousness is not here in this body. Your vitals are constant, but there is no sense of you. Just your corporeal body.]

~Huh. Okay.~

Glancing at the clock, McKenna saw it was only a bit after eleven. With a sigh she laid back down, searching for sleep. It came, but fitfully. By the time morning woke her up again, she felt almost more exhausted than she had been.

They headed back downstairs early, and were greeted by coffee and food to her relief. The three of them set to eating even as her stomach churned with worry and stress.

McKenna managed to finish a cup of coffee before the SecDef walked in, followed by Christopher. He nodded at her, grabbing coffee and making a bagel sandwich before he headed over, dropping down next to her.

"The president has been taken to a safe place. After what we witnessed we can't take any risks. Harold should be here shortly, but we're depending on you." Doug's eyes were hard. "You may need to kill them, and right now you're the only people who might be able to. Can you do that?"

INCOMING

All the food in her stomach congealed into a hard, cold lump, and she wanted to be sick. McKenna closed her eyes, mind racing.

You killed the people in the jungle calm and cold. You are not choosing this lightly. They are the bad guys. This is how you rationalized it to yourself before. Drug lords, no big loss. Enslaving aliens, no big loss.

With a concerted effort, she inhaled deeply then back out, sending all her stress and guilt with the exhale. She opened her eyes and looked at Doug.

"Yes."

Even as he closed his eyes, McKenna felt Perc and Cass agree with her. This price would be paid to save a world, a world with their loved ones in it.

Before Doug could say anything, Harold strode in, a handkerchief in his hand. "I don't think I've ever appreciated how much I hate the outdoors until I couldn't take allergy pills."

McKenna tilted her head, a thought sparking across her. "Why didn't you know you would be allergic to the trees?"

Harold snorted. "'Cause I grew up in Arizona. College in Phoenix. Dry desert, and then the last ten years I've been in DC which really has grass and a few other trees. Heck, I've never been to Central Park before. I checked and something called a sweet pepperbush is blooming like crazy right now. Guess what I'm allergic to?"

There was a dry chuckle around the area. It died quickly, but the act of laughter helped.

Christopher strode back in, and McKenna wondered how long he'd been up or when he'd last slept.

He had circles under his eyes and a focus that spoke of too many hours without sleep.

"Everything is ready to go. SWAT is here and set up in the trees. Everyone has their nose filters. The police are clearing out Central Park and have extra filters, if needed. At this point, we probably have all of them in a ten-mile radius, and orders out with Amazon to get more to this hotel ASAP."

Doug stood. "I'm being evacuated as well as most senior personnel. Christopher has volunteered to stay. Most government officials have been advised to leave, and the chief of police, as well as the head of UN security, know what's about to go down. They've seen Shanghai. Everyone is scared, so expect people to be short and trigger happy. Do what you can."

He paused, and McKenna thought he might say something more, but he shook his head and headed out the door, security personnel converging on him as he got outside.

"We need to get going to make sure we're there well before they come down. Their shuttles are extremely fast and maneuverable." Christopher's voice had flattened out as he scanned the room. "Make up coffee and food to go, we don't know if they'll surprise us or make us wait."

Ten minutes later, a large coffee with a lid and food in her hand, McKenna found herself, Perc, and Cass in a SUV barreling through the strangely empty streets. The world seemed to be holding its breath, waiting for the next act in this strange play.

~Everything okay?~ She needed to hear Charley's voice. Talk to Toni and JD. Part of her wished they had all come with her, it would make her feel better, even as it would put them more at risk.

~Kenna,~ Charley's voice filled her mind, his joy and worry a flavor like cherries and sour lemons mixed. ~Yeah. We're good. Toni won't let us watch TV anymore, so we've been practicing escape routes.~

~Oh?~ McKenna put a wealth of meaning behind that word, even as she made sure the conversation was public.

~The news is too scary for me to watch, I'm not letting them watch it.~ Toni's voice had a darkness to it, and McKenna wondered what else she'd missed. ~They're even interrupting the kid channels, so no more. This is it then?~ The question hurt. McKenna closed her eyes as she absorbed all the meaning behind those words.

~If we don't come back, know that I love you. All of you.~

~We know.~ The chorus of voices, kids and adults filled the space. ~JD?~

~Give me a minute.~ JD's voice was distracted, short. McKenna opened her eyes to see Cass with her eyes closed, a single tear running down her face, and it dawned on her who he spoke with.

There wasn't anything else to say, with a last burst of love into the links of her family she stepped out and focused on the now. Perc reached out and took her hand, and for a minute she wanted to lean into it. But for right now they needed the commander, and she couldn't lean on anyone, not if she wanted them to survive. McKenna squeezed back, but then disengaged. Perc's eyes narrowed then he nodded. They both went back to watching the city go by.

~Wefor?~ McKenna made sure that was private, outside their shared mindspace.

[Yes.]

~Is there anything else I can do? Anything that I should know, be aware of?~

[There is nothing in the databases that seems appropriate. If anything should appear you will be told immediately.] The AI's voice had a metallic feel to it, coppery.

That was it then. ~Thank you.~ McKenna let everything go. There was nothing else to do, no planning, no worry, she just needed to do her duty. A half-smile crossed her lips. At the end of the day everything always fell back to that. Doing her duty. Well then, there really wasn't a choice for the commander.

Chapter 35 - Once Again

After what happened yesterday, Central Park has been cleared of all people within a half-mile radius. The few reporters allowed there are all wearing filters to prevent what the government is calling 'pheromone-based psychosis.' We are watching to see if maybe the US will succeed where other countries have not. If you look carefully, you will see McKenna Largo is part of the group. Does this mean something? Is she on our side or theirs? ~ TNN Reporter

The four of them stood out there and waited, watching the silver ship come down. This time Perc stood with them, all of them creating a guard around Harold. Giving up on subtlety, they had all worn kilts and tank tops. Even though the morning breeze held a nip to the air, being able to shift and not be restrained now mattered more than anything. Standing next to Harold in his suit, with a handkerchief to his nose, they probably formed an odd picture. But maybe it made sense to the Elentrin as it echoed their own presentation.

The shuttle landed, and the ramp formed, letting its occupants out. Even knowing what to expect, McKenna felt her breath catch as Scilita walked towards them, her hair flowing like a cloak of rubies around her.

~Wefor, we are safe, right?~

[Yes, all your bodies have been adjusted to not respond to her pheromones. And if new ones are detected there will be an instance response to prevent them from reaching your brain.]

~As long as I don't think too much about HOW you will do that, it sounds great,~ Cass said, and McKenna shivered. She avoided thinking about this stuff as much as possible. That way led to insanity, and she already had enough problems.

"Good luck." Christopher's voice spoke in her ear, and she almost jumped. The sound surprising her. But she didn't reply, instead she shifted all her focus to the Kaylid in front of them, and the Elentrin they protected.

The lead Kaylid, she still didn't have a name to refer to him with, glanced at them, then the clearing. A half nod and he stepped back allowing Scilita to come to the forefront.

"Are you ready to allow us to help rescue you from the animals harassing your people? We can save you and all we ask is that some that we save come with us, to help us." Her voice was sweet, almost hypnotic, and Harold sneezed, a hard, violent sneeze making her flinch. It made her seem less ethereal.

The vision from last night popped into her head, and McKenna braced herself. ~This isn't going to go well. Be ready to shift.~

"Scilita, isn't it?" Harold asked, his tone staying respectful, but he didn't bow or look awed at all. Honestly, he looked miserable.

"Yes? Are you ready to help me in our time of need?"

"I fear you are mistaken. We have no animals that we need to be rescued from. Our people are fine. How else could we help?"

If McKenna hadn't been in meetings with him, she might have believed his concern. As it was, she watched the Elentrin, trying to be ready for everything and anything.

Scilita spun to look at the lead Kaylid, her eyes narrowed to red slits of long lashes.

"Why do they not bow to my wishes? They should be crawling to my feet to serve me." The same musical language as in the visions, but she understood all of it, sharing it quickly with Cass and Perc, though Harold looked confused.

"I do not know, my Siret. All should fall before your beauty and revere you," the Kaylid replied back in the same language, but to McKenna it sounded less heartfelt and more practiced.

"Could they either be immune or have developed a tolerance?" Scilita asked, her foot tapping.

"Unknown, my Siret. The information available for deciphering reactions is limited. Without others to run tests on or tools to take readings, there is not enough information to make a hypothesis. All we know is what we see."

McKenna bit back a sigh as all this flitted through her mind and she shared.

"Fine, then kill them and start the collection. We should be able to gather over a million from this continent alone. Use standard collection techniques. I wish to be off this planet. Their deaths should prove to them we are to be worshiped, appeased." The musical language and translating the numbers into concepts McKenna could understand distracted her, until it dawned on her what they were saying.

~Change, they've been ordered to kill us.~

McKenna reached for her warrior form and felt it move into her, filling her body with strength, even as she felt a strange alertness from Wefor and the others.

"As you will, my Siret." The few seconds it took for the leader to reply and turn to them even as Scilita stepped backwards were all she needed.

"Harold down!" The words were snarled out of her mouth as she finished shifting. The Kaylid lifted his weapon, but she saw the shock on his face as he looked at them. She didn't need to turn to see that Perc and Cass had also shifted, they felt different in her head in this form.

McKenna lunged. By the time the gun came up, she'd cleared the space between her and the lead Kaylid in a fluid leap. He blocked her attack by raising the weapon across his chest. McKenna grabbed, using her momentum to rip it out of his grasp and throw it away from them. Three sharp cracks sounded and the Kaylid flinched. She smelled more than saw the blood explode from the Kaylid surrounding Scilita.

"Don't kill her," she snarled, the earpiece sill in her ear. "We might need her, and this one."

With the weapon gone, the Kaylid attacked in a whirl of speed and claws that McKenna was sure would kill her. But her body responded, blocking and preventing his lethal claws from opening her up.

~Wefor, how do I subdue him? We need to talk to them.~

[There is no information in the databases as to anything specific. The same drugs that worked on you are probable to work on him, but the biology is different.]

"Get me manacles, chains, something." She yelled even as she ducked a blow that if it had connected would have ripped off half her face.

This close his bright blue eyes gleamed in the sandy coat, but while there was a thrill of action, she swore she saw something else in there. It almost looked like relief.

"McKenna, drop!" Christopher's voice rang in her ear and she launched herself away from the Kaylid. She saw two prongs embedded in his chest and the scent of ozone filled the air. His body jerked backwards, arching up for a time-defying moment, then slumped back down on the ground.

She glanced at him, trying to see if he had really been knocked out or was just faking it. But the blood where his teeth had bitten his lip and side muzzle indicated it probably wasn't fake. The other three Kaylid were dead.

~Where is Scilita?~ She spun, looking for her. Halfway to the shuttle she found her. Laying on the ground, her bright red hair looking like a cloak of blood around her.

"She isn't dead, is she?" McKenna asked as she ran towards the female. Three soldiers in full tactical outfits stood near her. Guns pointed at her as one of them talked into his headset.

"Elentrin captured. Three aliens dead. No causalities on our side." His voice sounded in her earpiece and in her ears as she got closer.

"Tazed?" she asked, looking at the limp figure, still so impossibly beautiful.

"Yes. Seemed the safest way to not deal with drug interactions."

She looked at the dead bodies and the ship, and firmly pulled her mind away.

Those are not your problems. You know autopsies and studies need to be done. Let someone else worry about them. You need to go with the two live ones and help with information gathering.

Her mind in a whirl wanting to ask about the ship, the crowd control, but McKenna kept her mouth shut. She turned at the sound of a vehicle approaching over the grass.

Christopher slipped out as it came to a halt. "Let's get them loaded up. An ambulance is coming for the dead. These two are being taken to a secure location. We contacted JD and had him verify what he could and couldn't break out of, so we're pretty sure it will hold."

McKenna nodded absently, turning around in a circle. ~Cass, Perc, where are you? Are you okay?~ She figured she'd have felt something via her connections if they'd been hurt. Right?

~We are fine, we got Harold out of there, and distracted the other Kaylid long enough for the snipers to take them out.~ Cass had an odd tone to her voice. ~But I need a shower.~

~But you aren't hurt?~

~No,~ Perc replied. You moved so fast giving us time, and the others didn't respond as fast as yours did. So when we rushed them, they panicked and fell back. That gave people time to take them out.~ Perc sounded steadier, and McKenna relaxed.

~Where are you?~

~Other side of field. We'll go back with them. They know to have food waiting for us, and some clean clothes and a shower for me. I have brains on me.~ Cass's mental voice went up just a bit, and McKenna couldn't help but shudder in agreement.

Looking around, she saw the bodies were gone, a big flatbed truck with a crane was being driven towards the shuttle, and people were carefully not looking at her in her warrior form. Suddenly self-conscious, McKenna lifted a hand to play with the large earring there.

"McKenna. We need to go. I doubt we have much time."

With a shake of her head, she entered the vehicle Christopher stood by and buckled in. No one spoke on the drive and McKenna replayed what had happened. It had been so fast.

~Wefor, was that learned memory or you? Because I can't fight like that.~ She left the question public in the mindspace in case it helped others.

[Both. The reaction time was sped up, but the memories of the fighting are laid into your cells, literally. Then the visions. Evidence is supporting that even when you didn't remember the dream training you have been training consistently for months to raise your training levels. This information didn't appear the databases.]

McKenna didn't know how to feel about that, but getting upset when it had probably just saved her life, seemed more than a bit stupid.

~Okay. JD, Toni, anything on the news we need to know about?~

~The news no, but social media is going crazy. Apparently someone had something out there filming, drone or something. They caught the takedown of the Elentrin, and people are freaking out. Butchers, animals, villains, all things being used. There is also one of you, though, that's where the controversy is, did he start to attack first? But with the Elentrin running, people are saying we attacked without provocation.~ Toni rattled all this off with a distracted attitude, and McKenna suspected she sat there going through social media watching all of this meltdown.

~So people aren't sure if I'm a villain or a good guy? Didn't they see what's happening in Shanghai?~ She tried to keep the exasperation out of her tone, but from the laughter from Perc and JD she figured it had still slipped through.

~I don't think most people know. All they see is happy people bringing things to the Elentrin there. And even the few things that have slipped out about the children have been pulled from the net. And then there is her beauty. She already has websites worshiping her, and requests for passage to Shanghai have spiked, even with all the airports closed.~

~Wow, you're good at this.~ Perc said.

~You learn to pay attention and see problems coming working the 911 center. Usually means we can get help moving that way before people call.~

Toni proceeded to fill them in on what was going on the rest of the drive in. Bottom line, the public didn't know for sure who were the bad guys, but right now they leaned towards the government.

~After all, who doesn't want to believe in friendly aliens that are beautiful, here to solve all our problems?~ Cass's comment set the tone as the vehicle pulled into a dark parking garage.

Chapter 36 - Interrogations

The ever-treacherous politically correct speech has a new minefield. With the shifters becoming a focus, how do you refer to people who aren't shifters to differentiate? Normals? But that implies shifters are abnormal. Non-shifters sounds stupid as most people can't shift. But if there is a difference, like what is coming out more and more with this alien threat, as they are only after shifters, what do we do? Are shifters even human anymore? Is that the answer, shifters and humans? What does that infer about the survival of our species? Will future generations merge? While the aliens approaching are a concern, what are the long-term ramifications of what is being discovered about the aliens living among us? ~ TNN Social Scientist

After the confusing whirl of dealing with prisoners - because that is what they were, pinging everyone, checking to make sure they were okay, and then setting up the lines of communication, McKenna found herself in a cell looking at the unconscious Elentrin - Scilita.

"And you want me to do what again?" she asked, trusting the earpiece to pick up even as she looked at the female strapped to a bed, hooked up to various machines, and snoring softly. She looked adorable. That was the scariest thing of all. After seeing the video from Shanghai, some people were getting pictures out via unofficial methods and the reality was chilling, nothing that evil should look that harmless and adorable.

"We need you to ask her questions. We don't know yet what the ramifications of Istanbul will be. Shanghai is a train wreck and unless the UN authorizes other countries to step in, we have to respect their official isolationist stance. All of which means we need information from that creature." Doug's voice sounded exhausted, and she knew he wasn't even in the city anymore. All high-ranking officials had been sent away to secure locations and nose filters were quickly becoming mandatory among politicians.

~And a few CEOs of major corps. The news is all over it, how they've been seen wearing masks over their faces. Anyone involved in the military or infrastructure is taking this threat very seriously.~ Toni dropped that bit of information in her mind and McKenna nodded.

"Okay, I get all that. I even understand why me. But what then."

"I don't know. Depends on what we find out. But we're already seeing ships heading for Istanbul, so I suspect we'll know soon how they're going to respond to those attacks. Gods, talk about examples of the two extremes. Total capitulation and total revolt. I hope Istanbul is well-armed."

McKenna just bit her lip, arms crossed over her chest. She remained in warrior form as changing back didn't seem worth it. Besides, it might make this invader think she could be turned into an ally. Maybe.

"Okay. But you'll have to tell me what to ask."

"Understood. We've got an expert interrogator coming in to help. So do what you can." His voice cut off, and McKenna figured he'd hung up. She turned to one of the agents; she didn't even know their names anymore, they switched out so much, though they were all competent and serious.

"Any chance of food? I should recharge and all this waiting is hard on the nerves."

"Yes. We have some sandwiches coming in. Should be here in twenty."

"Thanks." She turned back to the window, the snoring proving the Elentrin hadn't woken up. ~We were lucky. That could have been much worse.~

~It still might. We don't know anything about them, and Wefor doesn't have that information. So we have no way of knowing what's the truth or a lie. And we still don't know what the consequences will be for both of the other cities. How in the world do we fight a war where we can't get to the enemy?~ JD's voice didn't hold panic, but thoughtfulness, and she knew he sat there, a spinner in his hand as he mulled over the problem.

~I have no idea, but I don't know we're the ones to figure it out. I don't know what our capabilities are. Can we shoot them down? How do we get back the people already taken? The more I think about it, the more I want to run away and hide. I don't know how to save our world.~ McKenna felt her face tighten, and she wished she could cry, it might make all this easier to deal with. The simple life of being a cop seemed like a dream now, and part of her knew she'd never get it back.

~Kenna,~ four voices filled the mindspace, and she turned to stare at the wall trying to block out the caring and worry in their voices.

~Mom?~ Charley's voice cut through everything else.

~Yeah,~ she was perversely glad a tight throat didn't carry through in the mental voice.

~You're my hero. I want to be as brave as you when I grow up.~ His simple words almost undid her, her body pulled in tight, aching with the desire to hug him.

"Here's your food." The voice pulled her out of the mindspace, and she sniffed as she turned to face the agent. The scent of meat and salsa wafted from the bag he held out to her.

"Thanks." She took the bag and headed over to a small table to eat. He gave her a funny look but didn't say anything as he went back to working on a computer.

Toni fed her more information about the situation in China. Ships hadn't landed in Istanbul yet, so all they had were people filling social media with useless information that helped no one. McKenna talked to Nam and Charley and heard all about their day, the games and drills they'd been running to make sure they could get to the safe places. In the back of her mind, all she could do was hope they never needed it.

"McKenna?" The voice in her earpiece startled her. Which made no sense as she had people talking in her head all the time. But it did, nonetheless. It was Doug, which meant her time to relax was over.

"Yes?"

"We have the interrogator nearby, and the Elentrin is waking up." His voice held an odd note to it, but McKenna just nodded, shoving the last bite of a burrito into her mouth. "We'd like you there so you're the first person she sees."

"Okay." McKenna drained the bottle of water the helpful agent had provided and walked towards the room. The agent unlocked the door, an old-fashioned lock, heavy with no electronics, and let her in. The clang of it shutting behind her and the subsequent turn of the lock caused chills to run up her spine. McKenna moved her focus back to the bed the woman lay on. It looked like a heavy-duty hospital bed and restraints were located at her ankles and wrists. It was tilted to allow her to be sitting. Leads and other things were attached, and while she knew a few vials of blood had been drawn and were being treated like level five contaminates, she didn't have anything in her. Everything else was passive recordings.

The snoring had stopped, and the woman tossed a little, a moan coming out as she tried to raise her hand, it wouldn't move from where it was fastened. Another tug, then her red lashes fluttered open, looking down at her arm. A frown creased that perfect face as Scilita focused on her arm. Confusion followed. She lifted her head slowly, eyes tracing the equipment attached to her, then to the rest of the bed, then she finally scanned the room. Eyes locked on McKenna leaning against the wall, the door inset on her right, while there was an observing mirrored window on the left wall.

McKenna didn't know who stood behind the mirror, but she knew all of this would be recorded and dissected later.

"Show time, McKenna. Perc is here with us, so if the earpiece fails, we'll have him get you the information."

She didn't respond verbally, but nodded her head slightly, knowing the people watching would see her.

"You, release me." It was said in that liquid music language, one that sounded so much like song.

McKenna didn't say anything. This much she had down. Silence tended to make people talk, and while they might have the interrogator there, she knew how to ask questions. And leaning against a wall in this form should make anyone nervous, but who knew how the Elentrin would react?

"Did you not hear me? I said release me!" The command was snapped out, but McKenna didn't move, didn't do anything except watch. Scilita's eyes narrowed, and her gaze snagged on the earring in her ear. A sneer appeared on the beautiful face, and even then it didn't distract from her beauty. "You're one of the animals. But how did you achieve warrior form without us releasing you? The Ayl Mites never fail. How did you break out of your animal?" Her questions were sharp, rapid even as she pulled her gaze away, inspecting the room.

McKenna stayed silent as she heard a voice say her name via the earpiece.

"McKenna, I'm Darryl. I'll speak in your ear, just go with the flow, you know how this works." The new voice spoke, and McKenna let it flow in and tried to make the questions sound like they came from her.

"Ah, stupid. You are just an animal and have no way of knowing what I'm saying. I'll have to lower myself to your inadequate language."

"Oh, I understand you just fine. I just don't care. How can we make you leave?" She spoke in the same liquid syllables, and Scilita's head jerked up.

"Commander matrix. You should be required to obey me." Her body stiffened, and she spoke odd words that McKenna could translate but made no sense. "Execute Priority Siret Drakyn Servitude Zero Two Five Activate."

~Umm, did my language break?~

[Those are command words to activate the AI programming. All command words have been eliminated so they have no control over you. The original programming no longer exists for their purposes.]

"Sorry, won't work. Now answer the question."

Her eyes widened, making her looking so much like an anime character McKenna hoped a video of this never got out, people would go mad over her.

"That is not possible. The Ayl Mites are perfect. There are centuries of research to make them the perfect troop creation." Her indignation made McKenna want to laugh, but she just watched her, trying to keep her face blank. "Now release me. Where are my guards?"

"How do we make you leave?" McKenna repeated the question, not moving from her position on the wall.

Scilita sneered at her again. "You can't. Your world can't make us leave until we have the troops we need. Two more planets were found with the abominations on them. We must eradicate them,

INCOMING

then claim the resources." She almost spit those last words, her body straining against the restraints.

"No. So how can we make you leave?"

The female relaxed, leaning back, smiling at her. "Soon enough we will come and take what is ours. You can not stand against the might of the Elentrin. We have several systems under our control. Maybe we will decide to take this one also."

"And you don't think we'll fight?"

"*Pfft*, they always say that, then they fall to their knees to worship us." Her eyes sharpened again. "But you aren't. You did yesterday. Why are you not worshiping me today? That is the natural order of things, the Elentrin are perfect. They should be worshiped. Lesser races always worship us. It our due, our Glory."

McKenna blinked then narrowed her eyes.

~They mentioned that when I last had a vision. The Glory. Anyone know what that is?~

No one did.

"Follow up on that, though I don't think she has the mindset to even understand a loss." Darryl's voice spoke in her ear.

"Well, we won't go with you, nor will we let you take our people. We will fight you and you will lose."

She smiled back with a languid gesture, marred by the motion being stopped by the restraints. "We always win. We are the perfect people."

"This isn't getting us anywhere. Ask her about weapons or ship capabilities," Darryl suggested.

The next hour, McKenna parroted the questions being asked in her head, but for the most part they got the same type of answers they would have gotten if they asked McKenna about nuclear weapons.

She knew they existed and used some sort of uranium or plutonium, but anything more exact, she would have just gazed at you unable to answer.

That was what Scilita did. Facial expressions and vague explanations that did them no good at all.

McKenna laughed bitterly in her mind. ~Basically she's a politician. All the power and no idea how anything works.~

"Will they pay to get you back safe?"

Scilita just blinked at McKenna, her face a mask of beautiful confusion.

"Will they go away to get you back? If we threaten to hurt you?"

"Why would you hurt me? I am Elentrin and you are not the evil Drakyn." She seemed honestly confused and couldn't comprehend the idea of them trading her.

"Why wouldn't we hurt or kill you? We've already killed one of you."

Sharp teeth a pale pink that matched her lips and hair chewed on her lip for a moment. "Truth. His guards reported he had been killed. They were eliminated for their failure, of course. So precedent has been set." She tilted her head and looked at them. "But my Glory is better than Alairn's. Therefore, you should not kill me, and let me go back to my people, so we can collect the Kaylid we need to remove the Drakyn from this universe."

Darryl sighed in her head. "Go ahead and leave the room, McKenna."

McKenna turned and left the room, waiting for the agent to open the door from the other side. She ignored the questions from the female still restrained to the bed.

The agent met her outside the room and made sure it was locked again, then led her to a conference room. A teleconference was set up, and she saw Perc next to another man, dark skin, straight black hair, and handsome.

"McKenna, I'm Darryl. You did excellent. I'm just sorry we couldn't get the information we needed."

"So now what? I don't know what else I can get, and she does speak English."

The SecDef had an odd look on his face, and he shrugged. "Go home. There isn't anything else you can do, go spend time with your family."

"What about the Kaylid we captured?" McKenna asked.

"They don't seem to produce this 'Glory' or anything else. He is just sitting quietly in a very secure location. Since he can speak English also, there isn't any more reason to keep you guys here." Doug shook his head, dark circles under his eyes. "From here on out, it's going to be the people on the ground who are going to keep us alive and decide this war. We're watching ships drop into Istanbul right now. It'll be a bloodbath there. There are more being dispatched from the ships in the air." His smile had a sad finality to it. "Go home, McKenna. Caroline is waiting for you in a SUV with a police light bar if needed. You should be able to be with your family in about four hours. We can't really offer anything else except to thank you, all of you, for your service."

McKenna glanced at the image of Perc on the screen. He nodded.

~Let's go home, McKenna. Cass is grabbing some food right now. We should be there with them.~

McKenna stood and looked at the agent. "If you can take me to the car, I'm going to head out."

With that, the calls ended, and McKenna found herself back in a nondescript parking garage, a big black SUV idling there.

"Don't they come in any other color?" she asked as she got in. Cass was already there and handed her an iced coffee, which McKenna took with a sense of relief.

Caroline smirked at her. "What color did you want? Bright pink?"

"No, thanks." She looked around. "Where's Perc?" asking the same question in her mind.

~Coming, got delayed a bit.~ Even as his words rang in the shared mindspace, the elevator doors opened to reveal him with two large duffle bags. Caroline hit a button and the rear gate popped open. Perc threw the bags in, then climbed into the back with McKenna and Cass.

They sat together, the nearness of the others acting like a calming balm.

"So where to, ladies and gent?" Caroline asked, a half smile on her face.

"Why are you with us? Don't you have people to protect?" McKenna asked. ~Shouldn't she be with people more important than us? Especially since she can shift?~

Perc shot her a look, but before he could respond, Caroline did.

"The powers that be have decided that there could be more code words or other programming that might compromise me or those I protect. Given that, they feel it's safest to have me away from any of our protectees. And since you're still relatively important, they've decided to send me with you." She shrugged and tried to smile as if the demotion didn't bug her. But McKenna recognized that level of fake when she saw it. She'd forced the same smile more than often enough.

"I guess back to where Toni, JD, and the kids are," McKenna said slowly.

"That I can do. Buckle in people, and let's not get too complacent. People are really freaking out." With those words, Caroline shifted into drive and headed out of the parking deck.

Chapter 37 - Preparing for the Storm

With people walking around armed, most businesses boarding up, and only mandatory businesses still open, streets look empty. One keeps expecting to see people running down the streets with zombies chasing them. Instead, everyone is safe in homes and buildings. All homeless shelters have opened, and everyone is off the streets, fear tainting the air. All apartment complexes have locked down and everyone is serious about knowing who is near their homes. All police are active and walking, no one wants to be in a car unable to move if they come under fire. The world is watching what is happening in Istanbul and Shanghai, and the United States seems to be holding its breath while waiting for the reaction from the incident in New York City. I am sure historians will have opinions about this for decades to come, but for now we wait and see what will happen. ~ TNN News

Caroline drove the same way she'd done everything else McKenna had seen, with quiet competence. McKenna looked out the windows, her mind locked on the signals of the Kaylid linked to her. Her family, the strangers she had rescued.

Is it running away if you're going to be with those you love? Especially when I really can't do any more here?

The question ate at her as they drove out of the city. The streets were strangely empty. Caroline had the radio on very low, just loud enough they could hear it, but their voices would easily carry over it. The news was grim, everyone talking about China, or the current state of Istanbul.

Business were boarded over as they drove out of New York. The ever-present coffee and hotdog stands gone. Even the homeless seemed to have disappeared. A few cars drove, but the city seemed to be waiting.

McKenna became aware she was holding her breath, and forced it out, inhaling and exhaling. She was the only one still in warrior form, but it felt safer than shifting back to human. She settled into the warmth between the two bodies, and they listened to the news and watched the world go by.

It felt surreal, like the travel montage in an old black and white movie. Even the smaller towns seemed subdued. Stopping for gas once got them a few looks, but Caroline paid cash and people didn't say anything. More people walked about openly armed, and everyone kept an eye on the sky.

"Reminds me of stories my granddad told me." Perc said, even in the car his voice low. As if talking in a normal tone might change or shatter something.

"What stories?" Not really having any family, the idea of family stories had always fascinated McKenna. Maybe one of the reasons she'd enjoyed that afternoon with Jeremiah so much. Listening to someone talk about the family they loved was a new experience.

"Dad grew up in California. He said his mom, my grandmother, would climb up in a tower and sit up there for hours with a laminated card that had the silhouettes of various airplanes. There was a siren attached to the tower for her to signal an alarm if any of them matched." He looked at her and flashed a smile. "She was part of the Civil Defense the president talked about. Nothing glamorous, and neither the Japanese nor Germans got in far enough to make it anything anyone needed to worry about. But after Pearl Harbor, they didn't know that."

"Huh. Cool." McKenna closed her eyes and wondered what her father or grandfather might have been like. Now it didn't matter, she guessed. Her mother hadn't listed anyone on the birth certificate, and now she had her own family. Her mind drifted, and she lay her head on Perc's shoulder. Letting go of the worry and stress, for a little while at least.

The stopping of the car woke her. McKenna sat up, relieved she was still in warrior form. Eating just didn't sound good. Maybe at some point she'd store up enough calories so she didn't need to stress about eating every time she changed. Wefor had told them the calorie requirements had decreased once the nanobots completely populated the body, but since they were so low on fat, it still stressed resources to shift.

The house they had pulled into looked familiar, but it wasn't until Perc nudged her, saying, "Ready to go in? I bet they'll be out in a minute," that everything clicked into place. The seat belt was off and he got out of her way as she bolted out of the car. His prediction proved true as the door opened, and Charley came tearing out of the house. His white blond hair shining like a halo in the sun.

"MOM!" He slammed into her, his arms tight around her waist. McKenna felt the stress bleed away as he hugged her. Jessi and Jamie were next. She looked around, missing one.

"Where's Nam?" Jessi pulled back and looked around then heaved a very adult exasperated sigh.

"I'll get her. She's being silly." The black ponytail disappeared into the house at the same time JD and Toni came out, almost causing a collision. JD engulfed the two of them in his huge arms and body until Charley protested.

~Can't breathe, dying,~ even his mental voice had mock choking sounds.

JD laughed, the rumble making her feel like the world was alright again. He stepped back to see Jessi dragging Nam out of the house.

"I told you she'd miss you. Go," she ordered, and pushed the smaller girl towards McKenna.

McKenna recognized the look on Nam's face. The same one McKenna had made many times at Christmas and other holidays. Fear of not being wanted, accepted, of knowing you were an intruder. Charley and Jamie either sensed it, or Jessi was telling them what to do the more likely option, because they both released her.

She took two steps forward and swept the tiny girl up into her arms, hugging her tightly. "I missed you. All of you." Though her words were whispered into the girl's hair, she looked at her family, her pack surrounding her, and the world felt safe once again.

The moment was ruined by Caroline clearing her throat.

McKenna turned and looked at her, Nam still tight in her arms. She didn't see any reason to let the little girl down for a while. Since Nam had her arms and legs wrapped around McKenna, it worked out.

"Yes?"

"So not to ruin a moment, but we've probably got about three hours until something happens one way or the other. I'm yours to use. So use me."

McKenna almost choked at those words. "I am not going to use you. You're not disposable. That's how the Elentrin think, and I'll be damned before I fall into that mindset. I assume you got a bag in there?"

"Sure," Caroline had a wary look on her face, like she didn't believe McKenna's words.

"Then grab it and come in, find a place to crash. And while we are on that subject, Perc, what exactly is in those duffels?" She infused her words with welcome and caring and saw Caroline's cheeks flush a darker brown.

"Apparently Burby wanted to make sure we had supplies if it came down to the worst thing. I get the feeling most gun laws fell to the wayside with his speech. As did all the complaints about people stockpiling. Those are probably the most popular neighbors in town."

As he spoke, he popped the back of the SUV and pulled out the duffels, even as Caroline reached in and grabbed a serviceable bag packed to bulging.

"Bring it in, I'm probably freaking out the neighbors and I wouldn't mind cuddling for a bit." McKenna headed inside while everyone followed.

She curled up on the couch with Nam in her arms, Charley at her side, and the twins deciding sitting at her feet was the only place they wanted to watch a movie from.

While they did that, Perc laid out what had been packed into the bags. Automatic rifles, shotguns, pistols, hand guns, and more ammo than she knew what to do with. Being a cop, McKenna wasn't a stranger to weapons, but this amount had her overwhelmed. She couldn't identify half of what was on the table, much less have any confidence in how to load them, deal with them if they jammed, or even what ammo went with which weapon.

"I have no idea how to use more than half of that. And would probably hurt people if I tried," she admitted, her arms tightening on Nam enough the little girl whimpered softly.

~Sorry,~ she soothed and relaxed her arms.

JD and Caroline laughed. "No worries. Why don't you point out what each of you is comfortable with and I'll use the rest?" Caroline said, but then cast a speculative look at JD. "You know most of them."

"Yeah. I can use them. Not an issue."

"I can use a rifle, that's about it," Perc admitted. "Anything else has to be handed to me and explained. That was the entire point of the range trip. I have faith in my ability to aim and fire. Not much else. If you want me to know what to load it with, there are going to be issues."

Caroline shrugged. "That we can deal with. Worst case, all of us can shift and fight that way."

"They're going to be better than we are," JD warned.

"True. But they aren't fighting for their homes. For their families. That will always give us an advantage." Caroline's words had the ring of truth, and McKenna shivered and wrapped one arm around Charley, pulling him closer to her. He didn't protest.

Perc took Caroline upstairs, Cass's room had two beds so she could bunk there, though McKenna wondered if Cass would just move in with JD. Nam snuggled into her, and McKenna did her best to convince the girl that she was wanted, but she remembered those fears so well and knew only time would solve them.

Toni gave McKenna a smile, surrounded as she was by children, flipped on a movie for them and headed into the kitchen with Cass.

The simple joy of the Disney movie about family hit the spot with all of them, and though she stayed in warrior form ,McKenna felt more at ease than she had since that Sunday they were all kidnapped. Even with the aliens coming, people believed her, they'd done what they could, her family was here, they had plans and ways to protect themselves, and no matter what happened, they were here together.

She drowsed on the couch, Nam in her arms, Charley against her side, and Jessi and Jamie at her feet, both of them curled up, drawing as much comfort from her as she drew from them. Perc sat reading a book while she could hear JD and Caroline rearranging stuff upstairs.

Her mind drifted to Cass and JD, wondering when they would make it official, but he seemed happier and more at ease than she had seen him in a long time.

I guess he found his princess to rescue, and he likes that she doesn't need rescuing.

The thought made her happy, and she just dozed while the kids watched the movie. McKenna roused to full wakefulness at a sharp gasp from the kitchen and the breaking of something ceramic. Toni and Cass came out of the kitchen, their faces pale and something in their eyes that made her arms tighten around Nam.

"It's started." Toni's voice had no inflections as she walked out of the kitchen and headed to the TV. All attention turned to the TV as she set it to the TNN channel.

Chapter 38 - Special Report

"Please tune into our special coverage of what is going on in Istanbul currently. ~TNN Breaking News Istanbul

The camera shows dozens if not hundreds of figures plummeting to earth, a silvery wing deploying at the last moment slowing their descent. A pan up of the camera shows larger ships crisscrossing the area, dropping the figures. The camera pans back down to the city, and the city snaps into sharp focus.

"As you can see, invaders are being dropped across the city, and at least one of those larger ships has landed in a more secluded area, though we don't have any crews near there to verify what their purpose is. We are up here on the same hotel roof we were during the aborted negotiations."

Across the bottom of the screen scrolls the words 'Samuel Arons for TNN in Istanbul, live report'.

Sounds of screams and gunshots fill the area behind them. "One odd thing is that the local radio channels have been hijacked, and a voice, in what I have been assured is archaic Arabic, is repeating the same message over and over again. You should see a transcript of the message at the bottom of your screen."

INCOMING

As he speaks the words, the following is displayed across the bottom of the screen. "All Kaylid, if you wish to be rescued, come out in your warrior form, arms in the air and you will be collected. At this point all residents of this city are considered the enemy and will be eliminated."

The sound of guns and screaming filled the air behind the reporter, and he ducked as a red bolt splashed at the corner of the wall he stood at.

"Dang it. They've found us." Samuel continued to talk, crouched down, though the camera angle had changed to match his. "We have been authorized by TNN and the government of Istanbul to fight back." Behind him a man with a brown scarf wrapped around his head crawled to the edge of the wall and lifted a rifle over it, aiming down. Several sharp reports, and he looks back and nods. "Luckily it seems like their long-range weapons aren't as good as ours." The smile that crossed his face would have done any wolf proud.

The camera moved back over and took a look over the edge of the retaining wall. The sand-colored buildings with their vivid roofs had smoke drifting up between them. Bodies lay in the street, some with, some without, fur. As the camera pans, there is the movement of three invaders walking down the street. Their bulky guns and absolute lack of any color or personality on their garments giving away their origin. A woman darts across the street, her robes covering her from head to toe. One of them lifts its weapon and fires. A smooth, fast motion, the beam of red light impacts her and with a half cry she crumples to the ground. It doesn't take a doctor to know she's dead. The amount of blood staining the ground around her guarantees it.

"Those bastards." Samuel's voice is low and fierce. "Abram, can you take them out?"

The scarf-wrapped man moves back into the camera view, but this time he takes a minute to aim. Two sharp retorts, and the camera catches two invaders collapsing. A red beam bursts across the screen and Abram yelps pulling backward. An image of his rifle, the barrel deformed and melted, is shown as he pulls back.

"Jeff, we need to leave now. We need more weapons and ammo, and we don't have any here. I'll let you know when we are ready to be on the air again."

"Be careful, Sam. You're the only person we have on the ground there." Jeff's voice had worry in it as the feed ended.

The TV cut to a PSA explaining how to find your Civil Defense officials and urging all citizens to act responsibly.

The living room rang with silence as what they had watched settled into them. McKenna had to consciously loosen her grip on Nam. But she didn't let her go.

"I guess that answers that question," JD said quietly.

A general assortment of nods, but no one said anything. They sat there watching the news. A few drones had been dropped into Shanghai, and the Elentrin and their troops—it felt wrong to call them Kaylid—didn't seem to notice or they didn't care. The drones were getting pictures out of about ten different Elentrin in different parts of China, radiating out from Shanghai. At this point, most people were either hiding or were willingly going with the invaders. China's regime working against it as more and more people fell under the spell of the Elentrin.

If there had been some place to run to, McKenna would have put everyone in the car and fled. But there wasn't. Her own home would feel safer, but it didn't matter.

"So will we have any warning when they come?" Her voice low as the kids watched the news with wide eyes.

"The current plan is to sound sirens when they see the Elentrin start deploying. We figure New York, DC, LA, San Fran, Seattle, and maybe Denver will be targets, but we could be wrong." Caroline's voice had the same grave tone as McKenna's. "Most cities have an alarm system, either tornado, air raid, or tidal wave. In addition, the Emergency Broadcast System will be used to let people know where they're landing. As long as your TV or radio is on, you should be notified."

Cass and JD glanced at each other and rose. "I think we're going to bed. Night, people." They linked hands and headed up the stairs.

McKenna glanced at the clock, four in the afternoon. She couldn't even find the energy to tease them.

Good for them, I hope they enjoy.

"How about homemade pizza and ice cream for dinner?" Toni offered, her voice a bit shaky.

The kids just nodded, their faces pale.

"They're going to come after us, aren't they?" Jessi asked, refusing to look away from the scenes on the TV. Someplace in Istanbul now. McKenna wanted to shut it off, to protect her, to protect all of them from the stark reality laid out on the screen. But their lives were on the line too, keeping them ignorant put them in danger—as their little home alone adventure had proved.

"Yes," Toni answered for her, and McKenna looked up to see her blinking back tears.

Jessi swallowed. "Then I guess we better eat so we can turn quickly and run fast. Come on." She rose up and stalked to the kitchen heading to the fridge. Charley and Jamie followed her. McKenna could see them start to pull out supplies to make pizza with. Nam squirmed in her arms.

"You want to go help?"

"Yes, please."

"Go." McKenna released her, though her arms and heart ached as Nam left.

"Night is falling. And if they're busy with the other two locations, they may not hit us until later. We should sleep now. Christopher has promised he'll call me if anything changes or if they know anything. Sleep while you can, you might not be able to later."

Caroline's words hit like lead bricks. Cass and JD were together, she and Perc were still a maybe someday. For now she needed her family around her. McKenna looked up at Toni. "Sleep as animals tonight, all of us in a nest?"

She must have said it in her mind, too, because she heard JD and Cass respond. ~Yes, we'd like that.~ Toni and the kids all nodded with a fervor.

"I have to say I wouldn't mind," Perc said slowly.

McKenna looked at Caroline. "I know this might sound odd, but generally we don't dream in animal form, and there's a layer of comfort in being cuddled

INCOMING

together. Wefor said it helps the animal self and the nanobots." She shrugged. "You are welcome. Believe it or not, it's comforting after the first oddness."

Caroline looked at them and replied slowly. "It does sound odd." She glanced out the window, a pensive look on her face. "But not being alone and not dreaming sounds very good." Her short curly black hair created an odd shadow above her face, a reverse halo. "I'll try it. Worse case, it sucks, and I go back to my bed."

That seemed to have settled the matter. With the general mood quiet and serious, they ate, then created a huge nest in the living room. Weapons on the table in easy reach and phones near them. If they went off, people would hear them.

Caroline shifted in the bathroom, the rest just stripped and flowed into their animals, not caring. The pile of furred bodies curled around each other. Cass curled up with JD around her. Toni with her kids snuggled up next to her. McKenna lay with her back to Toni, touching, but not pressing, Nam and Charley curled up in the curve of her body. Perc framed her, his big cat body somehow fitting to surround the kids in a cocoon of fur. The cheetah that was Caroline paced out and finally decided on the base of Toni and McKenna, her golden fur and black spotted coat an odd counterpoint to the beige cougar and black jaguar.

McKenna inhaled, and the familiar smells of fur, sweat, cat, bear, wolf, flooded her senses and it felt like home. Peace settled into her, and she closed her eyes, letting herself purr. The gentle rumble acted like a lullaby, and after a few minutes everyone settled in, and she could feel them drop off to sleep as she fell herself.

Chapter 39 - Landfall

All medical personnel, city and county employees, firefighters, police, and utility company employees are being asked to report to work immediately. This is a call for all these employees to report to work. All other business are officially closed. Please stay home, arm yourselves, and watch the skies. Elentrin troops have started landing. At this point the orders are shoot to kill for all city or county employees. Residents are asked to stay home and protect themselves, but to not leave their homes. All shifters are asked to not take on their warrior forms unless absolutely necessary. National Guard troops are being deployed and the less confusion concerning citizens as opposed to invaders the better. ~ KWAK Alert

The shrill warning tone from six phones pealed out all at the same time, plus a shrill ringing from another one had everyone sitting straight up, looking around. Caroline flowed into human and dove for her phone. The one ringing.

"Yes?" Her voice sharp with tension. She stood there for a minute, unmoving, a statue even as McKenna watched, unable to look away.

"I understand. You, too." She lowered the phone, a faint disconnect tone coming from it as she turned and looked at them. "It's started. They're coming." The faint light slipping in through the blinds highlighted the tear tracks on her face.

Caroline turned and headed to the bathroom. McKenna and the rest stayed frozen for a moment. Then McKenna rose.

~Kids, stay in your animal forms. It's safer. Everyone else, make sure your earrings are on, get dressed in what you'll feel comfortable as warrior in, bright colors suggested. We're going to war.~

Toni shifted to warrior form, flipping on the news as she headed to her room. They could hear it from every room, their hearing good enough for that. The news made McKenna's stomach curl into a tight ball, eating would be something to do later. Right now even coffee didn't sound good. She pulled on her kilt, one of the best purchases she'd made in a while. Loaded up the pockets with stuff she'd need, then pulled on the brightest tank top she owned. A vivid turquoise blue that pushed towards neon.

If that doesn't say Earthling, nothing will.

Her earring caught the light reflecting it and she headed down to the weapons. Putting her standard issue 9 mm in an inner holster, she filled more pockets on the kilt with extra ammo for it, and one of the AR-15s.

~So what are we doing?~ It was JD asking, though he did it in the shared mindspace.

McKenna looked at the TV as she responded. ~We're going to protect our family and our world.~ The announcer was listing out the cities that could expect incoming invaders. All citizens were advised to be ready to defend themselves.

INCOMING

Hearing those words being spoken out loud, "All citizens are advised to take cover and shoot to kill. Distance is your best option," McKenna closed her eyes, inhaled through her nose, centering and facing what was about to come.

~Are we all good with this? The kids are going to stay here and hide. Not having any adults here will make this a safe place and the Elentrin troops should have no reason to come here. We are going to make sure this area stays safe. Charley, Nam, Jess, Jamie, you know where to go. You will stay safe and not come out until we come back. If we all die, you know who to find.~ They'd gone over and over, and the kids had the numbers of all the people they could trust. If everyone was dead, well, then there wouldn't be anything they could do.

All of them had shifted to warrior but Caroline, she admitted she felt more comfortable in human form, and knew her aim was better.

Toni stood there in warrior form, a kilt, vivid yellow tank top, and a handgun on each hip, with a .30-06 Savage in her hands. Even through the warrior facial structure McKenna could read her expression.

"You aren't coming."

"I can't. I can't leave my kids, not again." The words slashed like a knife through McKenna's heart, and she hesitated. All the worries and doubts rushed back in full strength, and she started to move towards Toni.

[The more adults that are present near the kids the greater the likelihood of the Elentrin finding them and you.] Wefor's voice sounded flat as usual. [They have already proved they are resourceful and strong. They would be safer alone.]

"I CAN'T!" The words came out of Toni in a roar, and McKenna found herself stepping away from the Jaguar Warrior Goddess standing in front of her. "I cannot leave them again, and I'll die to protect them before I let anyone hurt them."

The images of the figures falling from the sky, the casual way they killed people running from them, and the tight arms of Nam around her neck; all the images and emotions clashed in McKenna's head. But something told her she needed to be out there. Maybe the damn command module, maybe arrogance or hubris. But staying here felt wrong in a way she didn't know how to explain.

"Will you watch my children, too? Protect them, too?" Her voice broke though she tried to keep it steady.

Toni closed her eyes, then reopened them, the green all but glowing in the dark of the living room. "With my life, always."

The kids, all still in animal form twined around Toni's legs, a low whine emerging from their throats. McKenna moved, pulling Toni into a tight hug. "Thank you, for everything." Her whispered word containing everything she didn't know how to express.

Toni hugged back, claws digging in through McKenna's fur, but it didn't matter. They released each other, and McKenna crouched, petting each head and sending all the love she could down the mental links. With a force of will she stood and turned to the others, waiting for her. Of all of them only Caroline's all too human face betrayed the emotions they all felt, stress, fear, doubt, and a grim knowledge they couldn't hide and let others die for them.

"Let's go." McKenna said the words with a flat tone, channeling the AI as they headed out the door. The late summer morning had a strange calm beauty to it. Blue skies, mid-seventies, a light breeze, and beings falling from the sky. It felt like a surreal experiment.

McKenna made sure a round was in the chamber and looked towards the sky, calculating where the landing invaders were headed. She stood, letting what she saw filter into her brain.

~Wefor, can you tell where they're going?~
[Calculating.]

All of them stood there watching. The quiet bedroom community they had placed McKenna and the others in didn't have a large Kaylid presence. But McKenna hadn't paid much attention to the demographics of the area, plus with other people driving her around she felt a bit disoriented.

[It appears they are headed to Georgetown.]

McKenna had purposefully drawn Caroline into the shared mindspace, and she winced at Wefor but nodded.

"That makes sense actually. There's the Naval Observatory nearby. The area has lots of room for staging troops and equipment. Plus, I think a few pro-shifter rallies have been held near there."

"So? Do we head there? I can feel something itching at the back of my mind. Something big is going to happen and we, I, need to be there, but I don't know what it is or if it's me with my ego getting too big."

McKenna tried not to flinch at the looks everyone gave her, but the feeling coming through the links was considering, not anything more violent.

"It's near the capitol, and it wouldn't take much research to figure out that's our seat of government. Granted, most have been evacuated, but I would say yes. If they're going to do anything dramatic that would be a good stage. Not to mention the picturesque aspects," Caroline said thoughtfully.

"Go there? I don't see anyone here."

"Do you have a way to sense how many Kaylid are in the vicinity?" Caroline asked suddenly, turning quickly to look at McKenna.

"No," McKenna responded. "Wait, do I?"

[No. While other commanders may have equipment able to detect Aly Mite concentrations, that is not something possible just from standing here.]

"Then definitely let's head to the Mall. That will draw more there, help draw them away from here, and it would be a logical place for any leaders to focus on," Caroline said, an air of authority in her voice.

It felt right to McKenna. Heading to the car, she slipped in, followed by the others, while Caroline took the driver's side. As Caroline backed out of the driveway, McKenna saw faces peeking out of the window. She flooded the mindspace with love and heard Perc and Cass make an odd noise as Caroline slammed on the breaks. Her hands white around the wheel.

"What the hell was that?" Caroline gasped out, her voice shaky.

"What?" McKenna asked, confused.

"What you just did," Cass said, her voice just as shaky. "It felt like the best sex, orgasm, hug, buzz, and the sun on your skin all at the same time. What did you do?"

Caroline had her eyes closed and breathed deeply in and out.

McKenna looked at all of them, Perc had his fur-covered hands clenched, and she ripped her eyes away from the obvious evidence he'd been affected, too. "Umm, I just sent love to the kids and Toni. I wanted them to know how they felt. I put everything I felt into it."

Caroline shook her head and started to drive again, though her pulse still pounded in the side of her neck.

"I've felt waves of emotion before from you," JD said, his voice quiet. He sat in the third row of seats so she couldn't see him easily. "But this, this was that cranked to eleven. I'm not saying I didn't enjoy it, but next time, keep in mind what we're doing?"

"Got it." McKenna cleared her throat and locked her worries away. For now she needed to concentrate on what they were about to head into. The radio relayed information non-stop about where the invaders were coming down. From the sound of it, the military had removed the security from this information because everyone could see them incoming at the various radio stations. But they still could only give general areas. Not specifics.

Caroline focused on driving, but the rest of them kept the windows down and paid attention to the skies. The wind bugged her ears for a bit, but then McKenna realized how much she could tell from having the windows down and she learned to ignore it.

They could still see people dropping, but the pattern didn't make sense to McKenna. She started to talk out loud, more to help herself concentrate than anything else, though she made sure the words also ended up in the mindspace. Toni or the kids might have some insight.

"All the sequences or dreams we were in, they always worked in squads going through cities in a coordinated manner. Why does this seem more scattered and less organized? Shouldn't there be coordinating shuttles or something?"

Silence in the back for a minute.

"You know, I think you're right. So why would they be dropping randomly?" Perc said slowly, staring up at the sky.

"Caroline, is there an overlook or someplace we can get out and maybe get a view of this? I know the military can't take the time to look, but I have a thought," JD asked from the back, a thoughtful tone to his voice.

"Overlook, no. Not in this area. But there are a couple parking garages that are pretty tall. Want me to try that?"

"Please?"

McKenna didn't ask for details, just watched and tried to put the pieces together. "Caroline, do you have a way to tap into where shuttles are coming down?"

"Not from here, no. If I was in the office or had access to a real computer, maybe. But I can't get to those websites from my phone."

They reached the top of a tall parking deck on the outskirts of DC. Everyone piled out of the car and looked at JD who stood looking around, his bearlike face narrowed in concentration.

~Wefor, is there a way for me to make the nanobots increase my distance vision? Make it better to see the details?~

[Yes. You have enough commander module nanobots at this point. Order them to alter your vision to make it more accurate for distance.]

JD's eyes closed, his brow furrowed, then he opened his eyes and looked around. "Huh, it worked. 'Kay, give me a minute."

McKenna looked around, her heart seizing with each figure she saw coming down, then the various ships slowly dropping to earth. In the distance she could hear gunfire, but the world, at least here, seemed to be hiding.

Do I want to know what people are doing? What would I be doing if I wasn't here? Well, I'd be at work. Maybe that would be easier, someone else telling me what to do?

Her thoughts went multiple ways, but she still looked and watched.

"I think I have it," JD said, startling her out of her spiraling thoughts. She turned to look at him as the rest of them did. "They're landing shuttles in the middle of troop disbursement. I think they're either herding people in, or bringing captured Kaylid to the shuttle. We know they don't take prisoners, so I think they're collecting them, dumping them in the shuttles then going back for more. They aren't tied to the shuttles, they just dump their loads there and keep going."

They all turned and looked at the shuttles and the placement of people.

"I think he's right," said Caroline, her eyes sharp.

"So we should focus on the shuttles and free anyone they get. We can't get all the ones roaming about, but this way we can prevent anyone from being taken," McKenna said slowly as she worked out the logistics. The unspoken words of 'even if we can't stop them from killing' hung in the air.

Without anything else needing to be discussed, they got back in the car and headed towards where it looked like a shuttle had landed.

Chapter 40 - Walk the Path

Fighting has already started in New York City as five shuttles have landed in Central Park. Reports say a large number of the Kaylid aliens emerged, but one of the Elentrin was spotted as well. While there is speculation they may be looking for the ones captured earlier, most people are hunkered down. The NYPD has come out and said while they will not fire first, any alien seen with weapons will be treated as dangerous. Though the concern about the strange behavior around the Elentrin is concerning. There are some websites asking how anyone that beautiful could be so evil. As the situation changes, we will keep you updated. ~ TNN News

Caroline drove to about where they thought they had seen the shuttle. It was a mixed residential-commercial area and the quietness of the streets and city overall creeped McKenna out. But the emergency broadcast telling everyone to stay home and hide, to let people who knew how to fight deal with it, was still blaring from every station. The SUV slowed to a stop, and Caroline parked it.

"From here we probably need to move on foot." Her voice had dropped to a whisper and McKenna responded mentally.

~Agreed. Move out and listen, maybe we can make a difference.~ That mattered to her, and she checked the connects for Toni and the kids again. But they were still there, quiet and safe. If anything happened to them, she would know. Even as they got out she listened, expecting to hear more noise. How could a city so large be so quiet? She knew this city hadn't been evacuated, but it was like it held its breath, waiting.

Walking down the area she could hear some distant sounds; guns firing, vehicles revving, even what sounded like trashcans being knocked over. But nothing immediately near them.

~Wefor, can you sense or help us find the shuttle?~

The voice in her head didn't answer immediately as they kept moving forward. Just as she started to panic, thinking something might be wrong or that Wefor had been deactivated, the AI responded. [Not at this time. Possibility after the first one is found, future ones can be identified.]

She'd take that as a positive.

~Stop!~ Caroline's voice lashed out, louder and stronger that she needed to be in the mental space. McKenna froze, catching the others out of the corner of her eye doing the same thing even as she winced.

~There, the shuttle, and a Kaylid coming this way, carrying two people.~ Caroline pointed into a grove of trees and McKenna realized it was the edge of a park. Sure enough, a Kaylid, though she hated to think of the enemy by the name they'd taken as their own. But for now there wasn't much else they could do. This Kaylid had dark brown fur the color of a mink, but with white stripes breaking it up. It almost looked like a reverse zebra. It walked, a trolley floating behind it with two people laying on it.

McKenna assumed they had been knocked out as there were no obvious restraints and they lay there limp.

Rage flooded through her at the sight as well as the knowledge they had probably killed other people to capture these two. She started to move into the trees. ~Do we see anyone else?~

~No. What are you going to do?~ Cass had a tremble to her voice. For all her calm reactions in Colombia, McKenna knew she would have almost preferred to be home with Toni. Protecting yourself was easier than attacking.

~The only thing I can. Kill that Kaylid. We have no place to store them, and I won't allow any others to be killed because of my inaction.~ Her mental voice had lost all inflection, and she didn't know how to feel about that, but pushed the worry away.

Caroline had already followed her. ~I'll head over this way. Our best bet would be to take control of the shuttle but be careful about going into it. Many of our vehicles can be controlled via remote. I'd be surprised if theirs couldn't.~

~Agreed,~ McKenna responded, raising the M-16 to her shoulder. The Kaylid was clearly visible as it approached the ship. No one came out to meet it, which only reinforced the idea of remote ships. She waited another minute, watching the being. It walked with no fear or worry visible. Not arrogance, it just apparently didn't occur to it to be worried.

McKenna didn't allow herself to think, she pushed away all her training, all the warnings she was supposed to call out, sited in on the ear, and pulled the trigger.

The retort of the rifle sounded so loud against the silence it hurt her soul. The head of the Kaylid rocked to the side, and a spray of blood came out the other side as the figure crumpled to the ground.

~What the-~ The comment from JD broke off, and she ignored it, moving forward, still with the M-16 at her shoulder looking around. Listening with ears that rang slightly from the retort, but already the ringing was diminishing.

~Anyone see anything else?~

~No.~ Caroline's calm comment helped steady McKenna's pounding hear. She checked behind her to see where they were.

~Wefor, can we set that grid back up so I can see people and where they are in relation to me?~

[Working.]

A minute later a mental map appeared in her mind, showing the others. Nothing fancy but more of a knowing that ten feet behind her stood Cass. While twelve feet to her right Caroline walked.

~Cass, you have all the medical training, right?~

~In the dreams, I still don't know how much is going to transfer. I haven't actually pushed to see if it translates to treating humans.~

~Well, now's your chance. Please take a look at the two on the trolley.~

~Okay.~

McKenna could hear the trepidation in her mental voice, but part of her had shut off. The part that had time to worry about people's feelings. All she could do was focus on what they were faced with right now. Everything else would have to wait until later.

She kept walking, feeling JD on the other side as Perc watched over Cass. It made sense. JD and Caroline at least had experience with weapons, real world experience, while the other two only had the vision aspects. Right now she'd rather lean on JD, knowing how he would react.

~Movement,~ Caroline snapped out. McKenna spun towards where she sensed Caroline stood. She had dropped to a crouch, just barely in the clearing, pointing her gun towards a break in the trees. Over the top of her head McKenna saw another Kaylid walking in, this time with a body draped over its shoulder.

Thought didn't exist, only orders and an odd need to make sure no humans were taken from Earth if she could stop it. She aimed, making sure the human wouldn't be hit, and pulled the trigger. Once again the head rocked back and the Kaylid slumped to the ground, the human on its shoulder tumbling off.

~Perc, please collect that person. We need to find someplace safe to take them.~

She turned, scanning again. Part of her wondering where this competent unemotional person had come from, and part of her relieved that she was acting, and they were doing something.

~Yes,~ his mental voice stuttered a bit as he replied and she shot a glance over to him and Cass.

~You two going to be okay?~

The two Kaylid, her two friends, paused for a minute and turned to look at her, their eyes dilated wide, tension in their entire bodies.

Perc, his huge warrior form stood there like a monster from a Greek tale, with Cass crouched at his feet. She wished she had a camera to capture the image, but then it changed as Cass straightened.

~We'll have to be. They're fine, unconscious. Looks like an electrical method rather than chemical. Probably the same thing Charley told us about. First immobile, now a coma-like state. But I can't see anything wrong.~ Her voice distant, almost clinical, and McKenna relaxed. Perc moved towards the other body at the edge of the trees.

~Later,~ Caroline ordered as she moved to the edge of the shuttle and looked in. ~We're making news and will get attention soon. There are three people in here already.~

~I have movement coming this way, under a minute,~ JD added to the conversation, his voice a flat no-nonsense tone she'd only heard in really bad situations.

~Where do we take them? We can't leave them in the shuttle and out in the open, unconscious they're both vulnerable and a target,~ McKenna asked. She moved to focus on the direction JD faced.

~Give me a minute,~ Caroline said. McKenna glanced back to see her crouched next to the shuttle, typing furiously on her phone.

~Out of time,~ JD whispered in their minds as he drew up his M-16, aimed towards the trees.

Moving through them at a run were three figures, all fur-covered with bulky guns that looked like toys more than anything else. Her eyes checked automatically for earrings or colored clothing, there was nothing. Before she could get her weapons to zero in, JD fired. The sharp bark echoed through the clearing.

~Missed. Trying again.~ Another crack and she felt his joy as he hit. It took six more shots as they were now moving and diving behind trees as they advanced. Even so, for a weapon they didn't really ever use, it was good for shooting at this distance and while the targets were moving.

~Wefor, why are we being this accurate? I'd have thought we'd take a while, like we did at the range,~ she asked, though part of her didn't care.

[Enhanced hand-eye coordination, familiarity with the weapons, and the shared nanobots are being leveraged to create a triangulation system to increase accuracy.]

Wefor rattled off the information and it made sense as JD rose to inspect the bodies. ~They all the have same clunky weapons. But I can hear more coming.~ He moved his head one way then the other as if listening to things she couldn't hear.

~I've got a place for us, but we need to move. It's about three miles away. We need to get to the SUV and then get away from here,~ Caroline said, and that kicked all of them into gear.

JD ran back into the shuttle and grabbed two of the people in there. Perc came back with the other one and grabbed the remaining person in the shuttle. Cass had already turned and started guiding the trolley back the way they had come. Luckily it seemed to be dumb technology and floated with her as she pulled it. Even as they headed away from the shuttle, she could hear a weird howling sound.

[Warning cry, it carries for a long way,] Wefor provided as they moved. They broke into the street where they had left the car, and Perc cursed as he dove back into the cover of the trees. At least ten invading Kaylid walked towards them, weapons at the ready, two trolleys with six people collapsed on them, two in Kaylid warrior form.

~This is not good. We need to get out of here,~ Caroline called out. ~I've sent the address to all your phones. But we can't move fast enough carrying people. ~

~We aren't leaving anyone behind to get taken as slaves. Where are you having us go?~

~Military recruitment center. It has a skeleton staff right now, they're expecting us. It's all the help we can get. They're serving as a safe house.~ Caroline said dropping to the ground.

McKenna followed her example as Perc put his two down before hiding behind a tree. JD had laid his on the ground and had his gun up for a shot.

~Wait, hear that?~ Perc asked, his head tilting to the sound, back from where they killed the others and found the shuttle. McKenna turned her focus towards listening and felt her heart seize. A large number of beings were moving through the trees, and somehow she knew they were all Kaylid, and not those from Earth.

~We're about to be surrounded. We need to get out of here quick. ~ Even as the words were thought, the Kaylid coming down the street saw them. In that weird fluid movement she associated with hours and hours of training, their guns were up and firing at them. Red splashes of light that seared the trees and plants around them, creating an acrid smoke that burned her nose.

"Shit!" Perc called out as he covered one of the victims. McKenna glanced at him, then focused on the ones in front of them.

~JD, take the ones behind. Caroline, take the ones in front. Cass, Perc, see if you can keep those people protected. Shoot if you can, if not, just stay down.~ The orders came out rapid fire. She took a deep breath then focused on the ones shooting at them. This time she concentrated, but with incoming fire she had to duck more than once just as she pulled the trigger.

A scream at her left pulled her attention away, and she glanced over as the smell of burning hair and seared meat filled her nose.

Chapter 41 - Pay the Price

Current reports have placed the number of shifters taken by the aliens in and around Shanghai at over three thousand. With their spreading efforts and the government under the sway of the Elentrin influence, the real numbers may never be known. The only good aspect that can be seen is their death toll is almost nonexistent. The cultural reinforcement of what the leaders are saying about helping the invaders is troubling. While this might make an excellent historical study in retrospect, right now it is terrifying watching a nation being brought to its knees. The Elentrin is being escorted around by the leading officials of China and they all seem entranced by the woman. ~ TNN Report

Even as she watched, the light faded from Caroline's eyes as the hole in her chest steamed with fatty smoke. Her body folded in on herself and hit the ground with a dull thump. Her throat locked up and she couldn't breathe, unable to look away from the person she'd known, she'd liked. The light in her mind, the one that had been Caroline's, faded to nothing.

[Commander, you have to pay attention or you will be killed too, and then everything is lost.]

INCOMING

Wefor's voice snapped her out of the fixation on Caroline's body lying on the ground.

Her AR snapped up, and she pulled the trigger, adjusting as her first shot missed. The second took a Kaylid firing at them in the shoulder. It stumbled back but reoriented on her. Another pull of the trigger and it dropped, but as she moved to the next one she could see others coming in the distance. They were sending so many. Why were they all headed here?

Another burst of panic in the mindscape let her know Cass was trying to protect the unconscious humans from the blasts. A grunt of pain from Perc caused her to glance that way and she saw him firing back at the ones coming up behind them.

We aren't going to make it out of here. All this and we're going to die.

She didn't let her thoughts into the mindscape, as she kept shooting, her shots getting better and better, but there were more Kaylid coming. Their flashing light missing them barely and only because she'd hit the ground. The heat of one of the blasts seared across her skin, leaving burnt fur and blistered skin underneath.

~We can't hold, they're going to overrun us.~ JD's voice was grim, but only to her, a tight channel of worry. ~McKenna, you have to go. We can't lose you. You're the only reason the Earth has a chance.~

Outrage rippled through her, and she almost raised her head to glare at him.

~Joseph Daniel Davidson, if you think there is a chance in hell I am going to leave you guys, you must have had one of those beams hit your hard head.~ She shot and killed another one, but another scream of pain from Cass, then a muttered curse as she moved.

~The splash is hitting our people. I can't move them or get them any more covered,~ her voice frantic even as she lifted her handgun and fired. She didn't hit any, but she managed to make the oncoming attackers duck.

The certain knowledge they were all going to die settled into her bones. There were too many, Caroline was already dead, and not even nanobots could bring her back.

All I can do now is try to see if I can help make the cost so high maybe the Elentrin will change their minds.

The silence from Wefor told her she was all too correct. With grim determination she kept firing, trying to make every shot count. But as they hid behind vehicles, it became harder and harder to hit them. A roar of some sort of vehicle caused some Kaylid to look away from her little group, behind them.

McKenna didn't waste the distraction, she made another two drop. Then a third and a fourth dropped as three men in Army fatigues came around the corner, a Humvee painted army green following them with men on top.

The men on the top of the Humvee made quick work of the Kaylid in front of them. McKenna didn't waste time looking at them she spun focusing on the Kaylid shooting at them through the trees.

~Perc, Cass, grab the humans and get them over to the Army guys. They can help.~

"This is National Guard Captain John Carol." The words rang out behind her. Turning around would take too long.

"Good, nice to meeting you. Now come help me kill these others," she shouted behind her. "I've got friends bringing people to you that were captured by the invaders. They're still out of it."

~They're helping, though they flinched a bit, I think us walking over there holding the people helped. Two are headed your way.~ Perc said.

~Good, cause I'm almost out of ammo. I'm going to need more from the car,~ she replied, trying to see where that last flash of light had come from.

"Hi, ma'am. How many are there?"

She'd heard the rapid approach of feet, and since she'd known it wasn't Perc or Cass she'd figured it had to be one of the military guys. ~JD?~

~At least four more, but I can't see them.~

"We've got four. They have a shuttle in there, but we got the people that were in there out. They might have put more in, but we're worried they might be able to remotely recall the shuttles."

"Good call." His voice low. "I'm headed right. Stay here, then we can get you back to our base."

He crawled to the side through the low shrubs. A light flashed her direction hitting the bush next her, crating sweet smoke that served as an odd counterpoint to the burnt meat smell still in her nose. A sharp crack of a rifle from where he had gone, and she saw a shape collapse. In short order they proved why they were so much better at this than McKenna ever would be.

When they were all dead, and the captured people in the back of the Humvee, McKenna faced the officer. "Thank you. Our friend that was killed was Caroline Lance, a Secret Service agent. She said we could find a good place to retreat to here?" McKenna pulled out the phone and showed him the address. A smile lit up the young man's face.

"That's us. When you didn't show up, we got a bit worried. That mean you're McKenna Largo?" he asked.

She nodded, though right now she felt like a failure. He glanced back at the six people they'd rescued. "You did good. Let's get out of here."

Even as they talked, there was a weird sound, and she turned to see the shuttle rising up into the air. A sick feeling filled her stomach. How many people had she failed to rescue? How many parents would never see their children again? How many spouses had died while their loved ones were taken?

The ride to their base increased her feeling of surreality and failure. News of what was going on across the country and the world. People being taken, families being killed, all to grab one Kaylid. Some areas were making short work of any invaders; others, the more urban areas, had much higher casualty amounts. Every bit of news felt like a blow, and she closed her eyes wondering what else she could have done.

They treated her like a hero, and all she could see was her failures.

~Kenna?~ Toni's voice filtered in past her stressing.

~You okay? The kids okay?~ Her response instant. She tensed up, wishing she could fly, fly home to protect her kids.

~Yes. We're fine. There haven't been any here. This area doesn't have many shifters and we're staying below the radar.~

She blew out a breath. The back area had a place to smoke, she stood there, leaning against the wall. She looked around, but didn't really see anything.

~Kenna?~ Toni was back and she blinked.

~Yeah?~

~Stop beating up on yourself. We're all doing what we can do. You've helped.~ Her voice held reassurance, but the only thing McKenna could see was Caroline's dead body.

~Thanks. I'm going to get some sleep. Give the kids hugs for me.~ She shut down the connection, almost feeling like she contaminated them just by being in it. They had cots set up for people in the back rooms. Still in her warrior form, staying in that form made everything easier, she shut her eyes and tried to ignore the world as she went over everything she'd done. Trying to figure out what she could have done differently.

"Finally. Are all your kind this stubborn?"

McKenna felt her eyes snap open, but she didn't have eyelids or even eyes for that matter. She felt disjointed, almost like the first time Wefor had spoken to her, but she could see. Sort of. The feeling gave her the willies, and she began to thrash trying to figure out how to get out, but she didn't know what she was in or where out was. She floated in a space of nothingness, yet in front of her stood a figure, but she couldn't see colors or shapes, she just knew he was there.

"Would you please calm down? I don't have much time, and it took too long to find you, then to establish a connection. This is important."

His snappish words, rushed, yet familiar, had her focusing on the being on the other side of the nothingness.

"Ash?"

"Finally. Yes. Listen. Help is available, though you've done better than anyone else in all the times I've tried. But if your level of resistance keeps up, they will resort to kinetic weapons."

It dawned on McKenna he spoke in English rather than her brain interpreting what he said.

"You mean like sending asteroids to Earth, to impact our cities?"

"Exactly. I've managed to get the ships that are being deployed to the area you're in, routing from my ship. But the next ship will be here in a day or two, so you don't have much time."

"Time to do what? How can we make them leave?" It felt like she'd woken up and her brain started to work.

The sound in her head vibrated. "You can't. The Elentrin either take what they came for, or they'll destroy it all rather than allow someone else to have it."

"They've done that before?"

"Three times. All with worlds that had civilizations strong enough to fight them but didn't have an active space presence. One of them was my world." There should have been anger, regret, sorrow, some strong and deep emotion in those words but there wasn't. He made the comment as it if had happened so long ago the event no longer had any emotion attached to it.

"I'm sorry?"

"For? Never mind. This is wasting time. Listen. I've put a transmitter in all the shuttles that go down to your area of your world. You need to get into the shuttle and find the transmitter. It is small, and most of them I have hidden under seats. Tell your AI to look for this frequency. 2.36 mHz. It will only pulse once every thirty to forty-five of your minutes randomly to prevent anyone from noticing it. Most shuttles are supposed to stay on the ground for about 66 of your minutes, so you won't have long. You must find one of those transmitters and activate it. That will enable help to find you. "I can't guarantee all of them will have the transmitter, but I'll try. And in your area is a rough term. Your country is much larger than most. "

"Help? There is someone that can help us?" She waited for the spurt of adrenaline.

"I have to go. Find the transmitter and turn it on. You might be the only, the best hope for all of us. Now go, and by the Stars of Alara don't get yourself killed."

There was a weird jolt, and she found herself sitting up on the cot wide awake, looking around. The room had a low level light on in it, and three other people were asleep on the cots. She rolled out and went into the main area, Perc sat there, reading a book. McKenna dropped down next to him.

~Wefor, was that a dream? Were you there?~ She could feel others paying attention, which was why she had broadcast like that.

[Your query is not understood.]

~Huh, so that didn't register.~ Trying to make her words as descriptive as possible she relayed what

Ash had said and the weird frequency he had said to tell Wefor to monitor.

~What help could he be talking about?~ Cass wondered. She wasn't in the room, but McKenna could sense her and JD not too far away.

~I don't know, but should I do it? Should I go find that transmitter?~ It seemed like all her decisions were wrong lately, and she didn't want to risk any more lives.

~Absolutely.~ Toni's voice was firm. ~If they start dropping asteroids, our world is dead. Get the transmitter. If it is a trap, then it really doesn't matter given what the alternative is.~

McKenna glanced at Perc. He nodded and took her hand. "Yes. We'll find it."

Chapter 42 - Glimmer of Hope

The US is currently under martial law. All human shifters in warrior form are warned to wear earrings, bright colors, and make sure they are with people who know them. Aliens have been seen descending into most cities and shuttles are lifting up hourly with captured shifters. While attempts are being made to shoot them while they are coming in, efforts to shoot departing shuttles have stopped as the only people being killed are ours. The HALO (high altitude low opening) like drops are almost impossible to intercept with how our defenses are set and the Elentrin ships are too high up in orbit to be easily targeted. ~ TNN News

McKenna never went back to bed, her mind pulling apart each detail of the vision, what Ash had said. Wefor had no opinion, or at least not that the AI would share.

When morning showed up, she approached the de facto leader of their motley crew. About her age, the Captain, one Mark Alfonso formerly of Los Angeles, hid gang tattoos under his uniform. But he had a good eye for small squad tactics, which McKenna knew nothing about.

"Morning, Miss Largo. Any chance I can convince you and your people to head back home and hide out while the professionals take care of this?" His tone indicated he knew the answer, but from the hopeful look on his face she suspected someone up the chain had pressured him to ask.

"Hide in a corner hoping the monsters don't come after me?" she asked with a smirk. "Thanks, but no. But I do have a new mission, I guess you could say."

He sighed and sat down at his makeshift desk. The area had been the back hallway some smaller strip malls had. A folding table, a laptop, paper maps of the area and scribbled notes covered it.

"What exactly would that be?" He didn't sound excited but more resigned.

"Let me guess. You've been instructed to give me all possible aid and protect me at all costs."

"No matter how odd or strange the request might be," he said, almost smiling. "So what is this weird mission? And how many people are going to die?"

McKenna flinched at that and some of her good mood faded, Caroline's face flashing back before her. "Hopefully none, though it might take a day or two."

Captain Alfonso leaned back in his chair with a long suffering look. "Details."

"I need to see if I can get into one of those shuttles, possibly a few of them." Saying it out loud made her realize how insane it sounded. But she didn't have any other ideas, and if the news reports were correct, they didn't have many other options.

"The same shuttles that are remote-operated and could take you up to the ships above if they take off while you're in it." He paused, his brows drawn together, and he made a note on a pad, chewing his lip. After a minute he focused back on her. "That shuttle?"

"Yes. There's a possibility we have a friend among the Elentrin." She jerked her head up, but she kept her voice low. Tempers were high, and even alluding to this might be too much. "If that's true, there might be something on one of the shuttles that can help."

The captain sat up straight looking at her, eyes serious.

~For a young man he sure is suspicious. I thought military guys were supposed to be all gung-ho about jumping into danger.~ She commented, a bit wry, not sure how she'd explain all of this without sounding like a loon.

~Nope. That's the Marines. The Army considers things, then kills them.~ JD responded instantly, and McKenna had to resist rolling her eyes, the poor Captain wouldn't understand why.

"And why can't I or one of my guys get it?"

"I suspect I'm the only one that can find it or even figure out where it is. I could be wrong, but why risk anyone on what I may or may not know?" McKenna kept her voice logical though she tensed. This meant more than he could possibly know. Or she'd die horribly.

"They told me to support you no matter how crazy your request was. Okay. But I'll be damned if I go down in history as the one that let McKenna Largo get killed. I'm sending four of my best with your little group. The two of you aren't too bad. The other two are better as support. They don't shoot first and worry about it later."

~He has a point.~ Cass sighed. ~At the compound I didn't have time to think, and really I didn't do it as much as training. I can kill, I will, but it takes me building myself up to do it. If you wait that long I'll get you all killed.~

McKenna ducked her head. "Good. Use us. That, and we can heal from stuff faster than you."

Mark Alfonso shrugged. "Outside a burn, if they hit you with those damn rifles you tend to die. Unless you're telling me you can heal from that. If that were the case, I'd be asking you to change all of us." His voice had a bit of bitterness to it, and she flinched.

"No. Caroline was a shifter, and you can't heal from that. Only the minor stuff."

"Then it doesn't matter. Learn to duck. I'll have you going out soon. Any idea where a shuttle will land?"

"No. Only that I can figure out if what I need is on them."

"Then I'll add suspected shuttle landing locations and have them feed that down to us. One thing about this, it doesn't seem to occur to them to knock out our intelligence. Their orbit is too high to affect most satellites, so we still can see what's going on as they come down. I should be able to get us feeds for anything in a fifty-mile radius."

McKenna paused, remembering Ash's comment. "Can you make it a hundred-mile radius?"

He shot her an odd look then shrugged. "Your mission." He typed on his tablet then nodded at her. "Meet them out back in twenty. Get ammo and gear up. And make sure your shots count."

~Wefor, what is your range on that frequency?~ In this area it could take two hours to travel sixty miles, especially if it wasn't along freeway lines.

[At least twenty-five miles in this terrain. But be aware with a single alert we may not get there once it is detected prior to the shuttle lifting again.]

~We'll have to make it work. We need to find this. You guys hear that, ready to go?~

~Kenna?~ Cass's voice had a tentative quality to it.

~Yeah?~ McKenna frowned, she worried about the woman. Cass wasn't passive, but this actively going out to kill people—even aliens—made her uncomfortable.

~They don't have a medic here and my training is translating correctly. I'd prefer to stay and help with first aid. I'm better than anyone they have and they're still bringing in shifters that have been stunned or whatever it is.~

McKenna wanted to sag in relief. The matching relief from JD almost took her knees out from under her, and she staggered, leaning against the wall.

~That sounds like a great idea. I'll let the captain know. You two ready?~ She hated to admit how much she depended on JD and Perc, but their warrior forms were so huge it helped with getting people out of danger.~

~Yes.~ JD's voice rumbled in her mind and she turned to see the captain looking at her, an odd look on his face.

"Cass is going to stay and help you guys with medical stuff. So just me, JD, and Perc. That work?"

He cast a quick glance at all of them, but nodded. "Probably better. Those two take up more than their fair share of room in the back of a Humvee."

"True, but they're also damn useful to have around."

"There is that. I'll let the guys know." He dismissed her from his attention with one last sharp glance.

~Word about the telepathy is going to get out, you know,~ JD commented.

~Oh, well. That's their problem. I don't care if other people create the links as long as I'm not expected to carry everyone in my brain,~ she commented, heading back to use the restroom before they took off. Most of what she needed she had in her kilt pockets.

Two minutes before the deadline she showed up at the back of the building. Two young men who looked like they'd aged years in the last few days, leaned against the vehicle. One with skin the color of paste mixed with red dye, the other had skin that blended in with the tan paint of the Humvee.

"So hear you're the boss." The pale burnt kid had the name Lawson stenciled on his uniform.

"Boss? No way. I'll defer to your expertise. This is not anything I have training for."

[That is not accurate. You have both the information programmed into the nanobots and the sleep training to rely on.]

~That is not the same as actual training, and besides, these guys need to know I'm not going to take over. I don't need to be in charge of everything.~

The two men relaxed fractionally even as McKenna swore she could feel the AI pout.

"Well, then, ma'am, what is the mission?" Lawson asked, while the other kid, and they felt so young to her, climbed into the vehicle.

"We're going to track down shuttles. Looking for something specific." Perc and JD were getting in and arranging themselves.

He looked at her dubiously then waved his hand dismissively. "Ours is not to reason why," he muttered.

"I would really prefer it if we do, and do NOT die if it's all the same to you." McKenna smiled to take the sting out of her words. He flinched back a bit, and she remembered she was still in warrior form and a smile might not be reassuring. That made her want to smile more, but she fought it down.

"Sorry, I might be in this form too much. But yeah, no dying."

"That's my preference. I assume we're fine to take out and prevent any kidnappings?" His words had a layer of aggression there.

"Absolutely. Given that I'm hoping we're targeting shuttles, maybe we can interfere with some of return of prisoners. If were really lucky maybe we can get one landing and prevent any losses before they even get out of the shuttle."

A wolfish grin split his face. "Now that sounds like a plan, ma'am. Load on up and let's go invader hunting."

The soldier didn't flinch away from her smile this time. A few minutes later they were headed out. JD standing up, looking out the top to see if they could see any Kaylid on the street.

Lawson called back to her, "We've got a report of a shuttle headed down about fifteen clicks to the south. That one work for you?"

"Won't know until we get there. We might as well see if we can interact."

"Yes, ma'am."

~Ooh, getting ma'am'd now,~ JD teased.

McKenna didn't bother to look at him, she knew he'd smirk. Instead she focused on listening to the soldiers talk. A third sat in back with them. An older man who didn't open his eyes or anything, just let his body rock back and forth as they sped down roads.

"Got it. Just landed. If we move, we can get them as they're disembarking. On me." The orders were barked out, and McKenna followed, spilling out of the vehicle, and headed to the edge of a building. The shuttle had landed in a playground, the ramp already down as they peered around.

"They out already?" asked the older man, an M-16 in his hand and crouched in front of her.

"Don't know. They can't say for sure how long it's been down, below radar at this level. Wait, no, two more coming out now. Can you take them at the edge of the playground, Reg?" Lawson kept his voice low as the aliens moved towards the edge of the park, their weapons up and looking around.

"Yes, just waiting."

McKenna saw their ears twitch and ice clawed through her insides. ~We never told them how good our hearing is in this form, they're expecting human-level hearing. Shit and I can't tell them or they'll know. JD, are you at an angle you can take them out?~

~Yes, when they turn, I'll fire if you and Perc can grab our companions and yank them back, they are damn fast in firing.~

~Got it,~ she answered, and Perc confirmed. They shifted position a bit so Perc could grab two of them, and she could grab the third.

Chapter 43 - Hope made real

The events happening in Istanbul and Shanghai are well known at this point. The estimated death toll in Istanbul has risen to over a hundred thousand, and bodies are starting to rot in the heat. There has been fighting from all sides, and the dead lay mingled together. The number of people abducted from here is still unknown and may never be known as the ability to identify the dead has faded in the need to dispose of the bodies before disease sets in. Already the sound of flies can drown out the sound of gunfire. This is the worst sustained fighting seen since World War II. The city may never recover. ~ TNN Breaking News

~Now!~ Even as he said it, JD stepped out, the M-16 barking out loud cracks of sound that echoed between the buildings. As the word had entered their mind, Perc grabbed the two soldiers throwing them backwards almost as McKenna grabbed the one in front of her, pulling him to the side and out of the way.

Even as JD had stepped out, the aliens spun their weapons firing as they turned. The red light splashed across the corner they had been around, then tilted up.

"They're down," JD announced, lowering his rifle and turning to look at them. The two Perc had grabbed and thrown were shaking their heads, a bit stunned and out of breath. Lawson, who McKenna had grabbed, glared up at her.

"What the hell was that all about, Largo?" Anger coated his tone as he surged to his feet. He didn't quite tower over her warrior form, but he was taller than she, even if she'd been human.

"We hear really well in this form. Like if I concentrate I can get Reg's heartbeat. They heard you talking, and we realized you didn't know. It was the only way we could think of to not warn them and keep you all alive. I won't apologize for grabbing you, but people need to know they hear like a literal animal. You could never sneak up on a stalking cat, and the same goes with these guys. Radio traffic they can hear. All the agents I've been around have been using earpieces. If I want, I can hear both sides of those conversations. We just work on not listening and forgot they wouldn't be doing the same." She met his eyes as she talked, refusing to be cowed.

He glared at her, then at the shuttle and his men and cussed. "That explains a lot, and we should have thought about that. It's fucking obvious when you say it. Can you get what you need out of that shuttle?"

~Wefor?~

[Unknown. No signal has been detected.]

~Do I dare go see if I can search it?~

~I don't think we should take the risk until we know it is in there. Heck, even then I'm not sure you should be the one doing it. Let's wait and decide then.~ Perc's voice had a tightness to it that made

McKenna glance over at him. He looked at the playground and the dead bodies laying there, and for a moment McKenna thought she'd be sick.

This isn't how it is supposed to be. I'll do anything to stop this. If I have to die to stop this, I will.

A mix of emotions swarmed her, and she locked them down. Sharing them would not be wise, not now. Lawson came back, a dark look on his face. "That information has been shared out. It would explain why few of our ambushes have worked. Thanks," his voice grudging. "So does it have what you need?"

"We don't know. So for now we sit and watch and wait."

They collected the bodies after making sure there weren't any more beings inside, there was a place they were all being sent, they did sit and watch. The shuttle took off without any captured people, living invaders, or the signal being sent.

"I guess no? Next one then?"

"Yes, please." McKenna responded. They spent the rest of the day chasing shuttles but none of them sent out the signal Wefor monitored for.

Headed back to the headquarters, she checked up on everyone, the jolting of the vehicle almost comforting by this time.

~How are you doing?~ She directed it towards Toni and the kids.

~Fine, bored but fine,~ Toni responded. ~Only one sighting and a cop took it out. They have the cops on bicycles, it's quieter and they can cover areas pretty fast. Though I might kill my children if they don't stop whining about staying in animal form.~

The normalcy of the complaint made McKenna smile, and she heard a chuckle from Perc.

~Did you guys have any luck?~ Toni asked back.

~Wefor swears that frequency is being monitored, but no. We'll try again tomorrow.~ The rest of the conversation fell into friendly chatter, Cass sharing what she did during the day.

Captain Alfonso met them when they got out. "Thanks for that info. We're updating our tactics and doing more snipers. Anything else we should know about their abilities?"

McKenna laughed. "Probably. Perc? Wanna go do the show and tell?"

He laughed, his large shoulders shaking as sharp fangs were exposed. Human facial expression really didn't translate well to this form, but they were automatic for the most part. Half the people there took a step back.

"Sure. Can't let you and JD have all the fun. Come on guys, let's go have fun."

She laughed as the soldiers followed him like little ducklings to the storefront they'd taken over as a break room.

It took two days before Wefor caught the signal. By then they had become a rather efficient little squad. Tracking down the shuttles had become routine. Setting up sniper nests and picking off returning Kaylid worked well. They carefully didn't talk about the victims likely caused by the Kaylid in pursuit of capturing the Earthborn shifters.

The news got grimmer and grimmer. Istanbul was all but destroyed. China a confused waste land. Half the people crying for the absent Elentrin, the other half trying to pick up the slack.

As a whole, the US was doing pretty well. But if it went on much longer food shortages would start. So many people were armed and willing to fight that the cost was high to the invaders, and that created more stress for McKenna. But she hadn't had any more dreams. She'd feel better if she knew if that was a good or a bad thing.

[That one. It has been there for five minutes and the transmission was just detected.]

~Finally. Okay. I'm going.~

~Not alone, you aren't,~ Perc and JD said, basically in unison.

She started to argue but realized it wouldn't do any good.

"I need to go down and inspect that shuttle. It should have what I'm looking for."

The men they'd been working with over the last few days all instantly started packing up.

"What are you doing?" McKenna asked, looking at them.

"Coming with you, what does it look like? You're our responsibility. I'm not about to let you go into a shuttle by yourself that might kidnap you. Guys, ready?" he asked, glancing at the other two men who had finished packing up and stood with their rifles ready.

"Arguing with you isn't going to do anything but waste time is it?" she asked, giving all the men an annoyed look.

"Nope. So let's go." Lawson had the audacity to smile at her as they headed towards the shuttle.

~What is it about men?~ she muttered in her head.

Perc and JD just laughed while she got amused exasperation from Toni and Cass.

~Did you really think any of us would let you go by yourself? We can't lose you.~ The sentiment was reinforced by everyone, even the kids, and she sighed, both warmed and frustrated by their insistence on protecting her.

~Someday you're going to be on the receiving side of this, just saying.~

~Sure, bring it on,~ Toni said wryly while JD laughed at her.

They moved down from the building they had perched on top of. People helped the military right now, and no one wanted this to continue, so getting into and out of buildings to set up the sniper nests was easy. Going down and collecting captured people required a bit more risk. Either way, they moved with caution, the shifters listening and checking before waving them forward.

They took out a Kaylid coming back, but fewer and fewer had been coming back with any shifters. People didn't react well to being captured, and everyone fought.

The shuttle sat in the clearing, its silver presence a siren call.

"Have they managed to get in and inspect any of them?" McKenna asked softly.

"Not that I've heard. Other than the one they captured at the initial meeting, the others fly away if anyone goes in. Which means I'm reluctant to allow you to enter."

"Hmmm, any shifters go in? Or always just non?"

Lawson shrugged. "Above my pay grade. All I know is the one captured is the only one they've managed to study."

"Well, I have to go in. Maybe if I'm there, you won't trigger it."

Lawson smiled a wolfish grin at her. "Well, if they get us, they get us all. Not letting them get you."

A grunt of agreement from all the men had McKenna rolling her eyes, but they headed in, scanning for anything and everything.

Looking in the shuttle for the second time, McKenna paused, trying to pay attention to it this time. Last time she'd seen the people and hadn't paid attention to much else. Nets hung against the wall, in rows stacking up. It dawned on her this was probably how they meant to transport their prisoners.

Low benches on either side with harnesses every so often, and a center area where she would have expected a pilot's chair, but there was an odd-looking stand. Almost like a funky bar stool and some controls.

~Wefor, any idea what I'm looking for or where it might be?~

[No.]

~Well, that's no help,~ McKenna grumbled as she gingerly stepped into the shuttle, ready to spring back out the door at the first hint of it closing up.

Looking around, the lines all seemed clean and almost sterile. No hint of any type of personality to the ship.

~Okay, guys, I'm searching where he told me, but I'm not really sure what I'm looking for, and there are so many mixed smells in here I can't really sniff for anything.~

Lawson stuck his head in. "Get what you need?"

"No. I don't see anything that screams 'secret transmitter'. All I know is there should be a transmitter on this ship, but I don't know what should or shouldn't be here." Her frustration slipped out.

Lawson stepped carefully on the ramp as McKenna stood in the middle of the area.

"Okay, let me look. I love hidden object stuff."

Perc and JD stayed at the bottom of the ramp, both standing on it. They'd notice if it started to move.

Lawson moved in and started poking around, same as McKenna.

~I have no idea what the hell it could be. What does a transmitter look like for the Elentrin?~ Worry and the mental clock ticking down in her head drove her.

"Hey, look at this." Lawson was crouched next to where the nets and the chairs intersected. "Is this it?"

McKenna moved over and looked but couldn't see what he was pointing at. "What?"

He frowned, looking up at her. "You can't see that?"

"Lawson, I have no idea what you're talking about."

A pensive look crossed his face, and he reached out to pull something off the shadowed area. As soon as it detached, she could see a dull silver circular object with an opaque top.

"What the hell? I didn't see that at all until you pulled it off."

Lawson handed it to her. "No idea, but we can worry about it after we get off this shuttle. It makes me nervous as hell."

McKenna couldn't disagree, and they got out and headed out of the area. Once in the back of the Humvee she turned the object over in her hand. It looked pretty simple. A single press of the button would activate it.

[It was transmitting as it was pulled from its location. It stopped at that time. But there is no reason this can't be tracked where it currently is.]

Chapter 44 - Leap of Faith

The Elentrin made landfall in England today. Until this point, population centers in China, the US, and the area encompassing the Middle East have been the focus point for most of the aliens, but they are branching out. With the current disruption of communication, no one has any idea how many shifters have been taken, but counts of shuttles going up and down are worrisome, as are the larger ships setting down in China. Current guess is that each of those ships could easily hold a thousand or more shifters. No one knows what is happening to those who have been taken, but this war is quickly changing into a fight for survival. ~TNN News

"Lawson," McKenna blurted, sitting straight up. "Don't take us back. Take us to a big open park." She all but shouted the words, not wanting to take a chance of them not hearing her. All the men looked at her, brows furrowed. Lawson turned to glance at her, but he nodded. The truck slowed and turned down a street then revved back up, jostling them as it barreled down the empty streets.

The noise in the vehicle was too loud to really discuss anything. This needed to be done so everyone could hear her, so she didn't speak in the mindspace, instead turning the object over and over in her hand.

INCOMING

The vehicle rumbled to a stop, and the engine clicked off. McKenna leaped out and headed towards the grassy area, a chorus of questions following her. She ignored all of them and continued towards the middle of the park, though she listened and made sure she didn't hear anyone around.

She looked at the soccer field and sighed. The rest of the men all but surrounded her.

"Largo, what the hell is going on?" Lawson demanded, his tone annoyed though he kept his gun up and scoped out the area.

~Yes, Kenna, what's going on?~ Cass asked, and she could feel Toni and the kids all listening to her. Out of the corner of her eye she could see JD fighting to not cross his arms over his chest and glare at her, his fingers twitching with an invisible spinner.

"Okay, people, listen up. Here's the story. I got a message that this device could signal some help for us. I have no way of knowing if the person was lying or not. But we can't hold on much longer. Most cities are out of food as the trucks can't run, businesses are shut down. While we might be able to hold them off for a bit longer, the loss of life is going to start rising, and not for reasons of the Elentrin, but food, water, supplies, medicines." She swallowed, everyone looked at her, not moving. Even in her head she could feel the absolute concentration of the others listening.

"Cities are worst hit, and that's where the Elentrin are concentrating their attacks. They ever figure out how to bottle that pheromone stuff and spray it, we'll fold in a day," she said. McKenna knew she wasn't telling anyone anything they didn't know, just saying out loud what everyone was avoiding.

"And your point?" Lawson directed the question to her, but he kept scanning. Getting shot from behind never looked good on a service record.

"That this might be planted by the Elentrin, and I don't want to lead them back to where we're located. But at the same time it might be the only chance we have. We can't afford not to try it. I don't want to turn it over because this message was directed at me specifically. I have a feeling whoever or whatever is looking for me. Which means I need to do it, and the longer we wait, the more I'll overthink this." She shrugged and looked around. "At least if I do it here, the only person at risk is me. Everyone else get back in the vehicle and watch me from afar."

"No." The word chorused out around her and in her head, and she wavered from the emotional impact.

"McKenna, I get the hero thing, but we aren't doing this. Get over it and activate the damn device." Perc looked at her and didn't look away as she met his gaze.

"Argh, you are all idiots. This might get us killed." She didn't quite shout, but she glared at them.

"And what do you think what we've been doing will do? This is a dangerous time. Go activate it. We'll deal with whatever happens."

McKenna focused on the ground, hiding her face. She didn't know if she wanted to hug them all or beat them.

~You're loved. Suck it up and let's do this thing.~ Toni's brisk voice made her smile, and she lifted her head looking at the men who all just looked impatient.

[You are an odd creature. You have people who follow you, that would risk their lives for you, yet you push them away and risk your own. You are a commander, they should be honored to die for you.]

McKenna felt the sighs and amusement ripple through the mindspace as she walked a bit further into the clearing. The transmitter seemed to have a place that would depress if pushed.

~It doesn't work that way, Wefor. You protect the people who follow you.~

[Interesting. The existing information indicates that leaders are to be protected at all costs. This is a dichotomy.]

Making sure everyone was back away from her, McKenna pressed the transmitter and tossed it on the ground in front of her. Making the motion smooth and swift, then she backed up towards the others, her eyes locked on the silver object laying on the yellowish grass.

They all stood there looking at it, the occasional sound of a gun or car sharp over the rustle of tree leaves.

JD shifted his body, moving a bit. They all smelled a bit ripe from the last few days. Shower facilities were hard to get to, and they had found the warrior form smelled less than the humans did. But still, after three days they all wanted a shower and some fresh clothes.

Rustling behind her, but she didn't take her eyes away from the silver object, obscurely worried that if she did, she'd miss something important. "So how long do you think this should take?" Perc asked, his voice carefully neutral.

~What, did they all poke you to make you ask me?~ She didn't even try to keep the humor out of her mind even as she tried to calm down. Stress at being in the open, at not knowing what might happen, at what was happening everywhere, all ramped it up until she started to think she needed a spinner.

~Yes.~

She snorted mentally at his dry remark. "I don't know. But not like we all have hot dates or anything."

The laughter behind her derailed at a flash of light from the transmitter.

"Did you-" She broke off the question as it came again and this time it grew in the middle of the air above the small transmitter.

"Weapons up and trained on that, whatever it is. Don't shoot unless Largo gives us the clearance. Remember we might not know what the help looks like."

"If it is a Dalek, I swear to god I'm eating a bullet." Reg muttered darkly, and McKenna choked back a laugh. The last thing they needed was a fictional enemy intent on destroying Earth.

The air swirled and moved in a way that confused her mind and senses.

~Wefor, do you know what that is?~

Silence from the AI, but she got the impression of shock and amazement, which felt a little odd in her head.

It grew larger and McKenna took a step back, bumping into a body. Perc, she realized, as his hands came up to steady her, and she caught a glimpse of tawny fur with black marks.

"What the hell is that?" Lawson asked, but his voice remained steady.

"Your guess is as good as mine." McKenna heard her voice crack, but didn't look away.

Oh gods, what if this is a weapon? What if I've killed everyone?

Her hands clenched tight as it grew more. It stopped growing at about ten feet in height and roughly four feet wide. It hung there in the air like an ominous swirl of color and light.

Weapons ready, JD had grabbed hers and handed it to her when the light show started, they all aimed and waited.

"I think I see something. Is there someone walking out of the portal?" Lawson asked slowly, tension fraying his voice.

"Help, I hope." McKenna muttered, though she had no idea what form of help could come through a portal.

Even the wind in the trees seemed to stop as the figure stepped out of the portal and McKenna felt her heart stutter in her chest.

"Is that?" JD asked his voice hushed.

~What's going on? We can hear your mental voices, but we can't see anything. Guys, what is it?~ Cass's voice had a frantic aspect to it as she pinged them.

McKenna was still struggling to accept what she saw as the figure strode towards them. Tall, pushing about seven feet, humanoid in shape, in that it had two arms, two legs, and one head, but after that it was a creature from the visions. Scaled skin, fine patterns that reminded her of exotic reptiles. A neck that seemed shorter and stocker than the others she'd seen, and dark eyes that swirled with colors she didn't know how to name. But instead of the sleek elegance of the other Drakyn. This one looked like a tank. All power and danger. He made JD and Perc almost look tiny.

His strides were long as he headed their direction, but his hands were empty, and he had focused on her.

She felt an odd sensation as Toni paid attention to her reactions in the mindspace. For a minute her vision flickered then went back to normal. McKenna didn't have time to try to figure out what had just happened.

"Largo, what do you want us to do?" Lawson had a panicked aspect to his tone, but McKenna's brain had finally kicked in.

"Nothing, let me talk to him."

Swallowing past the lump, she took a step forward and tried to remember to not smile. Maybe she should change back to human? No, that would take away what few advantages she had.

The Drakyn stopped about three feet from her, not close enough to grab her, which gave her a measure of relief as she glanced at the four fingered hands with three long digits and a strong thumb. He nodded at her, not smiling, and she mimicked it.

"Are you the representative of this place, the one who might contact me?" He spoke English, but with a musical aspect, as if a cello could talk.

"Yes. You're here to help us against the Elentrin?" McKenna asked, and felt her heart squeeze tight.

This time the Drakyn smiled, revealing a mouth full of sharp teeth she didn't remember in any of the others.

"I'm here to help both of us put a stop to the Elentrin, permanently."

Epilogues

EMERGENCY BROADCAST: All citizens are urged to stay home and armed. Food supplies may be scarce for the next week and all residents are asked to be careful with shifting. If you shift into warrior form it is best to stay in it to conserve calories. Emergency rations will be available at Police and Fire stations in limited supplies. Ammo may be limited, and it is unknown how many attackers may be in your area. Make your shots count. Body collection in armored convoys will commence once needed. All bodies will be cremated per government instruction. ~ ESB

Raymond Kennedy sat in his Georgetown town home, a 1911 on the antique end table at his side as he watched the world come undone. Most of his plans were pushed to the back burner, but in some ways this might just give him more leverage. If they could chase away the invaders and survive, at least.

He leaned back, watching the TV. All prime-time shows had been suspended and other than networks focused on kids, everything centered on the invasion.

Making notes as he watched, he tried to see what he would be able to salvage from this.

A news item showing someone shift into what looked like a half-jackal, half-human monster, extend huge claws and fight with an invader had his eyes narrowing as he watched.

The privacy of his home was absolute. He'd made sure of that. A disgusted sigh slipped out of him.

"You'll never know. And you know you want to know." The words hung in the air. He glanced at the 1911 again thinking then shrugged. With quick efficient movements he stripped off his slacks, tie, shirt, and underwear, folding them neatly before placing them on the leather club chair.

Closing his eyes, he took a deep breath in and out, repeating it, then his body flowed into an animal form, low slung, vaguely cat-like face. A fossa, a more useless animal he couldn't have found, and had refused to even admit he could shift, avoiding it since that first day. With a soft snarl, the animal closed its eyes and flowed upward into the more useful warrior form.

He opened his mouth and a garble came out. A soft snarl, then another garble, though less. Another five minutes of practice and clear words came out of his mouth.

"This has promise. I'll have to keep it in mind for later." Raymond spent another fifteen minutes testing out the abilities of this form. The animal form had no use to him, but this, this had possibilities.

A blare of noise from the TV caused him to shift his attention. A scene of invaders landing in England, and the Royal Guard firing on them.

"Morons. I guess Britain will learn that having an armed populace has value in many ways." The sneer in his voice came through the Kaylid form intact. With a shake of his head he let himself go back to human. Dressing, he headed to the kitchen for some food. Minutes later, a sandwich in his hand, he kept taking notes about how this could be used. They would win of course, because if they didn't, well, none of this mattered at that point.

Plans are being made to attack the ships in orbit. The president has provided a press release stating: "All efforts are being made on altering existing weapons to attack the ships. We have no ETA at this time for when we will be able to successfully attack their ships, but understand we are working as fast as we can and coordinating with the space station to have them standing by to help rescue our people. We understand all the complications involved in this and be assured we understand the risks and are keeping in mind the danger to all humans." We will provide you more information as we receive it. ~ TNN News

"Shuttles incoming, all technicians report to shuttle bay 3 to collect incoming specimens. Culling and evaluations will happen prior to storage and education. Repeat all technicians are to report."

The announcements and sounds of clawed feet running through the halls were background noise. Ash tuned it all out as he sat in the tiny room that served as his office and his quarters. A high compliment for his ability and years of service. It proved he was a very well-trained pet. He blinked his eyes as he looked at the information on his display. A single word sat there, blinking at him meaning nothing to anyone, except it was the culmination of centuries of trying.

"Alara."

He gave himself another few moments to look at it, then he deleted it, rising to look out the mock window at space. A reward they'd said. It simply reminded him of everything he could never have - freedom.

But for the first time it had worked. Contact made with a Kaylid on the planet. A Drakyn brought in. Maybe, just maybe, he might see the Elentrin brought down in his lifetime. Or more accurately, before they realized that he had subverted his AI centuries ago and had been conspiring with the Drakyn to stop their madness.

"Good luck," he whispered, looking at the blue and white planet hanging in his view. "You're going to need it." He shifted his gaze to the shuttles heading out to start pulling in asteroids to send at the unsuspecting planet.

Authors Note:

I hope you enjoyed the third novel in the Kaylid Chronicles. Things are ramping up for Earth and does this visitor mean good or bad things?

Visit my website at www.badashpublishing.com to sign up for my newsletter and find out about the next books coming out in this series.

If you haven't already read my other books you can get them by these links.

[Kaylid Chronicles Book 1: No Choice](#)
[Kaylid Chronicles Novella 1: New Games](#)
[Kaylid Chronicles Books 2: Commander](#)
[Kaylid Chronicles Novella 2: Home Alone](#)
[Kaylid Chronicles Novella 3: Decisions](#)
Kaylid Chronicles Book 3: Incoming (well this one)

Expect book 4 in 2019!

Happy reading!

ABOUT THE AUTHOR

Mel Todd has three cats, none of which can turn into a form with opposable thumbs, which is good. If they could do that they wouldn't need her anymore. While writing and starting her empire, she decided creating her own worlds was less work than ruling this one.

Printed in Great Britain
by Amazon